W9-ANE-110

Praise for the Inspector Bordelli novels:

'A typically intriguing and thought-provoking Vichi crime novel ... will be appreciated by both new readers and established fans alike' *Good Book Guide* on *Death in Florence*

'A rich, detailed, traditional detective story ... The descriptions of Florence are delicious, dripping with atmosphere' *Saga* on *Death in Florence*

'Once again [Vichi's] depiction of Italian history and culture is both fascinating and complex ... As a portrait of a country struggling with its past, present and future, *Death in Sardinia* is a sharply observed slice of crime fiction with real depth.' *www.crimetime.co.uk*

'Vichi's prose transports readers to the deserted, sweltering streets of down-and-out Florence, thanks to a translation by Stephen Sartarelli that conveys the dialogue with a lyricism and tongue-in-cheek wit one instinctively senses were present in the original. Straight from the city that brought us da Vinci and Dante, Vichi is on a par with writers like Henning Mankell and Elizabeth George who have elevated the police procedural to a work of art.' *www.shelf-awareness.com* on *Death in August*

'Over the course of his police procedurals, Vichi shows us ever more secret and dark sides to an otherwise sunny and open city. But his happiest creation, in my opinion, remains the character of Inspector Bordelli, a disillusioned anti-hero who is not easy to forget.' Andrea Camilleri

Also by Marco Vichi

Death in August
Death and the Olive Grove
Death in Sardinia

About the author

Marco Vichi was born in Florence in 1957. The author of twelve novels and two collections of short stories, he has also edited crime anthologies, written screenplays, music lyrics and for radio, written for Italian newspapers and magazines, and collaborated on and directed various projects for humanitarian causes.

There are five novels and two short stories featuring Inspector Bordelli. *Death in Sardinia* was shortlisted for the Crime Writers' Association International Dagger 2013 in the UK, and *Death in Florence* (*Morte a Firenze*) won the Scerbanenco, Rieti, Camaiore and Azzeccagarbugli prizes in Italy. Marco Vichi lives in the Chianti region of Tuscany.

You can find out more at www.marcovichi.it.

About the translator

Stephen Sartarelli is an award-winning translator. He is also the author of three books of poetry. He lives in France.

MARCO VICHI

DEATH in FLORENCE

AN

INSPECTOR BORDELLI

MYSTERY

Originally published in Italian as *Morte a Firenze*
Translated by Stephen Sartarelli

HODDER

First published in Great Britain in 2013 by Hodder & Stoughton
An Hachette UK company

First published in paperback in 2013

6

Copyright © Ugo Guanda Editore, S.p.A., Parma 2009
Translation copyright © Stephen Sartarelli 2013

Paperback ISBN 978 1 444 71230 8
Ebook ISBN 978 1 444 71231 5

Typeset in Plantin Light by Palimpsest Book Production Limited,
Falkirk, Stirlingshire
Printed and bound by Clays Ltd, St Ives plc

Hodder & Stoughton policy is to use papers that are natural, renewable
and recyclable products and made from wood grown in sustainable
forests. The logging and manufacturing processes are expected to
conform to the environmental regulations of the country of origin.

Hodder & Stoughton Ltd
338 Euston Road
London NW1 3BH

www.hodder.co.uk

'What about Christ?' my mother asked. 'He saved us from corruption.'

'He died for no reason,' I said. 'His sacrifice didn't change anything. The good save themselves, but nothing can be done for the wicked. And man is wicked.'

Malaparte

Florence, October 1966

Still half asleep, he reached out with one hand, seeking Elvira's warm body, but encountered only coarse linen sheets. Then he remembered that she was gone. He rolled on to his back and stared into the darkness. Another woman had entered his life and then left in a hurry, like a bullet through flesh. Perhaps the right woman for him would not be born for another hundred years, or else she was born a long time ago and had already lived and died. Whatever the case, they would never meet.

Every time he found himself alone again, an unknown world appeared before him, in need of rebuilding. It was a little like being reborn, and he felt a new freedom slithering under the malaise . . .

What time was it? He glanced at the shutters and saw no light filtering through the slats. He felt like a wreck. The hope that the little boy would be found alive was growing slimmer by the day. Little Giacomo had vanished into nothingness five days ago. Just turned thirteen, chestnut hair, brown eyes, four foot eleven. An untroubled boy, studious and obedient. But what if he'd only run away from home? It's normal to do silly things at age thirteen . . .

He would have given anything for this to be the case, but he didn't believe it for a second. He talked about it often with Piras, his young right-hand man, but even he was pessimistic. They hadn't made any progress at all, hadn't the slightest lead to go on . . .

The ring of the doorbell gave him a start, and then he remembered Botta. It was Monday. His ex-con friend had wheedled him into promising to take him mushroom-hunting in the hills, at Poggio alla Croce. It was the right moment, Botta said. After many days of rain, there'd been a bit of sunshine and temperatures had gone up. Monday was an excellent day for it, since there wouldn't be any little families about on country outings, and very few hunters. Bordelli wasn't so crazy about mushrooms; he didn't know the first thing about them and had never gone looking for them. But a walk in the woods would do him good. Worrying about the boy was wearing him out.

He rolled out of bed and looked out of the window, feeling the cool air on his face. The sky was still dark, and he could barely make out a shadow on the pavement below.

'Ennio, is that you?' he called softly.

'No, it's the tooth fairy.'

'Come on up and have some coffee.'

Closing the window without making too much noise, he went and opened the door in his bare feet. Then he quickly slipped on a pair of trousers and washed his face with cold water to wake himself up. When Botta saw him in his vest, he threw up his hands.

'Don't tell me you were sleeping, Inspector . . . It's already half past five . . .'

'Put the coffee on, I'll be there in a minute.'

He finished getting dressed, took a pair of old hiking boots out of the wardrobe and rejoined Botta in the kitchen. They gulped down their coffee and went out. In the silence of the San Frediano quarter, Bordelli's VW Beetle made an infernal racket.

They pulled out into Piazza Tasso and turned left. Viale Petrarca was deserted under the black sky. When they got to Porta Romana, they turned on to Viale di Poggio Imperiale. Climbing uphill, the Beetle roared like a tank.

'Promise me one thing, Ennio.'

'Let's hear it . . .'

'Promise you won't cry if we don't find any mushrooms.'

'That's not possible, Inspector. We'll find so many that we'll have to leave a lot of them behind.'

'What makes you so sure?'

'You just do your job, which you do well . . . but don't bother with things you know nothing about.'

'I wish I were as much of an optimist as you.'

He was thinking about the missing boy, feeling almost guilty for wasting time hunting for mushrooms. But what else could he do? Sit in his office chewing his nails while looking at photos of little Giacomo? What good would that do?

'We'll have to arrange a dinner of porcini dishes,' Botta said with self-assurance. The inspector didn't reply. At that moment he had no desire for dinners with friends. First he had to find Giacomo Pellissari. But for now he had to stop thinking about him. His brain needed a rest. Going round in circles was more tiring than chasing prey.

They pulled up at Poggio alla Croce with their headlights still on and parked in a clearing of wet grass. Dawn was approaching. Bordelli put on his boots and they began to climb the slope in the cold morning air. The path was steep and full of rocks and mud. Botta trudged on with his basket swaying by his side. After just a minute of this, they were both panting heavily, steam rising from their mouths.

Beyond the hills the sky was turning greenish, and the birds of the forest began to go crazy. A thin layer of fog that smelled of rotten leaves hung stagnant in the air. In the half-light Bordelli saw a thin spider's web glistening with tiny dewdrops, and he remembered a morning in '44. He was returning from patrol with six men of his platoon, and he'd seen some droplets just like these, gleaming in the darkness along a wire as thin as a hair stretching between two trees. But it wasn't a spider's web. If torn, that string would trigger a 'ballerina' mine, a bomb which, before exploding, would bounce up in the air to the level of your belly. He'd seen a number of his mates die from those toys, their guts torn out.

'Over here, Inspector,' Botta whispered, as if other people might hear him.

Leaving the path, they dived into the woods, clambering up

the slope, grabbing on to the slenderest trees. Bordelli looked up at the sky through the boughs of the chestnuts. Watching the day break had always made him feel very sad, for no reason. During the war he'd managed to see the sun rise almost every day, and every time he'd thought it might be the last.

The sky turned violet, then orange, and a few minutes later it was day. Botta studied the ground, occasionally making sudden detours, as though following a non-existent trail. A few wild boar scampered silently away through sheets of fog, towards the hilltop, steam rising from their coats. For someone who went often into the woods, the sight would not have been anything special, but it gave Bordelli a childlike thrill. Only when patrolling the hills had he ever seen wild animals dashing through the trees, and every time he had aimed his machine gun with his heart racing. This time he could enjoy the spectacle.

They continued climbing. Botta refused to slow down, and at times seemed to speed up. The inspector could feel his heart beating fast, and his legs were already tired. The cigarettes and his fifty-six years were making themselves felt. And to think that in the days of the San Marco regiment he was walking up to fifteen miles a day, carrying a full backpack and weapons . . . But why did he always have to think back on that blasted war? Couldn't he just enjoy the outing?

Every so often Botta would bend down to the ground to examine a cluster of odd-looking mushrooms, some slender and whitish, others squat and dark, still others very fragile, then frown and mutter a few scientific or ordinary names. Then he would dismiss them and resume climbing.

'Why didn't you pick those? Are they poisonous?' Bordelli asked, following behind him. Botta shook his head.

'It's porcini or nothing,' he said solemnly, then fell silent again. At a certain point he stopped suddenly and opened his eyes wide.

'What is it?' Bordelli asked, worried. Botta looked at him, round-eyed.

'You're not going to believe this, Inspector . . . but I can smell porcini from afar. I don't need to go around scouring every corner of the woods.'

'Don't worry, I know an excellent psychiatrist,' said Bordelli.

'You don't believe me, eh?'

'I'm trying as hard as I can.'

'Voilà . . .' said Botta, as though inspired.

'What's happening?'

'The mushrooms are up there,' Botta said, pointing upwards, and a second later he dashed off. The inspector let him go on ahead, since he was unable to keep up with him. He could still feel the dinner of the night before in his legs: *Pappardelle alla lepre, arista con patate,* and Totò's Apulian wine at the Trattoria da Cesare. He watched Botta vanish through the black trunks of the chestnuts. He continued climbing, sweating from the effort. Fifteen minutes later he came out on to a broad path and stopped.

'Ennio . . . are you here?'

'Over here, Inspector,' Botta's voice called through the leaves. Bordelli caught a glimpse of him some fifty yards ahead, bending over amid the trees. He resumed walking and caught up to him.

'Careful not to step on them,' said Botta, alarmed. He was kneeling and delicately cleaning a few large porcini with an ordinary bristle brush. There were dozens of mushrooms all around them.

'So you *can* smell them . . .' said Bordelli, sincerely astonished.

'Do I make things up, Inspector?' Ennio was serious and concentrating, still carefully brushing the mushrooms with gestures that looked as though inspired by some archaic religion. Bordelli would have to wait for Botta to finish his work, and so he sat down on a rock. His gaze jumped from one chestnut tree to another, looking for wild animals. The only movement was that of the leaves falling from above. They would become suddenly detached and float slowly to the ground, as in a famous poem he knew nothing about. In the peace and quiet his thoughts turned back to Giacomo Pellissari, the boy's desperate parents, the long discussions with Piras . . . How could a little boy vanish just like that, into thin air?

'There must be at least two kilos here,' said Botta, weighing the full basket in his hand. He was beaming like the victor after a battle.

'I'm truly amazed.' The inspector sighed, rising to his feet. 'Let's have another look around.'

They resumed their climb, feet sinking into the bed of dead leaves as blackbirds fluttered between the trees. They forged on in silence, one behind the other, Botta inevitably leading the way.

'Can I ask you something, Ennio?'

'Go right ahead . . .'

'What are you doing these days to put food on the table?'

'Are you asking as a police inspector or as a friend?'

'As a friend.'

'I'm doing what I've always done.'

'Burgling and swindling?'

'What unpleasant words, Inspector . . .'

'I don't know what else to call it.'

'Let's just say I'm implementing a policy of redistribution of wealth while waiting for more honest laws.'

'I'm touched . . .'

'You can cry all you want up here, I won't tell anyone,' said Botta, still studying the ground.

'Why don't you just get a normal job, Ennio? I say it for your own sake. You've always had bad luck as an outlaw. You're always getting into trouble.'

'I'm never going back to jail, Inspector.'

'You could become a cook . . .'

'Well, it's possible I might open a trattoria sooner or later.'

'Where would you get the money?'

'If a certain job goes well for me . . .' Botta trailed off, stopped suddenly, and let out a long moan and opened his arms.

'Are you all right?' Bordelli asked, concerned.

'Look at this, Inspector. The first Caesar's mushroom of the season.' Botta sighed, full of emotion. An orangish sort of ball was poking up through the leaves on the ground.

'I'll try not to scream for joy,' said Bordelli.

'You can't understand, Inspector. It's like kissing a girl for the first time.'

'You don't know what you're talking about . . .'

'Amazing,' Ennio whispered, delicately picking the mushroom.

'Weren't you only looking for porcini?'

'There must be more of these around,' said Botta, ignoring him. He wrapped the golden mushroom in a handkerchief, put it in his pocket, and continued looking around. He found six more. He looked very satisfied.

'That's enough for today,' he said. 'We mustn't be greedy.'

Bordelli looked at his watch. It wasn't yet nine o'clock.

'What a beautiful place this is. It feels so good to be here.' He sighed, looking around. A moment later he slipped on a rock and fell on his bottom. He picked his aching body up off the ground, ignoring Botta's laughter. He'd muddied his trousers and his ears were ringing from the tumble.

'Bloody hell . . .' he said, picking the wet leaves off himself.

'You should never say out loud how great a place is, Inspector. The devil can't read our minds, but he can hear us just fine when we talk.'

'Did the nuns teach you that?'

'*Sah vah sahn deer*, Inspector,'[1] said Botta, who'd learned a little pidgin French in a Marseille prison.

They continued walking along the trails, forging on through the chestnuts and oaks, accompanied by strange birdsongs and the rustlings as the wind gusted through the branches. They saw a few more animals scamper off through the underbrush, and here and there they passed an old campsite, where the ground was still charred black from the fire. Old memories streamed confusedly through Bordelli's mind. Memories of

7

childhood, the war, old girlfriends now faceless. But elbowing its way through every thought was the mystery of the missing boy. Bordelli was beginning to think he'd been kidnapped by Martians . . .

Bordelli drove Botta back to his basement flat in Via del Campuccio then quickly dashed home to change clothes. It was already half past ten. After a long hot shower he began to get dressed, in no hurry. In his mind he could still see the dark tree trunks, the wisps of fog, the wild boar . . . but his thoughts were elsewhere. For the umpteenth time he reviewed in his head the reports of the disappearance of Giacomo Pellissari, in the absurd hope that he might finally discover a detail that would give him a lead to follow.

The boy had vanished the previous Wednesday, after coming out of his grammar school, the Collegio alla Quercia, in a torrential downpour. His father had taken him there at 8.25 that morning, as always. Normally when the school day ended, one of his parents was always there to pick him up. But that day, when his mother had gone down to the garage to get her Fiat 600, the car wouldn't start. She rang her husband at the office, and he'd got in his car immediately and headed for the Collegio. But he arrived more than an hour late, owing to an accident on the Viali caused by the downpour. Protecting himself with an umbrella, he'd gone into the school's entrance hall, expecting to find his son waiting there for him, but there was no sign of Giacomo. The school caretaker threw up his hands. He said the boy had waited for him until well past one o'clock and had even phoned home, but the line was always busy . . . In the end he'd left, running out into the rain, and there was no stopping him.

Bordelli lit a cigarette, again reviewing the matter down to the small details. By this point it was like watching a film. He

9

was quite familiar with the area between the Collegio alla Quercia and the Pellissaris' villa in Via di Barbacane. In fact he'd grown up in that very neighbourhood.

Barrister Pellissari had asked the custodian if he could phone his wife, but he, too, had found the line always engaged. And so he got back in his car and drove slowly along the route home: Via della Piazzuola, Viale Volta, Via di Barbacane. Giacomo wasn't at home. His wife was worried, but not terribly so. Perhaps Giacomo had ducked into a doorway to get out of the rain . . .

The barrister had gone over to the telephone in the hall and found the phone slightly off the hook. He upbraided his wife, and she began to get anxious. Pellissari went out again in his Alfa Romeo and combed the streets of the neighbourhood. He went up and down Via Aldini, a small, deserted street connecting Viale Volta and Via di Barbacane, several times. Giacomo knew the street well. It was just round the corner from home, and he liked to bicycle there with his friends . . .

At three o'clock the barrister had finally decided to call the police. Two patrolmen had gone to the Collegio alla Quercia to speak with the custodian, Oreste, a small man with very little hair and pink cheeks, who blanched upon hearing the news. They asked him to recount the sequence of events, and Oreste was very precise. After the usual chaos when school let out, he'd gone into the street to look at the rain. He'd found the boy in the doorway with his satchel between his feet, gazing anxiously out at Via della Piazzuola. He asked him whether he wanted to call his mother. Giacomo said yes and followed the caretaker to the porter's desk. He dialled his home number several times, but the line was always engaged. He seemed afraid, and Oreste had tried to reassure him. Somebody'd be along soon to pick him up, he'd said to him, there was no need to worry, it was obviously because of the rain. The boy went out again to look down the street, with Oreste following behind him. And then, less than a minute later, Giacomo had run out into the rain, coat over his head, satchel bouncing on his back.

Oreste shouted to him to wait, saying that he would walk him home himself, but the child didn't listen and kept on running. The caretaker had tried dialling Giacomo's parents' phone number again, but the line was still busy. In the end he'd decided there was nothing to worry about, and he stopped thinking about it.

A squad of policemen had questioned the inhabitants of all the buildings and houses along the road that went from the Collegio to the Pelissaris' villa, including Via Aldini. Only an old woman had seen from her window a young boy walking hurriedly in the rain at the corner of Viale Volta and Via della Piazzuola, around quarter past one. The clothes, the colour of the satchel, and the time left no room for doubt. The boy was Giacomo Pellissari. The old woman had been the last person to see him, and her testimony eliminated any shadow of a doubt as to the caretaker's sincerity. Nothing else had come out since, but that was to be expected. When Giacomo had left the school, it was lunchtime and raining cats and dogs, and everyone else was minding his own business.

Photos of the boy had appeared in all the newspapers and been broadcast on the national news and that of Channel 2, but nobody had come forward as yet. How can a boy disappear into thin air?

When he parked the car in the station's courtyard it was past
10.30. Mugnai popped out of the guardhouse and came up to
him, looking as if his dog had just died.

'Good morning, Inspector.'

'Hello, Mugnai . . . Why so cheerful?'

'The commissioner's got a stick up his arse, if you'll pardon
my language.'

'That's nothing new,' said Bordelli.

'It's not my fault the kid hasn't turned up! He treated me
like a blockhead.' He was very offended.

'Don't take it so hard, Mugnai,' said Bordelli.

'The boss said he wants to see you at once.'

'Fuckin' hell . . .' The inspector sighed.

'Prepare yourself. He's really pissed off today.'

'Too bad for him. Find Piras for me, would you? And tell
him to come to my office.'

He gestured goodbye to Mugnai and started up the stairs.
He went up to the second floor with a cigarette in his mouth,
promising himself he wouldn't smoke it before noon. He knocked
on Inzipone's door and went in without waiting. The moment
he saw him, the commissioner jumped to his feet, but certainly
not out of politeness. His eyes looked like burnt chestnuts.

'You must find that child, Inspector!' he shouted, shaking
his hands in the air.

'I want to more than anyone else, sir,' Bordelli said calmly.

'Then what's taking you so long? Have you read the papers?
POLICE POWERLESS! LAW ENFORCEMENT ASLEEP!' He came
towards Bordelli, waving *La Nazione* in the air.

'We're doing everything we can.'

'I'm not interested in your excuses! Get on with it, dammit!'

'He vanished into thin air,' said Bordelli, with a strong desire to light the cigarette between his fingers.

'Nobody vanishes into thin air,' said Inzipone. He tossed the newspaper aside and went and sat back down at his desk. Bordelli drew closer, still standing.

'We'll find him,' he said, more to himself than to the commissioner.

'I certainly hope so, Inspector, for your sake. I got a call this morning from the Deputy Minister of Transport. Barrister Pellissari is a very dear friend of his.'

'Ah, I didn't know. That changes everything. You'll see, we'll find the boy before the day is over.'

'Drop the sarcasm, Inspector,' said the commissioner, raising his chin with an air of menace. Bordelli put the cigarette in his mouth and lit it, before the commissioner's goggling eyes.

'Then I'll be clearer. I don't give a damn whose son he is.'

'And you think I do?' said Inzipone, furious at Bordelli's insolence.

'I can never speak for others, sir,' said the inspector, taking his leave with a slight nod and heading for the door. He heard the commissioner stand up again, making the legs of his armchair squeak.

'I don't like your way of doing things one bit, Inspector.'

'I am truly sorry,' Bordelli said without turning around.

'And you know I'm not the only who feels this way.'

'My respects, sir.'

'There must be a reason you're still an inspector at your age . . .' the commissioner muttered between clenched teeth, but Bordelli heard him just the same. He went out, closing the door behind him. He wished he was still up in the foggy hills with Botta, looking for porcini mushrooms through the rotting leaves. He went into his office and found Piras there waiting for him, sitting in front of the desk.

13

'At ease . . .' he said, but the young Sardinian had already shot to his feet. He still limped a little from the bullets that had shattered one of his legs a year before. He was barely twenty-two years old, but his considerable skills had convinced Bordelli to keep him by his side in every investigation. On top of this he was the son of Gavino Piras, a comrade of Bordelli's from the war, which made him even dearer to the inspector. Gavino had returned from the fighting minus an arm, but hadn't stopped living a farmer's life. But, all things considered, even he had been damned lucky . . . Bordelli still remembered the time Gavino had taken a grenade square in the chest, but it hadn't exploded. It just bounced off his uniform and fell at his feet like a rock . . . In the heat of the moment the German had forgotten to pull the ring, and Gavino cut him down with a single burst of fire. After the skirmish, he'd approached Bordelli.

'Even grenades are afraid of Sardinians, Captain,' he'd whispered, wild-eyed. He was well aware he'd been saved by a miracle . . .

'You wanted to see me, Inspector?' asked young Piras.

'Yes, I wanted to share my ball-aches with you.'

'Are you thinking what I'm thinking?'

'Unfortunately, yes.'

Without actually admitting it, they were now both convinced the boy was dead. No ransom demands, no anonymous telephone calls.

'Let's hope we're wrong, sir,' said Piras, who had sat back down in the meantime.

Bordelli went over to the window and looked outside. It was starting to rain again, for a change. The respite had lasted only two days.

'What should we do, Piras? Reread the reports? Eat them? Go and play a game of *bocce*? What the hell should we do?'

'If I can speak sincerely . . .'

'Go ahead.'

'Our only hope is to find the body.'

'Bloody rain,' Bordelli whispered, watching the large drops splatter on the asphalt. Dejected, he lit a cigarette. A receiver off the hook, buckets of rain, Signora Pellissari's Fiat that wouldn't start . . . A series of unlucky coincidences? Was it a premeditated kidnapping, or had chance stuck her grubby paws in this?

The internal phone line rang. It was the radio room. A car with two corpses inside it had been found a few hundred yards from the monastery of Montesenario. A man and a woman. At first glance it looked like a double suicide.

'All right, I'm on my way . . . Inform Diotivede and the assistant prosecutor,' Bordelli said calmly before hanging up.

'What is it?' Piras was already standing.

'I'll tell you in the stairwell,' the inspector muttered, taking a deep drag on his cigarette. He was doing his best not to smoke, but between women and corpses, it wasn't easy.

'Slow down, Inspector,' said Piras, limping.

'Sorry, I always forget.'

He slowed to the young man's pace and they went down into the courtyard. It was deluging. Mugnai saw them and came running out with a large green country umbrella that covered all three of them. While walking them to the Beetle, he asked what seven-letter word might describe the *Hill ever dear to Leopardi*.

'Forlorn,' Piras and Bordelli said in chorus. They got into the car and left, leaving Mugnai behind to his thoughts.

As they drove through Piazza delle Cure the rain let up a little, but the sky was still black. The inspector was thinking that it was a relief to deal with something concrete, even if it meant two dead.

Half an hour later they were at Montesenario. There was a pair of patrol cars there, as well as a few onlookers. It was still drizzling with a monotonous persistence that tried even the most steadfast patience. Bordelli approached the Fiat 600 and looked inside. A man of about forty with a hole in his left temple and a woman of about thirty with her hand on her bloodstained lap, both with their mouths half open. The back seat was stacked high with fabric catalogues.

'Keep those people away,' Bordelli said to one of the uniformed cops. He tried opening the door on the driver's side. It was unlocked. He stuck his head inside to have a close look at the corpses and bullet holes. The woman had been shot in the belly. Unlike hers, the man's eyes were wide open. He searched the man's jacket and the woman's handbag for their papers, then stepped aside to let Piras have a look. He was almost convinced he knew how things had unfolded, and wanted to see whether the Sardinian agreed. He waited patiently for Piras to finish.

'What do you think?' he asked him.

'It wasn't premeditated,' said the young man.

'Go on . . .'

'Two illicit lovers. They had a quarrel, he threatened her with the pistol, she perhaps made fun of him, saying the pistol wasn't loaded, and so he pulls back the slide and lets it go, not knowing that would make the gun go off. Seeing that he's killed her by accident, he loses his head and shoots himself.'

'Makes perfect sense to me,' said Bordelli, handing him the two poor souls' papers. The man was married, the woman too, but not to each other.

At that moment the Fiat 1100 of Dr Diotivede pulled up, as black and shiny as a politician's shoe. The old police pathologist got out with his medical bag in hand, also black, naturally. His snow-white hair gleamed in the morning light. As he approached the two lovers' car, he gave an almost imperceptible nod of greeting. He always wore a childlike frown on his face, as if he'd just been woken up to go to school. Opening his bag, he stuck his hands inside and then withdrew them already sheathed in rubber gloves. He ducked into the car to touch the corpses. Less than a minute later he peeled off his gloves.

'The woman died two hours later than the man, maybe even two and a half,' he said, jotting his first notes down in his notebook.

'Are you sure about that?' asked Bordelli.

'No, I was just kidding,' Diotivede grumbled, still writing.

'It wasn't really a question . . .'

'I have to go now, I have a rendezvous with an old lady,' the doctor said, putting his notebook away.

'Dead or alive?'

'What difference does it make?' said Diotivede, smiling, and he started walking towards his car, bag swaying at his side. A child with white hair, thought Bordelli, also smiling. The doctor swung the car around and headed down the hill.

Piras and Bordelli followed him moments later, descending in silence along the tortuous Montesenario road. There was no mystery to the tragedy, no secrets to uncover. There was no point in waiting for the assistant prosecutor. Prosecutor Cangiani wasn't the most pleasant person in the world.

And so the inspector found himself wrestling with the case of the missing boy again, and it was clear that Piras was thinking of the same thing. It had become a sort of obsession for both. It was the first time Bordelli had found himself in this situation, and he was having trouble swallowing it. When they got to Piazza delle Cure, Piras shook his head.

'Shit, Inspector . . .'

'What is it, Piras?'

'I just can't stand sitting here twiddling my thumbs like this.'

'What else can we do?' said Bordelli, lighting a cigarette. Piras rolled down his window and stuck his head outside, as though afraid he might suffocate. He found cigarettes disgusting and couldn't understand how an intelligent person could waste time smoking them. A cold wind blew in, insinuating itself under their clothing.

'I can throw it away, if you like,' the inspector said.

'And I can go on foot, if you prefer,' Piras said provocatively.

Bordelli took two or three drags in a row and threw out the cigarette, and Piras finally closed the window. After a minute of very Sardinian silence, he said that when he was about ten years old, a little girl had been murdered in his town. Raped and strangled. In all the towns around nobody talked about anything else. It took them several months to find the killer, and it was only by chance. One day, during mass in a nearby town, a little yellow ribbon happened to fall out of the priest's pocket. A woman who knew the young girl's family was almost certain she recognised the ribbon, and to be sure she went to the *carabinieri* after the mass. The little girl had worn her hair in a ponytail, and her mother would always make a bow with a yellow ribbon just like that one. The priest was questioned. At first he pretended to be taken aback, but he was visibly nervous. In the end he confessed. After one hour in jail he hanged himself from the bars of his cell with a sort of rope fashioned from shreds of his shirt . . .

'It's always nice to hear such cheerful stories,' Bordelli said, smiling bitterly.

'Well, at least they found the killer . . .'

'Not so fast, Piras. Nobody's said the boy was killed yet,' said the inspector, thinking the exact opposite.

'Thirteen-year-olds don't usually elope,' Piras muttered.

'Let's just wait . . . You never know.'

They were back at the station. Bordelli left the Beetle in the courtyard, took leave of Piras, and went on foot to the Trattoria da Cesare, on Viale Lavagnini. He greeted the owner and waiters and, as usual, slipped into Totò's kitchen, where the Apulian cook fought his daily battles between frying pans and clouds of smoke. It was also where the inspector had been taking his meals for years.

Totò was in fine form that day, more or less as he always was. Four feet eleven inches of sheer exuberance and nasty black hair sprouting from every pore. He greeted the inspector and recommended grilled pork chops with black-eyed peas. Bordelli nodded, resigned. He'd entered that kitchen many times swearing he would eat lightly, but rarely if ever had he kept his vow. He sat down and waited for Totò to fill his plate with those gifts of God.

'Have a taste of this, Inspector . . . . Allow me to teach a Florentine how these things should be made.'

'Thanks, Totò. It's just what I need.'

'That little kid still on your mind, eh?'

'Could you do me a favour and not mention it?'

'Of course, Inspector, of course.'

Totò was always busy but never stopped talking. He too told a few little stories of murdered children, down in the Salento, going into the details as though talking about how to make *spaghetti alla carbonara*. Bordelli listened in silence, washing down the pork with a red wine that made him weak at the knees.

After the short tales from back home, Totò started talking about long-haired hippies. He saw a lot of them about, these days. More and more, in fact. He liked them, actually, sort of like puppies. But he simply couldn't understand how a man could wear his hair like a woman without feeling embarrassed.

'In the past it was perfectly normal,' said Bordelli.

'I'd like to see what you'd look like with hair like a girl's,' said Totò, laughing and turning over a huge steak. He poured out a pot of pasta and a minute later set six steaming plates down on the counter of the serving hatch. Then with a smile on his lips he put a slice of apple tart and a small glass of *vin santo* down in front of the inspector.

Leaving the trattoria, Bordelli felt guilty for having succumbed to temptation. He lit a cigarette and started walking at a leisurely pace back to the station, thinking of the long afternoon ahead.

A beautiful girl in a rather short skirt walked past, and he turned around to look at her, very nearly crashing into a scooter parked on the pavement. He almost blushed, thinking he could be her father . . . if not her grandfather. He turned around again to look at her. But wasn't she cold, he wondered, with her legs all uncovered like that? He still hadn't got used to seeing such short hemlines, and they always had a powerful effect on him.

He thought of Elvira and their last night together. A night like all the others, except that the following day she'd left him, after the briefest of phone calls. She was very pretty, Elvira. She had a mole on her lip and another on her left breast.

'Poor old teddy bear, all alone again . . .' said Rosa, doing his fingernails with little scissors and emery boards. Bordelli was lying on the sofa with his shoes off, a glass of grappa resting on his chest. Every so often he raised his head to take a sip. The songs of Tony Dallara softly filled the room at low volume.

Rosa loved doing these little things for her policeman friend, especially when he was down. She would squeeze his blackheads, wash his face with creams, give him manicures, massage his back . . . Ever since she'd given up the profession she'd become a bit melancholy, but also sweeter. A tender retired prostitute with the soul of a little girl. Her big white cat, Gideon, was sleeping on a chair.

'I feel like Calimero,' said Bordelli.[2]

'You're always chasing pretty girls . . .'

'That's not true.'

'Yes it is.' She had a small, strange smile on her lips.

'At my age I'd like to find a nice, pretty woman who will stay with me till I die,' Bordelli said melodramatically. At least Rosa wasn't talking about the missing boy.

'I know the kind of woman you need.'

'I love it when you play Mummy for me . . .'

'I mean it.'

'And what kind of woman do I need?'

'I've noticed that you like dark women with long straight hair. Young and slender with dark, mysterious eyes . . .'

'Who wouldn't like a woman like that?'

'But that's not the kind of woman you need.'

'Oh no?'

'I could easily see you with a blonde of about forty, slightly chubby, always cheerful, who, whenever you came home, would throw her arms around you and drag you to bed.'

'Just the thought of it turns my stomach.' Bordelli sighed.

'You're not very nice, you know. I was describing someone a bit like myself,' said Rosa, pretending to be offended. Fortunately she didn't stop filing his nails.

'You're not the least bit chubby,' said Bordelli, trying to patch things up.

'Really?'

'I would swear to it under oath.'

'Well, I'm not exactly an anchovy, either . . . But maybe you're right, maybe I'm not chubby.'

'You're just a little . . .'

'A little what?'

'I can't think of the word, but you know what I mean,' said Bordelli, not daring to utter the wrong thing. Rosa finished with one hand, and picked up the other.

'Anyway, a little flesh is always a good thing,' she concluded, chuckling.

After a minute or so of silence, she started talking about her friend Tecla, who had fallen down the stairs, hitting her mouth and breaking a tooth, an incisor . . . and now her lips were all swollen and purple . . . But she'd been lucky, she could have left her hide in that stairwell.

'That friend of yours was right when he said we're all like leaves on a tree when the wind is blowing . . .'

'He's not a friend of mine, he's a great poet.'

'Have I ever told you about my Uncle Costante? He used to write poetry too. He died in Russia, poor thing . . . Oh, and have I told you my girlfriends and I are planning to put on another play?'

'I don't think so.'

'It's planned for Epiphany . . . But this time you really have to come.'

'I'll do my best,' said Bordelli, knowing he would as usual invent some excuse not to come.

'I wrote it myself,' said Rosa, all excited.

'I didn't doubt it for a second.'

'Would you like me to read you a few passages?'

'I'd rather let it be a surprise . . .'

'It's a touching story, but it's also great fun. It's about the friendship between a nun and a whore, who trade places in the end . . .'

'Interesting.'

'It starts with Suor Celestina praying in church, late at night. She's just come out of the room of a novice – just out of her bed, actually. She knows she has sinned, and so she's praying to the Madonna for forgiveness . . .'

They heard the sweet ding-dong of the doorbell, and Rosa sprang up like a jack-in-the-box.

'Never mind, at this hour I'm sure it's a prank,' said Bordelli, holding her back by the hand.

'I know exactly who it is,' she said, trying to free herself.

'You're expecting a visitor at eleven o'clock?'

'It's a little surprise for you.'

'A young woman with black hair and mysterious eyes?'

'Don't be silly,' said Rosa.

The moment Bordelli let go of her hand, she bounded towards the door, followed by Gideon.

'So who is it?' Bordelli called after her. She didn't answer, and disappeared on to the landing. Bordelli quickly put his shoes back on and smoothed himself out. He had no idea who it could be.

Rosa returned moments later, followed by a woman who, at first glance, looked to be about fifty, bundled up in an overcoat that went down to her ankles. Bordelli stood up.

'This is Amelia,' said Rosa.

'Pleased to meet you,' said Bordelli, making a slight bow. The woman responded with a mournful smile. She had a small head and a nose as narrow as a T-bone. And deep, sad eyes.

Rosa helped her take off her coat, and Amelia immediately became ten years younger.

'Amelia reads the tarot. She's very good.'

'Ah, how nice . . .' said Bordelli.

'She's here for you,' Rosa whispered.

'For me?'

'Aren't you pleased?'

'Of course I am . . .' He didn't want to offend Amelia.

'Would you like something to drink, Amelia?' Rosa asked. The woman declined with a faint tilt of the head. Rosa cleared the coffee table, pulled up a chair for the fortune-teller, and dimmed the lights in the room.

'All ready,' she said, chuckling like a child.

Amelia sat down and arranged the tarot cards on the table. She wore a jade necklace wrapped twice around her neck, and in the half-light the stones looked black. Bordelli was trying not to laugh.

'What would you like to know?' the seer asked in a whisper. He gave a slightly embarrassed look. He'd never believed in these silly things.

'I don't know . . .'

'Love, first of all,' said Rosa, speaking for him, and Bordelli shot her a worried glance.

Amelia started turning the cards over, studying them carefully. In the dimness her long, thin nose had something sinister about it. When all the cards were face up, she raised her head and looked Bordelli straight in the eye. Her gaze was now aflame, without a trace of sadness.

'A beautiful blonde woman, about thirty-five . . . suddenly broke off a relationship, a short time ago . . .'

'That's true,' Bordelli whispered, trying to hide his scepticism. Rosa must certainly have informed the fortune-teller.

'She wasn't the right woman for you,' Amelia said darkly. Rosa couldn't suppress a smile.

'You see? I was right,' she said, quite pleased. The seer took another look at the cards.

'Soon you will meet a beautiful, dark-haired young woman . . . a great passion will ensue, but it won't last long . . . Something horrible will come between you . . . And she's not the love of your life, either . . .'

'And will I ever find her? The love of my life, I mean,' the inspector asked, so as not to disappoint the two women. He couldn't wait to lie back down on the sofa. Amelia looked hard through her tarot cards and at last found something.

'In a few years . . . A beautiful woman, a foreigner . . . very rich . . . divorced . . . with two children . . .'

'I really don't see that happening,' the inspector muttered.

'. . . I can't tell you whether it will be for ever, but it will certainly be the greatest love affair of your life,' Amelia concluded, looking up.

'Are you sure about that?' the inspector asked, feigning keen interest.

'The cards never lie,' said the fortune-teller. She calmly collected the tarot cards and put the deck back together.

'Now for his health,' said Rosa.

'No, please . . . I don't want to know anything about it,' Bordelli was quick to say, just out of superstitiousness. The clairvoyant looked at him, waiting for him to ask something else. Rosa butted in again.

'Tell him something about his job, Amelia. The inspector is trying to find that boy who went missing.'

'Never mind about that, Rosa,' said Bordelli, but the fortune-teller was already lining the cards up on the table . . . A devil, a death's-head, a sun . . . and other images the inspector looked at without interest. Gideon had fled to the darkest corner of the room, green pupils glowing in the dark. Suddenly Amelia gave a start and brought her hands to her face.

'What is it?' Rosa asked anxiously.

The fortune-teller gestured to her to keep quiet and kept looking at the cards with an anguished expression. The inspector fumbled for a cigarette and lit it. In spite of himself he felt a long shudder run up his spine. The whole thing had taken him by surprise. He looked at the fortune-teller, waiting for her to say something.

'Tomorrow morning . . .' she stammered, unable to continue.

'Tomorrow morning what?' asked Bordelli, now gripped by the situation. To find little Giacomo, he was ready to follow any lead whatsoever, even the most absurd. But the psychic didn't answer. She collected the cards and stood up. Her gaze seemed far away.

'Amelia, what's got into you?' Rosa asked, as though feeling guilty. It was she who had asked her to consult the tarot about the missing boy. The fortune-teller put on her coat without saying a word. She gestured to Rosa to let her know she wanted to leave and headed for the door. Bordelli wanted to hold her back and ask her what she'd seen, but didn't have the courage. How could he let the power of suggestion make him believe such idiocies? How could the cards possibly know human destiny?

Rosa accompanied the card-reader on to the landing and stayed there for a few minutes. When she came back to Bordelli, he was already lying down with his shoes off, a small glass of grappa in his hand. She sat down beside him on the sofa, not bothering to turn the big lamp back on.

'Amelia refused to tell me anything,' she whispered in a dramatic tone.

'Could you massage my back with your golden hands?' Bordelli asked, already sitting up again.

'Of course, darling. Take your shirt off, and I'll go and get some cream,' said Rosa, and she got up and sashayed into the bathroom. It didn't take much to change her mood. Bordelli put out his cigarette, took off his shirt, and lay down on his stomach. Rosa returned with a jar of Nivea, took a big daub into her hands and, straddling his bottom, started massaging him.

'You've gained weight,' she said.

'No, it just looks that way to you.'

'I know about these things, you know . . .' she said with a

giggle. Bordelli was moaning with pleasure. Outside it started raining hard again. The wind picked up, and they heard a shutter slam. Weather for wolves. Gideon didn't give a damn. He was lying on top of the sideboard, belly up.

'Rosa, do you really believe that rubbish?'

'What rubbish?'

'The tarot, fortune-tellers . . .'

'Of course I do. My friend Asmara told me Amelia has read the tarot for her many times and has never been wrong, not even once, about the past *or* the future.'

'Give me an example.'

'Well, she told her her father had abandoned her as a child, and that her mother had died when she was six . . .'

'And about the future?'

'Last year she told her that she would have a small accident in January of this year, and it actually happened. She broke one of her little toes.'

'What else?' He liked to hear her talk.

'She told her she would be operated on for appendicitis, and that happened, too. She told her she would be receiving a small inheritance from a distant relative whom she'd never met, and that also came true. She told her one of her clients would fall in love with her and give her a beautiful ring . . . And it was all true, from A to Z.'

'Coincidence.'

'And she told you a blonde woman had just left you . . . What do you say about that?'

'A little bird must have told her . . .'

'I didn't tell her anything!' said Rosa defensively.

'Has Amelia ever read the cards for you?'

'Oh, no, I don't want to know anything about what's going to happen to me.'

'But you thought it was okay for her to read them for me.'

'What's wrong with that?' asked Rosa, kneading his spine like dough. Bordelli gave in to the pleasure, listening to the sound of the rain. He was trying not to think of the fact that sooner or later he would have to drag himself back to his flat. Rosa took a deep breath.

'Anyway, as I was saying . . . Suor Celestina's praying in the middle of the night when, all of a sudden, there's a knock on the convent door . . .'

The inspector was woken up at the crack of dawn by the ring of the telephone and threw himself out of bed. Even before answering, he knew what it was about.

'Yes?'

'Rinaldi here, sir. A hunter found a corpse buried in the wood, saw a foot sticking up from the ground. It looks like it belongs to a young boy . . .'

'Where?'

'La Panca district. We've already got a car on the way there,' Rinaldi said. The inspector couldn't help thinking of the last words uttered by Amelia: *Tomorrow morning* . . .

'Where exactly is this La Panca?'

'After the Strada in Chianti you turn left on to the Via di Cintoia and go on for another four or five miles. But to get there you have to take a trail that goes uphill towards the woods, in the direction of Monte Scalari.'

'I'll go and get Piras and then come up . . . . Call Diotivede—'

'What about the assistant prosecutor?'

'Wait a couple of hours to inform him: I don't feel like seeing him.'

'All right, sir.'

'Call the car and tell them nobody's to touch anything before I get there.'

'Yes, sir.'

As soon as Rinaldi hung up, the inspector rang Piras.

'I'll be by in ten minutes. They found a kid buried in the woods.'

'Shit, so it's him . . .'

29

'Try to be ready outside the front door.'

Bordelli got dressed in a hurry and went out without even drinking a cup of coffee. After a night of rain the sky was a clear, intense blue. The San Frediano quarter was beginning to wake up, and by now a few shops already had their rolling metal shutters half raised.

He stepped on the accelerator and was in Via Gioberti a few minutes later. Piras was already out on the pavement, eyes ringed with fatigue. He got into the car, frowning, and after a gesture of greeting, Bordelli drove off. The Beetle's persistent rumble echoed in the semi-deserted streets. Every so often they crossed paths with a scooter or another car. Dishevelled women appeared at the small balconies of their flats, coats over their nightgowns.

Leaving the city, they drove through Grassina. The Chiantigiana[3] was filling up with lorries and tiny, noisy three-wheeled vans filled with vegetables. The peasants were already out in the fields, toiling behind pairs of oxen or sitting atop modern tractors. The city was just round the corner, but out here it seemed farther away than the moon. The more or less smartly dressed, noisy and hedonistic youths who every evening poured into the streets downtown had nothing whatsoever in common with the wrinkled faces and dark gazes of a humanity that broke its back turning the earth.

They crossed Strada in Chianti and turned in the direction of Cintoia. After a mile or so, the road was unpaved, and the Beetle began to dance. To their left they saw forested hills standing out against the greenish sky. Past Cintoia Bassa, the curves grew tighter and tighter, and they had to slow down. A three-wheeled Ape van was struggling up the hill, spewing white smoke, and it wasn't easy to overtake it.

At last they arrived at La Panca, a hamlet of four houses around a bend in the road. They asked an old peasant woman for the road to Monte Scalari, and soon they were climbing a steep path. It was covered with rocks, and the car bounced this way and that. Wisps of fog gleamed white between the tree trunks. Some two or three hundred yards ahead, the main trail made a sharp turn to the right and continued upwards to Cintoia Alta, but they followed their directions and proceeded straight up through the woods. They came across a few busybodies climbing on foot, and Bordelli unceremoniously sent them back down. They ploughed on for another mile or so, sliding in the mud all the while. Round a bend appeared the squad car, parked in a clearing. The policeman on duty, Tapinassi, was standing by the car door, waiting. He came towards the inspector and stood to attention.

'Where's the little boy?' Bordelli asked.

'Over here, sir.'

Tapinassi gestured vaguely at Piras in greeting and led them towards the spot where the body had been found.

'Have you got a spade?' Bordelli asked.

'There's one already there,' Tapinassi replied.

They advanced another hundred feet along the path, then turned into the woods and continued climbing with effort through the trees. Every so often a strong gust of wind blew. In the spots where the carpet of dead leaves was thinnest, the sludge stuck to their shoes. The silence was beautiful, and Bordelli couldn't help but think of his walk with Botta.

'Tapinassi, do you know this area well?'

'No, sir. I'm not from around here, I was born at La Rufina.'

Moments later they saw the other policeman, Calosi, in the distance. Beside him was a man of about fifty with a double-barrelled shotgun slung over his shoulder and an Irish setter on a lead.

'Go back down and wait for Diotivede,' Bordelli ordered Tapinassi.

'Yes, sir.'

The young policeman headed back down towards the car. When Piras and the inspector reached the spot, Calosi leapt to attention and gave a military salute. Bordelli didn't even look at him. Together with Piras he went up to the freshly dug hole.

A small naked foot, half eaten by an animal and already decomposing, was sticking out.

'Wild boar,' Bordelli muttered. The nauseating stench of the corpse almost completely covered the crisp scent of the underbrush.

'It can only be him,' said Piras, a hand over his nose.

'We'll know straight away . . . Calosi, have you already taken pictures?'

'Yes, Inspector.'

'Pass me the spade.'

Bordelli started digging, trying to be careful. The hunter watched the scene with his mouth half open. The boy's leg appeared, then his thigh, bottom and back . . . And, in the end, his head. Completely naked. The smell was unbearable, and Calosi walked away, suppressing an urge to vomit. The boy lay face down. Bordelli turned him over with the help of the spade, and Piras frowned in disgust. The eye sockets were full of worms. The face was smeared with dirt, the features barely distinguishable. They heard a thud behind them and turned round. The hunter had fainted, and the dog started howling.

'Take care of that, would you, Calosi?' said Bordelli. He pulled his handkerchief out of his pocket and started cleaning the boy's face, careful not to touch it with his fingers. He felt as if he'd stumbled into an old painting about the plague. Every so often he had to turn his head away to breathe. He'd seen many corpses during the war. Children too, even newborns.

'It's him,' said Piras, immobile as a rock.

'Yeah, it's him,' the inspector muttered, tossing aside his muddied handkerchief. He'd seen only a few photos of the boy, but even so, it wasn't hard to recognise him. Giacomo Pellissari had finally been found. There he was, naked, soiled with mud, dead. The thought of having to tell his parents turned Bordelli's stomach. Meanwhile the hunter had come to, though he remained seated on the ground. The inspector approached him.

'Do you come up this way very often?' he asked him.

'Yes, I live in La Pescina, down by Lucolena,' said the hunter, looking away from the child's corpse. He was hollow-cheeked, with skin the colour of leather and ravaged by wrinkles. He must have been a peasant and was probably not much older than forty.

'Do you know the area well?' Bordelli asked.

'Like the back of my hand.'

'Are there any other roads that lead up here, aside from the one at La Panca?'

'There are several. From Figline, from Poggio alla Croce, and from Ponte agli Stolli by way of Celle, but all three are a lot rougher.'

'So a car can't make it up there?'

'No, too many rocks and holes. You'll drop your oil pan, you will . . .'

'And on foot?'

'On foot it's another matter.'

'Is Poggio alla Croce far from here?'

'Not very. Farther on there's the fork at the Cappella de' Boschi. You just keep to the left and it takes about an hour.'

'And where does the path on the right lead?'

'To Pian d'Albero, where Potente's[4] partisans were massacred. You can get to Poggio from there too . . . On foot, of course. They're nasty trails.'

'Thanks.' Bordelli lit a cigarette, thinking of his outing with Botta. Without realising, they had passed not far from the boy's corpse, but all they'd found were mushrooms.

'Can I go now?' the hunter asked.

'Just be patient for a little while longer. You're going to have to come down to the station to sign a statement,' said the inspector.

The sun was beginning to filter into the woods, spreading a golden glow between the black tree trunks. Piras caught Bordelli's attention with a whisper and pointed to two men approaching through the trees. It was Tapinassi and Diotivede.

The doctor gave a nod of greeting and went towards the

lifeless child without stopping. As soon as Tapinassi saw the corpse, he stopped dead in his tracks, white as a sheet. He stood there for a moment, slack-jawed, then turned away.

Diotivede opened his black bag, took out a towel, and laid it down beside the body. He carefully put on his rubber gloves, knelt down on the towel and bent over to examine the child, touching the body at various points. Nothing on his face gave any sign of the stench he was inhaling from just inches away. Turning the corpse over on to its belly, he continued studying it closely. Piras and Bordelli were a few steps away, anxiously awaiting information.

Moments later the doctor stood back up, put the gloves and the towel in a plastic bag, and tucked this into his medical bag. Then his customary black notebook appeared in his hands. He scribbled a few things in it and shoved it into his pocket. Bordelli came up to him.

'Strangled?'

'Not only that . . .'

'What do you mean?'

'First he was raped,' said the doctor. Bordelli exchanged a glance with Piras.

'How long has he been dead?'

'At a glance, I'd say three, four days.'

'I hope you're wrong. It's unthinkable that he was left for so many days in the hands of a monster.'

'God only knows what a wonderful time he must have had,' the doctor said darkly. He could have performed a post-mortem even on himself without any particular emotion, but the sight of dead children always put him in a grim mood. 'Can you tell me anything else?' he asked.

'You'll have to wait for the post-mortem.'

'Are you leaving straight away?'

'No, I'll be here a little longer . . . Give me a cigarette,' the doctor said. The inspector had seen him smoke only on rare occasions, and it always seemed peculiar to him. He offered him a cigarette from the packet and then lit it for him. The

34

doctor took a deep drag and then headed pensively up to the top of the hill, his bag swinging at his side. Bordelli went over to Calosi and Tapinassi, who both looked deader than the little boy.

'Call the morgue and tell them to send the van, and take that poor bastard back with you,' he said, gesturing towards the hunter.

'What about the dog?' asked Tapinassi.

'Bring him, too, it's the easiest thing.'

'All right, sir,' the two cops said in unison, having recovered their nerve a little.

'When the van gets here, be sure to walk the stretcher-bearers to this spot, and then you can leave.'

'All right, sir.'

Calosi and Tapinassi explained things to the hunter, and all three of them headed down the slope, followed by the dog.

Piras had asked them for the camera. After taking a few shots, he stood there staring at the little boy's corpse with eyes that evoked Sardinian vendettas. The city was far away. The city where the boy had vanished into thin air. At last they were making some progress. The body had been found. But if something else didn't turn up soon, they would be back where they started.

The inspector sought out Diotivede. He saw him some fifty yards away, motionless amid the trees, staring spellbound into space with his arms folded across his chest and his bag at his feet. He looked as if he were posing for a sculptor. Bordelli slowly caught up to him.

'We're going to need a little luck,' he said.

'Let's hope it's not like two years ago . . .' the pathologist said, alluding to the four little girls who were murdered in the spring of '64 before the killer was captured. They were months of hell . . .

A bird cawed from a treetop, and both of them looked up, trying to spot it.

'Give me another cigarette,' Diotivede muttered. Bordelli lit one for himself as well, throwing the match on the ground. A big mushroom rose up through the rotten leaves. Perhaps it was a porcino . . .

After facing the journalists with Inzipone at his side, the inspector shut himself in his office with Piras. It was almost four o'clock and they still hadn't eaten anything.

Bordelli ran his hand slowly over his already stubbly face, thinking of the delightful morning he'd had. Around eleven he'd gone to talk to the boy's parents, in Via di Barbacane. He'd wanted to go there alone. He saw Giacomo's mother fall to the floor like an empty sack, and helped her husband put her back on her feet. He didn't mention the rape, there was no need. He stayed with the Pellissaris for more than half an hour. Before leaving he had predictably vowed to catch the killer, to give the wretched couple something to hold on to. But as he was descending the stairs, he'd felt like a liar.

Commissioner Inzipone was blowing fire from his nostrils, having growled at Bordelli in private to get busy . . . As if up till then he'd only been scratching his balls, for chrissakes. Truth be told, he didn't know which way to turn. Giacomo had been buried in a hurry in a shallow grave. Whoever had done the digging certainly wasn't concerned with making the body disappear for ever, but only with getting it out of his hair. Maybe it was better the kid was dead. What sort of life would he have had after what he'd been through?

The inspector and Piras had searched the place where the body had been found for clues, any clue, within a radius of about fifty yards. But, aside from a few empty rifle cartridges, they'd found nothing. As if that wasn't enough, it had been raining all week, and the layer of rotting leaves didn't help.

Bordelli had sent a few patrols to La Panca a good while

before, to question the inhabitants of the area and check to see whether the other trails really were impassable for cars. Perhaps the hunter had been exaggerating.

The inspector was hoping there might be a witness who'd seen something important, or that Diotivede might make a discovery that would prove to be a turning point. He was hoping, but he wasn't terribly convinced.

'Let me smoke, Piras.'

'Can I open a window?'

'Do whatever you like, but let me smoke.'

He lit a cigarette as the Sardinian threw open the windows as if it were the middle of July. The rain had started falling again.

'We're going to solve this, Inspector.'

'Even at your age I wasn't so optimistic.'

'I can feel it . . .'

'We need a psychic,' said the inspector and, upon saying that, he thought again of Amelia. *Tomorrow morning* . . . the fortune-teller had said, before clamming up. To distract himself he told Piras the story of the tarot cards, and Piras loosened up and smiled.

'When I was a young boy, there was a sort of witch who lived in Bonarcado. People said she had the power to kill people from afar, and whenever I saw her on the street in town my legs would start to shake.'

Gusts of damp wind blew in through the open window.

'There's something I really want to do, Piras.'

'What's that?'

'Promise not to tell anyone?'

'Promise.'

'I would really like to have another little chat with that fortune-teller,' said Bordelli.

'Well, given our situation, anything's worth a try . . .'

'Thanks for the encouragement.'

The inspector picked up the receiver and dialled Rosa's number, hoping to find her at home.

'Hello?' said Rosa after the tenth ring.

'Ciao, Rosa, it's me.'

'Oh my God, I heard about the little boy on the radio . . . How horrible!'

'Rosa, how can I get hold of Amelia?' Bordelli asked curtly.

'She'd foreseen it . . . Do you remember what she said?'

'How can I reach her, Rosa?'

'Oh, dear God, I can't bear the thought of it . . . Poor little Giacomino . . .'

'Rosa, please, tell me where I can reach Signora Amelia.'

'Who on earth could have done such a thing?'

'Rosa! Can't you hear me?'

At last he got her to listen and repeated that he wanted to speak with Amelia as soon as possible.

'I'll try calling her,' said Rosa, and she hung up. Bordelli and Piras sat there in silence, waiting, shooting each other a glance every so often. The ring of the telephone made them jump in their seats. It was Diotivede.

'I can confirm everything. The decomposition process started not more than three days ago. He died of strangulation, and was raped first . . . by more than one person,' the doctor said. Bordelli felt a stabbing pain in his stomach.

'How many?' he asked, trying to remain calm.

'There were at least three . . . and don't ask me if I'm sure.'

'Why do you say *at least*? Usually you're more precise,' said Bordelli, exchanging glances with Piras. The police pathologist heaved a long sigh of forbearance before replying.

'When analysing traces of sperm it's possible to identify the blood type, and I found three blood types in the victim's rectum. On the other hand, if ten different men of the same blood type had raped him, I would find only one blood type. And that is why I said *at least* . . .'

'He was raped by at least three men,' Bordelli said to Piras, momentarily covering the receiver. The Sardinian shook his head and grimaced in disgust.

'Anything else?' the inspector asked Diotivede.

'An abrasion on the forehead, a bruised knee, a deep wound on the right thigh, caused after death, almost certainly by the shovel used to bury him. Under his fingernails I found carpet pile and a considerable amount of plaster dust, as if he'd dug a hole in a wall with his bare hands.'

'Couldn't that have happened at his house?'

'Certainly . . . if his father's a werewolf . . .'

'What do you mean?'

'Only tremendous fear can explain something like that. The fingernails are shattered.'

'Like in the gas chambers . . .' Bordelli muttered. He could still remember the films he'd seen of Auschwitz in which one could see the fingernail marks the dying Jews had made on the walls.

'Now comes the best part.' Diotivede sighed.

'Let's hear it . . .'

'He has large traces of morphine in his blood.'

'They drugged him . . .'

'That's what I just said.'

'Sorry, I was talking to Piras.'

'There's nothing else,' the doctor said.

'It would be a big help if we knew what house to look in for scratches on the walls . . .'

'I'll send you the report before the end of the day.'

'Better not say anything to the press, or anyone else, for that matter.'

'Not a word will leave this room, unless the dead start talking,' said the doctor.

They said goodbye with a sort of grunt, and Bordelli dropped the phone on to its cradle.

'Jesus fucking Christ . . .' he muttered, pressing his fingertips into his eyelids. He repeated to Piras everything the doctor had just told him, including the part about the seminal fluid and blood types.

'A bunch of perverts,' the Sardinian said between clenched teeth, brooding. Was it easier to catch a lone maniac or a group of sadists? He didn't know.

Disappointed, the inspector crushed his cigarette butt in the ashtray.

'These things are totally useless if we don't have a suspect.'

'Maybe we'll find one,' Piras said by way of encouragement.

'Please close the window,' said Bordelli. He couldn't stand feeling the humid air penetrating under his clothes any longer. Piras got up to close the window, and at that moment the telephone rang again. The inspector picked up the receiver with a sigh.

'Yes?'

'Your phone was always busy,' said Rosa.

'Did you reach Amelia?'

'She absolutely refuses to see you, but I managed to persuade her to talk to you over the phone.'

Rosa gave him the number. To judge by the first two digits, she must have lived in the San Gervasio area. Bordelli thanked Rosa and hung up. Though he no longer really felt like it, he rang Amelia at once. He told her the little boy had been found dead and heard her sigh.

'Is that what you saw in the cards?'

'Yes . . .' Amelia said warily.

Feeling embarrassed, Bordelli asked her whether she was willing to consult the tarot again about the matter, to see whether she could find out anything of use to the investigation.

'I'm sorry, Inspector, but perhaps you haven't really understood what the tarot is,' said the fortune-teller in a faint, hoarse voice.

'Well, I thought I'd try . . .'

'The cards can't reveal a killer's name; they can only tell what will happen to the person in front of me.'

'Perhaps you could find out if I'll succeed in capturing the culprit,' said Bordelli, feeling sheepish with Piras looking on.

'What must happen, will happen,' the psychic murmured.

'Exactly. So maybe—'

'Please, Inspector,' Amelia interrupted him in a weak voice.

41

'As you wish, then. Sorry to disturb you.'

'I can't help you, believe me.'

'Thanks just the same.'

Bordelli put the receiver down and leaned back in his chair. He briefly told Piras what Amelia had said. He felt relieved. Though he had yielded for a moment to the temptation, he really couldn't see himself paying heed to the tarot's prophecies.

'Let's hope something turns up at La Panca,' he said, without believing it for a second. At that moment somebody knocked at the door. It was Rinaldi with the first results. The paths through the woods had been carefully checked. To get to Monte Scalari by car one had no choice but to go by way of La Panca. The other trails had large stones, deep holes and impassable, tortuous bends that even a jeep in wartime would have had trouble negotiating.

'Anything else?'

'Nothing else, Inspector,' Rinaldi said dejectedly, as if it were his fault.

'All right, you can go, thanks,' the inspector said, even more disappointed than him. Rinaldi vaguely gestured a military salute and left in a hurry. Evening was falling, and the sound of torrential rain rose up from the street below.

'What the hell are we going to do now?' Bordelli asked, worrying an earlobe.

The following morning he left home before eight o'clock and headed for La Panca. He felt the need to go back there, although he was convinced there was no point in it. He couldn't bear sitting behind his desk, staring at the wall, crushed by a feeling of powerlessness that had been weighing on him for days like a sense of guilt.

He stopped at Porta Romana to buy the Florentine daily, *La Nazione*:

LITTLE GIACOMO FOUND DEAD
RAPED AND STRANGLED

He tossed the newspaper on to the front seat and drove off, reviewing in his mind the reports of the policemen who had questioned the inhabitants of La Panca, Cintoia Alta and Monte Scalari. They were all more or less the same: nobody had seen anything unusual. There were, moreover, a number of inhabited houses on the hill, as well as an abbey, and the wooded area was often frequented by hunters and people foraging for mushrooms. It was normal to hear cars driving by at all hours; nobody paid any attention.

In short, they were getting nowhere. The only new information was from Diotivede, and for the moment it was useless.

He arrived at La Panca with his morale in tatters. As he went up the path in the car, he realised he'd finished all his cigarettes and half-cursed between clenched teeth. Crumpling the empty packet, he hurled it out of the window. After a few bends, he parked the Beetle in the same clearing as the day before. He opened the glove compartment, to check whether there wasn't perhaps a spare cigarette in there, but all he found was a little box of Tabù-brand liquorice drops. Tapping the box with one finger, he let a few of the bitter drops roll into his mouth.

He put on his hiking boots and set out slowly towards the spot where the body had been found, knowing he was wasting his time. From the ground, still wet with rain, rose a sharp smell of putrefaction, as a breath of damp wind caressed his face. The silence of the woods was broken only by birdsong, the rustling of his footsteps and, now and then, a distant gunshot. The upper boughs of the trees stood out against a colourless sky, as the sun formed spots of light on the carpet of rotten leaves.

He trudged on, breathing heavily, expecting at any moment to see a German pop out from behind a tree and start shooting at him. That had actually happened to him in the forests of the Abruzzi, as he made his way up the Italian peninsula, biting the tails of the retreating Nazis. Luckily he had not figured among the dead, and when he returned to camp he'd marked the eleventh notch on the butt of his machine gun. He didn't yet know that in the coming months he would add another sixteen. He had never felt guilty about having killed; there wasn't anything else he could have done in those moments. But they weren't good memories. He remembered the distress of a comrade of his in the San Marco battalion who couldn't forgive himself for pointlessly killing a Nazi. During a rather tempestuous firefight, he'd seen this hulking German running towards him and instinctively cut him down with a burst of fire. A moment later he realised he'd riddled with bullets a wounded man who was collapsing to the ground. He never gave himself a moment's rest, as if he'd killed an innocent . . .

Bordelli recognised from a distance the hole in which the boy had been buried, and he gritted his teeth. Reaching the spot, he stopped in front of the loose earth, hands dangling at his sides. In his mind's eye he could still see the small naked foot sticking out of the ground, the mud-smeared body, the worms writhing in the empty eye sockets. Not far away he heard a tree trunk creak in the wind, and at that moment it seemed the saddest sound on earth. He started walking around, looking at the ground, moving the leaves with his feet in the absurd hope of finding something. All he saw were the usual cartridges and a few shabby mushrooms. He was pointlessly wasting time, but what else could he do? Sit in his office warming his chair?

He moved away from the makeshift grave, walking in a spiral motion, in ever broader circles, examining every inch of earth carefully. In spite of everything, he still had hope. It was a senseless illusion, but it was all he had. He wasn't asking for much, for Christ's sake. Just a button would have been enough, or a cigarette butt, a spent match . . .

After half an hour of this, he stopped circling the grave and headed deeper into the woods. His hope had run out, and his search turned into a solitary walk. He wanted only to enjoy some silence undisturbed. He ambled along slowly, letting the beauty of the place fill his eyes. He didn't even feel much like smoking. He felt good, there in the woods. It had taken Botta's mushrooms to make him realise this. He had to come back to these hills more often. The best thing was letting his thoughts travel up unknown paths, or remain suspended in the air. Through the trees' black trunks he saw a large hare race breathlessly away and disappear into a thicket. It was safe for now, but sooner or later a hunter would gun it down and it would end up as sauce for a pot of *pappardelle*.

He kept on walking, breathing deeply, lost in his memories. Every so often he heard a shot ring out in the valley. He went down a hillside and found himself back on the trail. He was almost certain that if he turned to the right, he would end up back at the car, and so he went in the opposite direction. His mud-caked boots reminded him of the long marches with the San Marco battalion, blisters burning the soles of his feet, sweat saturating his uniform. He could still almost hear the extravagant curses of Mosti, a giant from Massa as big as a wardrobe, who hated walking. Bordelli would remind him that if not for the war, he would still be rotting in jail, and the beast would only sneer.

He arrived in front of a small chapel that stood at the crossing of two trails. It must have been the fork mentioned by the hunter: to the left, Poggio alla Croce, to the right, Pian d'Albero. Bordelli went to the right and proceeded at a slow pace, his mind clouded by old memories. A light wind washed through the branches like an invisible sea, making the leaves fall and dragging a mollifying smell of death through the air. Here and there a secondary path broke off in another direction through the woods, disappearing amid the trees.

On the hillside opposite him he glimpsed an abandoned house through the vegetation, its shutters closed and the roof half caved in. One saw more and more such houses these days, here and there in the Chianti. A horror of the rural life had driven the young people to the cities in search of a less laborious, more entertaining way of life. He couldn't blame them, really; a peasant's life was hard, miserable. But they soon discovered that the poor weren't any better off in the cities. It was just a different sort of poverty, in some ways much more profound.

He found himself looking up at a slope of large, jagged rocks. The hunter was right. If you took the car up there, you would surely drop the oil pan. To the right the view opened up on to a broad valley, and he stopped to look. A bank of dark clouds was rising up over the gloomy horizon of hills, covering the entire vault of sky. He became entranced, watching a falcon flying in broad rings until, at last, it nosedived straight down and vanished.

Who knew how long it would take to get to Pian d'Albero? He knew the story of the Nazis who, one June day in '44, had massacred partisans and defenceless civilians there, but he'd never seen the site of the slaughter. He followed the path for a little over a mile, then decided to turn back. He would go to Pian d'Albero another time.

He walked along unhurriedly, savouring the moments of solitude. Passing the Cappella dei Boschi again, he continued down the path that led to La Panca. The wood's animated silence relaxed him. It wasn't like in wartime, when silence was full of deadly traps.

He trudged up a short incline paved with ancient flagstones, and past the bend, through the vegetation, caught a glimpse of a tall stone building. Almost certainly the abbey of Monte Scalari. As he continued on his way, the abbey disappeared behind the trees, and a hundred yards up the path he saw a shrine in *pietra serena* with an empty niche. With a flutter of wings, blackbirds flew out of some brambles, diving into the underbrush, chirping their alarm amid the shrubs.

He stopped in front of the shrine. To the left, a narrow, rocky trail descended steeply towards the bottom of the valley. How much misery must these woods have witnessed? Sculpted on the grey stone of the shrine, near the top, were the words: *Omne Movet Urna Nomen Orat*. Bordelli attempted to translate them, trying to unearth the Latin he'd learned at school. Every. Move. Urn. Name. Prays. What the devil was that supposed to mean? He gave up trying to understand and resumed walking. Moments later he found himself in front of the abbey, a vast construction suffering from the weight of the centuries. There were loophole windows here and there in the wall of *pietra serena*, and a small sort of tower rose up from the top of the wall, over the main entrance gate. He imagined great rooms peopled with ghosts, monumental fireplaces, frescoes with the stories of saints. In a flat open space to the side was a large Peugeot with its sides spattered with mud. Who knew who lived there, in such an isolated place? Whoever it was, Bordelli envied them. He would love to live in a sort of fortress like that, far from the city and his fellow men. Perhaps together with a beautiful, beloved woman, blonde or brunette, it didn't matter . . .

Better to forget about dreams and keep his feet firmly on the ground. How many years had he been tossing about this idea of moving to the country? He need only make up his mind. It wasn't long before he could start collecting his pension, and he wanted to spend his final years tending a vegetable garden and picking olives. It shouldn't cost too much, an old abandoned house with a bit of land. If he sold his flat in San Frediano he could easily buy one and fix it up. Still walking, he whispered a promise to himself: after he found Giacomo Pellissari's killers he would get on with looking for a house in the country.

Caught up in these thoughts, he started looking around at the land again, really wishing he could smoke a cigarette. Out of the corner of his eye he saw something move, then turned round and managed just in time to see a head disappear over the top of the hill. Who the hell could it be? He quickened his pace and reached the top, heart thumping in his ears. He spotted a hunchbacked man moving hurriedly away through the trees, and started running after him, yelling at him to stop. At first the man sped up, as though trying to flee, but when the inspector yelled again, he stopped and turned round. When Bordelli caught up to him, he found an old man with a basket full of mushrooms, looking at him warily.

'Police . . .' the inspector mumbled, panting, hand on his chest. The man kept staring at him. He had a long, cavernous face, lined with deep wrinkles of toil, and towy hair.

'Why didn't you stop?' Bordelli asked, knowing it was a stupid question. The old man shrugged feebly.

'When hunting the mushroom, too much talking spells doom,' the old man said in utter seriousness.[5]

'I just wanted to ask if you have a cigarette.'

'I don't smoke. Can I go now?'

'Of course, I'm sorry . . .' Bordelli muttered. The old man turned and went on his way, disappearing through the trunks of the chestnut trees. A moment later it was as if he'd never existed.

The inspector returned to the trail, demoralised. In his mind he asked God or chance to let him find something, and he even made a vow: if he found something, even so much as a clothespin or button, he would smoke less. He precluded stopping altogether, lest he prove unable to keep his promise. But merely smoking less was a great challenge: the first week he would get down to ten, the following week down to five . . . He tossed these thoughts around in his head like a child, even if he felt a little ashamed of it . . .

He passed under the powerful branches of an enormous oak, whose trunk would have taken at least three men with arms extended to encircle. At its feet someone had built a tiny chapel of stone and brick, and he wondered, *Why ever?* Glancing inside, he spied a picture of the Virgin with seven swords thrust into her heart, painted by an unskilled hand. He continued down the path, and a short while later the Beetle suddenly appeared round a bend. His stroll through the woods was over. A useless stroll. Now he could smoke as much as he wished. He'd already slipped the key into the door, preparing to leave, when he suddenly changed his mind. Spurred on by one last illusion, he continued walking towards La Panca, like a castaway searching his desert island for signs of life for the hundredth time. In reality it was merely an excuse not to return just yet to the office, where he would have felt like a caged animal.

He strayed repeatedly off the track, penetrating the forest through the trees, scanning the sea of leaves carefully. Cartridges, nothing but cartridges. Here and there an indistinct bootprint, or confused tyre tracks in the dirt. Signs that were, in any case, totally useless. There certainly was no lack of people trudging through these woods.

After a gentle uphill climb, he came out on to a broad plateau with very tall pines. He stayed for a few minutes to look around, charmed by the stillness, then decided that it was time to return. He was heading back to the car with his tail between his legs when he heard a sort of peeping sound. He stopped and tried to figure out where it was coming from. It must have been behind the brambles that lined the path. When he tried to look behind them, his clothes got all tangled in the thorns, but he managed to see a very small black and white animal toddling unsteadily through the ferns, sounding like a little bird. For a second he thought it was a baby magpie that had fallen from the nest, though it wasn't the right season . . . A moment later he saw that it was a tiny kitten, all wet and spattered with mud. It was mewing desperately. Perhaps it had woken up too soon after the last suckling and had strayed from its refuge before Mamma had returned. He stood there looking at the little ball of fur, which kept peeping, staggering on its tiny legs. He wondered what to do. In the end he circled round the brambles and went towards the kitten, after checking to make sure the mother wasn't somewhere nearby. He almost ended up trampling on the carcasses of three other kittens of about the same size as their surviving sibling. They were whole, as if they'd starved to death. And it hadn't been long, at first glance. A day at the most.

As he was about to bend down and pick up the kitten, he spotted a piece of paper a little farther away, folded in two, sticking out from under the leaves. He went excitedly to get it, as if it were a gold nugget. It was a telephone bill, half faded and sodden with rain. Though it wasn't easy, he could make out the address: *Panerai Butcher Shop / Livio Panerai / Viale dei Mille 11r / Florence.* The payment deadline dated from seven days earlier. Bordelli bit his lip. Viale dei Mille was very close to the area where the little boy was last seen. Was it only a coincidence? He had to remain calm. That piece of paper didn't mean anything. It was only a bill that had been lost in the wood; he shouldn't give it too much importance . . . But hope had already seized hold of him. He felt like a lovelorn youth, consumed by desire, who mistakes a simple glance for a promise of love.

He put the bill in his pocket and returned to the kitten, which wouldn't stop squealing. The moment he picked it up, it stopped, and then nearly fell asleep in his warm hand.

Going back to the car, he wiped the kitten with a handkerchief. He crumpled up *La Nazione*, turning it into a sort of bed, then laid the tiny animal in it. He hadn't yet started the car up when the cat started mewling again, but not as desperately as before. It sounded much calmer. It was he, Bordelli, who felt restless. Turning the car around, he headed back towards La Panca, checking every second to make sure the kitten hadn't fallen on to the floor.

'Briciola!' Rosa cried out as soon as she saw the kitten.

'You've already found a name?' asked Bordelli, handing her the tiny animal.

'Can't you see she's got a little face just like Briciola?'[6]

'Maybe it's a boy.'

'You know even less about cats than you do about women . . . You're a girlie kitten, aren't you, Briciola?' Rosa said to it, holding it in her hands and rubbing her nose on its little head.

'It's women who don't understand men,' Bordelli grumbled, following Rosa into the kitchen.

'Poor thing, it has a bad eye.'

'It may have been a thorn; I found her in the middle of some brambles.'

'Look who's here, Gideon!' said Rosa, putting the kitten down in front of the big white tomcat. Gideon sniffed the intruder for a few seconds, looking perplexed. He walked around the little thing, which could barely stand up, then with a fairly benign blow of the paw made it roll on the floor.

'Gideon, what are you doing! That's naughty!' Rosa shouted, picking up the kitten.

'He realises he won't be Mummy's little darling any more.'

'Poor Briciolina, who knows how long it's been since she's eaten . . . I must call the vet at once. When they're this small they sometimes have trouble surviving,' said Rosa, heading for the entrance hall.

'I'm leaving her in good hands,' said the inspector, following behind her. Rosa found the number in the telephone book . . .

Before the vet picked up, Bordelli blew her a kiss by way of goodbye and left.

As he was descending the stairs he pulled out of his pocket the telephone bill he'd found in the woods. If not for the mewling kitten, he would never have found it, and he hoped it was a sign from destiny. He read the name of the subscriber: *Panerai Butcher Shop.* Three thousand two hundred and thirty-five lire's worth of phone calls. He put the bill back in his pocket with a shudder, even though the butcher might well have dropped it while hunting or looking for mushrooms. The discovery proved nothing concrete, but it was still a tiny flame in what had been total darkness.

He went back to the station, knowing he had next to nothing in his hands, but at the same time he had trouble controlling his excitement. He told Mugnai to send for Piras at once, then went up to his office. Flopping into his chair, he lit a cigarette and tried to calm down. He started studying the telephone bill, as if seeing it for the first time. It had been paid seven days before, but who knew when it had been lost? It was hard to tell. Anyway, there was no guarantee that Livio Panerai had paid it in person. Maybe his brother-in-law, or a friend, or an errand boy had gone to the post office to pay it in his stead. But what if in fact it was he who had buried the little boy? Maybe he'd dropped the bill when he pulled out a handkerchief to mop his brow, and the wind had carried it away . . .

He heard a police car drive off with tyres screeching and siren blaring, but didn't care to know what had happened. His mind was on the telephone bill. He continued to study it carefully, as if somewhere it might contain, in code, the killer's name.

At last he looked up and started gazing at the sky through the window. Lacking any real clues, he had three options before him: the frontal attack, the spider's web, and the keyhole. Which was the right one? Frontal attack had one advantage: surprise. You batter the presumed culprit with firm accusations, hoping he'll collapse. In short, a bluff by the book, but if you didn't bring home the goods, it was the same as in poker: you lost everything. The spider's web was a work of embroidery that aimed at exhausting the suspect with vague but incessant insinuations, like Porfyry Petrovich with Raskolnikov. Obviously, it didn't always work. Everything depended on the suspect's nerves. And anyway, to put it into practice you needed a lot of time and, most importantly, you had to be a good actor. The keyhole approach was a long operation, one which required patience and skill. Stakeouts, tailing, endless searches. And if you had the right person on your hands, sooner or later something would come out. It was the most demanding approach, but also the least risky. You just waited in the shadows for someone to make a wrong move . . .

There was a knock at the door, and he gave a start. It was Piras, with dark circles under his eyes. He limped to a chair and wrinkled his nose, smelling the stale cigarette smoke in the room. Bordelli noticed but pretended not to. He showed Piras the telephone bill he'd found and told him about his walk in the woods, the kitten, and all the rest. Lastly he laid out the three options for him.

'What would you do?' he asked, though he'd already made up his mind. Piras bit his lip before speaking.

'The likelihood that this bill was dropped by the killer is very slim, extremely slim, in fact. But that doesn't mean it's impossible, and it happens to be the only lead we've got. The best thing is to spy through the keyhole and hope we get lucky.'

'I agree,' said Bordelli, blowing smoke out of his mouth like Godzilla. Piras fanned the air with his hand and then went and opened the window without asking permission.

'Didn't you want to quit smoking, Inspector?'

'I've been wanting to quit ever since I started, Piras.'

'So for now you want to force me to smoke, too.'

'I want to go and see what he looks like,' said Bordelli, standing up.

'Who?'

'The butcher.'

'If you don't mind, I'll go with you,' said the Sardinian, limping towards the door. Who knew how much longer he'd be walking like that? In the end, however, he'd been lucky. The robbers had shot to kill.

They got into the Beetle and drove off. It was just eleven o'clock, and almost all the people on the streets were women, shopping. After the viaduct of Le Cure, they turned on to Viale dei Mille. The inspector kept an unlit cigarette between his lips, puffing on it as if it were lit. Not far away, in Viale Volta, was the house he'd grown up in. He didn't know the Panerai butcher shop. Maybe in his day it didn't exist yet, or he'd simply never noticed it. His mother had always bought meat in Via Passavanti.

They went the entire length of the Viale, keeping their eyes on the numbers of the buildings. They'd gone almost all the way to the municipal stadium when at last they saw number 11/r, *Panerai Butcher Shop – Chicken, Rabbits, Game*. They drove past it and parked in front of Scheggi's, the most famous grocer in the area.

'Shall we have a panino, afterwards?' said Bordelli.

'Sure, why not?' said Piras.

'Wait for me here.'

The inspector got out and walked towards the butcher's shop. On the pavement he crossed paths with a good-looking chestnut-haired girl in a decidedly short skirt and a face somewhere between cute and haughty. He forced himself not to turn to look at her. It didn't seem like the right moment. But the call of the forest came anyway, and in the end he turned round . . . Only for a second, but it was enough to make him suffer. Shaking off the vision, he slipped into the butcher's. It was a clean, brightly lit shop, with a crucifix hanging on one wall and a lot of beautiful, bleeding meat. The butcher himself looked to be a little over forty. Fat, square face, blue eyes, and a merchant's smile. His head was bald and shiny but for two tufts of hair at the temples, and he ran his tongue continuously over his lips. The inspector felt an instinctive antipathy for the tubby hulk and his blustery manner, but this certainly wasn't proof of his guilt. Indeed, over the years he'd met more than a few charming murderers and unbearable innocents.

There were two customers there, a rich lady in a fur coat weighted down with bracelets and a stout man with a huge nose and deep-set eyes. The woman was very demanding and just as indecisive. She took a very long time to choose. The butcher had the patience of a spider and didn't miss a chance to let drop a couple of double entendres. The lady smiled with bourgeois detachment, visibly amused.

The inspector observed the butcher, trying to figure out who he looked like. At last it came to him: he looked exactly like Goering. If he'd had more hair, he could have been his twin. He continued studying Panerai, his movements, his eyes, his facial expressions . . . He seemed like the perfect sex maniac, capable of rape and murder. But Bordelli was well familiar with the power of suggestion. To free himself of all prejudice he tried imagining that someone of authority had told him that Panerai was a scientist. And the butcher turned into a scientist. He imagined someone had told him he was mentally ill, and the butcher was transformed into a madman making incomprehensible gestures. He continued the game, transforming him into a do-gooder, a loan shark, an accountant, an orchestra conductor . . . A useless exercise that could go on for ever.

The fur-clad lady at last overcame her reservations and declared to the world what she wanted. The butcher threw a large piece of meat on the chopping board, as if it were an enemy he'd just killed, and started working on it with his knife. '*Amor, ch'a nullo amato amar perdona . . .*'[7] he declaimed, pursing his lips like a rose. The lady shuddered with vanity. Then she paid a considerable sum without batting an eyelid and left, carrying the meat-filled package almost with disgust.

'What can I get for you?' the butcher asked, turning to Bordelli.

'Wasn't the gentleman ahead of me?' asked the inspector, gesturing to the customer beside him.

'Go ahead, thanks, I'm in no hurry,' said the man.

'You're very kind . . . I would like a steak for the grill,' Bordelli said to the butcher, looking at the slabs of meat spread out in the refrigerated display case. He was thinking he would bring the steak to Totò and eat it that same evening.

'This is Chianina,'[8] said the butcher, putting a gorgeous block of meat on the chopping board. He took two large knives, rubbed them together with the grace of habit, and thrust the blades in.

'So, it's mushroom season again,' the inspector let drop, the way people do in shops while waiting to be served. He wanted to find out whether the butcher went up into the hills for reasons other than for burying a corpse.

'For those who know how to find them,' said the butcher, picking up a cleaver to break the bone. At that moment a transparent little old man popped out from the back room, looking as if he was breathing his last. He had a submissive gaze and the manner of a fairy-tale grandfather, which clashed with his bloodstained apron. The butcher changed expression and looked at him harshly.

'You already done?'

'Yes,' the old man whispered, intimidated.

'Don't just stand around twiddling your thumbs, go and take care of the pig . . . What, you're still here?' he said, proud of his power. The little old man vanished without a word, silent as a cat. The inspector imagined the miserable life he must lead, spending his days cutting up animal carcasses, hands covered with blood . . . He felt sorry for him.

'A few days ago I found a lot of porcini at Poggio alla Croce,' he boasted, resuming the conversation.

'You're either not really a mushroom hunter, or you're fibbing,' said the butcher, smiling again, lowering the cleaver to the bone and breaking it with one blow. The man knew what to do with knives.

'I swear I found some,' Bordelli insisted, trying to get him to open up.

'Whoever finds mushrooms never tells where he found them,' said the butcher, shaking his head in a friendly way.

'There were so many I decided to be generous,' the inspector explained, realising his mistake.

'There are never enough,' the butcher grumbled.

'You found some?'

'Very few.'

'Where?'

'Up in the woods . . .' said the butcher with a grin, glancing at the customer, who was in no hurry.

'I've learned my lesson. From now on I'll keep my secret to myself,' said Bordelli, throwing his hands up.

'A sacred vow . . .' said the butcher. He clearly was a mushroom hunter, and there was nothing odd about his going around in the woods. He could easily have lost his phone bill bending down to pick a porcino.

'Have a look at this thing of beauty,' the butcher said, holding up the steak, which he then dropped on to the scale.

'How much do I owe you?'

'A thousand seven hundred . . . well spent,' replied Panerai, wrapping the meat up. Bordelli paid and returned to the car.

'Still feel like that panino, Piras?'

'What was the butcher like?' the Sardinian asked.

'A fat guy with a bald head who looks like Goering,' said the inspector, tossing the steak on the back seat.

'A likeable sort, in other words,' said Piras.

'And a mushroom hunter . . .' muttered the inspector, shaking his head as though disappointed.

They went into Scheggi's. There was a bit of a queue and they had to wait. When their turn came, they ordered two stuffed panini, Bordelli's with *finocchiona* salami and Piras's with mortadella. They set to them straight away, with gusto. The moment they got back in the car, the inspector saw the man who had let him go first walk by on the pavement. He had a slight, rather comical limp, head bobbing lightly every two steps. Bordelli followed him distractedly with his eyes, with the strange feeling that something had escaped him.

'What is it, Inspector?' asked Piras.

'Nothing . . .'

'Don't tell me I limp like him.'

'No, no, compared to him you move like a dancer,' said Bordelli, starting up the car.

Giacomo's mortal remains were returned to the family, and the funeral was scheduled for the following morning at the Badia in Fiesole. The inspector was half tempted to attend, then decided that there was no point in it. He phoned Signora Pellissari to reiterate his condolences, but above all to ask her what butcher shop she patronised. The woman gently replied that she went normally to Mazzoni's in Piazza Edison, a bit taken aback by the strange question. Bordelli assured her that the investigation was proceeding without delay, then left her to her grief.

The butcher was put under round-the-clock surveillance. He didn't take a single step without being watched. The men in the radio room had the phone numbers of all the places where they could reach the inspector: home, trattoria, Rosa. In the event of big news, they had orders to ring him at any time of the night or day. No matter what happened, at the end of each surveillance shift, he was brought a detailed report of Panerai's movements. Bordelli never missed a chance to repeat to the men in the field that they should use the utmost caution, change cars frequently, and never get too close. The butcher must never suspect anything, even if this meant losing him when he was being tailed.

There wasn't much information to be had on Livio Panerai. Forty-four years old, son of Oreste Panerai, an honest butcher who'd died seven years earlier, and Adelina Cianfi, still alive and living in Via del Ponte alle Riffe. An ordinary past as a Fascist Youth, then as a *repubblichino*,[9] but without any major blots. No recorded political activity since the end of the war. He'd grown rich with his butcher's shop. Five years ago he'd bought a ground-floor apartment in a small three-storey villa in Via del Palmerino. He'd married Cesira Batacchi in 1948 and they had a seventeen-year-old daughter, Fiorenza, who attended the Liceo Dante. Clean record. Hard worker. Licence to bear arms for hunting. Owned a dark grey Lancia Flavia and a cream-coloured Fiat 850, which he used to drive to work. Didn't do anything out of the ordinary during the day. Seemed to live only for his family and his work. One morning before going to the shop he'd gone to the post office to pay a bill. In short, unless proved otherwise, it was probably him who had lost his telephone bill in the woods. One afternoon he'd closed the shop ten minutes early to go and buy a box of shotgun cartridges at the armoury at Ponte del Pino. On Sunday he'd taken his little family to lunch at his mother's. He almost always stayed home after dinner, though it was true that the constant rain didn't make one want to go out. In one week, he went out only once, with his wife, to the Cinema Aurora, to see *The Incredible Army of Brancaleone*. And that was all.

In short, a goody two-shoes. Perfectly innocent. But Bordelli didn't want to give up on the only clue he'd sniffed out, and so he kept having him watched. As for requesting authorisation to have his phone tapped, he hadn't even tried. He already knew that Judge Ginzillo would never grant it: *Let me get this straight, Inspector Bordelli. You want to violate the intimacy of a free citizen of the Italian Republic because of a telephone bill? Which you found over two hundred yards away from where the corpse was buried? I wonder, are you mad? You need much better clues than that, my dear inspector . . .* That was more or less what the rat-face would have said. Not out of procedural zeal, but for fear of getting into trouble. He'd never forgotten some small 'trifle' which according to him had very nearly derailed his brilliant career.

Commissioner Inzipone was getting increasingly nervous and making no effort to hide it. He harried Bordelli with useless telephone calls, always repeating the same things . . . *Have you seen the newspapers? What the hell are you waiting for? Why are you sitting on your hands?*

The inspector was patiently waiting for the surveillance teams to turn up something new, but as the hours and days passed, his hopes were beginning to crumble. Jack the Ripper, too, was never caught, like so many others. What if the band of monsters killed again?

During the long wait, there was another suicide he had to deal with one morning. A pretty girl of humble origin had hanged herself with the sash of her dressing gown in a luxury apartment she owned in the centre of town. The body had been found by the cleaning woman, the morning following the death. The girl's mother explained between sobs that Matilde would never have committed suicide and must have been murdered. She was bewildered, having been unaware of the existence of that apartment and wondering how her daughter could possibly have bought it, since she worked as a salesgirl at the UPIM department store. Bordelli likewise thought it seemed fishy and got down to work. It didn't take long to figure things out. The girl had got sacked almost three months earlier and was the mistress of a sixty-year-old industrialist from Prato. Bordelli paid a call on him, and the businessman immediately owned up to his affair with the girl. He said he was deeply saddened by it all. He made no mystery of all the money he had spent on her. He'd given her the apartment as a gift and even paid the cleaning woman. Appealing to male complicity, he begged Bordelli not to let the matter get into the papers. The inspector smelled a rat. He asked him to come with him to the station and started pressuring him. After less than an hour of questioning the businessman confessed. They'd had a furious row and the slaps had started flying. The girl fell, hitting her head against the corner of a table and died almost instantly. In a fit of panic, he'd hung her from the sash of her dressing gown, to make it look like a suicide. He hadn't wanted to kill her, it was the last thing he wanted, it was an accident.

'She wasn't dead,' said Bordelli.

'What?'

'When you hanged her, the girl was still alive.'

'That's not true . . . it's not possible,' the businessman stammered, teetering in his chair.

'Read the post-mortem.' Bordelli passed him Diotivede's report. The girl had died of suffocation. The blow to the head wasn't serious. It had only knocked her out.

The man sat there in shock for a few moments, openmouthed and round-eyed . . . Then he burst into sobs. Bordelli turned him over to two guards and had him taken to the Murate prison. He wouldn't stay there for long, with all the money he had. As it happened it was a case of manslaughter following a failed unintentional homicide. Whatever the case, the whole matter had been cleared up in no time. Whereas the murdered boy . . . Damn it all . . .

'Let me get you something, Inspector,' said Totò. Lasagna, sausages and beans, the usual flask of red and endless chatter about a thousand topics, from politics to women. Only once did the cook make a reference to the murdered child, and Bordelli was able to change the subject immediately.

After dinner he drove slowly home, burping up essence of sausage. He parked the Beetle, and when he was slipping the key into the main door, he froze. The idea of sitting alone in front of the telly smoking and drinking made him feel depressed, and so he thought he would go into the centre of town and see a film. The last shows would be starting in half an hour. He headed off on foot with an unlit cigarette in his mouth, determined not to light it. To keep out of the annoying drizzle that kept falling without ceasing, he walked right up against the buildings. Their dark façades were dotted with the luminous rectangles of windows, which glowed with the changing bluish light of television sets. Every so often a shadow passed on the pavement, and two eyes shone in the darkness.

The Cinema Eolo was showing *La Grande Vadrouille*, but Bordelli didn't feel like seeing a comedy that night. He walked past the Gusmano bar, which as usual was full of elderly people playing cards with a flask on the table, some of them still in their overalls. Some youngsters had formed a circle round a pinball machine, spellbound as they watched the little steel ball bounce around.

He went down Via di Santo Spirito, and a woman surfaced in his memory: Milena, a beautiful young Jewess who had turned his brain to mush. She was a member of the White Dove, an organisation that hunted down Nazi war criminals who had escaped trial at Nuremberg, and she'd gone away to continue her work elsewhere. Who knew where she was now, what she was doing, or whether she thought every so often of the old inspector who'd lost his head over her? Without realising it he lit the cigarette and inhaled deeply. He didn't want to think about the women he'd lost, but about those who had yet to appear . . . if any. At his age it was no longer easy to charm a woman. Being born in 1910 wasn't so lucky. When he was a kid it was very hard to have a real relationship, unless one happened to find an open-minded girl or to get married, and now that there was more freedom he was pushing sixty.

From high up in one of the buildings he heard the scratchy bars of an old tango, and his heart gave a tug. He'd first heard the song in the days of Mussolini, and it felt as if a century had passed since then. At that moment even the war seemed far away, almost like a dream. At other times it weighed so heavy on him that it felt as if it had all happened yesterday. But he didn't want to think about the war just now . . .

He crossed the Ponte Santa Trinita, hoping to find a film to suit his mood. There was a great deal of bustle in the centre of town. People walking, on bicycles, on motorcycles, in cars, groups of youngsters, couples, husbands and wives . . . There they all were, in the city's convivial drawing room. In Via degli Strozzi there was a queue of traffic that advanced at a walking pace, and the air reeked of exhaust fumes. The multitude in ferment evoked no sense of joy in him, but merely made him feel lonely. Maybe it was just his black mood nipping at his heels, but he couldn't lie to himself: he didn't like Italy. He loved it in his way, in spite of everything, but he didn't like it. An Italy decayed first by war and now by dreams of wealth. The Italy of the throngs at Piazza Venezia and the throngs in Piazzale

Loreto . . .[10] The grumblings of an old man, he thought, throwing away his cigarette butt with a sigh.

He came into Piazza della Repubblica with its pompous buildings. It was full of parked cars, well-dressed men and women in little hats. He went to see what movies were playing in the two cinemas under the arches. The Edison was showing *The Battle of Algiers*, the Gambrinus *The Good, the Bad and the Ugly*. He needed to relax, and so chose the western. Before entering the cinema he went to the Giubbe Rosse café to ring the station and had another coffee while he was at it. He asked Tapinassi whether there was any news of Panerai. All normal. The butcher had gone home at 8.40 and hadn't come back out since.

Bordelli headed for the cinema, fiddling with the cigarette packet in his jacket pocket. In the middle of the piazza, he saw an old flame of his walking towards him like a vision. At least ten years had passed, but she still looked quite young. She was laughing, arms around a tall, pale, distinguished-looking man. Their eyes met for an instant, and she gave a barely perceptible start and kept on walking, pretending she hadn't seen him. Bordelli turned round to watch her walk away, wondering, with an unexpected twinge of jealousy, how a woman could choose two men so utterly different.

He slipped into the cinema and went up to the balcony, hoping it would be less crowded. The lights had just gone down and he had a little trouble finding a place to sit, groping around in the dark. Smelling some feminine perfume in the air, he turned and saw a girl with a fine profile seated next to him. He'd better forget about her if he wanted to enjoy the film.

The newsreel began. New cars at the Turin Salon, movie actors smiling, motorcycle races, industry thriving, beautiful Italy looking to the future and marvelling at the wealth it didn't have. Even the advertisements talked about carefree worlds where life was comfortable and cheerful, the women attractive and families happy. That was how one governed a poor country: by making it dream.

At last the film began, and between one gunfight and the next, Bordelli managed to distract himself. Then it was time for the intermission. The moment the lights came up, a dense mumble of voices rose from the floor. The inspector turned to look at the girl. Very pretty, with black hair and a fine little nose. Instinctively he thought of the words of Amelia the fortune-teller: *Soon you will meet a beautiful dark young woman . . .*

Beside her sat another girl with chestnut curls. They were both wearing skirts short enough to make one seasick. He kept ogling the dark girl, fascinated by her mischievous face. All at once she turned and looked at him. She had magnificent eyes animated by a treacherous childish sparkle. It lasted only a second. The girl looked away and whispered something into her friend's ear, and they both giggled. He blushed at the thought that they mere making fun of him. When the ice-cream man appeared with his box of frozen delights strapped around his neck, it was a relief. Bordelli bought a chocolate-covered cone and bit into it with gusto, as he used to do as a child. He tried to ignore the girls. Every so often he would catch sight of their naked legs and melt into impossible dreams. He couldn't help it. Women's legs had always had a powerful effect on him. Their ankles and feet, too, were fascinating. Often, after making love, he would fall under the spell of a small foot sticking out from under the sheet, as though he were looking at some mysterious, archaic sculpture. Sometimes a woman would catch him staring and ask him what he was looking at, and he would change the subject, lacking the courage to tell the truth . . .

The two girls next to him must have had superb little feet, to judge from their hands and their slender ankles. Better not to think about it. There were so many other girls all around him there. Most of them were in couples, and there was a lot of passionate kissing going on. Then darkness returned, and the film resumed. It was gripping, and you could have heard a pin drop. Whenever a close-up appeared of the good guy, who was also good-looking, one could hear a buzz of female voices. Bordelli watched the screen but was unable to forget about the dark girl next to him. He could hear her breathe, feel her move lightly in her seat, and at moments he could smell her real scent under her perfume. The girl smiled, and Bordelli saw her bright white teeth glimmer in the dark. With childish stubbornness he wanted to believe that the fortune-teller had been right, that this was in fact the young woman foretold by the tarot. Damn, he felt as if he was already falling in love. It was always like this, whenever he went out alone. He could fall in love with two slightly parted lips, a batting of eyelashes, a naked shoulder blade he saw passing in the street. Perhaps it was his secret remedy for feeling less alone, so he could keep on dreaming.

He decided to forget about the fortune-teller's predictions and concentrate on the film instead. The final duel had the whole audience holding its breath, even though everyone knew that the handsome chap would win . . . . And he did. In the final scene, too, it was Mr Good Looks who was lord and master. He rode away on his horse, alone as every hero must be, full of money, victorious, riding off to new adventures . . .

The lights came on and the two girls were the first to stand up. Bordelli remained seated. He took it hard. Though unable to admit it, he had been hoping that when the film was over the two girls would say he was a wonderful man and invite him to have a drink with them. Foolish old fogey. He stood up, sighing, and joined the mob descending the stairs. He saw the two girls in the distance and tried to work his way through the crowd and rejoin them. He fantasised about introducing himself and inviting them for a drink at the Giubbe Rosse or perhaps at Gilli's.

When at last he came out, he saw them walking leisurely under the arches. He pulled up beside them, heart beating fast. Then he turned to look at them and even opened his mouth to say something, but the girls only gawked at him in bewilderment, and so he gave up, walking away quickly, telling himself that they weren't so pretty after all. There was a lesson to be learned in the fable of the fox and the grapes.

There are worse things in life, he kept repeating to himself as he walked home. There were worse things than seeing a pretty girl and desiring her hopelessly. He lit a cigarette, blowing the smoke skywards. Crossing the Ponte alla Carraia, he turned down Borgo San Frediano. On the opposite pavement was old man Nappa leaning against a wall, coughing and spitting up pieces of lung, cursing with the little bit of breath he had left. Bordelli gave him a slight nod of greeting and continued on his way. He saw a big red cat crouched on the roof of a Fiat 500, lazily watching the night around him, and he thought at once of the kitten with the bad eye. Who knew whether Rosa would manage to save it?

At the corner of Piazza del Carmine two drunkards were discussing the great themes of life, staggering on gimpy legs. Bordelli turned round for a second to look from afar at the building in which, barely a year before, a loan shark had been murdered, stabbed in the neck with a pair of scissors. It hadn't been hard to put himself in the killer's shoes.

At last he arrived home. He took a hot shower, feeling as if he was washing away several tons of sadness. Then he got into bed and turned out the light. Though very tired, he couldn't fall asleep. Confused memories merged gently in his head, taking him on a melancholy journey through time. Little by little, from the sludge of remembrance, a clearer vision surfaced, like a monster rising up from the tranquil waters of a lake . . .

One day in the Abruzzi, he and Molin had gone out together on patrol. There was silence all around. The same silence as in other villages they'd passed through after the Armistice, when they could feel behind the closed shutters the distrustful gaze of women and old folk who could no longer stand to see any more outsiders, be they Italian, American or German. They only wanted whoever came to leave just as fast.

They trudged up to Torricella Peligna, a small stone village at the top of a mountain, which looked out on to the Majella massif. Molin was a giant from the Veneto with a heart of gold, but the sight of him was frightful. His broad, flat face was the opposite of harmony. Whenever he ducked into a farmhouse to ask for a piece of lard or a little cheese, the women would scream and run and hide.

It was early June. The line of resistance at Cassino had just been broken, at the cost of tens of thousands dead. At that altitude the air was cool, and the climb got one's blood running. They were both sweaty and smelly. The bulk of the Wehrmacht was close by, and aside from the high street, the hilltop town was a spider's web of narrow passages. It seemed purposely made for playing hide-and-seek. They advanced slowly through the deserted streets, machine guns in hand, checking every corner and window. It seemed quiet enough, but appearance was the worst sort of deception. Suddenly four Stukas flew overhead at low altitude, making an infernal racket. Bordelli and Molin flattened themselves against a wall. The Luftwaffe didn't kid around. They waited for the planes to pass, then resumed walking, but the sudden noise had put them on edge.

They were continuing their climb up a tortuous little street, when suddenly they smelled some cooking in the air and exchanged a glance of understanding. They were hungry. It wasn't a normal hunger they felt. It was the desire to taste something different from hard tack and tinned meat. They would have given their right hands for a boiled potato or a fried egg, an eye for a sausage. Molin was a born curser. Out of every three words he uttered, two were curses. At times it was hard to follow him, since the effort of removing the swear-words from his argument made you lose the thread. And on that day he was, indeed, hungry.

'Jesus fuck, I just can't stomach that Allied shit any more! What I wouldn't do for some pork fat! I'd kiss the old pig Badoglio on the lips, I would! If I see a chicken anywhere, I'm gonna open fire, Blessed Fascist Virgin!'

Bordelli gestured to him to pipe down, and Molin lowered his voice. There wasn't so much as a dog about. The only sounds were those of the bolts and windows shutting as they passed.

'Who are we fighting this war for anyway, Molin?' Bordelli said, discouraged. The Venetian spat on the ground and wiped his lips with his hand. He remained silent for a minute, then started listing the different parts of the pig, spouting curses in between. And every part he named he translated into all the dialects he knew. When he got to the trotter he suddenly froze, closed his eyes, and breathed deeply.

'Holy Fascist Virgin, can't you smell it? That's cooked meat, for the bleedin' love of God. Pork . . .'

Bordelli took him by the arm to make him keep walking, but the gorilla had dug himself in like a mule. He was sniffing the air noisily and deeply enough to make his lungs burst, as if that would suck the meat into his mouth. All at once he goggled his eyes and yelled:

'Bleedin' Nazi Virgin, I swear that's pork I smell!'

At that moment Bordelli noticed, some fifty paces ahead, a pair of shutters that were only pulled to, both on the first floor. Amid the thousands of other closed shutters, the two left ajar were cause for concern. He didn't have time to say anything before the shutters flew open and the machine guns opened fire. A burst of bullets crashed in a cluster into the stones just over their heads. In a split second Bordelli was belly down on the ground. He fired a burst at the shutters on the right and the slats splintered apart. The shooting stopped. Turning towards Molin, Bordelli saw him still standing, sniffing the pork-imbued air.

'Get down!' he shouted.

'That's pork, Commander!' The bursts of machine-gun fire resumed with redoubled fury from both windows. Bordelli returned fire, for longer than the first time. As soon as he stopped he jumped on Molin, dashing him to the ground a second before a cluster of bullets would have pierced the gorilla's chest. They got back up and started running breathlessly downhill. The Germans' bullets smashed into the stone houses like blows of a pickaxe, ricocheting everywhere, leaving a cloud of stone dust floating in the air.

They reached the lower town with hearts thumping in their ears, and could hear the Nazis swearing, clear and sharp, above them. Once they were safely in the wood, Bordelli started touching himself all over. He felt a pain in his side, and his uniform was wet in that area. He ran his fingers over it and sniffed. It wasn't blood. The Nazis' attack had punctured his wine-filled canteen, but the bullet hadn't passed through to the other side.

'Molin, if you ever do that again I'll shoot you myself, is that clear?'

'It was pork, Commander! We have to go back there.'

'The pork is in your brain,' said Bordelli, clapping him on the shoulder.

Molin made it through the war alive, but Bordelli had lost

touch with him. Most likely he'd taken up the peasant's life back in the Veneto. Who knew whether he too remembered that morning in Torricella Peligna, and the smell of grilled pork that nearly got him killed?

Another long morning with no new developments, at least on the butcher front. During the night there'd been burglaries, brawls, family rows . . . the usual stuff. In the station's offices people typed and people smoked, and every so often a police car screeched out of the courtyard. Piras had spent the night keeping watch over the Panerai residence until dawn and was now asleep in his bed. His report consisted of three words: *Nothing to report.*

And what the hell were these big fat flies still doing around in late October? A particularly large one was flying lazily from one end of Bordelli's office to the other, buzzing sickly like a biplane that has been hit by enemy fire. The inspector watched it, happy not to be able to concentrate. He was about to light his umpteenth cigarette of the day but then dropped it on the desk with the matches. He would smoke it after lunch. It was almost one o'clock. He picked up the phone and dialled Diotivede's lab.

'I bet you have a liver in your hand,' he said, as soon as he heard someone pick up.

'Who is this?' said a young man's voice.

'I'm sorry, I must've dialled the wrong number.'

'Who were you trying to call?'

'Forensic Medicine . . .'

'Oh, who would you like to talk to?'

'I was looking for Dr Diotivede.'

'Please wait just a minute and I'll see if the doctor can come to the phone,' said the lad. Bordelli was dumbfounded. Through the receiver he heard some footsteps walking away, then after a long silence some more steps approaching.

'Yes?' It was Diotivede.

'Since when do you have a secretary?' Bordelli asked.

'He doesn't cost much, I just feed him the leftovers from the post-mortems.'

'He must be the happiest man in the world.'

'I hope this isn't one of your useless calls.' The doctor sighed.

'I wanted to know if you felt like having lunch with me.'

'Are you feeling lonely?'

'Well, there's a big fat bluebottle in here, keeping me company, but it doesn't talk much.'

'I'll be free in about half an hour.'

'I'll be waiting patiently.'

'All right, then, see you in a bit,' said Diotivede, hanging up.

The inspector rose slowly, said goodbye to the fly, and went down to the courtyard. It was starting to rain. Driving out in the Beetle, he waved to Mugnai, then saw him get out of the guard booth, gesticulating. He rolled down a window.

'What is it?'

'Inspector, could you do me a really big favour, sir?'

'What?'

'Could you buy me the *Settimana Enigmistica*?' he said, putting a hundred-lira piece in the inspector's hand.

'Tell me something, Mugnai. Have you ever managed to complete one of their crossword puzzles?'

'I certainly have, sir . . .' said Mugnai, seeming hurt.

Bordelli slapped him on the belly and left, the windscreen wipers screeching against the glass. The viali were packed with cars, most of them driven by mothers on their way to pick up their children at school. The pavements were a confusion of umbrellas. He stopped at the kiosk in Piazza della Libertà to buy *La Nazione* and the *Settimana Enigmistica* for Mugnai.

When he got to Viale Pieraccini it was raining buckets. It was really an October to forget. Parking at the bottom of the staircase to the Forensic Medicine Institute, he killed some time skimming the newspaper.

At last Diotivede appeared under a large black umbrella. He came down the stairs, spry as a young lad, and got into the Beetle.

'Who was the kid who answered the phone?' asked Bordelli as they drove away.

'A resurrected corpse.'

'You could have invited him too.'

'I decided to let him work. He's a young graduate who wants to specialise in the art of the post-mortem.'

'His mum must be so happy.'

'That's enough of this silliness. It's a wonderful profession,' Diotivede said in all seriousness.

'A gravedigger once told me the same thing,' Bordelli said, laughing. He wanted to laugh a little, to dispel the tension of waiting. The doctor heaved a long, provocative sigh but ignored the challenge.

'Where shall we go to eat?' Bordelli asked.

'Feel like going to Armando's?'

'Armando's it is.'

'On Thursdays they have *baccalà*.'

'You don't seem like the *baccalà* type to me.'

'I found some in a dead man's stomach the other day and felt like having some,' said Diotivede.

'You could have eaten his, while you were at it,' said the inspector.

'Still nothing on the boy?' the doctor asked, changing the subject.

'Not yet.'

'Sons of bitches . . .' Diotivede said under his breath.

The inspector was astonished. He'd never heard him talk that way before. They both fell silent. It was still raining, and there were a great many cars on the road.

They arrived in San Lorenzo. The Trattoria da Armando had few tables, and they were all taken. All men, except for two American women. Diotivede and Bordelli had to wait for fifteen minutes in front of the counter, continually changing position to let the waiters pass. People were talking loudly, mostly about hunting, mushrooms and football.

At last a table became available, and they sat down. They ordered *baccalà alla livornese* and a litre of wine.

'Have you ever gone walking through the woods outside of town?' Bordelli asked.

'I always have and still do,' said Diotivede.

'Ah, I didn't know . . .'

'When did you last pee?'

'This morning at the station . . . Why?'

'Ah, I didn't know,' the doctor said with a cold smile.

'Well, now you know and can sleep easy,' said Bordelli, filling the glasses. He wanted to enjoy his lunch and not think about going back to the office to wait for news that might never come. Diotivede decisively changed the subject.

'I'm engaged to be married,' he said, point blank. Bordelli stopped chewing.

'Are you serious? Since when?' He was truly astonished. The doctor normally never opened up like this.

'Aren't you going to ask me how old she is?' asked Diotivede, a sparkle in his eye.

'How old is she?'

'Forty-two, but she looks thirty-five.'

'Then be careful, she must be mad.'

'Brilliant people are always considered mad.'

'Did you tell her you spend your life in the company of corpses?'

'That was the very reason we fell in love,' said Diotivede with another icy smile.

'What's her name?'

'Marianna.'

'You must introduce me to her,' said Bordelli.

'Better not. I say this for your sake.'

'In what sense?'

'You might die of envy.'

'Is she really so beautiful?'

MarcoVichi

'She's gorgeous,' said Diotivede, taking a long swig of wine.

'Are you sure she's in her right mind?' Bordelli asked, trying to provoke him.

'Absolutely. She told me she hates police inspectors.'

'Well, she hasn't met *me* yet.'

'I'd rather she didn't know I keep bad company.'

'I get it, you're the jealous type,' said the inspector, feeling a genuine twinge of envy.

'Look who's talking. It's been twenty years and I've never known a single one of your girlfriends.'

'I never quite get to know them myself, as far as that goes.'

'Maybe you should change your brand of aftershave,' said Diotivede, lustily chewing a mouthful of *baccalà*.

When Bordelli pulled back into the courtyard of the police station, it was past 3.30 and drizzling. Mugnai ran up to him with an umbrella.

'Inspector, Piras has been looking for you for the past hour.'

'Here you go,' said Bordelli, handing him the *Settimana Enigmistica*.

'Thank you, sir.'

'Where's Piras?'

'I think he's in the radio room,' said Mugnai, scanning the cover of the *Settimana*.

Bordelli went at once to the radio room, and Piras came towards him with his hands in the air.

'Shit, Inspector . . .'

'What is it?'

'After lunch Panerai left his flat an hour earlier than usual, and they followed him as far as Piazza Alberti, but then they lost him.'

'It happens,' said Bordelli, suppressing a curse.

'They're searching every street in the area for him, but still haven't found him.'

'Just keep looking.'

'I'm staying here, sir. I'll let you know as soon as they pick up his trail again.'

'What time does the butcher's shop reopen?'

'At four.'

'I'm going upstairs.'

The moment he entered his office he heard a moribund buzzing over his head and realised that the fly didn't have much time left. He flopped into his chair with a cigarette in his mouth and a song by Little Tony in his head, which he hummed from time to time.

It was a long, boring afternoon. Only one new development: the big black fly decided to die right on his desk, beside the Giacomo Pellissari file. Bordelli picked it up by a wing and dumped it in the wastepaper basket.

At eight he went and had a bite to eat in Totò's kitchen, and as soon as he came out he felt the need to be coddled by Rosa. Actually, it hadn't really been just 'a bite to eat'. He'd gorged himself on pasta and meat and had knocked back nearly an entire one-litre flask of wine. Not that he felt drunk or anything. He could always hold his alcohol. At the end of the war he had even happened to seize a railway car full of cognac headed to Germany. He would drink whole cupfuls and at the most would feel a light sense of euphoria. But tonight he really had eaten too much, and a little stroll would do him some good. He drove the car home and left it there, then headed for Via dei Neri, an unlit cigarette in his mouth and a rainproof hat rolled up in his pocket. The sky was covered with threatening clouds, but at the moment it wasn't raining.

When he was a little kid those streets were full of carriages, bicycles and a few rare cars, but most people wore out their shoes on the pavement. Everything was different now. There were more and more cars and motorbikes, driven by younger and younger kids. Many of them dressed bizarrely, rather differently from the young people of his day, who by the age of twenty were already fully adult and by forty on the verge of old age. Nowadays it seemed as if the young didn't ever want to grow up, and Bordelli liked this. He felt as if he was absorbing some of this youth, at least until he saw his reflection in a shop window.

An Alfa Romeo Spider overtook him on the Lungarno, wildly honking its horn, and he just managed to glimpse behind the windows the blonde hair of a couple of girls . . . Unless they were long-haired boys. There were more and more of them about these days. He'd even sighted five in a single day once. And he would often misidentify them. He would see long hair, turn round to look at the woman and find instead a man with a beard. It upset him every time.

Crossing the Ponte alle Grazie he noticed that the Arno was swelling and slowed down, fascinated by that mass of dark water sliding silently through the city, cutting it in two.

A moment later he rang Rosa's buzzer and waited a good minute before the front door opened. He climbed the stairs slowly. He was mildly surprised not to find Rosa waiting for him on the landing. The door was ajar, and he slipped inside. Rosa was in the sitting room feeding the half-blind kitten some milk through a syringe without the needle, as Gideon observed the scene from his perch on the sideboard.

'Look how cute she is . . . She eats like an ox. By now she's out of danger,' said Rosa.

'I hardly recognise her,' said Bordelli, sitting down on the sofa. Indeed, the kitten had gained weight and her fur looked shiny. She was digging her claws into the syringe as though afraid it might be taken away. She seemed full of energy.

'If you want something to drink, help yourself.'

'Perhaps a bit later . . .'

'You have no idea what I had to do the first day to make her poo.'

'Can't they do it all by themselves?'

'Not when they're this little. And if they don't poo, their intestine gets blocked and that's the end of them. I had to rub her bottom with cotton, the way the mama kitty does with her tongue. I was at it for a good fifteen minutes. Finally this little thing as hard as a rock came out . . . and I cried for joy.'

'You're such a good little mum,' Bordelli commented.

'Wasn't that yummy?' Rosa said to the kitten, kissing it on the head and setting it down on the carpet. Gideon jumped down from the sideboard, ready to square off. The kitten ran towards him and jumped on him, trying to bite his nose. Despite the bad eye, she seemed to see quite well. Gideon flopped down on the floor and started swiping at her with his paws as though toying with a mouse.

'They've already made friends,' said Rosa, touched. Even after ten years of brothels she could still blush and feel moved like a schoolgirl.

The cats carried on playing. Briciola would attack Gideon, who then defended himself. Suddenly the kitten stopped wrestling, took a couple of little steps back and forth, then collapsed on the carpet.

'Is she unwell?' the inspector asked, alarmed.

'No, no, she always does that. She'll play and play and then suddenly fall asleep.'

'I wish I could do that.'

He looked at Briciola, thinking that if he hadn't passed by those brambles, she would have suffered the same fate as her little brothers and sisters. It was chance, or fate, that saved her. And he hoped that chance or fate might deign to lend him a hand in his investigation as well.

'Would you like a little grappa?' asked Rosa, rescuing him from his thoughts.

'You're a sweetheart . . . I've also got this pain in my neck . . .' Bordelli said, in all seriousness. Rosa went up to him and wrinkled her nose at him the way one does to children.

'You chase after every skirt you see, but you'll never find someone to spoil you like your Rosina, not in a million years,' she tittered. She picked the kitten up from the floor, and without waking her put her in a little box with an old sweater inside.

'She sleeps like a rock, the little thing.'

She filled two small glasses with grappa, took off her purple stilettos, had Bordelli lie down and then straddled his bottom. She started massaging his neck with soft but decisive movements, laughing as he moaned with pleasure. But it wasn't just pleasure he felt. Rosa's little massages also had the power to empty his mind and suspend his judgement of the world, a rather relaxing thing.

'I must admit you really know how to use your hands,' he managed to say between groans.

'If you only knew how many overgrown little boys I've massaged while they complained about their bitchy wives and witchy mothers-in-law . . .'

'I am *not* an overgrown little boy,' he grumbled.

'You're the most childish of them all,' she laughed, massaging harder.

'At any rate, I haven't got any wives or mothers-in-law . . .'

Hearing the roar of the violent, driving rain outside, Bordelli remembered he'd come on foot.

'You're going to have to lend me an umbrella; I walked here.'

'You walked here?' Rosa asked in surprise.

'It's a pretty easy walk.'

'Why don't you sleep here tonight? Just listen to the weather outside . . .'

'It's not the end of the world if I get a little wet. I can take a nice hot shower when I get home.'

'Well, I've got all the umbrellas you want,' said Rosa, a little disappointed. But luckily she didn't stop massaging him.

'Why don't you tell me some old story about your family?' Bordelli mumbled. He loved listening to Rosa reminisce about times gone by. She was a good storyteller, and she liked doing it almost as much as she liked shopping for shoes and provocative little dresses.

'Have I ever told you about the time Zia Asmara fell in love with the parish priest?'

'I don't think so,' Bordelli lied, happy to relive yet again the travails of Zia Asmara, painful to the one who had lived them but most amusing to listen to.

'Zia Asmara was my mother's little sister. At twenty she was the prettiest girl in Cerbaia, and all the men in the area would have given their right hands for her. Not just boys, old men, too. But she fell in love with a young village priest who'd just arrived from Bologna, and she used to go to all the masses, at all the different times of day, just to see him . . .'

After two hours of torrential downpour only an insistent drizzle remained, as streams of dirty water flowed down the pavements. It was well past midnight. Aside from the occasional passing car, there was nobody about. Bordelli hugged the walls of the buildings as he walked, huddling under the small pink umbrella Rosa had lent him. He'd nearly fallen asleep in her miracle-working hands, and had to yank himself violently out of that limbo.

He passed under the Uffizi arcade, just to avoid returning by the same route he had come by. His feet were cold and wet. Leaving the Ponte Vecchio to his left, he continued along the Lungarno. The rainfall was letting up by the minute, but he still needed the umbrella. Without stopping, he cast a glance over the parapet. The Arno was more swollen than ever, heaving in great muddy splashes and flowing fast with a dark murmuring sound. It would not have been much fun to fall in just then. When he got to the corner of Via de' Tornabuoni, the rain suddenly stopped, and he closed the absurd umbrella with a sense of relief. The moon was smothered by a thick mattress of clouds, looking like a torch trying to make its way through the fog.

Crossing the Ponte Santa Trinità, he noticed some youths on Vespas and Lambrettas proceeding slowly alongside the Via Maggio pavement across the river, gesticulating at a man who was walking peacefully along. Then they put their scooters up on their kickstands, got off and surrounded the man. Bordelli quickened his pace, and as he approached he heard the youths' mocking voices. There were five of them, all about twenty years old.

'Homo . . .' one of them yelled, running his hand over his crotch. 'You wish, eh?'

'Pan-sy, pan-sy, pan-sy,' chanted another.

'When d'ya last take it up the arse, eh?'

'Tomorrow,' answered another, guffawing.

'So you like little kids, do you? Pervert!' said the one who seemed like the ringleader, and he dealt the man a slap that resounded in the quiet street. At that point the other four started slapping him around as well, and the poor man fell to the ground. The insults grew more violent, and they started kicking him in the face. The youths didn't even notice the burly man approaching at a quick pace.

'Hey, bed-wetters . . .' said Bordelli, drawing up behind them. They all turned round at once, all with the same surprised sneer on their faces.

'Ah, what a pretty little umbrella,' said the ringleader.

'One fairy draws another,' said another, as the others laughed.

'There's plenty for you too, Gramps.'

'Show us how you bugger each other,' said the leader, swaggering towards Bordelli. 'Gramps' dropped his little umbrella and punched him square in the face, sending him rolling on the ground. The other four hesitated, full of rage. Bordelli looked each one of them in the eye. They were well dressed, with clean faces. Rich kids.

The ringleader got up slowly, trembling, his jacket covered with blood and a hand over his mouth. The inspector thrust his hands into his pockets with self-assurance. He felt like the good-looking hero of the film he'd seen at the Gambrinus. He was well aware that if they all jumped on him at once, he was screwed. He had to play the fear card, but he wanted to do so without pulling out his badge.

'I'll give you guys two seconds to disappear, and then we start counting teeth,' he said, pulling his fists out of his pockets. They all gave a start and looked at one another. One step forward was enough . . . The boys jumped on their scooters and were off at full speed, shouting insults and laughing.

Finally Bordelli went to help the victim, who was still on the ground, from where he'd witnessed the scene. His face was bleeding, and he was breathing heavily. The inspector had seen him walking about the neighbourhood in the past and had immediately understood that he didn't like women.

'Everything okay?'

'To be honest, I was feeling better before,' the man muttered, slurring his words. But he managed a smile. He looked to be about the same age as the inspector. He was thin, with a long, gaunt face, and two watery eyes like a beaten dog's. The orange silk scarf around his neck was blood-stained, like his shirt and jacket.

'Would you like me to take you to Casualty?'

'Do you really not recognise me, Bordelli?' said the man. The inspector took a good look at him, and suddenly remembered.

'Don't tell me . . . you're Poggiali . . .' he said.

'Or what's left of him,' Poggiali said, smiling. He got to his feet with Bordelli's help, and then leaned against the wall to keep from falling.

'It was the same story even at school, remember?' Poggiali touched his teeth to make sure they were still all there.

'My memory's a bit hazy,' said Bordelli, shrugging. In truth he remembered his school days perfectly well, when the Fascist regime glorified the sort of masculine man who impaled women. Even in middle school the boys used to make sport of queers and sometimes even beat them up, although many of them used to follow them into the bathrooms and let them masturbate them for a few cents.

'You pack quite a punch,' said Poggiali.

'I used to box a little as a kid.'

'God bless boxing.'

'I live just round the corner here, come and tidy yourself up,' said Bordelli, picking up Rosa's umbrella.

'I live nearby too, why don't you come to my place?'

'As you wish,' said the inspector, curious to see where

Poggiali lived. They started walking down Via Maggio side by side. Poggiali was still wiping the blood off his face, limping almost like Piras.

'Only you and a couple of other friends used to leave me alone,' he said.

'I have to confess that at the time I didn't have much sympathy for people like you.'

'What about now?'

'Good question . . .'

'What exactly is it about us poofs that bothers you all so much?' Poggiali asked, with a frankness that made Bordelli smile.

'It's not an easy subject for people of our generation,' the inspector admitted.

'Nor for today's youth, apparently.'

'There have always been idiots and there always will be.'

'You should all be happy to have fewer rivals hunting for birds, no?'

'I'd never thought of it that way.'

'In other words, what do *you* care if we like men?' said Poggiali, turning on to Sdrucciolo de' Pitti. Bordelli didn't know how to reply, and his old school chum smiled.

'Whenever you see a queer you immediately think of some perversion, something sexual and nothing else. You imagine the sight of two men fucking and it disturbs you.'

'I suppose you're right,' said the inspector, realising that Poggiali's orange scarf had immediately made him think of the boy who'd been raped and murdered.

'And yet I assure you that we homos have the same full range of feelings as you humans,' Poggiali said blithely.

Arriving at a door with the paint peeling off, he pushed it open and they climbed the stairs to the fourth floor. Poggiali's flat didn't look very big, but even the entrance had something elegant and unusual about it. They went into a small sitting room cluttered almost obsessively with statuettes, theatre masks, ceramics, crazy paintings, terracotta animals, busts of generals and ephebes, and bouquets of dried roses. Two walls were covered with bookshelves up to the ceiling. Poggiali opened up a little bar lined entirely with mirrors on the inside.

'Help yourself, I'm going to the bathroom to freshen up a little,' he said, leaving the room.

Bordelli calmly rifled through the bottles and found a French cognac. He filled a small glass to the rim, then flopped on to one of two sofas upholstered with imitation tiger skin. He'd never seen a room like this before, and his gaze got lost in the countless different objects vying with one another for space. There were a great many turtles of every shape and size. One was on the floor and must have been over a yard long, while the smallest was ridiculously perched atop a Fascist fez. A strange, miniature museum where one would have needed a whole afternoon to examine each piece . . . The exact opposite of Bordelli's place, which was bare and disorderly, even sort of lugubrious.

'Here I am, good as new,' said Poggiali, in a fluttering purple dressing gown and slippers. Despite his swollen lip and a cut on one cheekbone, he looked untroubled.

'I guess you like turtles,' said Bordelli.

'It's a question of affinity. In the face of danger, they withdraw into their shell, like me.'

He made himself a martini and sat down on the other sofa, facing his guest. Surrounded by his inanimate objects, he looked like a monarch in a gloomy fairy tale.

Bordelli realised he was fighting off unpleasant thoughts of the sort that Poggiali had been talking about. It had even flashed through his mind that destiny had brought him to one of Giacomo Pellissari's killers . . . Simply because Poggiali was a *homosexual.*

'So, how's life?' he asked, to avoid thinking about it.

'I don't want for anything. I'm retired and own another apartment that I rent out.'

He went on to say that he'd held a number of different jobs, from postman to manual labourer, and that when his parents died he'd inherited the two flats.

'Mine are dead, too,' Bordelli muttered. He already knew that sooner or later he would ask Poggiali what he thought about the murder of Giacomo Pellissari, but he was waiting for the right moment.

'Every now and then I see your name in *La Nazione* . . . Inspector here, inspector there . . .'

'Until you see it in an obituary, everything's fine.' Bordelli refilled his glass and asked Poggiali what he'd done during the war.

'I didn't fight, I was rejected for service. Officially for respiratory insufficiency, but you can imagine the real reason. I stayed in Florence the whole time, keeping far away from the stinking Fascists.'

'And after the eighth of September?'[11]

'I escaped to the hills and almost ended up by chance in Potente's band.[12] I saw my share of corpses, dear Bordelli. I even fired a gun a few times, but that's not my cup of tea. Even among those valiant lads there were a few who couldn't bear having me around. But I also spent some rather eventful nights with a few others,' Poggiali said, with a smile between naughty and nostalgic.

'Don't tell the communists, they'll burn you alive.'

'I think I'd ask to be hanged first, like Savonarola.'

'Have you heard the news about the little boy who was raped and murdered?' Bordelli asked, no longer able to put it off.

'Poor thing . . .' Poggiali said, nodding.

'Mind if I ask you a question?'

'You can even ask me two, if you like.'

'I'm just curious . . . Since you know about these things . . . Yes, well . . . Is it normal for a homosexual to be sexually attracted to children?'

'Of course, just as it's normal for all Jews to be moneylenders, all Neapolitans pizza-makers, and all women whores.'

'I didn't mean to offend you.'

'I'm not offended. I just happen to know that you *normal* people think that way. I'm used to it, my friend.'

89

'I can't blame you, but maybe it's not entirely our fault.'

'Tell me something. Do you sleep with ten-year-old girls?' Poggiali asked, sitting up from the sofa.

'Do I have to answer that?'

'That's exactly my point. I like young flesh, like everyone else. But it's nothing to do with children.'

'Do you know anyone who sees things a little differently?'

'I know every kind of person, fags and non-fags. There are some who like to watch other people fuck, there are others who like to have people piss in their mouth, others who mastur-bate while licking a woman's stockings, and others who fuck animals . . . I really don't give a damn about what people do for pleasure, unless they're making somebody suffer for it.'

'I'm just trying to understand what kind of people would rape a child.'

'Well, don't expect them to be monstrously ugly like the ogres in fairy tales. People who do that sort of thing are sick in the head, but they could easily be your friendly dentist or your neighbourhood baker. People who lead perfectly normal lives. The worst perverts I've ever met were rich bourgeois with spotless reputations,' said Poggiali, emptying his glass in one swig.

'Thanks for the cognac.' Bordelli sighed, getting up.

'Already off to bed?'

'It's late . . .'

'Worried I might molest you?' Poggiali asked, faking a woman's voice. The inspector smiled.

'You know what I've always thought? That if I'd been born a woman, I would still like women.'

'You're an incurable male, but at least you're not a policeman.' Poggiali laughed. He saw Bordelli to the door, and they shook hands.

'Good luck, Inspector.'

'I'll need it . . . See you around, Poggiali.'

'Goodbye,' said Poggiali, more realistically.

The inspector slowly descended the stairs. As soon as he

was outside, he lit a cigarette. He too knew that they weren't likely to see each other again soon. He couldn't picture himself inviting Poggiali to dinner or for a stroll about town. Even though he felt deep down that they could have become friends. The old poof actually seemed like a lovely person.

The rain had started falling hard again during the night and still showed no sign of letting up. When Bordelli pulled into the station courtyard it was past nine. He'd been stuck in traffic for a good half-hour. He got out of the car with his overcoat pulled up over his head and ran to the main entrance, dripping wet. Rinaldi came up to him with dark circles under his eyes and a pale face, to bring him up to speed on things. Panerai had gone out at ten minutes to eight that morning and taken his Lancia Flavia. He hadn't gone to the butcher's shop, but had stopped in Via Lungo l'Affrico near Via d'Annunzio to pick up three men who'd been waiting for him under their umbrellas. The Flavia had left the city and gone south, past Pontassieve, Rufina and San Godenzo, and had just taken the road to Muraglione.

'Who's in the unmarked car?' Bordelli asked, heading for the radio room with Rinaldi at his side.

'Piras and Tapinassi, sir,' said Rinaldi, suppressing a big yawn.

'Go and get some sleep,' Bordelli advised him, patting him on the back.

'I'm not tired, sir . . .' the policeman said, shrugging. When they entered the radio room, the inspector immediately got in touch with Piras. The connection was bad, and Piras had to repeat himself several times in order to be understood. It was raining where he was, too. The butcher and his friends were proceeding at moderate speed. They'd stopped only once, to have breakfast and get petrol, just before San Godenzo.

'Try not to lose him,' said Bordelli. He got a long crackle

by way of reply, faintly modulated by a metallic-sounding voice. A few seconds later they lost the connection, thanks to the Apennine mountains.

'Call me as soon as you hear something,' Bordelli said to the men in the radio room.

He went up to his office, took off his wet raincoat and opened the window to air the place out. It was raining cats and dogs and seemed as if it would never stop. He lit a cigarette and smoked it with his elbows on the windowsill. The passing cars raised great bow waves.

Piras wasn't able to re-establish contact until another hour later, and Bordelli dashed at once to the radio room. Now the Sardinian's voice came in loud and clear. He named the towns they passed through along the trunk road: Il Poggio, Il Bagno, Bocconi, San Benedetto, Rocca San Casciano, Dovadola, Pieve Salutare . . . Panerai's Flavia forged on without hesitation, as though the butcher or one of the passengers knew the route well.

'Where the hell are they going in this rain?' the inspector asked under his breath, running a hand over his face.

'They've turned right,' said Piras. When the unmarked police car reached the intersection, the Sardinian read the names on the road sign: Fiumana, Trivella and . . . Predappio, Mussolini's birthplace. So that was where they were headed.

'Today's the twenty-eighth of October, Inspector,' Piras croaked over the radio waves.

'A leopard can't change its spots . . .' said Bordelli, disappointed. Panerai's and his comrades' nostalgia was pathetic, but it certainly didn't make them guilty of the murder of Giacomo Pellissari.

'What should I do, Inspector?' asked Piras, equally chagrined.

'Stay on his tail.'

Bordelli leaned back in his chair and lit his umpteenth cigarette of the day, as Piras continued chronicling his journey. After a series of gut-wrenching bends, the road became straighter, and at San Lorenzo in Nocento the butcher turned right again.

Fiumana, Trivella . . . and, at last, Predappio. *Duce, Duce, eja eja alalà!*[13]

The inspector pressed his eyes hard with his fingertips and heaved a desolate sigh. He was well aware that many of the functionaries whose paths he crossed daily were nostalgic for the old regime, including the commissioner. He thought sadly that Carlino, the former partisan fighter who owned the bar near Rosa's place, was right: deep down, the Italians were incurably Fascist. Children in need of an authoritarian father so they could feel protected, so they could hear somebody tell them: *Sleep easy, I'll take care of everything.* The important thing was to sleep, eat, have an easy job, a quick tongue, and money to go to the beach. A nation of poor bastards seeking redemption in dreams of power. This wasn't the sort of Italy for which Franco Bordelli had shot all those Nazis . . .

Piras got back to the station late that afternoon, having followed Panerai's car all the way back to his house and been relieved by another unmarked car. He limped up to Bordelli's office, collapsed in a chair, and began recounting their pleasant outing to Predappio in the driving rain. In some of the shop windows they saw busts of 'Bighead',[14] lictor's fasces, the symbol of the regime, death's heads of the 10th Assault Vehicle Flotilla,[15] black T-shirts with the words *Me ne frego!* written on the front.[16]

A few hundred people, mostly men, had gathered in the monumental piazzetta Mussolini had built in front of the modest house he was born in. They included not only people who had lived under the regime, but also youths who had only heard tell of that period. Piras and Tapinassi had mixed in with the crowd, always keeping an eye on the butcher and his friends.

Fascist songs, battle cries, tears, banners, signal flags, *eja eja* and choruses of *alalà* . . . It was all there. Round about noon the butcher and his mates had gone to the San Cassiano cemetery to visit the sacred tomb of Il Duce in the Mussolini family chapel.

'People younger than me were kneeling down with tears in their eyes, like they were thanking the Madonna for miraculously curing them,' Piras commented, a half-smile playing on his lips.

'Mussolini made Italians dream far more than the Madonna ever has,' said Bordelli, getting up and thrusting his hands in his pockets, waiting to hear the rest.

'At lunchtime . . . hunger won out over devotion,' said Piras, who just couldn't take that pathetic gathering seriously. A convoy of cars had come down from Forlì and the restaurants had been taken by storm. He and Tapinassi managed to find a free table in the same trattoria as Panerai and his comrades, which was mobbed with 'pilgrims'. Gnocchi, tortelli, lasagna, tagliatelle, *strozzapreti*, pork, stews, rivers of Lambrusco, laughter and songs from the good old days. To avoid attracting attention, he and Tapinassi had joined the chorus, pretending to know all the words. The restaurant owner smiled at the thought of all the money he was making. For the occasion he'd put a bronze bust of Il Duce, with a fez on his fat head, on the bar in full view. When the time came for grappa, a little man of about fifty and half-drunk stood up and made a speech, a garbled panegyric of the Duce and his noble deeds. He concluded with a rousing shout of *Boia chi molla!*[17] To deafening applause, followed by more songs . . .

'An unforgettable day,' said the Sardinian. Around four o'clock the butcher and his confrères got back on the road in the driving rain and returned to Florence. Panerai stopped in Via Lungo l'Affrico to drop his friends off and then went home. The shop had remained closed all day. On the rolling metal shutter was a sign with the words: *Closed for family reasons.*

'Devotion works miracles,' said Bordelli, realising that the butcher had sacrificed a whole day's earnings just to go and pay homage to Papa Mussolini. He obviously hadn't felt confident leaving the shop in his old assistant's hands.

'While he was at it, he could have written: *Closed for national holiday*,' said Piras, standing up. Tomorrow he would have to get up at dawn to continue the surveillance of Panerai. He said goodbye to Bordelli and went home to bed.

Bordelli finally lit a cigarette, still walking round the room, looking at the walls. Every so often he glanced out of the window and saw only rain. So the butcher was nostalgic for Il Duce . . . So what? There were a lot of Italians just like him, and they frightened him less than some dark souls who called themselves anti-Fascists. But most importantly, that sentimental journey to Predappio had no objective relation to the little boy's murder. Another dead end. He was wasting his time chasing ghosts. Perhaps he should resign himself to the likelihood that the butcher had nothing to do with the murder. He would wait another week and then call off the surveillance . . .

He flopped into his chair, feeling exhausted. He wished he were somewhere else, maybe even some*one* else. In his twenty years with the police it was the first time he didn't know which way to turn, and the idea of failure obsessed him. But there was no point in tormenting himself. All he could do was wait and hope.

He tried to distract himself with other concerns . . . There were four years left before retirement. He had no children, no wife. He ate too much, drank too much, smoked too much. He had to change his lifestyle, buy a house in the country, stop smoking, marry a beautiful woman and tend a vegetable garden. His curmudgeonly cousin Rodrigo hadn't wasted any time. In February he'd sold his flat in Viale Gramsci for several million lire and for a song had bought an old peasant house with two hectares of land up from Bagno a Ripoli. After restoring it he still had plenty of money left over. He lived there with a woman he was crazy about, and at the tender age of fifty-four he was planning to have at least three children. Bordelli had learned all this from his Zia Camilla, Rodrigo's mum. It had been a long time since he'd heard from Rodrigo, and so he picked up the phone to give him a ring. A little chat with his cousin was just what he needed to distract himself. He and Rodrigo were so different that the best way for them to understand each other was to avoid each other. But this was exactly why he wanted to talk to him, to smile at the continuous misunderstandings that arose from their surreal conversations. He dialled the number, but after some ten rings, he hung up. Too bad, he had been primed for it.

It was raining harder and harder, the sound like an enormous frying pan sizzling. He lit another cigarette and went out of the office. Just to be sure, he dropped by the radio room to hear the very latest on the butcher. Nothing unusual, no news.

He went home, cursing the bloody autumn weather, blaming it for all the tension that was biting at his heels. In the hope of calming down, he stayed a long time under the hot rain of the shower, singing old songs from back in his day . . . *Mamma son tanto felice, perchè ritorno da te* . . . He had to stop thinking all the time about the murdered boy . . . *La mia canzone ti dice, ch'è il più bel sogno per me* . . . But he would find the killers, he had to . . . *Mamma son tanto felice, viver lontano perchè?* . . .[18]

Still humming, he slipped on his bathrobe and went into the kitchen to look for something to eat. There wasn't much choice. He prepared himself a plate of pasta with tomato sauce, following Botta's instructions. He sat down to eat it in front of the telly, which was already on, keeping the wine within reach. The National channel was showing a science programme that he couldn't manage to follow. His brain kept worrying fruitlessly, turning round in circles like a stripped screw.

He finished the pasta, with compliments to the chef. In spite of everything, he'd managed to enjoy his *penne al pomodoro*. He emptied his glass and lit a cigarette. Blowing the smoke up towards the ceiling, he sighed like a soul in purgatory. Now that his hunger was slaked, a subtle anxiety clouded his every thought. He felt old. A poor old wretch defeated on all fronts. He imagined himself already retired, senile and spending his nights counting the change in his purse as he'd seen his grandfather do. Broth, hot-water bottles and a great deal of rest . . . Then, one day, death and amen.

It was barely ten o'clock. He didn't feel like spending the whole evening staring at the telly, entertained by delightful thoughts about the meaning of life. He needed to go outside and change his mood, have a little conversation with somebody . . . He thought of Dante, the half-mad scientist who lived in Mezzomonte in an old villa with its doors always open, a giant full of energy with long white hair flying in all directions. He'd met him in the summer of '63, when investigating the death of Dante's sister Rebecca. They'd become friends, even though they saw each other rarely and still used the formal address with each other. Dante was a night-owl and at that hour had probably just gone down to his underground laboratory.

He stubbed out his cigarette in the ashtray and went into the entrance hall to phone him. He let it ring for a long time, and finally he heard someone pick up.

'Dante here . . . Who is it?' asked the scientist in his deep ogre-like voice.

'Good evening, Dr Pedretti. Am I disturbing you?'

'Ah, Bordelli . . . How are you?'

'That's what I'd like to know. And you?'

'I am still curious about the world.'

'I wish I were too . . .'

'But you are, otherwise you wouldn't be a policeman.'

'Perhaps you're right.'

'Why don't you come and see me, Inspector?'

'That's exactly why I called.'

'I'll be waiting.'

'I'll be there in half an hour . . .'

He covered his head with an umbrella as he got out of the car, then entered Dante's big house through the front door. Lighting his path with a match, he groped his way down the stairs to the large underground laboratory, which was as big as the entire floor plan of the house. It had been created by knocking down the old basement walls in the name of science.

He entered the great, silent room, which was shrouded in darkness, a pair of candlesticks spreading a lunar light that licked at the shadows. At first glance it looked like a dark church lit up with candles, and the old bookcases overflowing with books along the walls were the tabernacles. Dante's altar was a great big workbench covered, as always, with open books, bottles half filled with coloured liquids, various gadgets and every manner of incomprehensible contraption. The scientist was standing with his elbows propped on the workbench. He was writing something in a red-bordered notebook of the kind children use in primary school.

'Hello, Inspector,' he said, hearing Bordelli approach in the darkness. He didn't even raise his head. He seemed to be concentrating.

'I hate to bother you while you're working.'

'I was just playing,' said Dante, dropping the pen on to the bench. They shook hands. Dante's handshake was powerful, almost brutal. His white mane looked like a flame of magnesium.

'Grappa, Inspector?'

'That's why I came . . .'

'I must have put it somewhere here . . .' Dante muttered, searching among the bottles on the bench.

Bordelli glanced at the inventor's open notebook and saw an entire page covered with a dense pattern of mathematical formulae. That was the game he was talking about. Dante raised a large, half-empty bottle, with no label, in the air.

'Here it is,' he said. Then he fished two miraculously identical glasses out of the Gehenna. They eased into the only two armchairs, keeping the bottle within reach. Dante relit the cigar he had in his mouth and blew a ball of smoke towards the ceiling. At the first sip of grappa, the inspector felt his legs slacken.

'Does the barn owl still come to visit you from time to time?' he asked.

'Now and then. She always appears suddenly, unannounced, then disappears for a month . . . the way women do sometimes.'

'Maybe one day she'll decide to stay.'

'I doubt it. I know women well,' said Dante, and he burst out laughing.

'I'd like to buy an old farmhouse around here.' Bordelli sighed, imagining the peace that reigned in that house.

'There are as many as you like in the area. Most people still hate living in the country.'

'I can understand that.'

'But you should hurry up, if you're serious. Before long the old abandoned houses will cost an arm and a leg.'

'Are you really so sure?'

'Ask me whether Monsieur Lapalisse was still alive a moment before he died, and I'll give you the same answer.'

'Then I'll start looking soon. First I need to take care of some business.'

'You mean the murdered boy?' asked Dante.

The inspector nodded. They both remained silent for a spell, thinking. Only the light ticking of a clock was audible. Who knew whether it was still raining outside? The inventor stood up slowly and planted himself in front of Bordelli, surrounded by dense swirls of smoke.

'For primitive man, violence meant survival. Today man no longer needs to hunt in order to eat; he goes to the supermarket and fills up the trolley. The powerful animal strength that dominated him for thousands of years now sits down in front of the television, shaves with the latest Philips razor, and goes on outings with the family every Sunday . . . And every now and then the beast appears with the bill.'

'If only it was every now and then.'

'Human consciousness is the most devastating illness in nature,' decreed Dante, staring into space.

'That's encouraging.'

'The madman Nietzsche invited man himself, rational man, thinking, self-conscious man, to cure this unforgivable illness of nature by voluntarily annihilating himself in the species. He invited consciousness to put itself in the service of nature, to restore to the human race its animal strength and purity. Instinct obliges the animal to fight so that only the best may impregnate the female, and according to him, man should achieve the same result through rational choice. It's the most absurd proposition in the world, though fascinating. Nietzsche was trying to make bricks without straw, a bit like Marx . . . And both gave birth to monsters.'

'And we're left with the Christian Democrats,' said the inspector.

'Hallelujah . . .' muttered Dante, sitting back down. He took two or three deep drags of his cigar, and his face disappeared behind a cloud of smoke. When it slowly reappeared, there was an ironic smile on his lips. Bordelli refilled his glass.

'I can understand wickedness, but cruelty escapes my comprehension,' he said sadly. He was feeling unpleasantly sorry for himself, unable as he was to do his bloody job as a cop. He emptied his glass in one swig and refilled it again. The inventor's voice seemed to come to him from the bottom of a well.

'The wild beasts we call ferocious have no sense of being cruel or even wicked,' said Dante, his eyes following the lazy arabesques of smoke rising up to the ceiling.

'Some men however are just and true, now and then.'

'A microscopic minority, rather like a soap bubble in a sewer.'

'I'm touched by your optimism,' said the inspector, who deep down didn't really disagree with him. Dante smiled.

'I'd like to tell you a fable . . .'

'Go right ahead,' said Bordelli, searching for his cigarettes. He asked for nothing better to distract him from the thoughts still obsessing him. Dante waved away the smoke with one hand, in an unconsciously priestlike gesture.

'Once upon a time there was a very intelligent mouse who one fine day decided to write an important treatise. He wanted to recount, in minute detail, the customs and habits of the human race. During the day he would go out of his mouse hole and mill about here and there, observing the life of men, and then at night he would return home and patiently write by candlelight about what he had seen. He was a very sensitive and discerning mouse. Nothing escaped him. He caught every nuance and could see through appearances. After a year of this he finished his book, which came to exactly one thousand pages. By a strange quirk of fate his treatise ended up in the hands of a scholar who wanted to translate it at all costs. It took him many years of effort before he was able to decipher the mouse language, but at last he found the right key for it. He translated the treatise and was truly astonished. He could hardly believe it: the little mouse had described the life of the human race better than any man could ever have done. He was very anxious to meet the enlightened little mouse who could grasp the subtlest mechanisms regulating human society. He sought him far and wide, hoping to shake his little paw and pay homage to his knowledge. But when he finally discovered where the little mouse lived, he threw up his hands in dismay. Riddle me this: why?'

'The mouse had turned into a man?'

'Much simpler: the mouse had his hole in a concentration camp,' said Dante, smiling majestically.

'That's the kind of story they should be telling the little children . . .'

Saturday morning he arrived at the office with his spirits in tatters. He collapsed in his chair and lit a cigarette, inspecting the various objects and papers covering his desk. It had rained all night, and was still raining. The monotonous sound of the water was the perfect background for his state of mind. Time seemed at a standstill. The wait was becoming unbearable. What sense was there in holding out hope? The butcher led the most normal, banal of lives. He was a blackshirt, but it stopped there. The Giacomo Pellissari file lay on the desk; by now Bordelli knew it by heart. There was a knock at the door, which opened slightly, and Rinaldi's head appeared.

'Here we go again, sir,' he said softly, with a dark look in his eye.

'What are you talking about?'

'Inspector Gorghi . . . He's interrogating a lad . . . in his usual way.'

'Bloody fucking hell,' said Bordelli, standing up with a sigh. He followed Rinaldi, his hands itching. They trotted down the stairs to the ground floor.

'Who's the lad?' Bordelli asked.

'Some student.'

'What did he do?'

'Inspector Gorghi found some anarchist broadsides in his pocket.'

'The animal's probably trying to get him to confess to crucifying Jesus Christ,' said Bordelli. He'd detested Gorghi from the first time he ever saw him, and always did everything possible to avoid having anything to do with him.

As they turned down the corridor where Gorghi had his office they could hear the young man's cries. Bordelli told Rinaldi to wait for him in the radio room, then barged in without knocking. He found Gorghi with his fist raised, ready to strike again. The kid had a broken lip and his glasses were on the floor, crushed from having been trampled on.

'Bordelli, how nice to see you,' said Gorghi with a worried sneer, lowering his fist. The youth was looking anxiously at Bordelli's angry face, fearing that the beating was about to continue with four hands.

'What has this terrible criminal done?' Bordelli asked, breathing into the face of his underling.

'That's what we're trying to find out,' Gorghi said defiantly.

Bordelli had no more words at his disposal and so decided to let his hands do the talking. Without warning he dealt Gorghi a punch square in the face, which sent him flying backwards. Gorghi fell on to the desk, as pens and papers went flying all over the place before the young student's astonished eyes. When he raised his head again, blood was flowing from his nose, which he covered with a handkerchief that immediately turned red. The boy didn't know where to look, but a hint of a smile began to appear on his lips. Gorghi was glaring at Bordelli with hatred, swearing under his breath. The inspector ignored him and started humming a little song. He picked up the phone and rang the radio room.

'Send me Rinaldi at once; I'm in Gorghi's office,' he said, then hung up.

Gorghi was panting, livid with rage and embarrassment. He'd been made to look like a nincompoop in front of that little bastard with a head crammed full of bullshit ideas, and he couldn't stand it. He was percolating revenge in his mind, but didn't dare breathe a word for the moment. Bordelli calmly picked up the youth's broken glasses and handed them to him.

'I'll have someone take you home.'

'Would you please explain to me what's going on?' the lad asked, standing up.

'A difference of opinion,' said Bordelli, smiling.

'Are you . . . a policeman?'

'No, I'm the baker from across the street.'

They heard footsteps, and Rinaldi came through the door, out of breath.

'Your orders, Inspector?'

'Please take this gentleman home.'

'Straightaway, sir.'

'So I owe thanks to a police inspector,' the student said with a tinge of bitterness.

'There are worse things in life.'

They shook hands before the dark, glaring eyes of Gorghi. The kid shot a malevolent glance at his tormentor and left the room, with Rinaldi following behind.

'You shouldn't have done that,' Gorghi muttered, pale as a corpse.

'Pull another stunt like that and I'll have you shipped off to Orgosolo to hunt down Mesina,'[19] said Bordelli, leaving the room without turning round.

He went upstairs to his office and lit a cigarette, watching the raindrops drip down the window panes. The whole thing had left him with a slight feeling of nausea. He'd never been a violent man, but bastards like Gorghi made him come out fighting. Actually, such individuals weren't worth the time of day, and a minute later he'd already stopped thinking about him.

All at once he decided to go and pay a call on Panerai, without any precise plan in his head. It was a few minutes before seven. He crushed his cigarette in the ashtray and went out of the door, suppressing the desire to light up another one. He descended the stairs slowly. In the lobby he grabbed an umbrella at random, then went and got into the Beetle. The windscreen wipers were old and left streaks of water on the glass. He wanted to see the butcher again, look him in the eye, exchange a few words . . . What was he expecting? To read in his eyes that he was the killer?

Some ten minutes later he parked in Viale dei Mille. He looked around for the unmarked car with Piras and Tapinassi in it, and when he found it, he nodded vaguely in greeting. He entered the butcher's shop dripping wet, and Panerai greeted him as he might a favourite customer. At the counter was a girl clutching a large handbag, rather shabbily dressed and with a submissive air about her. Clearly a cleaning woman doing the shopping for her employers. At second glance she turned out to be rather pretty, and the butcher was teasing her with racy quips. The girl tittered and rocked in her place. These must have been the most amusing moments of her unhappy day. Panerai ceased chopping up the rabbit for a moment, and, with the knife in the air, looked the girl in the eye.

'*What I like best in life is to find myself in a dark wood . . .*' he whispered, oozing double entendres and winking at Bordelli. The girl turned bright red and suppressed a chuckle, pleased with the man's coarse flirtation.

'You shouldn't look at me that way . . .' she said, pronouncing all her vowels too sharply. She must have been Sicilian. The butcher resumed chopping the rabbit, then wrapped it up.

'That'll be eight hundred lire, *bedda sicula*,'[20] he said, wet-lipped. The girl paid in a hurry and ran out with her hand over her mouth. Panerai followed her with his eyes, smiling.

'I like that Sicilian girl,' he said, sure of Bordelli's male complicity.

'Very pretty.'

'Well, it's better not to think about it . . . How was the steak?'

'Excellent. In fact I'd like another.'

'Those who come to Panerai's always return,' said the butcher, picking up the slab from which he cut the steaks and laying it down on the bench with a thud. Then he rubbed two sharp knives together, as usual. Bordelli started humming an old song from the Fascist era, for which he'd forgotten the words. Panerai froze, and his lips broadened into a smile. Then he started singing, waving the tip of the knife around in the air.

'. . . *nella parte dei violini, | mine magnetiche e sottomarini, | ed al posto delle trombe, | bombe bombe bombe bombe . . . | Il sassofono tenore, | lo farà l'incrociatore . . . ed invece dei tamburi, | siluri, siluri, siluri in quantità . . . | siluri, siluri, siluri, in quantità . . . | siluri, siluri, siluri, in quantità! | Serenatone, serenatone, | per la perfida Albione . . . | Boom, boom, boom, boom . . .*[21] Ah, those were the days . . .'

'Sacred words,' said Bordelli, trying his best to sound convincing.

'"There is no greater sorrow / than to recall happy times / when in misery . . ."' and this your teacher knows,'[22] recited the butcher, shaking his head ruefully.

'We'll be back,' said Bordelli, egging him on. Panerai lowered his voice.

'Yesterday I went to see Il Duce. I go twice a year, for his birthday and for the anniversary of the March.'[23]

'You don't say! I couldn't take the time off, unfortunately.'

'It was him, not Garibaldi, who made Italy.'

'Absolutely right.'

'What the hell are they waiting for to rid us of those three-nostrilled Jews[24] who are constantly plotting against the state?' asked the butcher, thrusting a knife into the meat.

'We have to wait for the right moment.' Bordelli sighed. It was the first time he had played the role of Fascist reactionary, and it cost him some effort.

'If it was up to me . . .' The butcher couldn't finish his sentence because a woman came in holding a small boy by the hand. He finished cutting the meat and the bone, casting glances of tacit understanding at Bordelli. He wanted to give him the steak free of charge, and Bordelli had to insist on paying. When it was time to go, they exchanged a Fascist salute by way of goodbye. Opening his umbrella in the doorway, Bordelli felt relieved to get away. It was still raining hard, but he felt almost happy. The water seemed to be washing the world's filth away. He didn't feel like going back to the station. He went to his car, tossed the steak inside, and after another look at the unmarked car, he headed off on foot along the avenue in the direction of Le Cure. A little walk in the rain would do him some good. He felt quite discouraged. Panerai was a hunter, a mushroomer, a pathetic Fascist who pretended to be in love with his customers. He belonged to the ranks of hit-and-run males, following in the footsteps of Il Duce. In short, he couldn't picture him doing certain kinds of things with little boys. But then why couldn't he bring himself to call off the surveillance? Because he didn't want to throw away the only lead he had? Because he didn't feel like sitting in the office twiddling his thumbs? Or was he still hoping it was worth the trouble? He didn't know the answer, but for now it was best to stop thinking about it.

He turned down Via Pacinotti, shoes soaking wet by that point. The water was streaming fast down the drainage channels. The Cinema Aurora's neon sign looked terribly depressing in the rain. He started looking in shop windows without interest. He just needed to move, to walk. When he passed in front of a clothing store, a vision took his breath away: a dark, beautiful girl was arranging the window display in her stockinged feet.

He kept on walking, breathing with his mouth open. After some twenty paces, he froze, heart racing. He already knew he would turn back to see her again. He had to remain calm. She was just a pretty girl with an Egyptian-style haircut, while he was a mature man with a good deal of experience behind him . . . It was no use, his heart refused to calm down. This always happened, every time he saw a woman he seriously liked. He turned round and headed back towards the shop, thinking about Amelia's prediction. He would have given his right hand for the dark young woman foretold by the tarot to be her. Summoning his courage, he stopped in front of the display window and started looking at the girl with a serious expression on his face. She barely cast him a glance and carried on working, moving about with a certain animal elegance. She was sheathed in a short dress and had some pins in her mouth for fastening the clothes. Beautiful, refined, dark but luminous . . . Bordelli realised he was already falling in love, like a teen-ager dazzled by the prettiest girl in school. He could not take his eyes off her. He followed the graceful movements of her arms, her small feet caressing the footstool, her wavy hair . . .

The girl finished arranging the last dress and then turned towards the strange man eyeing her from outside, oblivious to the rain. The inspector steeled his nerves and nodded, as if to say that the window display was perfect. The dark girl stepped down from the stool and put her shoes on, moving like a chamois. She came out of the shop and ran under Bordelli's umbrella to look at the results of her labours. The inspector did not turn to look at her, but was watching her out of the corner of his eye. He felt his elbow lightly graze the girl's and secretly inhaled the lovely scent wafting in the air. He would have liked to say something but was afraid his voice would quaver. How could he possibly be still so inhibited at his age? A few words, any words, would have sufficed to break the ice. Two stupid words, even one . . . But which? He was just about to make up his mind when the girl shrugged and went back into the shop without saying anything. She went behind the counter and started thumbing through a magazine rather distractedly. Bordelli kept eyeing her through the window, his heart beating wildly. One second more and he would push open the door. She was just a pretty girl, he kept telling himself. Or should he say woman? How old could she be? Twenty-six? Twenty-seven? If Amelia's cards hadn't predicted the appearance of *a dark young woman*, he would have left by now. He was almost certain of this. The oracle of the cards was guiding his will, as if the past could change the future . . . Taking a deep breath, he went inside the shop, leaving the umbrella outside the door.

'Hello,' said the girl, looking up from her magazine.

'I'm not sure you recognise me; I'm your umbrella,' he said, seeming to have left his inhibitions outside on the pavement.

'I'm sorry, I didn't even thank you.'

What a beautiful voice she had.

'I should be the one thanking you.'

'What for?' she asked, sincerely puzzled.

'For making such a beautiful window display . . .' He was really getting bold now, surprising even himself. It really must be fate, he thought. The girl stared at him with a vaguely devilish smile, like certain of Correggio's angels. Seen up close, she was even more attractive . . . But why was she so quiet? After a few eternal seconds of silence, Bordelli felt unsure again.

'I was looking for a shirt . . . I don't know what colour yet . . .' he stammered.

'I'm sorry, but we only have women's clothing,' she said, amused by the poor embarrassed man.

'Yes, of course, I meant to say *blouse*,' he said, trying to recover.

'What sort of style are you looking for? Dressy? Simple? Cotton or silk?'

'Could you perhaps give me a little advice?'

'Is it for a special occasion, or just everyday wear?'

'Just for everyday wear.'

'Age?'

'Twenty-five.'

'What size?'

'More or less the same as you,' said Bordelli. He realised he was sweating. The girl went to get some blouses off the shelves and set them down on the counter.

'This one's cotton, form-fitting, quite simple, actually. This, on the other hand . . . is silk . . .'

She was laying them out delicately, inviting him to feel the fabric with his fingers. Bordelli obeyed, feigning keen interest.

'What about this one?' he asked, pointing to a white blouse and trying hard not to look at the girl.

'This one's flannel, feel how soft it is,' she said. The inspector took a corner between his fingers and nodded, convinced.

'All right, I'll take it.' He didn't want to come off as one of those annoying customers who turns the whole shop upside down and then doesn't buy anything.

'Excellent choice,' she said, folding the blouse.

'How much is it?'

'Four thousand nine hundred. Would you like it gift-wrapped?'

'Please, yes.'

Damn. Who would ever have imagined it would be so expensive? But he didn't want to seem miserly, and so he took out his wallet with great nonchalance. The show was about to end. He had no more excuses for staying, unless he kept on buying presents for a non-existent woman. He waited for the girl to finish gift-wrapping the package, never once taking his eyes off her. He was desperately trying to think of something to say, but his head remained utterly empty. He paid without batting an eyelid, and after stammering a 'thank you' he left without turning round. Outside, he headed down the pavement, package under his arm, feeling as if he were walking inside a bubble. He felt like an imbecile, but by now he knew what he was like. If he hadn't gone into the shop, he would never have forgiven himself. It made no sense to regret it. He

turned down Viale dei Mille without even remembering that
he was just a few steps away from the house in which he'd
learned to walk and talk. The Beetle was far, far away; he
would have to cross the sea to get to it.

He dropped in on Totò to entrust him with the Fascist steak. He would eat it another day, nice and ripe. The cook asked him whether for dinner he would prefer sausages and beans *all'uccelletto* or *baccalà alla livornese*, but Bordelli didn't feel like staying.

'Your namesake's on TV tonight,[25] and I don't want to miss it,' he said.

'You can watch 'im here too, Inspector,' said Totò, pointing at the twelve-inch telly on the shelf with the pickling jars.

'I'm going home, Totò, I'm tired.'

'I just got some grappa that can raise the dead,' said the cook, trying to persuade him to stay. Bordelli thanked him, but that evening he really wanted some peace and quiet. He said goodbye and went home, cursing the bloody rain, which showed no sign of letting up.

He made himself a nice plate of penne with butter and Parmesan cheese and a lot of black pepper. He went into the dining room to turn on the telly, settled into the sofa with the plate on his lap and a flask of red wine within reach. He watched the last segment of the evening news without a great deal of interest. There was no point in trying to kid himself. The brunette salesgirl had got under his skin. Beautiful, gorgeous, what eyes, what a mouth, what legs! . . . Damn, God only knew how many guys were drooling after her. She could have any man she wanted, she only had to choose. Why on earth would she want an old police inspector who loosened his belt when he ate? He'd better forget her. A girl like that. Nor was it the right moment to waste time chasing after a woman. He had other things to think about . . .

Colonel Bernacca, the weatherman, said that there was an improvement in store for the next day and, marking up the map of Europe with his felt-tip pen, he explained the movements of the clouds to the Italians.

Bordelli finished his pasta and poured himself another glass of wine. *Carosello*, the adverts programme, began. After the jingle for Paulista coffee, it was Nino Benvenuti's turn, as secret agent 00SIS. He slew his enemies, hopping around like a cricket, while a voice off-camera listed his qualities: elusive, overwhelming, indomitable, unpredictable, explosive, irresistible . . . and all because he drank Cavallino Rosso brandy. Maybe agent 00SIS even had the power to conquer the dark girl in the dress shop . . . But hadn't he just said he didn't want to think about that?

He lit a cigarette and put his feet up on the coffee table. Enrico Maria Salerno advised Total petrol for driving faster. After topping up his Giulietta Sprint with Total Super, he left all the other cars on the autostrada in the dust, exulting: 'Now *that's* driving!' Would the dark girl like Salerno, or was he also too old? But there was old and old, and at any rate one could do nothing about it. Gregory Peck must have been about fifty, like Anthony Quinn, Lino Ventura, Yves Montand . . . and James Stewart must have been pushing seventy by then. Old charmers who had all the women in the world falling for them. And he, in fact, did look a little like Lino Ventura. Almost every woman he'd known had told him this. Except that he wasn't a great actor, he was a chief inspector who should have been made commissioner long ago. He hadn't risen any farther in the ranks because of his strange understanding of his work, and perhaps also because of his 'excessive anti-Fascism'. But he didn't give a damn about becoming a commissioner. He didn't want to end up getting fat sitting behind a desk, and power didn't interest him.

He refilled his glass again. *Carosello* wasn't over yet. After Mariarosa *l'invidiosa*, there was the skit with Gringo, who kept Montana-brand meat in his holster belt. Bordelli grimaced. Seeing that stuff in a tin made him think of the war. The Allies had brought in tons of tinned meat, and the Italian troops quickly learned to detest it. They sometimes buried those damned tins deep in the ground, so as not to have to carry them in their backpacks. They preferred picking fruit off the trees, even if unripe. He imagined telling these things to the dark salesgirl, and it made him feel very old. When he was going up the Italian peninsula jabbing the Germans in the arse, she was still wetting the bed.

Studio Uno began.[26] Mina was wearing a long black dress down to her feet that left her back exposed, which was more or less what she always wore. She launched immediately into a song with a pulsating rhythm, swaying her hips. Bordelli went to fetch some grappa and fell back on to the sofa, lying down. After a ballet number and a sad song, Totò at last made his entrance to thunderous applause. No matter what he said, people laughed. Nobody else had a face like that . . .

Bordelli woke up aching all over. Past 2 a.m. He'd fallen fast asleep right after Totò's segment. The day's programming was over, and the television set was crackling, a blizzard filling the screen. Not very pleasant to the ears. He got up with a groan and turned the set off. He dragged himself into the bathroom to brush his teeth, not daring to look in the mirror. Spitting the toothpaste out into the sink, he watched it swirl down the drain.

He undressed and went to bed. The moment he turned out the light, he thought of the dark-haired girl again, her strong, delicate hands, her animal way of moving her hips . . . He had to stop being so silly . . . Retirement was just round the bend, he shouldn't forget that. How many women did he see on the streets each day? Some made more of an impression on him than others, but in the end he forgot them all. And even the

beautiful dark salesgirl was destined to be forgotten. It was
better for him to forget her. What point was there in still thinking
about her little stockinged feet, her porcelain ears, her insolent,
childish mouth . . .

When he opened his eyes, it took him a few moments to realise what was different: he couldn't hear the rain. It had stopped raining. Light filtered through the slats of the shutters, and he could see the hands of the clock. Quarter past eight. He got up slowly, took a long shower, and went out. A stiff wind made his hair stand on end. The streets were deserted except for a few old women on their way back from mass. He walked to Piazza Tasso and ducked into Fosco's bar, one of the few in the neighbourhood that was open on Sunday. The jukebox was already blaring a song by Celentano.

'Coffee, Inspector?'

'You read my mind . . .'

'Life treating you well?' Fosco asked, busy with the espresso machine.

'Let's not exaggerate. And how are you?'

'Getting along all right. I work like a fool and all my money goes to the government.'

'It's not easy for us Italians to grasp, Fosco, but the state is *us*.'

'Us or them, the money flows out like piss either way.'

Fosco had set up the bar a few months earlier with the proceeds from years of smuggling and selling stolen goods, activities he hadn't really ceased, truth be told. Everybody in the neighbourhood knew it, and everybody respected him. On the back of his hand near the thumb he had a tattoo of a die with the number 5 face up, symbolising the criminal underworld and the time he'd spent in jail. And yet to look at him he could have been a retired schoolteacher embittered by life. Bordelli had known him since before the war and had never had the displeasure of arresting him.

'Looks like Colonel Bernacca finally got it right this time,' he said, to change the subject.

'Let's hope it lasts,' Fosco muttered, setting a steaming espresso cup down on the counter. Seated over in a corner and nodding off was Stecco, who by that hour had already knocked back several glasses of wine. Bordelli nodded in greeting to him and gulped down the coffee.

'Got a token, Fosco?'

'Go ahead and use my phone,' said the barman, inviting him behind the counter.

Bordelli phoned the station to find out whether there was any news. Tapinassi read him Piras's and Rinaldi's radio communications: the butcher had gone out at 6.30 a.m. in his Fiat 850, taking his hunting rifle with him. There was hardly anyone about at that hour on a Sunday morning, and so it hadn't been easy trying to tail him without being noticed. Panerai had gone as far as Cintoia Bassa, not far from La Panca. He parked the car on a side path and went up the hill on foot, rifle slung over his shoulder. Piras hadn't felt like following him into the woods; not only would he have risked being discovered, but he would have had to hide in the bushes and perhaps been shot at. He and Rinaldi had retreated a bit along the Cintoia road and stopped the unmarked car at a point from which they could see the butcher's 850. They were still there now and would probably remain there for a few more hours. Bordelli told Tapinassi he'd come by the office a little later and then hung up. He returned to the other side of the bar.

'Thanks, Fosco.' He sighed, pulling out his wallet.

'For what?'

'What've you got to smoke?'

'The usual stuff, Inspector . . . Rothman's, Chesterfield, Pall Mall, Stuyvesant, Lucky Strike, Turmac . . .' Needless to say, they were all contraband.[27]

'I'll try the Turmac, I've never smoked them before,' said Bordelli, laying a one-thousand-lira note down on the counter.

'Red or white?'

'Red . . .' said Bordelli, choosing at random. Fosco disappeared behind a little door and returned with the cigarettes.

'The coffee's on the house,' he said, giving him the change. The inspector thanked him and went out of the bar, lighting a cigarette in the doorway. He headed off down the pavement, crushed by a feeling of resignation. The wind blew in warm gusts, bringing a vague smell of dead leaves from the hills. He was never going to find Giacomo's killers. The butcher had lost his phone bill while searching for mushrooms or hunting. Simple as that. There was no point in tailing him any longer. The inspector had let himself be seduced by a telephone bill, pinning all his hopes on that silly piece of paper. He was in the dark again and would probably never come back out. Unless some saint interceded and gave him a hand, the boy's killers would get off scot-free. It was a pill too bitter to swallow.

He walked past his own block of flats and continued on as far as Borgo San Frediano. Hearing a woman call his name, he looked up. The powerful Signora Aneris was waving a large hand, holding a panino worthy of a stonemason in the other. Bordelli waved back. He'd never exchanged a single word with her, but they always said hello like old friends.

He pushed open the glass door to the shop of Santo Novaro, the barber who never laughed. They called him the Undertaker around the neighbourhood, and he knew it and was proud of the fact. Nobody had ever seen him laugh, but his eyes burned with a harsh Sicilian irony. Proud and handsome, he looked like a miniature copy of Amedeo Nazzari at the time of *'A plague on him!'*[28]

'Bacio le mani, Inspector.'[29]

He'd come to Florence as a boy with his parents after the war, but still amused himself playing the Sicilian.

'Ciao, Santo.'

They shook hands. Santo's was bony and as hard as an olive branch. There were no other customers in the shop, and Bordelli settled into the swivel chair. The Sicilian covered him in a light blue canvas sheet, which he tucked in round the neck, then he grabbed a pair of pointed scissors.

'A little trim?'

'But not too much.'

'I hope you don't want to become a hippy, Inspector,' said Santo, taking his first snips.

'I have to confess I wouldn't mind, if only I were thirty years younger.'

'Men should be men.'

'In the olden days men used to wear their hair long, too,' said Bordelli, looking at him in the mirror. Santo remained silent for a moment, contemplating the inspector's words, but without interrupting his work. After each snip he would scissor the air emptily, making a nervous, swishing sound that was quite familiar to Bordelli's ears and set him at ease. He was looking in the mirror and thinking of the salesgirl. If only he were thirty years younger . . .

'I know some things I wish I didn't,' Santo whispered gravely.

'What things?' Bordelli asked with a shudder, as if the Sicilian were about to reveal the names of Giacomo's killers.

'Cowlicks,' said Santo, still snipping.

'Cowlicks?'

'Cowlicks, Inspector. They're passed on from father to son, like sins.'

'Explain yourself, Santo.'

'There are fathers who aren't their sons' fathers, and sons who aren't their fathers' sons. Cowlicks never lie. I see them, and I know.'

'What do you know?'

'I could give you a list of all the sons in the neighbourhood who are not in the right family.'

'Are you serious?'

'Unfortunately, yes, though I'd rather not know.'

'Tell me something, have you ever come across a son of

mine?' Bordelli asked, smiling, though waiting for the barber's answer with a certain apprehension.

'Don't worry, Inspector, I won't tell anyone,' said Santo, still serious.

'You're only joking, I hope?' said Bordelli, slightly worried.

'Of course I'm joking; in fact I'm going to tell the whole neighbourhood.'

'And who's the bogus father?' Bordelli asked, to keep the game going.

'I am . . .' said Santo, raising a shining scimitar. Before it came down on his head, Bordelli woke up. The barber was shaking him by the shoulder.

'You snore like a tractor, Inspector.'

'What's that? . . .'

'Put your head under the tap, I have to wash your hair.'

'What? Ah, yes . . .' muttered Bordelli, leaning forward as if to lay his neck down on the guillotine. Santo rubbed his soapy head hard, twice, then rinsed. He turned on the hair-dryer and two minutes later the inspector's hair was dry. Looking at himself in the mirror, Bordelli barely recognised himself, so clean and well groomed. The barber removed the light blue sheet and brushed the hair clippings away from his neck.

'Now you look like an American actor, Inspector.'

'Haven't you mocked me enough today, Santo?' Bordelli said, standing up. At that moment a man came in, dragging behind him a little boy with a defeated expression on his face.

'I want you to shear this lamb,' the man said with a frown.

'It's *not* long,' the boy muttered, pushing the hair behind his ears as if to hide it. Santo and Bordelli silently looked on.

'You look like a monkey,' the man said scornfully.

'It's not long,' the boy repeated, huffing in frustration.

'Damned Beatells . . .' the man said, emphasising the last syllable.

'It's Bea-*tuhls*, not Bea-*tells*,' the boy said, correcting him.

'You make me feel ashamed.'

'I don't want a crew cut . . .' The child was about to start crying.

'Can't you see how disgusting it looks?'

'I like it this way,' the boy muttered gloomily. His father cuffed him on the back of the head.

'That's enough whining, now just get over there and shut up.' And he unceremoniously pushed his young son into the smaller chair, emitting a long sigh by way of conclusion.

'Taper it high, please . . . the Beatles be damned.'

Then he dropped on to the bench and opened the day's edition of *La Nazione*.

'The butcher returned home at twenty past eight with a hare and two pheasants.'

Piras had dark circles under his eyes, which seemed to express the same feeling of resignation as Bordelli felt. The inspector ran a hand over his face, looking disconsolate.

'We're chasing shadows, Piras.'

'We're doing the right thing.'

'We've been tailing day and night some poor idiot who cuts up meat for a living, a butcher who still knows the words to Fascist songs by heart and flirts crudely with every woman he sees . . .'

'There's nothing else we can do right now, sir.'

'Don't you think it's time to forget about him?'

'And do what?'

'That's not a good reason for wasting time.'

'Let's wait a few more days, Inspector.'

'What for?'

'I don't know, but . . . Just think about it. If you had killed a little boy, what would you do? You'd sit tight and keep a low profile for a while, no? If in fact the butcher had anything to do with the murder, he certainly wouldn't take the chance of doing anything out of the ordinary . . . even if he wasn't aware he was being followed.'

'Why, do you think he might be aware?'

'You never know, sir. Maybe he's wise to us and is playing dumb. He might not be as stupid as you think.'

'We can't go on for ever like this, Piras.'

'Ten more days . . .'

'One week, and not a day more. If nothing turns up, no more butcher. There are other things we could be doing . . . Probing pederast circles, for example, or plastering the boy's picture all over town, offering a reward . . .'

It would have been useless, and he knew it. He had to resign himself. Nobody was going to pay for Giacomo Pellissari's death. He put a cigarette in his mouth but gestured to Piras to let him know that he wasn't going to light it. The telephone rang. It was Rosa.

'Hello, monkey. How are you? You have no idea how much Briciola has grown! She's become a proper little demon, climbing up curtains, jumping on beds, getting into everything . . . The most lovable little pest you'll ever see. But what a terror! Even Gideon's afraid of her, big as he is . . . But what did I want to tell you? Ah, yes . . . I've decided that tonight you must invite me out to dinner . . . To a good restaurant, mind, the kind where they uncork the wine in front of you. Come by to get me at half past eight . . . And don't be late. I hate waiting for men.'

'Rosa, what's got into you?'

'Don't tell me you won't be here before nine . . .'

'I'm sorry, but I'm really not up for going out tonight.'

'If you're worried about the money, I'll pay for it myself, don't worry.'

'It's not that . . .'

'They really don't make men the way they used to, dammit!'

'Be a sport, Rosa.' Bordelli sighed, chewing his unlit cigarette. Rosa unfurled her little-girl voice.

'Come on, monkey, you don't want to leave your dear Rosina alone at home, do you? The one who gives you all those nice massages and wants so badly to go and eat in a good restaurant? You're not really so heartless, are you, you big, ugly teddy bear?'

'All right, you win. I'll ring your buzzer at half eight. But don't take an hour to come down, I beg you. I hate waiting more than an hour for a woman . . .'

'I'll be right on time, ciao ciao, darling,' said Rosa, hanging up.

The inspector dropped the receiver into its cradle, imagining the restaurant bill, and looked at Piras in resignation. The Sardinian stood up.

'I'm going to the radio room, Inspector. So you can smoke in peace.'

'Do you really find it so disgusting?'

'I sincerely hope that one day you'll find it disgusting too, sir,' said Piras, and he limped out of the room.

Bordelli left the station on foot and went to have a bite to eat in Totò's kitchen. Knowing he would be eating out that evening, he decided against Panerai's steak, which was lying in the fridge. He tried to eat as lightly as possible, fighting off an insistent Totò, who wanted to stuff him as usual. He managed to avoid drinking the rue-flavoured grappa that the cook had shoved under his nose, and escaped at last from that place of perdition.

He felt like stretching his legs a little, and instead of going straight back to the office, he went for a walk in the centre of town. After drinking another coffee in San Lorenzo, he kept wandering aimlessly about. There was a great deal of bustle at that hour on a Sunday, and as he walked amid the crowd he heard a father talking to his little boy of about ten, whom he held by the hand. The man was dressed expensively and wearing a hat, a big gold wristwatch and very shiny shoes. He spoke softly to his son, teaching him the ways of the world, and the boy listened with his mouth half open.

'You mustn't pay any attention to things that don't concern you . . . Don't worry about others, you must think only of yourself . . . Do you know what I mean?'

'Yes, Papa.'

'Other people only want to cheat you. If you're nice, they take advantage of you, if you give them an inch, they'll take a mile. Nobody ever does anything for nothing, remember that. You must do what's good for you. Don't look anyone in the eye and just go your own way . . . Do you know what I mean?'

'Yes, Papa . . . Can I have those marzipan fruits now?'

And they turned down a side street, continuing their lesson in living. Bordelli shook his head and smiled. Hearing that rich father's words was like looking through the keyhole of the Italian bourgeoisie's soul. It was only one more confirmation of what he had always thought. There was nothing more rotten than the Italian bourgeoisie, than the families of the upper, middle and petite bourgeoisie, steeped in the rot of Fascism and that of the Liberation. It was all quite horribly simple. The rich thought only of becoming richer and didn't give a damn about how the rest of the world fared, so long as they could plunder it and accumulate wealth. They didn't give a damn about Fascism or democracy. They merely wanted to be left in peace to make money. They were greedy, petty and stupid, with the sort of pettiness and stupidity that the rich are so fond of, because therein lies the strength that enables them to get richer and richer. They got rich on the backs of people they disdained, as has been the case in every other epoch and every other nation on earth. They were scornful, greedy, banal, obtuse, licked their fingers as they counted their money, locked themselves up inside their villas thinking they'd left the rest of the world outside, believed they had no connection to the world barely scraping by just outside their garden walls. They were even convinced they'd shut death out, and when one of them died, they looked at each other with terror in their eyes, shocked that so much wealth couldn't protect them from death.

He thought of the *commendatori*, oil men, lawyers, bankers, businessmen and builders who were ruining the city, and he burst out laughing. He thought of all the bourgeois who were so impressed with pomp – the pomp of the king of Italy, the military pomp of Mussolini, the decadent pomp of d'Annunzio's Vittoriale villa, the hidden, imagined pomp of democracy – and he burst out laughing. He thought of all the drab, banal bourgeois who dragged themselves along behind the rules and customs of their fathers and grandfathers, thinking that it would go on for ever. Didn't they look their sons and daughters in the eye? Didn't they see the vipers in their bosoms? Didn't they know that their children didn't want any more rules and were itching for their own share of power, authority and money? Didn't they understand that their children, raised in arrogance, had naturally become arrogant towards the rest of the world? Didn't they realise that their children were only waiting to inherit their wealth, their fathers' wealth, and had no use for their rotten rules? Didn't they realise their children wanted to undermine their authority and have no bosses so they themselves could be the bosses? Having grown up in luxury, crushed by iron-clad rules, those young people had the rage of the unredeemed in their eyes, a universal disdain. All they wanted was to knock their fathers off their thrones and take their place. They were worse than their fathers and mothers, wanted to be even more rich and powerful than their parents, and the seeming hunger for freedom was nothing but a desire for power and money. But even more ridiculous was that nowadays even the workers, even the clerks, the paper pushers, wanted to be like the rich they had always served. Envy took the place of pride. They too wanted to be rich and powerful, they wanted a villa and garden to lock themselves up in and leave the world out of, with all its poverty, suffering and death, the way you leave your rubbish outside the door for collection . . .

He walked slowly back to the station, hands thrust deep in his pockets. Nodding hello to Mugnai, he went upstairs to his office, dropping into his chair like an accused man taking the stand. A child had been killed, and he was getting nowhere. He was frittering away the time with outlandish and useless reflections on the disgusting human race as a way of not thinking about his failure. He even felt a little stupid, but what could he do if, even at a moment like that, he couldn't get the pretty salesgirl in Via Pacinotti out of his head?

Late that afternoon a jewellery-store robbery threw the

police department into disarray. There was a chase up Via Bolognese, and then the burglars' car flipped over on the curve at Pian di San Bartolo. Two men died on the spot and a third was on the way to the hospital. The jewels were recovered down to the last diamond, and they all lived happily ever after.

At 8.30 sharp the inspector rang Rosa's buzzer. After an eternity she poked her head out over the balcony and shouted for him to wait 'another minute' and she would be right down.

When the front door finally opened, Bordelli had already smoked three cigarettes. Rosa appeared in all her splendour, teetering atop red patent-leather stilettos, eyes swollen with make-up, and wrapped in a short, scarlet cashmere coat with a fur collar. Her lips were bursting with red.

'Don't worry, it's me . . . Stop making that face.'

'You have a very subjective sense of time, Rosa.'

'Don't start with your usual male arguments.'

'It's ten past nine, but since I'm a gentleman I won't mention it.'

'It's your fault for always arriving on time,' she said in all seriousness. Bordelli stood there for a moment, open-mouthed, then shook his head and said nothing. They got into the Beetle, and Rosa said she'd reserved a table at Alfredo's, in Viale Don Minzoni.

The moment they entered the restaurant, the murmur of conversation fell silent. Everyone turned to look at the strange couple: a middle-aged man with a vaguely unkempt air and a flashy blonde wearing too much make-up and piercing the floor with her high heels. The women stared with malice in their eyes, while the men gawked with feigned indifference. Bordelli felt a little embarrassed but didn't show it. Rosa left to Bordelli the honour of taking off her coat, which revealed to the world a tight red dress that hugged her hips as though painted on. They sat down at a table apart from the rest, and finally the hum of voices resumed. Bordelli took thirty seconds to decide what to eat, then waited patiently for Rosa to overcome her indecision. An impassive waiter with a long, thin face uncorked a bottle of Amarone before their eyes, filled their tulip-glasses and scampered off. Inside their black circles of mascara, Rosa's eyes sparkled with joy.

'What shall we toast to?'

'I don't really feel like it, Rosa,' Bordelli muttered, thinking of the murdered boy.

'Ah, I know what: a toast to the woman who succeeds in dragging you to the altar . . . Aw, come on, don't make that face.'

'I don't think I'm cut out for marriage, Rosa.'

'At mass this morning, Father Mauro said some very beautiful things about marriage . . . It almost made me want to get married.'

'You go to mass, Rosa?' Bordelli asked in astonishment.

'I've never missed a single Sunday. Why?' asked Rosa, seeming almost offended.

'So you used to go even when you . . .'

'Even when I what?'

'When you worked at the little house?' the inspector said in a whisper.

'Ah, you mean when I was a whore?'

'Sshhh, speak more softly, please,' said Bordelli, looking around.

'What's wrong? Are you embarrassed? Even Jesus Christ was fond of whores, you know.'

'There's no need to tell the whole world.'

'Everybody knows it, it's in the Gospels.'

'That's not what I meant . . .'

'Well, whatever the case, all my prostitute friends go to mass, to confession, and even take communion.'

'I didn't mean to offend you.'

'Deep down, we're all saints. Do you think it's easy to play mamma to a bunch of overgrown little boys with their brains in their pants?'

'I'm sure you're right,' Bordelli admitted. The waiter arrived with the first course, and their hunger reduced them to silence. A little later Rosa gave a little smile and said in a soft voice that she'd recognised a former client of hers there in the restaurant.

'The one with the glasses and white hair sitting across from that hag . . . who's his wife, actually.'

'Don't be mean.'

'She's ugly as sin, look for yourself.'

She waited for her gaze to meet that of her former client, then smiled and waved her fingers in the air at him. The man stiffened and, after a few seconds of bewilderment, started speaking rather heatedly with his wife.

'You've ruined his evening,' said Bordelli.

'He's a judge. He always wanted me to pronounce him guilty and spank him. After all the things I did for him, he should be on his knees, kissing my feet, instead of pretending not to know me. Don't you think it's funny?'

'Not for him.'

'I think it's funny.'

She waved at the man again, this time winking as well. The judge turned white as a sheet.

'If you carry on that way, tonight it's his wife who's going to be spanking him,' said Bordelli, smiling.

'I can't help myself, I'm having too much fun. D'you know how many of my old johns I've run into, arm in arm with their wives? You have no idea of the things they do to avoid being discovered. One guy pretended to faint, another nearly got hit by a car – but the funniest are the ones who throw themselves on their wives and start kissing them passionately . . . it's so amusing . . .'

'They're the ones who paid for your flat.'

'After what I did for them they should have bought me the Pitti Palace.'

She waited for the judge to give in again to the dangerous curiosity of looking at her, and then she shook a scolding finger at him, as if he were a child. His wife realised something was up and turned round to see what was happening. Rosa blew a fire-red kiss at the judge and relished the scene in all its detail: the wife opened her eyes wide, gave her husband a withering look, then stood up calmly, grabbed her coat, put it on, and left the restaurant without turning round. The judge remained paralysed, staring into space. Everyone in the restaurant had witnessed the scene, and silence descended on the room. A waiter went over to the judge's table to ask whether something was wrong. The judge didn't answer, then put five thousand lire down on the table and staggered out of the restaurant. A few seconds later, between stares and giggles, the buzz of voices started up again.

'You're a witch,' the inspector whispered, chuckling to himself.

'And you're a dear. Any other man would have got angry.'

'About what?'

'You're dining out with a woman who blows kisses at other men.'

'It's the least I can do for you.'

'You're such a sweetheart . . .' Rosa whispered, caressing his cheek.

'It's all the Amarone's fault,' said Bordelli.

The dinner continued serenely, with the help of a second bottle of wine. Bordelli still had the salesgirl on his mind, but preferred not to bring up the subject. He did, in fact, have a strong desire to talk about her, to describe all her beauties in detail, and even emit a few sighs like the forlorn admirer he was. But he certainly didn't feel like hearing that he was too old for a woman like that. He was already all too well aware of it.

They ate like pigs, making small talk. And between idle chatter and grappa, it got to be almost midnight, at which point Rosa leapt out of her chair.

'Oh my God, Briciola! I haven't fed her!' she said.

Bordelli asked for the bill and paid without flinching, even leaving a handsome tip. It was money well spent. He'd had a pleasant evening, having managed to clear his mind for a few hours.

They emptied their grappa glasses and stood up, unsteady on their feet. A young waiter helped Rosa to put on her coat, and she thanked him with a lipstick-bright smile. They went out of the restaurant, followed by the curious gazes of the few remaining customers.

'How nice! It's not raining!' said Rosa.

'I don't see any stars. I'm afraid it's going to be the same old story tomorrow,' said the inspector, his defeatism beginning to resurface. They got into the Beetle and drove off. The wind was blowing, tossing the trees' bare branches in the air. When they were outside Rosa's building, the inspector remembered the blouse.

'I have a present for you, Rosa.'

'For me? How sweet!'

'Just a little thing I picked up.' He searched the back seat for the package with the blouse and handed it to Rosa.

'You're such a dear . . .' she said, all excited, and unwrapped the package. She tore the paper and held up the blouse. After giving a little cry, her face changed expression, darkening.

'I'm not twelve years old any more,' she muttered, frowning as she looked at the blouse.

'What do you mean?'

'Can't you see how tiny it is?'

'Don't you even want to try it on?'

'How do you expect me to fit into this . . . this sock?' said Rosa, dropping the blouse into his lap like some kind of rag.

'All right, I'll go and exchange it tomorrow,' he hastened to say, happy to have an excuse to see the pretty salesgirl again. His enthusiasm made Rosa suspicious.

'Men normally hate wasting time exchanging articles of clothing, except . . . I smell a woman in this,' she said, reading the name and address of the shop on the card inside. Bordelli blushed.

'There's no woman . . .'

'I know you better than you think, sweetie,' said Rosa, grinning like a protective mother.

'What size should I ask for?' Bordelli queried, to change the subject.

'What's her name?'

'Rosa, there's no woman.'

'Liiiiii . . . ar! Liar!'

'I'm not a liar.'

'Careful going through doors with that nose, Pinocchio.'

'Come on, Rosa, tell me your size.'

'Well, if it were up to me, I would rather have a red blouse.'

'And the size?'

'A thousand dollars, dead or alive.'

He drove down the viali in the rain, blowing his smoke out through the open vent. As if everything else weren't bad enough, the rain added the finishing touch. There weren't many cars about, as many Florentines had left town. The long All Saints' Day weekend had already begun, but not for everyone. The schools would remain closed for the entire week, though many shops were open. But not the one the beautiful girl worked in, unfortunately.

He'd gone that morning, around nine o'clock, to the shop in Via Pacinotti, heart racing. And he'd found a sign on the rolling metal shutter: *Closed Till Sunday 6 November.* He'd got back in the car with his tail between his legs, tossing the blouse on to the passenger seat. He would have to wait a whole week before he could see the salesgirl again.

He'd even passed by the butcher's in Viale dei Mille. The shop was open, the unmarked car parked nearby with Piras and Rinaldi in it. They'd greeted him with a look, and he'd kept on going, feeling more and more convinced that the Pellissari file would end up in the archives on the 'Unsolved Cases' shelf.

It was a long time since he'd last gone to the cemetery to see his parents. Two days hence the cemeteries would fill up with flowers and black-clad people, and the faded photos of the dead would smile at the relatives come to pay their respects. The Day of the Dead.[30] You could also call it the Day of the Living. And Friday would be Victory's turn to have its day, the victory in the Great War. Another Day of the Dead, actually: half a million of them, buried under flags and medals and so many grand speeches. A war of peasants' sons executed by their generals because they didn't want to die for no reason.[31]

He stopped for a few moments on the Ponte Vespucci to look at the Arno, which was roaring over the Santa Rosa weir like the sea in a tempest.

Minutes later he parked the car near the gate of Soffiano cemetery and got out with an umbrella over his head. A beautiful girl passed him on the pavement, not deigning so much as to look at him, and it occurred to Bordelli that the salesgirl would have done the same.

Entering the cemetery, he walked leisurely until he came to his parents' tomb. His father looked more nineteenth-century than ever and seemed to be smiling. His mother instead stared at him with concern . . . And he looked back at her in turn, at her well-combed hair, her sad eyes, her tight-lipped mouth that looked as though about to utter a cry. He relived the moments of her death, when he held her hand and smiled for her.

'May God forgive you, Franco . . .' his mother had whispered one evening.

'Forgive me for what, Mamma?'

'All the men you killed . . .'

'It was war, Mamma.'

'You took the life of other men and must repent.'

'Mamma, you have no idea of the things I saw . . . If you'd seen what I saw . . . It was war, Mamma.'

'The laws of Heaven are different from those of the earth . . . I'm very afraid for you, Franchino.' She was dying, but she was afraid for *him*, for *his* soul.

'I do repent, Mamma. I've already repented many times over. God knows me well . . .' he said, so that she might die in peace. His mother smiled.

'Go now, you have so many things to do. Don't waste time on me.'

'I don't have anything to do, Mamma. It's nice just being here with you.'

'I have to die just to have you beside me . . .'

'Don't say that, Mamma.'

'I'm sorry, that was mean.'

'Do you want me to read you something, Mamma?'

'Read me something, Franco . . .'

At that moment Franco had wanted to cry. But he didn't cry when, a short while later, his mother died, and he didn't cry when he threw the first handful of dirt on her coffin. Only then, at her bedside, had he felt like crying. But he'd smiled instead, got up, and gone to look for a book to read to his mother. He found a very old edition of d'Annunzio's *Alcyone*, its pages spotted with mildew. To bring back memories of school days, he started reading the famous poem 'Rain in the Pine Grove', relishing its sublime, empty music . . . *Through the branches | one hears not | the hiss of the rain, | silvery, cleansing, | the whisper that varies | branch by branch, | now denser, | now finer* . . . And while he was reading, his mother died. She died with a smile on her lips and her eyes shut, accompanied by D'Annunzio's crisp lines. Her hands on the blanket looked still alive, like the hands of a woman asleep. He had a feeling of infinite emptiness, and liberation as well, and guilt, and shock, all sweetly, agonisingly mixed together. He looked at his mother, expecting her to open her eyes and talk to him, even though he knew she was dead. He wished she would open her eyes and ask him about the war, wished she would ask him what the war had meant to him. He knew she was dead, and yet he expected her to open her eyes. He would have listened to his mother's questions and replied by looking into her eyes. He would have said: Mamma, those who fought in the war, those who killed in the war, continue to see, for the rest of their lives, bellies torn open, heads blown apart by bullets, arms and legs severed from bodies, children crushed by rubble, women raped, eyes wide open, corpses covered with worms, and to them, every flag is stained with blood, even the flag of victory. When those who have killed in war see people walk by on the street, women, men, children, boys, girls, they see dead people walking, people who are dying, who are about to be killed, stamped out, slaughtered. They see this and try not to think about it, not to believe it, try to see luminous women, cheerful children, smiling men, but they see only the death that has generated that light, that cheer, those smiles. They cannot forget what they have seen, for the rest of their lives their eyes will be full of the war dead, those they killed and their friends who were killed, there is no difference, they're all one great mountain of corpses they've had to climb over to get to the other side, and no flag, no love of country, no medals of valour, no official speeches or solemn commemorations can erase this memory. Killing in wartime is a curse that lasts a lifetime, killing in wartime is normal, if you kill in wartime you've done your duty, and that is what is impossible to forget. I would have told you this, Mamma, but you died before I could tell you. While you were alive I was afraid that sooner or later, in a moment of weakness, I would tell you all this, but now you're dead and I'm no longer afraid. You were good to me, Mamma.

He'd turned out the light a good hour earlier, but was unable to fall asleep. The very air weighed down on him. The sound of the rain lashing the street kept him company. It hadn't let up all day.

For dinner he'd finally eaten Panerai's steak, prepared by the peerless Totò. A steak the shape and size of a 45-rpm record, and four fingers high. He'd washed it down with a flask of red and then hung around chatting with Totò till one in the morning, with the help of a bottle of grappa.

Back at home he'd looked at old family photos, still drinking. Without realising it, journeying through the past he'd finished the bottle . . . Then why couldn't he fall asleep? As he lay there immobile in the dark, he felt a thin veil of death enfold him. Even when he moved and changed position, he felt the delicate veil of death enfold him again.

To forget his anxiety, he tried to imagine the beautiful salesgirl lying beside him . . . He even invented a whole story about her . . . They'd just finished making love for the fourth time . . . She'd fallen asleep like a stone and was breathing softly, so softly he couldn't even hear her . . . There she was beside him, naked, warm, pleasantly exhausted . . . If he reached out he could touch her, caress her belly, breast, face . . . But he didn't want to wake her . . .

He began to take it so seriously that he found himself wondering apprehensively whether she really loved him . . . If he wanted to stay awake all night, he was on the right track. He had to find another method. He started telling himself the story of Little Red Riding Hood and fell asleep right before the wolf ate Granny . . .

When he woke up it was almost ten, and yet he felt as if he'd slept for only a few minutes. He staggered to his feet and went and looked out of the window. The sky was still dirty with clouds, but it wasn't raining.

He had no desire to shave and wash, and had to force himself. He didn't want his mood to get the better of him. Personal care was very important, especially at certain times. So he'd learned from Capo Spiazzi at the time of Monte Cassino. Spiazzi demanded that all the men on the front lines look smart: close-shaven, clean uniform, buttons sewn on tight, boots polished. It was just stupid military zeal. He'd understood that strict formality helped keep morale high. After an absurd war 'alongside our German ally', everything had been suddenly turned upside down. Italy had already lost the war, and now she had to keep on fighting to pay for her disastrous choices. Winning a lost war was the best that one could hope for. It was a humiliating situation. Maintaining one's appearance between bombings helped to keep oneself focused, to preserve, at least, a shred of personal dignity.

He went out and decided to walk to the station, to work off the dinner of the night before. It wasn't too cold. In the few passing cars he saw families dressed up in their Sunday best. He'd resolved not to smoke until midday. At the end of the war he'd met an English officer who smoked every other year. And every other New Year's Eve, after twelve months of smoking, he would enjoy his last cigarette, and then, after a year without smoking, on New Year's Day, he would relish his first cigarette. No Italian would ever be capable of doing such a thing.

When he got to Piazza della Repubblica he stopped at the Giubbe Rosse café to take a coffee comfortably sitting down. Two tables away from his there was an attractive woman of about thirty, rather provocative and a little vulgar. She was with a nondescript man. She knew she was attractive, and though she didn't look at anyone, it was clear she knew she was being looked at by everyone. Bordelli, too, was looking at her. Her beauty was the sort that caught the eye. Blonde, fleshy lips, almond eyes. A bit behind her sat another woman, also attractive, but with a completely different kind of beauty. Fine, delicate, with perfect little ears and chestnut hair tied in a short ponytail. She too was with a nondescript man. She did not attract attention; hers was a connoisseur's beauty. The salesgirl, for her part, had both kinds, a blend of different beauties. That was what Bordelli liked about her.

He carried on looking at the two women, imagining what their lives were like. Was the blonde married to a rich man whom she tried to milk as much as possible? Like a sort of high-class whore? And was the other one perhaps a young mother who had left her beloved child with Grandma so she could go out for a drink with her husband?

He heard someone say something in Latin behind him, and turned round. Seated behind him was a slender, handsome elderly gentleman of about seventy, smiling. He was well dressed, with pure-white hair and the moustache of a Habsburg general. He had an upper-class air about him, and his black suit was from another era.

'What was that?' Bordelli asked, taking an instinctive liking to the man.

'*Man is never what he appears to be, and woman even less so,*' the old man translated for him, an ironic gleam in his eye.

'Juvenal? Seneca?'

'Manlio Ceramelli de' Lupi Scarlini, that is, yours truly,' the man introduced himself, holding out a bony, well-manicured hand.

'Pleased to meet you. Franco Bordelli Casini Postriboli,'[32] said the inspector, making the old man smile. They shook hands, and the gentleman's eyes gestured discreetly towards the two beautiful women.

'Have a good look at them . . . The striking blonde lady is a devoted wife who would rather be burnt alive than betray her husband. The other one, the little nun, is also married, but has the bad habit of sleeping in a different bed every night.'

'How did you know I was thinking about them?' Bordelli asked in amazement.

'I'm under the illusion that I can intuit what is going through the minds of others.'

'Apparently it's not just an illusion.'

'At any rate, I was lying. I don't know the first thing about those two women, but I always try to avoid the lure of my first impressions. My greatest fear is the enslavement of prejudice.'

'I'll try to do the same.'

'You work with the police?'

'I'm beginning to think you're a sorcerer.'

'I'm not. A few months ago I happened to see your picture in the newspaper, and I'm lucky enough still to have a good memory,' said the old man, lightly touching his temple with an index finger. Bordelli felt increasingly curious about the strange gentleman with three surnames.

'And what do you do, if it's not too indiscreet to ask?'

'I squander inheritances. It may seem a rather simple occupation, but in reality it hides a whole host of insidious obstacles.'

'Such as?'

'A sense of guilt, the fear of poverty and scorn, common morality, reflection, fits of parsimony, far-sightedness . . . I could go on, but I'd rather not bore you.'

'It must be tiring work.'

'Extremely tiring, I assure you. Because of these contrary forces I've managed to save just one home, the last one remaining. A penthouse flat in Via de' Bardi, with a view of the Ponte Vecchio. As you can see, I'm not a terribly good inheritance squanderer, otherwise I should already have taken up residence under a bridge, perhaps *dans un château de carton*.'

'How romantic.'

'You're probably wondering why I'm speaking so lightly of my personal affairs to you, a complete stranger. I confess I don't really know why; it's the first time this has happened to me. But it's just the sort of thing I like, the fact that at my age I can still sometimes surprise myself.'

'I wish I could do the same.'

'*Homo faber fortunae suae* . . .'[33] said Manlio Ceramelli de Lupi Scarlini, smiling.

'Do you know Latin well?'

'Just enough to have fun with it.'

'Do you think you could translate a phrase for me?'

'I could try.'

'It's carved over a shrine at the crossing of two paths in the woods, just a few steps away from an ancient abbey . . . *Omne Movet Urna Nomen Orat.*'

'Well, let's see . . . Firstly, if that's really the way it's written, it's untranslatable. If it were: *Omne movet urna nomen . . . Ora*, or *Orate* or *Oratius*, or more precisely *Horatius* with an *H*, it would translate as follows: "The urn shakes every name. Pray." It's more or less a line of Horatius Flaccus, Third Book, First Ode, which begins thus: "*Odi profanum vulgus, et arceo . . .*"'

'So it's famous . . .'

'You must certainly have read it at school . . . *I hate the vulgar rabble, and keep them away*. The quote on your shrine is the last line of the fourth stanza, which is thus: *Omne Capax Movet Urna Nomen.* The transcription omitted the word *Capax*, but it's not necessarily a mistake – actually I'm convinced it was left out on purpose. For the Romans the urn was a receptacle in which they put lots to be drawn, lots with names on them for the gods to read. In a Christian context it means: *Pray so that your names will be the fortunate ones* . . . Which is probably an echo of the Book of Revelations, where it says that the names of the saved are written in the Book of Life. What seems unusual and interesting to me is that they use a line of Horace that to common mortals must sound rather sybilline. I would have been less surprised had the phrase been inscribed inside the abbey. Quotations of that sort might be quite familiar to the majority of the monks, many of whom were scribes and recopied ancient codices. But it might have been simply the whim of a cultured, humanist monk, perhaps the abbot himself . . . More than that I can't tell you. I'm sorry . . .'

'I think that's more than enough,' said Bordelli, in a bit of a daze. In front of this inheritance-squandering old man, he felt like a perfect ignoramus.

'Do you mind if I ask you a question myself?' asked Manlio Ceramelli de Lupi Scarlini.

'If it's not too difficult.'

'It's quite easy, actually. Would you be so good as to lend me a thousand lire?'

'Well . . . yes, of course . . .' said Bordelli, reaching into his jacket for his wallet. He took out a one-thousand lira note and handed it to the old man.

'You're very kind.'

Ceramelli de Lupi Scarlini put the filthy lucre in his pocket with the utmost elegance and crossed his legs. His eyes had clouded over with nostalgia like those of an old stationmaster seeing a steam engine again after many years. The inspector would gladly have given him another thousand lire but was afraid to offend him. He turned round to look at the two women, but in the meantime they'd both left.

'Excuse me for just a minute,' Bordelli said, getting up. He went to the men's room, and when he returned the old gentleman was gone. He went up to the cash register to pay, but the barman said his coffee had already been taken care of. As he was leaving the Giubbe Rosse he noticed that a tip of three hundred lire had been left on Ceramelli de Lupi Scarlini's table, and he couldn't suppress a smile.

Early the following morning, Bordelli set out to make the climb from La Panca to Monte Scalari on foot. He'd put on his hiking boots and an anorak with a hood, in case it rained. He wasn't looking for anything in particular. He just wanted to take a long walk in the woods. He felt he really needed it. Having left his cigarettes in the car to avoid temptation, he trudged up the path, breathing deeply, wanting only to grant himself a few hours of peace and quiet. He couldn't get the bitterness out of his heart. He felt defeated, and not only as a law enforcement officer. His life was a disaster. Alone and womanless. He was even getting fat. And his work was a miserable business. What, in reality, did he do? Merely try, as best he could, to sew up the small tears in a tattered, worn-out piece of fabric, rather like trying to heal a blemish on the body of a leper. When things went well, he would feel as if he had accomplished some sort of mission, and when they didn't, he felt incompetent. A magnificent line of work, really. Four more years and they would put him out to pasture, perhaps with the title of deputy commissioner. Better not to think about it . . .

It took him about half an hour to reach the top, where the trail more or less flattened out. Great mud puddles made passage difficult, as streams of water, fed by the prior day's rain, poured down the slopes. The dark trunks of the chestnuts and oaks were enveloped in a bluish haze given off by the damp earth. For November it wasn't too cold. A sort of dim glow, at once spectral and light, rose up from the dead leaves rotting in the mud and highlighted the combination of colours of the forest.

He thought again of the old gentleman he'd met at the Giubbe Rosse and wondered how he lived. He would have liked to see him again, to hear his ancient voice again. He'd even looked the man's name up in the telephone book but found nothing. Maybe one day he would run into him again, minus another portrait of Giuseppe Verdi.

He passed under the great oak, walked past the abbey of Monte Scalari and continued up the path that led to Pian d'Albero. It was All Souls' Day. At that hour the cemeteries were already besieged by people and flowers, and the freshest graves would enjoy a few tears. He imagined Mr and Mrs Pellissari at the cemetery, hand in hand, staring incredulously at the photograph of Giacomo.

He stopped on a hilltop that afforded a view of the valley below. Across the horizon a thin strip of blue hovered above a ridge of hills. The luminous azure radiated hope, like a prison door left ajar. The rest of the sky was an oppressive, spotted dome of lead, a dome in motion. He waited for the strip of blue to vanish, then resumed walking.

The trail continued rising and descending, following its tortuous path. To the right was a steep descent down to an invisible stream. Every so often there appeared a secondary trail that led farther into the woods, and Bordelli thought he'd like to explore them all one day. At one point, where a huge puddle blocked the way, he had to walk along the edge of the chasm, stepping on wet, slippery rocks.

He noticed a metal object half buried in the ground and bent down to dig it out. It was an unexploded machine-gun cartridge. He put it in his pocket and kept on walking, head full of memories of the war. A dirty war set in motion out of weakness by a weak man posing as a strong man . . . A weak, powerful man, a tyrannical child driving a tank. A child who dragged Italy into a stupid, ferocious war that the Italians pretended not to have lost, so as not to feel ashamed . . . not realising that victory would have been more shameful than defeat, an even deeper wound. Good thing they did lose the war. Still, the shame of defeat had entered the people's blood and bones and it was useless to pretend . . .

He heard a large animal running through the scrub at the bottom of a slope, but didn't manage to see it. A moment later, silence returned, a silence made up of a thousand sounds and rustlings, the silence of the forest. A long blast of wind brought a flurry of dead leaves that fluttered in the air like d'Annunzio's flyers over Vienna.[34]

Underneath his every thought was her, the beautiful salesgirl of Via Pacinotti. She was a ghostly presence, a kind of scent he felt permeated with. He saw once again her impertinent eyes, her fine, impish mouth . . . Perhaps she too, at that moment, was in a cemetery, taking flowers to a dead grandparent.

He continued walking for over an hour, until he saw, beyond the trees, a large structure of stone and brick. He'd arrived at Pian d'Albero. Quickening his pace, he soon reached the end of the wood and came into a large clearing. To the right was the house of the massacre, standing against a sky the colour of wet ash. The path curved and then led straight to the house, while another, smaller path forked to the left and into the trees. He followed the broader trail, which went slightly uphill. He could almost hear the sound of the German machine gun cutting down the resistance fighters. It was a quite familiar sound to him.

Farther up was another fork. The path to the left had to be the one that descended towards Figline. He pushed on as far as the house and stopped to look at it. A large, abandoned house, which nobody would ever live in again.

He turned towards the valley. From up there he could see the Valdarno plain, and in the background a soft horizon of hills crushed by clouds. He sat down on a big rectangular rock, to rest his legs. It occurred to him that he had almost stopped thinking about Giacomo's killers, as if he were resigned never to find them. When he'd found the butcher's phone bill in the wood, a flame had been lit in the darkness – a flame that was now going out.

Half an hour later, he began to head back, pleased to

recognise the stones, trees and puddles he had seen on the way up. Who knew what the colours were like in other seasons? He would soon find out. By now he couldn't do without these solitary walks.

All of a sudden he heard a soft but deep murmur. A light drizzle was falling, barely wetting his hair, the kind of misty rain that sometimes falls during the first weeks of spring. It lasted only a few minutes, just long enough to paint the vegetation in livelier colours.

When the abbey of Monte Scalari came into view his legs were aching. He wasn't used to walking mile after mile like this. He was thirsty. He'd been a fool not to bring a canteen of water along with him. He came up to the shrine with the Latin inscription and read it again, but without stopping, satisfied to know what it meant. Leaving the abbey behind him, he continued walking, without haste, hand in his pocket, fingering the bullet he'd found along the path.

Suddenly he saw another person moving through the woods, some thirty paces ahead of him. A young lad was coming down a slope, practically sliding, holding his arms out to keep his balance. When he reached the footpath he stopped and looked around as though lost. He had very close-cropped hair, and his clothes danced on his body as though hung from a coat hanger. Bordelli walked towards him, curious to know what he was doing. The youth noticed him and waited for him to approach, immobile, head hanging.

'Hello,' said Bordelli, drawing near. The lad still didn't move, and his lips were contorted in a sort of grimace. At first glance he looked as if he might have a screw loose.

'Hello,' the inspector repeated, stopping in front of him. He wasn't really so young after all, and looked to be about thirty.

'The Madonna has it in for me,' the man whispered, with a sort of smile on his lips.

'Why do you say that?'

'She has it in for me . . .'

'Did you do something to make her angry?'

'She's wicked . . . she hates me . . . everybody knows that . . .' he said, head swaying slightly.

'Do you live around here?' Bordelli asked him paternally.

'Have you got a cigarette? Eh, have you?'

'No, I'm sorry.'

'The woods are full of the souls of the dead,' the young man said, gesturing broadly with his hand.

'Yes, I've seen them.'

'You smell that stink? Eh, you smell it?' He sniffed the air like an animal.

'What stink?'

'Bachicche's stink . . .' said the young man, upset, looking past the inspector. Bordelli turned round and saw a man advancing slowly on the path at a distance, a rifle resting on his shoulder.

'Do you know him?' he asked the madman.

'Bachicche . . . Bachicche . . .' the young man muttered, then quickly crossed himself and ran off in the direction of La Panca with arms flailing. Bordelli waited for the man with the rifle to approach, then greeted him with a nod of the head.

'Good morning.'

'Greetings,' said the man, stopping in front of him. He looked to be a little over sixty. Slender, with a square head and skin as tough as parchment. His small, intelligent eyes looked like pebbles removed from a brazier.

'Not even a sparrow?' Bordelli asked, looking at the empty game bag hanging from the man's belt.

'I don't feel like shooting any more. Haven't felt like it for years.'

'Then why do you go around with a rifle?'

'Habit,' the man said with a shrug.

'A few minutes ago I ran into a rather strange young man,' said Bordelli, just to make conversation.

'I saw him. That's Giuggiolo . . . He's not quite right in the head.'

'I noticed.'

'Poor lad, he had a bad time of it when he was a boy.'

'Why, what happened?'

'It was in '44, round about Christmas time . . . Are you coming down to La Panca?' asked the man. Bordelli nodded, and they headed down the trail together. The old man remained silent, staring into space as if collecting memories. Bordelli was curious to hear the story of Giuggiolo and waited patiently. They came to the great oak, which looked more and more imposing every time Bordelli saw it. The old man came to a halt directly under its boughs and looked up. His eyes were on one branch in particular, a long, gigantic branch that loomed over the trail.

'It happened right here . . . The Germans had their base at the abbey and patrolled the woods during the day with their dogs. One morning they caught the miller with his backpack full of bread and realised he was taking it to the partisan fighters. They hanged him and his whole family from this oak, with their hands tied behind their backs. Father, mother and three children. Then they forced everyone in the area to come and see. I was there, too, and I remember it as if it was today. The women were crying like calves. They hung Giuggiolo from up there, where you see that big knot. He was eight years old. They did him last, and he got to see his whole family hanged. First Papa, then Mamma, then his sixteen-year-old brother, and his ten-year-old sister. One by one, he saw them all stop kicking in the air. Then it was his turn. The Germans put the noose round his neck and pulled him up. Giuggiolo kicked more than the others, and as soon as he stopped, the Germans started singing a song . . .'

Bordelli looked up at the oak's thick black branches and saw five bodies swaying in the wind.

'At a certain point Giuggiolo's rope snapped, and he fell to the ground. He rolled down that slope over there for a good twenty yards, with his hands still tied. The Germans were sure he was dead and so they left. We were sure he was dead, too, since we'd seen him die with our own eyes. We didn't have the courage to go and get his body and bury it, and so we went home to chew on our anger. Giuggiolo remained in that spot for two days and two nights, without moving, and on the third day he rose up like Christ . . . But his brain had gone to the dogs,' the man concluded.

Bordelli remained silent. The sky was overflowing with huge, oppressive clouds the colour of lead, looking like boulders piled up at the bottom of a river. The dark green of the oaks seemed to spread through the air, wrapping everything in a greenish glow, as in certain ancient paintings. The old man ran a hand over his face as if to remove a spider's web.

'To this day I can't stand to hear German being spoken,' he said, and resumed walking.

'It's the same for me,' the inspector mumbled. Whenever he saw a German over forty years old on the streets of Florence, he couldn't help but think of the war. Every time he would ask himself whether that mild-mannered tourist on holiday with his family had killed one of his comrades or massacred women and children, like at Sant'Anna, or perhaps at Sant'Anna itself.

'They're a nasty race, those Germans,' the old man said.

'The Italians did the same things and worse, but the generals who ordered them died in their own beds,' said Bordelli. He was thinking above all of Graziani and Badoglio, who had used chemical weapons on African villages, on defenceless people whom the glorious bombs of Fascist Italy had skinned alive with high-speed leprosy. He was thinking of the Italian soldiers who had killed women and children, who had raped, tortured, humiliated, destroyed. The schoolbooks didn't tell of these things. They told of Enrico Toti tossing his crutches and of Pietro Micca, but not of these things. And so Italians continued to think of themselves as good people who brought civilisation to the uncivilised and paved roads, built hospitals and schools for savages, a generous people who conquered more with spades than with rifles.

The old man said nothing, keeping his share of the shame to himself. They made their way down the path in silence, side by side like old friends. Half an hour later they were at La Panca, where they parted ways, saying goodbye with a nod of the head.

He didn't look at his watch until after he'd started up the Beetle to go back into town. Ten to two. Descending by way of the unpaved Cintoia road, he avidly sunk his teeth into the panino with prosciutto that he'd bought in the village's only shop, a small wine tavern that didn't even have a sign outside. His long walk had made him hungry as a wolf, as in the days of the San Marco batallion, when after a twenty-mile march they would stop to sleep in a stable. Now he knew for whom he had eaten tinned meat and killed Nazis, he knew for whom he had borne the weight of that bloody, stupid war. He'd done it for Giuggiolo and others like him. For those who had always been losers and who would never win. Now at last he knew for whom he had killed.

He stopped at the Osteria della Martellina to drink a glass of wine and then continued down the Chiantigiana. As he drew nearer to the city he began to feel more and more dejected. He could already see himself in his office, squirming in his chair, the Pellissari file on his desk. He'd been wrong to imagine that a telephone bill could lead him to the killers. As if that wasn't enough, the commissioner had asked him to be present on 4 November in Piazza della Signoria for the raising of the flag in the Victory Day celebrations. Commemoration ceremonies depressed him, and even before ending his phone conversation with Inzipone he'd already been trying to think of an excuse not to go.

Back in town, as he was crossing the San Niccolò bridge, he saw small groups of people craning their necks over the parapets. They were looking at the Arno racing fast under the bridges, darker and more swollen than they had ever seen it before.

At the station, he rang the radio room as soon as he sat down in his office. They put Piras on, who had just finished his surveillance shift.

'There are some new developments, Inspector.'

'Not over the phone. Come upstairs.'

Hanging up, Bordelli lit his first cigarette of the day. He smoked it in front of the open window, enjoying it as he hadn't done for years. One had to wait a long time to earn a little pleasure.

A minute later, Piras came in, and without saying anything he started polemically waving his hands in the air. He looked tired, his eyes sunken. Settling into a chair, he started immediately giving his report: the butcher left home at twenty past nine in his Lancia Flavia, together with his wife and daughter. They stopped in Le Cure to pick up Panerai's mother, and in Piazza della Libertà they pulled up alongside a baby-blue Fiat 1500 with an elderly couple inside, probably the wife's parents. The two cars then went together to the San Felice cemetery at Ema. At a quarter to one the two vehicles parked in front of Panerai's place, and everyone went inside. A few minutes later the butcher came out again, alone, and took the Fiat 850. He took Viale Righi to the end and continued down Via Lungo l'Affrico, as on the day when the unmarked car had lost him. This time, however, they were able to follow him: through Piazza Alberti, Via Gioberti, Via Cimabue, Via Giotto . . . all the way to Via Luna, a narrow little one-way street. Piras jumped out of the car and followed him on foot, lest the continued presence of the car should arouse the butcher's suspicions. After two curves, Panerai's Fiat made its way with some difficulty into an even narrower street, off to the right. Piras stopped round the corner to listen. He heard the engine of the 850 being turned off, the car door opening and closing again, then the sound of a front door slamming. When he came out, he saw that the little street was rather short and widened as it came to a dead end. On the opposite side was another narrow street, only slightly longer, which also came to a dead end in a sort of small piazza. The buildings were working-class tenements with old plaster on the façades. Farther ahead there was an arch, which led to Via Gioberti.

'I know that little street,' said Bordelli, remembering an old girlfriend who used to live in the area. Throwing his cigarette butt into the road, he pulled the window to and started pacing back and forth as Piras continued his report.

Piras had gone back to the car and told Rinaldi to drive round the block as far as Via Gioberti. They parked about fifty yards away from the arch in Via Luna. The little street was one-way, and Panerai would have to pass that way. Some twenty minutes later the butcher's Fiat 850 finally came out on to Via Gioberti, and they followed him back to his home. Piras meanwhile had called for another car, and he and Rinaldi went back to Via Luna. In the dead-end square where Panerai had parked there were only two storefronts with their rolling metal shutters down and one old front door of dark wood, with no doorbell or name. There were no windows. No cars. The sky was hidden by a corrugated plastic roof, which covered a good two-thirds of the little piazza. It had probably been put there by a mechanic or craftsman to create an outdoor space usable even in the rain.

'And that's about it,' Piras concluded.

'Well, compared to nothing, it's something. I want to know as soon as possible in whose name the building is registered; maybe something useful will turn up. We must leave no stone unturned. As soon as the offices open, I want you personally to go to the Land Registry and Conservatory. I'm asking you and not somebody else, because it won't be a simple matter.'

'If they take tomorrow off for the long holiday weekend, they'll reopen on Monday.'

'Oh, they're off tomorrow, don't you worry . . .'

'So there's no need to hurry.'

'Go home and get some rest, Piras. You look like a ghost.'

Marco Vichi

'Thanks, Inspector,' said the Sardinian, standing up. He vaguely gestured a military salute and went out. Was he limping a little less each day, or was it just Bordelli's imagination?

The inspector continued pacing about his office with his hands in his pockets, already knowing what he would do. He had to get inside that place and see what there was behind that old front door in Via Luna. A warehouse? A depot? Or maybe a slaughterhouse? For bringing women or children to? As usual, he was getting ahead of himself. He mustn't forget that the only evidence he had was a telephone bill he'd found in the woods . . . And it wasn't even evidence, but simply a hope, a very fragile, irrational hope that chance had put him on the right track. It made no sense to ask for a search warrant from Judge Ginzillo, whose only reply to such a request would have been to laugh hysterically, like an old aunt protecting her slice of pie.

As soon as it was dark outside he left the station. He drove straight to Via Gioberti, parked the Beetle and, torch in his pocket, continued to Via Luna on foot. The street was deserted, and there wasn't anybody at the windows. Turning left, he found himself in the small dead-end piazza. He went up to the door, hoping he could spring the lock. It was Botta himself who had taught him the art of picking locks, but he'd never attained his teacher's level of skill. He turned on the torch to study the lock, and had to bite his lip. It was a hard one, the kind that Botta called 'trouble'. He tried just the same, checking to make sure nobody was coming. Over his head was the corrugated plastic canopy, shielding him from the view above. He fiddled with his miraculous metal wire for a few minutes with no results. He had to resign himself. He would never open it, except perhaps with dynamite. It was a job for Botta. It wasn't the first time he had had to turn to him. Going back to the car, he headed for San Frediano. Since Botta didn't have a telephone, one had to go directly to his basement flat to talk to him.

Bordelli pulled in to Via del Campuccio. There was no light filtering out of Botta's pavement-level window. He bent down just the same, to tap on the pane, hoping Ennio was inside, sleeping. He knocked harder and harder, and called out. Nothing. The building's front door didn't close securely. He pushed it open, descended a flight of stairs and knocked on the door. Silence. Tearing a page out of his diary, he wrote: *Ring me at any hour, it's extremely urgent.* No need to sign the message, Ennio knew his handwriting well. He slipped the note under the door and left. All he could do was wait.

It was just half past six, and he returned to the station. He collapsed into his chair, exhausted. He stared at the phone as if expecting a beautiful woman to call. He could barely wait to open that door. Maybe be would find something in there, anything, a concrete clue that would show him the way, maybe even the evidence he was looking for . . . or maybe not, maybe it would all be useless except to make him decide to leave that wretched Mussolini-loving butcher in peace.

By a quarter past eight, still no Botta. Perhaps he'd been arrested for one of his 'business deals'? Bordelli rang the Murate prison and identified himself, but they told him there was nobody named Bottarini among the latest arrivals.

He went back to Botta's flat, but everything was still turned off. He looked up at the sky. The moon was being suffocated by a thick mantle of black clouds. At any moment it would start raining again.

He went home, feeling discouraged and anxious. Perhaps there was no need for all this haste, but by now he'd got it into his head to open that door and wanted it done as soon as possible. He had to try to relax.

He went into the kitchen to make some spaghetti. Since he didn't even have any tinned tomatoes, he dressed the pasta with olive oil, pepper and grated pecorino cheese. Then he brought it all into the dining room and turned on the telly. On Wednesdays there was a film on Channel 2 that must have just started. It was an old American movie, exactly what he needed to distract himself. Settling into the sofa with wine beside him, he put his feet up on the coffee table and started eating. The spaghetti wasn't bad at all, and he regretted having made so little. A minute later there was none left. Setting the empty bowl down on the coffee table, he refilled his glass and lit a cigarette. He felt relaxed, at long last . . .

He woke up to the sad sound of the music announcing the end of the broadcast day, neck aching. He'd fallen asleep, chin on his chest, before the film had ended. Ennio hadn't called, dammit. He thought for a moment of going to see whether he'd come home, but felt so lazy that he decided not to bother. It was better to go to bed. Botta would call sooner or later. Getting up from the sofa with his knees creaking, he turned off the telly before the screen turned to snow. Leaving everything as it was, he went into the bedroom. Sooner or later he would have to wash the dirty dishes. He undressed and got under the covers. A nice long sleep would do him good . . .

Despite his fatigue, he was unable to drop off. All he did was toss and turn, trying not to think of Via Luna, Botta or the salesgirl in Via Pacinotti. To free his mind he started rummaging through his memory. He skipped over the war, going farther back, to the more distant past . . . Faded images blurring into one another, women now faceless, friends never seen again, school benches, working up a sweat in the playground playing football all alone . . . He saw his mother again, cooking pasta at home on a Friday evening, his father listening to Mussolini's speech on the radio, the young widow from the floor above making eyes at all the men she passed, the horse-drawn carriages, the cars driving by now and again on the Viale, the teachers who practically dislocated their shoulders giving the Fascist salute to Il Duce, the Saturday Fascist rallies in Balilla uniform,[35] the first girl over whom he'd lost sleep and appetite . . . as beautiful as the sun, and treacherous . . . that was how he remembered her . . . And starting with her he began in a daze to review all the women who had left him, counting them like sheep . . .

He woke up feeling even more tired than before, and with a swollen bladder. Through the shutters filtered the wan light of dawn, but there was no sound of rain. So as not to wake up entirely, he did not turn on the light when he went into the bathroom, but groped his way there, dragging his fingers along the walls to orientate himself. Once back in the bedroom he closed the internal shutters, and in total darkness got back into bed. He had goosebumps from the cold. To warm himself he curled up like a child, wrapping the covers tightly round his body. He remained that way for a long time, with his eyes closed, hoping to fall back to sleep. But it was hopeless. By now he was awake and his head already churning. Whatever had become of Ennio, dammit? He almost smiled at the thought that a murder investigation could be held up by a burglar's absence.

He felt like a wet rag. Muttering a curse, he got up and opened the shutters. It wasn't raining, but the vault of the sky was still swollen with dark clouds. He took a long scorching shower, calmly got dressed and made himself some black coffee, which he drank in front of the French door in the kitchen, in small sips. The weather promised nothing good. It was the rainiest autumn in memory.

He headed off on foot, came out into Piazza Tasso and turned down Via del Campuccio. When he got to Botta's place he bent down to tap on the window pane. No reply. He went into the building and knocked on his door, calling out his name. Ennio wasn't there. Where the hell was he hiding? There was no point in asking the neighbours or at the local bars. Nobody would say a word more than necessary, especially if the person asked actually knew something. It was an unspoken agreement, and they all benefitted from it.

Bordelli went back to his block to fetch the Beetle. While crossing the Ponte Vespucci he saw the Arno, swollen as a whale's back. The fall at the Santa Rosa weir looked frightening, but it wasn't the first time. When he got to the station he shut himself up in his office to wait for Ennio's phone call, taking care of a few overdue matters by dint of sighs. No news about the butcher . . . but he'd better be ready to be disappointed.

At eleven o'clock Commissioner Inzipone rang for his umpteenth useless scolding concerning the Pellissari murder. As usual he started citing newspaper headlines accusing the police of somnolence and incompetence. Bordelli cursed him in silence.

'I'm following a lead, sir . . . As soon as I've got any news . . .'

'What lead?' the commissioner asked impatiently.

'I'd rather not say for now.'

'More secrets, Bordelli . . .?'

'I'm superstitious, you ought to know that by now.'

'Well, this time I hope it works,' Inzipone grumbled, then hung up without saying goodbye. He could go to the devil, thought Bordelli.

A bulletin came in from the north. Maximum alert: a terrorist from the Alto Adige[36] was on his way to Rome. Apparently he intended to set off a bomb at the National Monument to Victor Emmanuel II the following day, to celebrate Victory Day in his own way. Roadblocks were set up everywhere in a big hurry, and every traffic patrol car was to have a photo of the suspect.

At a quarter to one, Bordelli already had hunger pangs and walked to the Trattoria da Cesare. It was nearly deserted. The waiters stood in the doorway watching the cars go by on the Viale, and Cesare complained that it was all the fault of the long All Souls' Day weekend and the bloody weather.

'Enjoy a day of rest,' Bordelli advised, patting him on the back, and then went and sat down in Totò's kitchen, letting

himself be led by the hand into the sinful world of Ciacco[37]
. . . crostini, salami, fried polenta . . .

'You've been looking a little down the last few days,' said
Totò.

'Must be the rain.'

. . . *pappardelle alla lepre*, sausages, big tumblers of red
wine . . .

'An October to be forgotten, Inspector.'

'You can say that a little louder, if you like.'

. . . grilled pork chops, *fagioli all'uccelletto*, a bowl of custard
pie, a nice cup of coffee, and some home-made grappa to
finish things off.

He couldn't carry on eating like this, he wasn't twenty years
old any more. He swore it would be the last time. He often
made vows of this sort as the grappa was being served. He
glanced at his watch and downed the glass.

'Time to go back to the henhouse, Totò,' he said, getting up
with difficulty. He felt like a barrel packed full of stones.

'You mustn't miss dinner here tonight, Inspector. I'll give
you a taste of a *peperonata* that can raise the dead.'

'We'll discuss that this evening, Totò. If I think about it now,
it'll make me sick.'

He patted the cook on the back and went out of the kitchen
with his knees buckling. It was raining hard outside, and Cesare
lent him an umbrella.

He came out of the restaurant with a cigarette between his
lips and crossed Viale Lavagnini in a hurry. The minute he
turned on to Via Duca d'Aosta, it started deluging. Tossing
aside the now drenched cigarette, he broke into a run. He
arrived back at the station panting heavily and with shoes
completely soaked, and dragged himself up the stairs to the
first floor. Aside from the sound of the rain, you couldn't hear
a thing. Everyone was at the windows looking out, fascinated
by the downpour.

He ducked into the men's room to towel-dry his hair, then
shut himself up in his office and removed his wet raincoat.

Without bothering to sit down, he grabbed the internal telephone and called the switchboard. No news of Botta. He couldn't stand waiting any longer twiddling his thumbs. Lighting a cigarette, he too went and stood in front of a window to admire the deluge. The rail fell with unheard-of force, and the streets had turned into torrents. A cold shiver ran down his back, and he instinctively touched the radiator. It was as hot as a pan on the fire. So why did he feel cold? Must be from indigestion and his wet clothes. He blew the smoke against the window pane, head full of thoughts. From the start of this affair he'd felt as if he were playing chess with destiny. One wrong move, and his king would be dead. The next move was his to make, and it was Via Luna.

He went and sat down, huffing with impatience. Picking up the Pellissari file, he opened it on the desk, almost angrily. Seeing the photos of the body again, he felt his stomach tighten. Giacomo's killers were free, to eat, drink and live in peace. He couldn't stand it.

And why the hell didn't Ennio call? He stubbed out his cigarette in the ashtray with such force that it crumbled. One second later there was another cigarette in his mouth, but with an effort of will he managed not to light it. His throat was dry. He took a sip of water, and it tasted bitter. He was trying to buck up. Soon it would stop raining and he could go with Botta to force open that damned lock. He needed only to be patient and wait . . . and wait . . . There wasn't even a fly in the room to keep him company. He felt downcast and tired, and everything seemed gloomy. Had a genie appeared out of a bottle at that moment, he would have asked to be reborn in Lapland among the reindeer.

Another shiver shook his whole body. His shoes were dripping wet and his feet frozen. He'd probably best dash home to change clothes if he didn't want to catch a chill. He really didn't feel like facing that wall of rain, but he had no choice. When he got up to go, his legs felt weak. His joints ached into the bargain, and he realised he was sick. He must already have a bit of fever, damn it all. What a time to fall ill. He rifled through his drawers, found a box of aspirin and swallowed a couple. A few times in the past a couple of tablets had been enough to nip the flu in the bud, though at other times it was the flu that nipped him in the bud. Before anything else, he had to take off those wet clothes. He was already in the doorway when the ring of the telephone made him start. If it was Botta, he couldn't be calling at a worse time. He staggered back to the desk, shivering all over.

'It's Mr Pellissari the lawyer on the phone for you, sir.'

'All right, put him on,' said Bordelli, sitting back down. He heard a crack, and the background buzz seemed to change.

'Hello?'

'Inspector Bordelli?'

'Hello, Mr Pellissari . . .'

'Tell me the truth, Inspector . . . Is there any hope the monster will ever be found?'

'We're following a very promising lead, but at the moment I can't tell you anything else.'

'I want to be able to look my son's killer in the eye, I want to ask him how he could ever . . .'

'We'll catch him, I can promise you that,' said Bordelli, hoping he was right. Shivering with cold, he patiently listened, without interrupting, as Pellissari unburdened himself. He didn't have the heart to tell him that his son had been raped by at least three men. Before hanging up he repeated that the murderer's days were numbered. He was about to get up when the phone rang again.

'Yes?'

'Have you seen how it's raining?' said Rosa, munching on something.

'It's been raining for weeks, Rosa.'

'Not this hard . . . What if this is the Great Flood?'

'That's already happened, Rosa. I don't think God repeats himself.'

'My friend from Prato . . . Milena, remember her?' she said, and then Bordelli heard her bite into a biscuit.

'Rosa, I can't stay on the phone.'

'She brought me some Mattonella *biscottini*, and some *Brutti ma boni*, too.'[38]

'Rosa . . .'

'I'll save a few for you, monkey, don't worry. But don't come tonight, I've invited some girlfriends and we don't want any boys around.'

'Rosa, please stop for a second.'

'Why, what is it?'

'I can't stay on the phone. My clothes are soaking wet and I have to dash home to change.'

'Oh, come on . . .'

'I don't feel well, I think I'm running a temperature.'

'Oh, go on, you never get a temperature . . . Don't you want to hear what I'm making for dinner?'

'I'll call you back later,' said Bordelli, and he hung up without giving her time to respond. He was feeling worse and worse. He started down the stairs, grabbing the banister like an old fogey. Crossing paths with Inspector Silvis, who was on his way up, he let him know he was going home for a few minutes to change clothes.

'Are you feeling all right, Inspector?' Silvis asked, looking him up and down.

'I feel great. Like an earthworm crushed by a boot.'

'If you don't mind my saying so, you look to me like you're burning up with fever.'

'Nah, I'm sure it's just a touch,' the inspector muttered, knowing it wasn't true.

'Have you heard about the bomb?'

'What bomb?' Bordelli asked.

'An anonymous phone call . . . A bomb at the Sita station . . . They're on their way there now, with a team of explosives experts.'

'One of the usual jerks, I'm sure.'

Bordelli continued down the stairs, and when he looked out into the courtyard it was like being behind a waterfall. Pressing the umbrella over his head like a sombrero, he ploughed his way to the Beetle. And, defying the temperature and the deluge, he drove off. The sound of the rain almost drowned out that of the car's engine, and the tyres raised great waves of water on both sides. He felt terrible. His bones ached, he was shivering, and his nose was running. He certainly would not be able to attend the Victory Day celebrations the following day. Maybe that was why he'd caught the flu, to bail out of the 4 November ceremonies.

Without ever shifting into second, he ventured towards the centre of town. The windscreen wipers were useless. He was able to proceed simply because he knew the way.

As he drove down the Lungarno, great splashes of mud fell on the windscreen, only to be washed away at once by the rain. He caught a passing glimpse of a crowd of people along the parapets, huddled under umbrellas, looking out at the river. Common sense dictated that he should avoid going out again into the rain and race straight home and make some broth, but he didn't want to give in to this stupid flu. During the war he'd slept in meadows, stables or outside in the snow . . . There was no need to panic over a couple of degrees of fever.

He parked the car with two wheels on the pavement, got out with the umbrella pressed down on his head and, wiping his nose with his hand, looked out at the Arno. It looked like a scene from the Apocalypse. A huge mass of muddy water coursed violently under the bridges, crashing against the pillars, rumbling like a squadron of aeroplanes. It was so close to the parapets that you could almost touch it. But it wasn't something to get too worried about. It had happened before, and the Florentines were used to these sorts of scenes. In a few places in the countryside around the city it would burst its banks, flooding a few acres of farmland. But two days later, all would be back to normal.

He got back in the car, crossed the Carraia bridge and went on as far as Via del Campuccio. Without getting out, he stopped outside Botta's windows, but the lights were still off inside. He drove off again, teeth chattering from the chill, and he felt almost pleased. He really wasn't up to going to Via Luna, but he knew that if Botta had been at home, the temptation would have been too hard to resist.

He parked in front of his building and went inside. He climbed the stairs dripping like a tree after a storm, nose running. But he was safe at last. He'd never felt so happy to be home. He filled the bath and immersed himself in the boiling water, hoping to cook the feverish shivers out of him. Staring at a cobweb that undulated gently in a corner of the ceiling, he steeped in the tub for a long time, imagining that the beautiful salesgirl from Via Pacinotti was waiting for him in bed, already half naked, rubbing her little feet together between the sheets with impatience . . . Dreaming was cheap.

When he got out of the bath he felt extremely weak, got dressed in a hurry and put on two woollen jumpers. Outside it was already dark. The rain continued to come down with frightening force. It was the first time he'd ever seen such a downpour.

The thought of eating nauseated him. He heated some water in a saucepan, poured it into a glass and dissolved two spoonfuls of honey in it. He drank it in very small sips, to get the bitter taste out of his throat. He swallowed two more aspirin and, shaking like a leaf, went and lay down in bed with the thermometer in his armpit. His heart was beating in his ears and it felt as if there was a boulder on his head. He hadn't been this sick for years. He felt like a war casualty and wished he had a pretty nurse with sweet eyes to look after him or, better yet, the dark salesgirl . . .

He checked the thermometer. Thirty-nine point three. What a fuss over a little temperature. In the days of the San Marco, he'd machine-gunned Germans with a forty-degree fever, and yet now he felt as if he didn't even have the strength to peel an apple. He was old, he had to accept it. A bowl of broth, a hot-water bottle, and a whole lot of rest . . .

He glanced at the clock, unable to bring its hands into focus. It took him a few moments to realise that it was a few minutes before seven. He desperately needed to sleep. Picking up the phone and setting it down on his belly, he rang headquarters, said he felt bad, really bad, actually, and added with feigned regret that he would not, unfortunately, be in any condition to attend the 4 November commemoration.

Summoning his strength, he got up and took all the blankets he owned out of a chest of drawers and laid them down on the bed, one on top of the other. A good sweat was what he needed. He closed the shutters, both inside and out, and even unplugged the telephone so that nobody could wake him up. Sliding under the stack of blankets, he turned off the light. He sank his face into the pillow, crushed by a limitless sadness. He felt like the loneliest man on earth. Who knew where the pretty salesgirl was at that moment? Lying on a sofa, listening to the rumble of the rain? Or in the arms of a handsome young man? Perhaps both . . .

A minute later he was snoring like a train . . .

While Bordelli sleeps, the rivers of the Mugello and the Aretino burst their banks, flow downstream and further swell the Arno. The Valdarno is flooded, as is Pontassieve, where a bridge collapses and a house is washed away . . .

> *The night falls on our heads*
> *the rain upon us pours*
> *the people smile no more.*

A little while later the Arno begins to splash against the tops of the Ponte Vecchio's arches and overflows in the La Lisca district of the town of Lastra a Signa. The Tuscany–Romagna trunk road, and all communications between Florence and Empoli, are cut off. At 2 a.m. the Mugnone bursts its banks and floods the Parco delle Cascine. The stables there are full of horses. The thoroughbreds are saved in a hurry, but less attention is paid to the others, and they drown. At half past two, the Arno bursts its banks at Nave, Rovezzano and Villa Magna . . .

> *The world is changing presently*
> *and will change again by and by*
> *But take a look up and you'll see*
> *big patches of blue in the sky.*

At 3 a.m. the great spate of the Arno reaches Florence. On the left bank, between the Ponte alle Grazie and the Santa Trinita bridge, the drains are chucking up mud. The river is now as high as the parapets on the Lungarno. At half past three the Anconella aqueduct is overwhelmed by the wave of mud, and an overseer, Carlo Maggiorelli, becomes the first casualty of the Florence flood. He was on the phone, answering a call from someone telling him to get out, when he was swept away by the water's fury. Basements flood, a few boilers explode, home taps run dry . . .

We see an old world come
crashing down upon us now . . .
but what fault is it of ours?

At 4 a.m., in the already flooded parts of the city upstream, *carabinieri* and army personnel with boats and dinghies ferry people to safety. The Arno bursts its banks at Rovezzano and floods the districts of San Salvi, Varlungo, Gavinana and Ricorboli. Gavinana is under a foot and a half of water. Only half an hour later, the river has conquered the Lungarno Cellini, courses down Via dei Renai and submerges the San Niccolò quarter. Mayor Bargellini is asleep at home in Via delle Pinzochere. He is woken up by a phone call from the commissioner of police, gets dressed in a frenzy and goes out. A car takes him to the Ponte Vecchio, where he meets the commissioner, the prefect and a few journalists. The river rumbles like force-nine seas, and the iron railing around the statue of Benvenuto Cellini is vibrating like a string on a double bass. Uprooted trees bourne on the swell thud loudly against the pillars of the bridge. Amid the muddy waves one sees carcasses of cows, cars, splintered wardrobes, a large bus caracoling like a dead whale. The men on the bridge do not know yet that there are areas both downstream and upstream from Florence that are already well under water: San Colombano, Badia a Settimo, Vingone, Rimaggio, Guardiana. Bargellini would like to go home to warn his family but the streets have become impassable because of the torrents of mud flowing fast everywhere. He stops in at the offices of *La Nazione*, inaugurated just a month ago and still sparkling new, then continues on towards Palazzo Vecchio.

> *How many times have they smiled sadly and said*
> *the dreams of the young are all smoke*
> *They are tired of struggling and no longer*
>   *believe in anything*
> *now that they're so close to the goal.*

By order of the prefect the jewellers of Ponte Vecchio are alerted by the night patrols and run to save what they can from their shops. At 5 a.m. the sewage drains of San Frediano are spewing muck. A putrid stream flows down Borgo Ognissanti, and a short while later the Baroque church and old barracks of the *carabinieri* are flooded. All night Dante Nocentini, head of the Florentine office of the National Press Agency, has been walking up and down the Lungarni to monitor the river's progress. In the end he decides to stop in Piazza Cavalleggeri, in front of the unsightly Biblioteca Nazionale, which at night takes on a gloomy and simultaneously ridiculous appearance. Suddenly the Arno rises over the parapets and a stream of slimy water begins to inundate the cobblestones. Nocentini starts running towards Piazza Santa Croce, chased by the water advancing inexorably down Corso dei Tintori. He runs to Via dei Pucci, to the offices of the National Press Agency, races up the stairs and broadcasts the news to Rome: the Arno is flooding Florence.

> *It will be a fine society*
> *founded on liberty.*

By 6 a.m. Borgo Ognissanti has become a raging torrent and Piazza Gavinana is under ten feet of water. The Arno enters

Borgo San Jacopo and Via Maggio in triumph, and at half past six is coursing from Bellariva towards the centre of town, churning down the Via Aretina. Moments later, the parapet at Piazza Cavalleggeri collapses, and the raging Arno vents its fury on the Biblioteca Nazionale and the Santa Croce quarter.

> *It matters not that someone on life's path*
> *should be prey to the ghosts of the past*
> *Money and power are deadly snares*
> *that have worked for so very long.*

Nearly the whole city and a few neighbouring towns are without electricity, gas or telephone service. Around seven o'clock the river inundates Piazza Alberti, San Frediano, Santo Spirito, Piazza dei Giudici, the Lungarno degli Archibusieri, Por Santa Maria . . . It courses with frightening speed, overturning cars, crashing through front doors and metal shutters, pouring out into the streets what it stole in the Valdarno: dead animals, trees, shattered furniture, oil drums . . . The Lungarno degli Acciaioli collapses, along with certain stretches of the Lungarno Corsini. By eight in the morning, in Via dei Neri, where Rosa lives, there are ten feet of water, and the level keeps rising . . .

> *And if we're not like you*
> *there must be a reason*
> *and if you don't know it*
> *what fault is it of ours?*

He opened an eye in the darkness and, hearing the dull sound of the rain, huffed in annoyance. He was surprised to see thin shafts of light filtering through the cracks in the inside shutters. It couldn't possibly be morning. How long had he slept? Twelve hours at the very least. He hadn't slept like that since childhood. He felt a mountain of blankets weighing down on him and smelled a strong odour of sweat from the night. Groping beyond the edge of the mattress, he found the lamp switch and pressed it, but there was no light. As usual, he didn't have any spare bulbs and would have to unscrew one from the light fixture in the entrance hall. He didn't feel like turning on the overhead light. He couldn't stand bright electric light right after waking up. Without sitting up, he opened the drawer in the bedside table and pulled out an electric torch. He always kept it within reach, a habit he had picked up during the war. Turning it on, he lit up the clock. Twenty past eight. He thought he heard someone talking loudly in the street. It was strange, on a holiday like that.

He still felt weak, but the fever seemed gone. He reached out and grabbed the thermometer, which he stuck under his arm, then lit up the ceiling with the torch. He knew every single crack and little stain in the plaster. They hadn't changed for years, and were like unshakeable certainties. Little by little, something began to surface from the dark well of his memory, a long night of rain during the war, inside a tent with three men from his battalion, drinking cordials and talking about women. Never had so many lies been told in a single night, but it was merely a way to keep the thought of death at bay.

Thirty-six point seven. He'd done it. He'd beaten the fever. And it had taken only one night. He was a sapper from the San Marco, after all. That must be worth something. He turned off the torch, rolled on to his side and closed his eyes. Perhaps it was best to wait for it to stop raining before sticking his nose outside. He could hardly rush off to Piazza della Signoria for the commemoration ceremony. Any doctor would have forbidden it. He would sleep for a few more hours and then dawdle about the flat, enjoying a bit of *dolce far niente* as he hadn't done for centuries. A nice cup of coffee, a few phone calls, a hot bath . . . It would be interesting to see what was on the telly in the morning. He imagined these trifles with great pleasure, like a child waiting for his mother's goodnight kiss. He remained in bed, snug and warm, head full of hazy memories ceaselessly overlapping. In his drowsiness he thought he heard an explosion in the distance, but decided he'd probably dreamt it.

Before long he got tired of lying in bed and decided to get up. Setting his feet down on the floor, he yawned with gusto. He felt much better than he had the previous night. When his eyes adjusted to the penumbra, he finally stood up. Taking his trousers from the chair, he slipped them on, staggering. He went over to the window to open the blinds, then peered through the slats in the shutters . . . and his jaw dropped. Where the street had once been there was now a river of muddy water coursing fast towards Piazza Tasso. Throwing open the window and the shutters, he saw dozens of people looking out of their windows, wrapped in overcoats. Incredulous like him, staring at the flooded street. The rain was still falling just as forcefully as the night before. The water was almost high enough to cover the front doors of the buildings, flowing swiftly and carrying with it cars, trees, broken furniture . . .

He looked at the spot where he'd parked his Beetle, but it was gone. Why hadn't anyone called him from headquarters? He ran to the phone and picked up the receiver. It was silent. Then he remembered unplugging it. He plugged it back in, but there was still no dialling tone. He tried turning on the overhead light. Nothing. All power had been knocked out. He put on his coat and returned to the window.

'It's still rising,' he said to himself out loud. The turbid river was swelling before his eyes, carrying debris away and staving in shutters and doors. A number of women wept in silence, scratching their cheeks with their fingers. Small children looked out, wide-eyed and bewildered. One storey below him, old Signora Cianfroni was leaning out over the windowsill with her little dog in her arms. Somewhere a newborn was screaming desperately.

'The shop . . . the shop . . .' whimpered a man above him whom he couldn't see. The water continued rising. Bordelli lived on the third floor. The water could never rise that high, he repeated to himself.

'Down there . . . a dead body . . .!' a woman cried.

And indeed, a stiff corpse floated by on the water, one arm extended over its head. Bordelli realised it was only a mannequin washed out of a shop somewhere but said nothing. He didn't feel like talking. He went into the bathroom with the torch and set it down on a shelf. After flushing he turned on the tap, but only a dull gurgling sound came out. Cursing, he went back to the window. The water had risen even more. Seeing a man at the window smoking a cigarette, he went to look for his own. He quickly counted how many he had left in the packet. Just six. He would have to make them last, not knowing how long he would be held prisoner by the flood. He lit one and rested his elbows on the windowsill to smoke it, resigned to waiting. The smoke fluttered indifferently in the air, swirling and vanishing. In the distance he heard the melancholy sound of a helicopter.

He smoked till his fingers burned and then tossed the butt below. Touching the radiator, he found it almost cold. The water had flooded the basement and the boilers were no longer functioning. With the window open, his flat was getting cold. He thought of Botta in his basement flat. If he'd gone home last night, had he managed to escape in time? Or had he been overwhelmed by the mud in his sleep? At any rate, the few things he owned were lost by now. Poor Ennio. He also thought of Rosa, who lived almost right next to the Arno, in a 'hole', as the Florentines called it. He imagined her looking out from her little terrace, which gave on to Via dei Neri, eyes downcast and puling while the cats played in the sitting room. She was in no danger on the fifth floor. Diotivede likewise was safe. To reach as high as l'Erta Canina where he lived, the water would have to submerge the Palazzo Vecchio. Piras lived on the third floor in Via Gioberti, and by that hour should already have been on duty at the station. He thought of his cousin Rodrigo. He'd never seen his new place, but had heard that it was at the top of a hill. Zia Camilla, Rodrigo's mother, lived in Via Boccaccio, almost at San Domenico, where Dante watched over Florence from the hilltop.

Bordelli heard the sound of a few transistor radios and remembered he had one. Turning it on, he went back to the window, holding it close to his ear. They were saying that the Arno had burst its banks in Florence and the city was under water, isolated and cut in two . . .

Suddenly the water sort of hiccupped and started rising even faster. Ten minutes later it had come up another two feet, coursing ever faster and bubbling, dragging away everything in its path. Cars crashed against buildings, banging into one another, knocking down street signs. The helicopter was still flying over the city, but nobody could actually see it. A Volkswagen Beetle floated by like a boat. After uprooting a street sign it went and smashed into the corner of Via dell'Orto before continuing on towards Piazza Tasso. It was probably going to keep his car company, Bordelli thought, suppressing a desire to light up another cigarette.

After the initial shock and despair, a sort of feeling of resignation settled in. Nobody was talking any more. It was as if a community of ghosts had come to watch the end of the world. The only sounds were from the rain and the swashing of the mud. The level continued to rise. Good thing the fourth of November was a holiday, Bordelli thought. If this had happened on a regular workday, the city would have been full of people, cars and parents taking their children to school . . .

Time seemed to have stopped. The only thing moving was the sludgy mass flowing through the streets, gaining inch after inch on the façades of the buildings. There was nothing to do but wait and watch the muddy monster as it swelled between the blocks of flats. One man started taking photographs and was soon imitated by others.

Over the radio the reporter Marcello Giannini, trapped inside the RAI offices in Via Cerretani, lowered a microphone out of the window so that listeners could hear, live, the sounds of the river of mud coursing towards the railway station. It was announced that Mayor Bargellini would speak, and everyone brought their portable radio closer to their ears. A hollow-voiced Bargellini asked people to remain calm and wait for the rescue teams. Whoever owned any kind of floating craft was requested to bring it as soon as possible to Palazzo Vecchio. The news programme continued with lists of other areas of Italy hit hard by the bad weather. Everywhere landslides, floods, isolated towns. There was also mention, of course, of the Victory Day celebrations. Government politicians were busy with the ceremonies all across the country. Bordelli turned off the radio so as not to use up the batteries. He stuck a cigarette between his lips but didn't light it. He had only five left.

Long hours of waiting and cigarettes passed, and around two o'clock it finally stopped raining. The water had risen halfway up the first floor of the buildings, but the current had slowed. Everything imaginable had floated by, including a coffin lid with a large crucifix on it.

The radio said that an emergency rescue centre was being set up in Campo di Marte, which the flood waters hadn't reached and couldn't reach owing to the high wall of the railway. Emergency rations, mineral water and medical supplies were being collected. Amphibious vehicles and tankers were soon to arrive from nearby cities unaffected by the flooding. All the doctors in the province were requested to go to Careggi hospital, the only serviceable facility in town. It was announced that Aldo Moro and Minister Taviani were out of Rome to celebrate Armed Forces Day, the former in Gorizia and the latter in Bari. They were informed at once of the disaster and were already busy coordinating a massive relief effort. It was also reported that over eighty inmates had escaped from the Murate prison and were moving across the rooftops and through dormers and windows opened for them by the inhabitants of the quarter. Some were dangerous criminals, and citizens were advised to use extreme caution.

And so the hours, minutes and seconds went by. People were powerless to do anything except watch the putrid water flow down the street. A nauseating smell festered in the air, and many had covered their faces up to the eyes with hand-kerchiefs and scarves.

Round about five o'clock the sky started to darken, and the

people at their windows gazed upwards in dread. Others crouching on rooftops looked like huge frightened birds. In the gloomy glow of sunset, the river of mud assumed a terrifying aspect, and one could not help but think of the rivers of Hell mentioned by Dante . . . *They course from rock to rock in this valley, / form the Acheron, the Styx, and the Phlegethon*[39] . . .

Then night fell. Dozens of candle flames appeared on the windowsills, and the perspective of buildings became the columbarium of an enormous cemetery. The river of mud slowed down further, lapping softly against the walls of the buildings. Then suddenly it stopped altogether, and a tomblike silence descended on the neighbourhood. It was the same oppressive silence Bordelli used to hear during the war on certain winter nights.

He stuck a cigarette in his mouth but didn't light it until he couldn't hold out any longer. It was the last but one. The smell of heating oil and sewage was by now familiar to him. He couldn't stand looking out of the window any more. One could only imagine the chaos at the police station, the traffic police command, the *carabinieri* headquarters, the fire station, the Comiliter, the Prefecture and Palazzo Vecchio . . . and there he was, stuck at home doing nothing, with no water, electricity or telephone line.

He dropped the cigarette butt, following it with his eyes until it was swallowed up by the water. He closed the window and went out on the landing, torch in hand. He shone its light down the stairwell, illuminating the motionless surface of mud below. It would be impossible to go out. He felt trapped. He went down to the floor below and knocked on the Macciantis' door. The husband came and opened up, candle in hand, wrapped in a red jacket. His eyes were ringed with dark circles and he was unshaven. His little workshop in Via dell'Orto had surely been destroyed.

'Have you got an extra candle, by any chance?' Bordelli asked.

'Come in . . .' Maccianti said gloomily. He was a small man

with little hair on his pear-shaped head and always gave off a faint smell of machine oil. Bordelli followed him into a dining room with dark furniture. A number of candles burned in the room, their flames long and motionless. Maccianti's wife and two children were standing at the window huddled tightly together. Seated around the table were the first-floor tenants, a retired labourer with his wife and mother-in-law. Bordelli made a gesture of greeting, which was returned in silence. Faintly visible in one shadowy corner were two large suitcases, bulging like those of refugees. Maccianti rummaged through a drawer.

'I can give you these,' he said in a whisper, handing Bordelli two candles.

'Thank you so much, it's more than I could have hoped for,' the inspector said in relief. A few hours earlier a couple of candles meant nothing, but the Arno's fury had inverted the order of meaning.

'My wife buys them by the box, for the little statue of the Blessed Virgin we have in our bedroom.'

'I've got an extra bedroom and a sofa, if anyone needs a place,' said Bordelli, saying goodbye to the people gathered and going back upstairs.

He had a hole in the pit of his stomach. He hadn't eaten for almost a day. He went into the kitchen to see what there was. All he found was a small piece of pecorino cheese, some old bread and half a box of biscuits. He also had a bottle of water on his nightstand. He couldn't sleep unless there was a bottle of water on the nightstand. He ate standing up, having laid the torch down on the table. He thought of the poor wretches who had lost everything, and he felt lucky. Until yesterday, living on the upper floors of a building without an elevator had always been a nuisance.

He went back into the bedroom, lit both candles and lay down in bed with all his clothes on. The flames flickered ever so gently, casting tremulous shadows. A thought resurfaced in his mind. Giacomo Pellissari. Whoever killed him could only benefit from this disaster. The flooding would occupy the authorities' attentions for a long time, and everything else would fade into the background. He thought of Via Luna, wondering how high the waters had risen in that neighbourhood. The mud might have even destroyed the apartment, wiping out all traces of evidence and washing away the only hope there was of making any progress in the investigation. The case of the boy's murder was in serious danger of being shelved.

There was only one cigarette left. He preferred holding out to being left without, but he would have to distract himself in some way to avoid smoking it. He picked up the torch and went into the dining room and cast the light on the spines of his books. He saw several volumes of Herodotus's *Histories.* They were a present from a woman some years ago, but he'd never read them. He took the first volume back to the bedroom, set the torch down on the bedside table, stuck two pillows behind his head and started reading . . .

The book was quite engrossing and almost made him forget about the flood. He kept reading for a good while, suppressing the desire to smoke. Particularly amusing to him was learning about the customs of certain ancient peoples. The Babylonians, for example, had to pay a tax before they could marry a beautiful woman, so that only the rich could afford to do so. The money was then allocated for dowries for ugly or disfigured women, who obviously were married off to commoners . . . Who knew how much he would have had to pay, in Babylon, to wed the beautiful salesgirl of Via Pacinotti?

Around ten o'clock he went and looked out of the window again. Candles flickered gloomily on many windowsills. In the half-light he saw ghostly spectres leaning on their elbows, the incandescent tips of cigarettes glowing bright as they took deep drags. He turned the torch beam downwards and couldn't help but smile a little. About a foot and a half above the waterline on the building façades was a thick line of black oil dripping down. The waters had begun to recede, flowing slowly back towards the river. If they kept up this pace, in a few hours he would be able to go out. He had no desire to remain there counting the minutes and inches. He shut the window and went back to bed. Pulling up a few blankets, he rearranged the pillows and resumed reading.

He woke up with the book on his chest. When he exhaled he could see his breath. It was very cold, and the room was flooded with daylight. It was almost 8 a.m. He'd read late into the night and then nodded off. The candles were guttered, their dried wax running down the side of the nightstand. He went and opened the window. Under clear skies the spectacle was even more dismaying. The mud was almost all gone, leaving behind shattered cars, broken doors and gutted shutters, all manner of debris brought there by the fury of the current. A thick, still-damp ring of oil marked the walls at a height of over ten feet. In the distance he heard the melancholy wail of numerous sirens and the even whirr of helicopters. The ghosts of the night were beginning to come out of their homes, pale, exhausted, incredulous. They swashed around in the muck in boots or shoes wrapped in plastic bags fastened around their ankles, looking around with sleep-deprived eyes. Every so often a siren would rise above the chorus and seem to draw near before continuing on in another direction and blending in again with the rest.

He went into the kitchen to load up the coffee pot, blessing the gas cylinder and the half-bottle of water he had left. He felt decidedly better. Perhaps the emergency itself was the cause. He changed his clothes but still smelled bad. Searching around in a storage cupboard he found a pair of rubber boots in good condition. The coffee tasted better than ever before.

Putting his torch and transistor radio in his coat pockets, he ventured down the stairs. As he descended, the stench got stronger and stronger. The last two flights were quite slippery, and he very nearly fell. One wing of the double front door hung from a single hinge, while the other had come off and was floating in the entrance hall. He pushed it aside and went out into the street, where the water came almost up to his knees. The air was unbreathable. The human figures moving about amid the piles of debris looked like the damned. At the bottom of the street, towards Borgo San Frediano, a tree had got stuck in the entrance of a building. It all felt like a city after a bombing raid. The modulating sounds of sirens merged together into a single distressing wail.

He headed towards Piazza Tasso, paying close attention to where he stepped. There might be all manner of things hidden under the muck, and one could get hurt. He turned to look at the shrine at the corner of Piazza Piattellina; the black mark of the oil ran just below the Baby Jesus's head. He continued on, taking small steps, circling round a Fiat 600 on its side that blocked half a lane. Looking out from a first-floor window was a woman wrapped in a blanket, shivering.

'I've lost everything . . . everything . . .' she muttered, head swaying back and forth. Men were hoisting old and young on to their backs to carry them to the dry areas. Here and there a few transistor radios could be heard croaking. A man was telling everyone to be extremely careful; there was an open manhole in the middle of the street, hidden by the mud, and a woman had fallen in and broken her leg.

In Piazza Tasso the oily line on the walls was barely a yard above the ground, and the remaining muck was much shallower. Just off the pavement the carcass of a large dog surfaced, black with oil. Along the Viale two or three cars rolled along at a walking pace. In the public gardens a number of ruined cars lay piled up between the flower beds. There were even two Volkswagen Beetles, caked with mud only halfway up the doors. One was his. He went up to it and walked around it. It was dented on every side, and the headlights were broken. He looked inside. The interior was intact. On the back seat he saw the blouse he needed to return, spared by the flood, and it forced him to think of the pretty salesgirl. Not even in that hell could he manage to get her out of his head.

He started walking towards Botta's place, sloshing through the stinking mud. The blue sky promised a beautiful sunny day. He still had that last cigarette, all crumpled up, but wanted to resist a little longer. He would light it before entering the first open tobacconist. In Via del Campuccio all that remained was about an inch of black slime, and the mark left by the oil was very low. Men and women were sweeping the mud towards the manholes with brooms and mops, emptying out basement flats with buckets, rummaging through ruined shops.

Drawing near, Bordelli saw Botta come out of the front door of his building with a bucket in hand, covered in mud, and made a gesture of greeting. Ennio poured the putrid water into the street.

'Good morning, Inspector. I'm afraid I can't invite you inside for a cup of coffee today,' he said, forcing a smile.

'Another time, then,' Bordelli replied, patting him on the back. Poor Ennio. He never had any luck. The flood hadn't reached much farther than his place, stopping only a few yards up the street.

'If they hadn't woken me up in time I would have drowned like a rat, Inspector. With all the mud pouring down, climbing the stairs wasn't easy.'

'Did you manage to save anything?'

'I brought a bundle of clothes up to the first floor, to Signora Maria's flat. But I didn't have much more than that.'

'So it could've been worse . . .'

'My grandfather always used to say that sometimes it's better to have nothing, and now I know what he meant.'

'So where were you hiding all this time, Ennio? I've been looking for you for the past two days.'

'I was away on business,' said Botta, smiling only with his eyes. The inspector didn't bother to ask what kind of business.

'When did you get back?'

'Thursday night. I got your note, but it was raining so hard, and I didn't feel like going out to look for a telephone . . . What did you need?'

'I'm afraid there's no longer any need.'

'Are you just going to leave me in suspense?'

'I'll tell you another time. Have you got a place to stay until you've finished cleaning out your room?'

'I haven't given it any thought yet.'

'You can come and sleep at my place, if you like. You'll never believe it, but I even have a guest room,' said Bordelli.

'If I can't find anything else, I'll definitely come and impose on you.'

'I'm not sure when I'll be back home. You can go there whenever you like, since you don't need keys. The room's at the end of the hall.'

'Thanks, Inspector.'

'Ciao, Ennio, I'm going to try to go to the station.'

'Have a good day,' said Botta, disappearing into his building, bucket in hand.

The inspector went back to Piazza Tasso, which was filling up with people trudging through the mud. He got into his Beetle and put the key in the ignition without much conviction. It couldn't possibly start. He tried all the same, and to his great astonishment the small engine started to turn, making its usual whirring sound. The car lurched and the pistons were misfiring . . . As the battery began to show signs of fatigue, the engine backfired twice and then fell into a regular rhythm. People gawked at him as if they had just witnessed a miracle.

'Damned Germans . . .' he muttered to himself, shaking his head. Hitler's 'car of the people' was born the same year that Mussolini instituted the 'racial laws', but it had survived Nazism. Further proof that good things can sometimes issue from bad.

He checked the petrol gauge; a little over half a tankful. He began to manoeuvre, pushing away the other cars blocking his path. At last he came off the pavement. The tyres slid this way and that in the mud, and driving wasn't easy. Pulling out of the piazza, he started looking for a parking spot on the uphill Via Villani. He wanted to go to the centre of town, but preferred to go on foot, not knowing what he would find. The street was full of salvaged cars, but in the end he found a space for the Beetle.

Retracing his route on foot, he glanced at his watch. Nine-twenty. He crossed Piazza Tasso again and went up Via del Leone. The water had receded even more. Dozens of brooms swept the mud away from the building entrances, while silent shadows moved about inside the flooded shops.

He made a right turn into Piazza del Carmine, which was strewn with wrecked cars and large clumps of brush. Despite the sun, everything was opaque, dead. He heard the helicopters flying over the city but still couldn't manage to see them. The great portal of the church had been forced open by the flood, and a Fiat Giardinetta had ended up on the staircase in front. There were animal carcasses everywhere – dogs, cats, but also chickens and rabbits washed in from the countryside.

He crossed the piazza diagonally, exchanging long glances with the people he passed. In Borgo San Frediano the muck was a bit deeper. He walked past the carcass of a cow, black with heating oil, lying on its side with two legs suspended in the air. A bit further on he had to climb over a large tree and very nearly fell into the slime.

Legions of people were sweeping the mud out of entrance halls, as detritus from the shops was piled up on the pavements. It looked like Italy just after the war, or worse. A tiny woman with a scarf round her head wept in silence while carrying armfuls of rotten vegetables out of her shop.

When he came out into Piazza Nazario Santo, he heard the Arno rumbling. The small square was cluttered with ruined cars, some of them belly up. A twisted Fiat 850 had ended up on the roof of a large saloon. It was anybody's guess how long it would take to get things back in order.

He continued on to Via di Santo Spirito. The scene was the same everywhere. Devastation, detritus, mud. Sulking faces and elbow grease. Every so often he heard a bitter wisecrack, which met with ironic smiles. The layer of smelly muck stagnating in the streets added further gloom to a city already marked by centuries of bloody conspiracies, violent intrigues, betrayals, deceptions and swindles, a city forever dominated by morbid tensions hidden under the false playfulness of wit. As they shovelled up the mud they were already cracking jokes about the flood, inventing jokes in a never-ending effort not to succumb.

He arrived at Piazza Frescobaldi. Borgo San Jacopo was jammed with automobile carcasses and debris, so he turned towards the Arno. The flood hadn't quite reached the Ponte Santa Trinita, and it was a relief to walk for a stretch without slipping. The huge mass of water coursed majestically, roaring like a four-engined plane, making the cobblestones vibrate underfoot. A small group of people on the bridge were looking at the chasms left by the collapse of the Lungarno Accioli and the Lungarno Corsini. Another public works project that would soon strike up another dance of kickbacks and graft, Bordelli thought sadly. Catastrophes had always been good for business. Nothing new there. The Italy of the boom years had found its vital lymph in corruption, shady business and tax evasion. Which was fine for everyone, so long as there was more money in their pockets and they could lie on the beach in summer. The Italians had no more sense of state than a flea, perhaps less. They were infected with a taste for privilege and cronyism, fascinated by the rich and powerful, devoted to nepotism and whoring. They'd been nursing this mentality for centuries and would probably never be rid of it. In *The Leopard* Lampedusa said there was no hope for Sicily, but he could easily have extended the concept to the whole country . . .

As he was about to turn on to Via Tornabuoni, he slipped on the slime. Looking at the desolation of the collapsed Lungarno, he'd actually felt a twinge of pleasure, as if some sort of vengeance had been achieved at last. If only the Ponte Vecchio had also collapsed, and with it the Duomo, Palazzo

Vecchio and all the Philistines with them . . . Florence thought
she was saved by her glorious past, like a degenerate son resting
on the laurels of his father and grandfather. Even Panerai the
butcher and the offal seller in San Lorenzo believed that in their
veins still coursed the blood of Dante, Michelangelo, Leonardo
and Brunelleschi coursed still. All the beautiful things you see,
as you look around in awe, are the work of our very own hands
. . . The work of us Florentines. From here came the spark that
renewed the world, and all must bow before our genius. Come
and spend your money in the birthplace of the Renaissance,
buy our knick-knacks, our artistic postcards, our statuettes of
the David, our jewels forged in the soul of Benvenuto Cellini,
sleep in our hotels, eat our steaks, our *pasta e fagioli*, our offal,
our lamprey, take a ride in a horse-drawn carriage, touch the
snout of the Porcellino . . .[40] Why should we care about creating
new immortal works of art when we can sell the ones
we've already got? Our true soul has always been commerce
– the god who protects us is the god of thieves . . .

And today Florence trembled because her treasures
were spattered with mud. Rich or poor made no difference.
The rich were cynical and indifferent, and the poor
envied them, dreamt of being like them, of becoming even
worse than them . . .

Lost in these thoughts, he turned down Borgo Santi Apostoli,
which the Arno had submerged in ten feet of water. Piazza del
Limbo looked like a rubbish dump. In front of the tunnel that
led to the Lungarno, an old woman looked on with a broom
in her hand, all wrapped up in a coat and scarves.

In Por Santa Maria, Bordelli saw a number of traffic officers
standing in front of the Ponte Vecchio and went up to them.
One of the officers raised his hand.

'Nobody is allowed to pass this way,' he said in an authoritarian tone.

'What's going on?' Bordelli asked, flashing his badge. The
officers sprang to attention.

'At ease, at ease . . . What are you two doing here?'

'We're making sure nobody gets close to the Ponte Vecchio, because of the jewellers' shops.'

'Gold first and foremost,' the inspector grumbled, and moved on. Behind the two policemen he caught a glimpse of some jewellers rummaging through the sludge in search of lost treasures. Finally forced to dirty their hands, he thought. He set off along the Lungarno Archibusieri and then turned round to look at the Ponte Vecchio, which seemed to be in pretty bad shape. The jewellery shops were half in ruins and great clumps of shrubbery, and even a whole tree, had accumlated above the arches.

He went under the portico of the Uffizi. He was getting rather good at walking in the slippery muck. From the corner of Via della Ninna he glanced back at Piazza della Signoria, which lay entirely under a thick layer of slime. In the middle of the square a small crowd of people had gathered round a tanker, waiting their turn to fill bottles and plastic cans.

Walking alongside the Palazzo Vecchio, he found a good foot and a half of water at the end of the sloping street. He turned down Via dei Neri, keeping to the pavement to gain an inch or two. Tired faces looked out at him from the windows. Men and women in rubber boots made their way through the mud. He crossed paths with a lanky chap with a bitter smile on his face.

'Bloody Arno . . . Jesus bloody Christ . . . Why couldn't it wash away my wife instead of my car?' he muttered, shaking his head. Further ahead a wooden scow slid silently through the mud, ferrying old folks and children.

When Bordelli arrived at Rosa's front door, he found it smashed in by the flood waters. Ducking into the building, he went up the dark stairs, lighting his way with the torch. Behind one door he heard some shouting and a little girl crying. By the time he reached the top floor, his legs were giving out. He knocked at Rosa's door. No reply. He knocked harder. At last he heard the sound of high heels drawing near.

'Who is it?'

'It's me, Rosa,' said Bordelli.

The door opened and Rosa appeared in her short red coat, the little kitten in her arms. Her pallor seemed to indicate that she hadn't slept, but she hadn't forgotten to make herself up.

'Darling . . .! I was so scared . . .' she said with tears in her eyes, laying her head on his chest.

'It wasn't the Great Flood, but it was close,' Bordelli whispered, stroking her blonde hair. Briciola was between them, clinging to their coats with her claws. Rosa was sniffling.

'Early yesterday morning . . . I went out to look at the Arno . . . In Corso Tintori I saw a man running . . . running away from the water, which was chasing him. I raced back home . . . I tried to ring you, but there was no answer . . .'

'I had a high temperature . . . I unplugged the phone . . .'

'. . . I went out on the terrace and saw everything . . . the water got higher and higher . . . stronger and stronger . . . cars were crashing against the buildings . . . they sounded like bombs . . . I even saw some corpses floating by . . . oh, God, what a fright . . . what a fright . . .'

'The worst is over now.'

'Good Lord, do you stink . . .' said Rosa, raising her head with a grimace.

'I had a good sweat last night and haven't been able to wash,' said Bordelli by way of explanation. Rosa sniffed him again, wrinkling her nose.

'You smell like a circus . . . it's like sniffing a lion's bum,' she said, a hint of a smile on her lips.

'No woman has ever paid me such a sexy compliment before,' he said. 'Can I come in for a minute?' He needed to sit down, even if only for a minute.

'Not with those filthy boots you can't,' said Rosa, horrified. Bordelli sighed and took them off, setting them down on the landing.

'Is that better?' he said, waiting for Rosa to give him the go-ahead.

He shuffled into the sitting room, leaving damp footprints on the floor. He sat down on the sofa, not taking off his coat, and leaned back. The day had barely begun and he already felt like a wreck. But he had no cause for complaint, since he'd felt much worse the night before. Rosa sat down on the armrest beside him, smothering the kitten with kisses as the animal tried to squirm away.

'Naughty little pussycat . . . Where do you want to go?'

Rosa was back to her usual self, as though nothing had happened.

'You wouldn't happen to have a glass of water, would you, Rosa?'

'I've got a whole case of the effervescent stuff. Would you like a bottle to take away with you?'

'Just a glass'll be fine,' said Bordelli, hoping to get some of the bitterness out of his mouth. Rosa set Briciola down on the rug and went to the kitchen to fetch the water. The kitten took advantage of the situation and jumped up on the table. In a matter of seconds she had managed to reach into the fruit bowl with her little paw and take out a hazelnut, which rolled on to the floor. She then jumped down and started playing with the nut, batting it back and forth across the room. Bordelli glanced at his watch; it was already half past ten. He stood up and went to intercept Rosa, who was returning with the water. He emptied the glass in a few gulps, with more pleasure than he could ever have imagined.

'I have to go,' he said, heading for the door.

'You'd better wash as soon as you can; it's not easy to be around you,' she said, following behind him. Bordelli put his boots back on, said goodbye to Rosa, and headed down the stairs, starting to shiver again. He hoped his fever wasn't coming back.

The Santa Croce area was still flooded. To get to Piazza Beccaria without trudging through the water, he had to take a long detour by way of Piazza d'Azeglio. It was the same everywhere: dead animals, uprooted trees, water heaters, television sets, piles of rotten fruit reduced to mush, and hundreds of automobile carcasses, free gifts for the car wreckers. He even saw a large expanse of dead fish and a couple of grounded scows.

In the areas now free of water, the piles of rubbish accumulating outside the shops were getting taller and taller. The smell of oil polluting the air made it hard to breathe, especially in the narrowest streets. Every so often one saw amphibious military vehicles drive by, as well as a few jeeps, fire engines and ambulances. The sound of the sirens rolled across the roofs and cast a sorrowful pall of uncertainty over the city, but the most familiar sound was that of brooms sweeping away the mud.

The Piazza Beccaria gate rose up amid a pile of cars stacked one on top of the other. The streets leading to the centre of town were blocked by military vehicles. There was traffic on the Viali, the cars' wheels sloshing through the slime. Bordelli crossed the Piazza and went down Via Gioberti, eyeing the black line of heating oil cutting halfway up the first-floor windows. He walked slowly, legs aching. He passed under the Via Luna archway, which had been completely submerged during the flood. He was about to do something totally useless, he was well aware of that. He turned down the little street that had fed his illusions, and stopped in the square. As he expected, the door of interest had been smashed in by the water. He crossed the threshold just to taste his defeat. Four rooms utterly devastated by the mud. The floors were covered with detritus. A small door led to a basement still brimful of water. He lit his last cigarette, tossing the packet to the ground. The Arno had wiped out his last hope, cutting the very fine thread, the only thread, that might, perhaps, have led him out of the labyrinth.

He returned to Piazza Beccaria, headed for Piazza Donatello along Viali, which was clogged with cars advancing a few feet every ten minutes. The ambulances and fire engines struggled to get through the traffic, as a few mud-spattered traffic cops hastily tried to clear a path for them in the middle of the boulevard.

The flood waters had stopped just past the English Cemetery, so there was no problem walking down Viale Matteotti. It was a real pleasure not to have slime under one's boots. He continued on as far as Piazza della Libertà. The newspaper kiosk was open, and people were queuing up. He went to have a look round the corner of Viale Lavagnini. No trace of flooding: Cesare's trattoria had been spared. And what about Totò? He knew he lived in Via Pisana but couldn't remember on what floor. He retraced his steps and turned on to Via San Gallo, picking up his pace. It was only two days since he'd last left the station in Via Zara, but it felt like ten years. The boy's murder seemed a distant memory, buried by time. There was no way, of course, for him to keep up with his investigation in the midst of the catastrophe. There were far more urgent matters to attend to. With a bitter taste in his mouth, he had to admit that it had almost been a stroke of luck, since he hadn't known which way to turn anyway.

Police headquarters had been spared as well. The courtyard was mobbed with people who'd had to leave their homes and didn't know where to rest their weary bones. The back-and-forth traffic of military vehicles continued unabated. The atmosphere was a combination of patience and agitation. Small children looked around with fear in their eyes, while the oldest still hadn't forgotten the disaster of the war. Mugnai was pale and looked as if he'd lost weight. He was keeping busy amid the confusion, along with several other officers. As soon as he saw Bordelli, he came running towards him.

'Inspector! Aren't you supposed to be at home with the flu?' he asked, as if he'd seen a ghost.

'I'm feeling much better . . . Where are they taking them?' he asked, indicating a lorry that was boarding a group of evacuees.

'Wherever there's room . . . Barracks, convents, a few schools . . .'

'Was your place flooded?'

'Everything's fine, Inspector. I live in Le Cure.'

'What about Commissioner Inzipone?'

'He was here for about half an hour last night, then he went to the mayor's. At the moment he should be at the Prefecture.'

'Have we got phone service?'

'Everything got knocked out, electricity included. We're making do with generators.'

'Is Piras in?'

'I really don't know. It's been total chaos here since yesterday morning.'

'Go and get some rest, you're pale as a corpse.'

'Not now, sir,' said Mugnai, and he turned and went back to the evacuees.

Bordelli went straight to the radio room. You could cut the smoke with a knife, and everybody's face was drawn. Maps of the province and the city were spread out over the tables, and there were empty espresso cups scattered everywhere. The murdered boy was the farthest thing from everyone's mind . . .

They brought Bordelli up to speed on the situation. During the night the entire force had been called to report for duty, including the married men. They were trying to count the dead, rescue the living, draw up plans for repairing the aqueduct, the power lines, the telephone lines, the gas lines and the sewers.

A few of the escaped inmates had been brought back to the fold, and one of them had drowned after trying to grab on to a tree trunk. People were already turning their attention to damaged artworks, devastated churches, museums and libraries. Rome was getting ready to send President Saragat the following day, as stormy meetings were held at the Prefecture. Only recently had instructions been issued for police and military to take autonomous action on the basis of need and not to wait for specific orders.

A relay system had been organised. Some police officers were making rounds of the city, checking on the situation and reporting back to headquarters. Emergencies were communicated by radio to the Comiliter and the military encampment set up in the stadium at Campo di Marte.

Deputy Commissioner Draghi had managed to organise a network of ham-radio amateurs, placing one at the Prefecture, another at Palazzo Vecchio, and another at police headquarters. They communicated with other radios broadcasting from areas that still had electricity, relaying calls for help to the fire department and ambulance services. Almost all of the operators were clandestine radio aficionados, previously working outside the law, but it was thanks to them that pregnant women and the seriously ill and wounded were brought to safety.

Bordelli asked whether anyone knew where Piras was. They said he'd gone out at dawn to take part in the rescue efforts and hadn't been seen since.

Tinny voices kept coming over the radios through a thousand crackles. At Le Cure a small group of men and women had sacked a delicatessen. In Borgo Allegri a looter was caught rummaging through a flooded house and was nearly lynched by a mob. Word came that a household goods shop in Via dello Statuto was selling boots at six or seven thousand lire a pair, brooms for three thousand, and so on.

'I'll go and look into this myself,' said Bordelli, searching for his cigarettes. Then he remembered finishing the packet and asked the others. He found himself with half a packet of Alfas in his hand, and immediately lit one upon exiting the radio room. In the courtyard he chose a grey Fiat 1100 from among the squad cars. Driving away, he immediately noticed it wasn't a normal 1100 but had a souped-up engine.

The Viali were clogged with traffic. Two exhausted-looking traffic cops were trying desperately to remedy the situation, yelling and blowing their whistles. Bordelli even gave the siren a toot, and soon they cleared a path for him.

Driving with two tyres up on the pavement, he arrived at last in Via dello Statuto, an area the flood hadn't reached. Spotting the shop on the opposite side of the street, he parked the car and made a beeline for it. With the sun that was beating down, it was hard to imagine that the centre of town had been inundated with mud.

He entered the shop and queued up with the others. There were some five or six people in front of him, and the air stank of smoke. The shop owner was in the process of selling a pair of boots. He was rather gaunt, with a pointy face and cheeks ravaged long ago by acne. His lower lip hung like a pork chop, and two little chains dangled from the stems of his glasses.

'Seven thousand?' said the customer, incredulous. He was about forty, with a round head and a moustache.

'That's how much it is today, it can't be helped,' the shop-keeper muttered with a shrug.

'Normally they cost about five hundred lire,' the client persisted.

'What do you want me to say . . .?'

'You're taking advantage of people in need.'

'If you don't want them, just give them back, I'm sure I can sell them to someone else,' said the shopkeeper, taking back the boots and acting offended.

'Just give them to me anyway,' the customer said angrily. And he threw the money down on the counter and headed for the door, grumbling through clenched teeth. The inspector stopped him in the doorway, inviting him to accompany him back to the counter. The man followed him, looking confused.

Bordelli pulled out his badge and stuck it under the shopkeeper's nose.

'Police. I believe this gentleman's seven thousand lire ended up in your wallet by mistake.'

'What's that?' the shopkeeper muttered, frightened. The customers in the queue followed the scene with bated breath.

'Perhaps I haven't made myself clear. I'm ordering you to give the gentleman back his seven thousand lire.'

'But I . . .'

'I'm losing my patience.'

'But what are you saying? I . . . I'm not . . .' the man stammered.

Bordelli slapped him square in the face.

'I'll give you one more second, and then I'll arrest you for extortion,' he said, with the same look in his eye as he used to get when shooting at Nazis. He had more respect for thieves than for characters like this man. The shopkeeper was terrified. With trembling hands he took a bulging wallet out of his pocket and extracted seven thousand lire. Bordelli accepted the notes and handed them to the customer.

'Boots are on the house today,' he said, smiling. Then he went around asking the customers what they needed, told the owner to serve them, then sent them off without paying. When he was at last alone with the shopkeeper, he looked him hard in the eye.

'Now I want you to take out all the boots and brooms you've got, and don't make me say it twice.'

He followed the man into the back room to make sure he didn't try to pull a fast one. He ordered him to take the boots and brooms out of the shop and line them up on the pavement. In the street a long queue of cars was proceeding at a snail's pace, spewing clouds of smelly exhaust.

'Now close your shop,' said Bordelli.

'Why?' the man whimpered, taking a step back.

'Close it up,' said Bordelli.

The man hurriedly pulled down the metal shutter and turned the key in the lock.

'Can I go now?'

'Give me the key.'

'What are you going to do?'

'The key,' said the inspector, extending an open hand. The shopkeeper took the key off its ring and put it in Bordelli's palm, looking desperate. Bordelli stepped down from the pavement, bent over and dropped the key into a sewer drain. The shopkeeper opened his mouth but didn't manage to say anything.

'If you reopen your shop before the month is out, I'll personally escort you to Murate,' said Bordelli. Then he turned on his heels and, cutting through the traffic, went back to the Fiat 1100. As he started it up he noticed the shopkeeper walking down Via dello Statuto, bent forward as though into a stiff wind. He felt terribly sorry for the wretch, and hoped he wasn't raising any children.

The inspector decided to go to Campo di Marte. The idea of holing up at the police station didn't appeal to him at all. He would rather jump into the fray. To avoid the clogged Viali, he went by way of Via Bolognese, taking the steep descent past the Badia and coming out at San Domenico.

At last he reached the stadium. The field was swarming with people and military vehicles and was being used as a landing pad for helicopters. Supplies and provisions were being collected under the Marathon stand, where a small field infirmary had been set up. Red Cross nurses and soldiers were keeping very busy. Lorries came in, escorted by traffic police motorcyclists and loaded with bread, sugar, salt, fruit, bottled water, tinned food of various sorts, and mattresses. Some non-commissioned officers were consulting a map of the city spread out over a field table.

Bordelli started helping the soldiers unload crates, concealing his fatigue and ignoring the painful twinges in his back. He wanted to show these little boys what a Methuselah who'd fought with the San Marco battalion was made of. Meanwhile it occurred to him that Panerai's butcher's shop was only about a hundred yards away, and he felt defeated.

Someone turned on a small transistor radio at high volume. The city authorities were issuing directives. No one was to use their car except in cases of emergency . . . Anyone in need of medical assistance was to go to Careggi hospital . . . Medical supplies, food provisions, candles and blankets could be had at the Campo di Marte stadium. Tankers were distributing water in Piazza del Duomo, Piazza della Signoria and Piazza Santissima Annunziata . . .

The chaos grew by the hour. Volunteers were arriving from districts untouched by the flood, from nearby towns and villages, from other regions, and even from other countries. They included men and women of all ages. From Siena came a lorry loaded with bread, paid for by a private citizen. A number of wholesalers spontaneously brought foodstuffs from their warehouses.

A number of amphibious vehicles set off for areas still under water, and Bordelli asked to go with them. They took the more lightly injured to the field hospital, and the more serious and sick to Careggi. They rescued children, pregnant women, elderly people suffering from the cold. They distributed emergency provisions to families, mostly bread, bottled water and milk for the little ones, but also pasta, sugar, flour and fruit.

The great marble statue of Dante in Santa Croce looked down in disgust at the smelly muck stagnating at his divine feet, as a wicked glint seemed to shine in his scornful eyes. All around were ruined metal shutters and doors, damaged cars, fragments of furniture, twisted metal, great clusters of shrubbery, mud piles, animal carcasses and trees brought in from who knew where. A bomb would have done less damage. The stench made one gag. A thick black line ran across the church's white façade. It didn't seem possible for the water to have risen so high.

After sunset, a military floodlight was turned on from Piazzale Michelangelo high above the city, its powerful beam illuminating the small Piazza dei Cavalleggeri, where dozens of students had formed lines and were tirelessly passing from hand to hand the precious volumes of the Biblioteca Nazionale.

Bordelli managed to secure a parcel of provisions for Rosa, including milk for the one-eyed kitten. He spent the whole day going back and forth from Campo di Marte to the most devastated streets of the city's centre. He forgot to eat, but not to smoke.

That night he found himself on a wooden scow in the still-flooded streets of Gavinana, sliding over the stagnant water with a lamp in his hand like demon Charon, with embers for eyes . . .[41]

By the time he parked the squad car in Viale Petrarca it was almost midnight. His clothes were all soiled with mud and his feet ached. He felt exhausted, drained. He was getting too old for such exertions; normally he needed at least a few hours' rest in between. Walking in the moonlight, torch in hand, he crossed Piazza Tasso, where there were still a few shadows moving silently about.

Climbing the stairs to his flat, he felt like Ulysses with Ithaca in his sights. In his pockets he had four half-consumed candles. He'd stolen them from the little church of the Madonna della Tosse, begging the dead to forgive him. At any rate, they no longer needed them.

Entering his flat, he noticed a glow coming from the dining room, and more importantly, he smelled the aroma of good hot food.

'Ennio, is that you?' he asked, going down the corridor. When he entered the dining room, he smiled. Botta was sleeping on the sofa with his mouth open, snoring lightly. A number of candles, inserted into empty bottles, burned on different pieces of furniture about the room. The table was spread with a floral-pattern tablecloth and settings for two, with water, bread, wine and all the rest. It was truly touching. He went up to Botta and shook his shoulder lightly.

'Ennio . . .'

'Eh?'

'The mushrooms are calling you,' Bordelli whispered.

Botta opened his eyes wide and raised his head. Seeing the inspector, he sat up with a groan.

'I wasn't asleep, you know . . . I was just thinking . . .' he said, arranging his hair with both hands.

'Am I wrong, or did you cook something?' Bordelli asked, sniffing the air.'

'Good thing you had a bottle of gas.'

'I'll ask the pope to beatify you at the very least.'

'Don't expect anything special . . .'

'What could be nicer than a candlelit dinner?' Bordelli asked, gesturing towards the table. Botta stood up, still half asleep.

'Go and wash your hands and change your clothes. Then come and sit down at the table,' he said, heading out of the dining room with a candle in hand.

'Shall I wash with wine or vinegar?'

'There's a full can of water in the bathroom.' Botta yawned, then disappeared into the hallway.

The inspector went into his bedroom to change clothes, having put the torch on the bedside table. It disgusted him to put clean clothes on his dirty body again, but there was no alternative. His feet were covered with dried mud, and he rubbed them long and hard with an old towel. The best part was when he could finally put on a pair of normal shoes.

He looked at himself in the bathroom mirror. He had a couple of days' growth of beard, and dark circles under his eyes. Sticking a plug in the basin, he washed his hands, pouring out as little water as possible. As Botta was busying himself in the kitchen, he went back to the dining room and sat down at the table. The candle behind him projected the enlarged shadow of his head on the wall in front of him. He nibbled a bit of bread and a chasm opened up in his stomach. On a chair he noticed some newspapers. The headline of the 4 November edition of *La Nazione* screamed: ARNO FLOODS FLORENCE. In the middle of page 1 there was a short article in bold type: *Latest update: Six a.m. Each new report is more dramatic than the last. The embankment at Lungarno Acciaioli . . .*

Bordelli thumbed through the other pages, skimming the different articles on the flood. On page 4 he found an article that made him smile: CITY CELEBRATES SOLDIERS. Details followed on the Florentine commemoration of the 4 November holiday, giving the times and places of the different events. At 10.30, flag-raising in Piazza della Signoria; at 11.30, speech by the president of the National Association of Combat Veterans in Palazzo Vecchio; stands set up by the armed forces in various piazzas of the city to display to the public the latest novelties in radio communications and health services . . .

Bordelli opened *Il Resto del Carlino*, hot off the presses: FLORENCE UNDER WATER / CITY TRANSFORMED INTO LAKE. On the right there was a large insert in bold lettering: *To the readers of* La Nazione: *The stately new office building of* La Nazione *has shared the fate of the rest of the city of Florence and been devastated by flood waters. While waiting for the daily's normal services to resume, its sister newspaper,* Il Resto del Carlino, *a product of the same publishing company, has prepared the present special edition for the entire province of Tuscany, specifically to fill the role normally played by* La Nazione . . .

Botta finally made his entrance, candle in one hand and a steaming pot in the other. Setting everything down on the table, he started filling their dishes with pasta. *Spaghetti alla carbonara.* Bordelli tossed the newspapers aside and felt his mouth begin to water, as used to happen during the war on those rare occasions when he smelled roast beef in the air.

'Forget the beatification, they should make you a saint straight away,' he said, rolling a mouthful of spaghetti on to his fork. The candles shed a dim, yellowish light in the room, turning their faces into waxen masks.

'The second course leaves a lot to be desired,' Botta said modestly.

'There's even a second course?'

'Well, there's even a side dish, as far as that goes.'

'And maybe even a dessert . . .?'

'*Biscottini di Prato* and *vin santo.* We could do worse,' Ennio said, smiling.

'Where'd you find all this stuff?'

'A little here, a little there.'

'Afterwards you must tell me how much you spent . . .'

'Never mind about that, Inspector. At the moment I'm not hard up for cash.'

'So that little job you mentioned went well?' the inspector asked, refilling his glass with wine.

'Precisely.'

'A lot of money?'

'Enough . . .'

'Did you sell a monument to an American tourist, like Totò?'

'Practically.'

'If you don't tell me I won't be able to sleep.'

'Am I talking to the police inspector or to the man?' Botta asked, as he always did before owning up to his crimes.

'You're speaking to a starving man who has every intention of getting drunk,' said Bordelli, chewing an enormous forkful of spaghetti.

'I sold a drawing by Guttuso,' Botta said with a serious face.

'A forgery?'

'The guy who bought it thinks it's real.'

'And who's the lucky man?'

'A Milanese industrialist.'

'Then it's not a crime,' said Bordelli, taking a long draught of wine. It didn't bother him at all to know that rich Milanese businessmen were buying fake Guttusos.

'Who's the brilliant counterfeiter?' he asked.

'You're looking at him.'

'You?'

'*Mwah* . . . What's so strange about that?'

'I didn't know you knew how to draw.'

'I even had a show once, at the Gorgona prison.'

'I'll bet you can also play the piano and write sonnets.'

'I've never written any poetry, but I can scrape a fiddle a little, given half a chance . . . Still hungry, Inspector?'

'I'm in your hands.'

'I'll be right back,' said Botta, heading off to the kitchen.

He returned with a frying pan full of sausages and beans, and they had no choice but to uncork another bottle of wine. They recounted to each other what they'd done during the day. Botta had helped a family clean all the mud out of their house, letting his own flat slide for the moment. Towards evening he'd queued up for water, and then gone out in search of food to eat.

At last they finished their meal. They were dead tired but didn't feel like going to bed just yet. So they spread out on the sofa with their *biscottini* and *vin santo*. In the half-light, the silhouette of the lifeless television made a sorry sight. Bordelli knew he stank and was dreaming of a nice warm shower.

'Now you can tell me,' said Botta.

'Tell you what?'

'Why you were looking for me . . .'

'It doesn't matter any more, as I said.'

'If you don't tell me, I won't be able to sleep,' said Botta, turning the tables on him.

Bordelli sighed. 'Well, I wanted you to open a door for me.'

'For a change . . .'

'If you're looking for bread, you go to the baker's, no?'

'Is it related to the case of the murdered boy?' Ennio asked. Bordelli nodded.

'It was my last chance to follow some sort of lead, some sort of clue . . . if it really existed at all. But we'll never know.'

'And where's this door?'

'Near Piazza Beccaria, but the flood made sure it was entirely smashed in.'

'Too bad . . .' said Botta, disappointed. It gave him great pleasure to pick locks on behalf of the state.

'Don't worry, Ennio, you'll see, sooner or later I'll need you again,' said Bordelli, smiling wearily. They carried on chatting, nibbling biscotti and drinking *vin santo*. Jumping from one subject to another, they ended up talking about women. Bordelli still had his mind on 'his' salesgirl, but made no mention of her. Ennio, on the other hand, opened up and told him about his most recent love affair with a blonde of about forty who worked as a cashier in a supermarket. He loved her to death, and she likewise seemed properly smitten. In short, it was all going swimmingly, but then the blonde had started complaining a little, saying they weren't meant to be together, they were too different from each other . . . they didn't understand each other . . . something was missing . . .

'The usual rubbish women say when they want to dump you.'

'Don't I know . . .'

'At any rate, she left me high and dry, the slut,' Botta concluded, refilling his glass.

'Try not to think about it, Ennio,' said Bordelli, who felt consoled by their common fate.

Every so often the candle flames started flickering, then a moment later they were straight as arrows again. Sip by sip Bordelli and Botta ended up telling each other their childhood memories. Ennio drew his words out slowly, staring at the ceiling with eyes half closed and a smile on his lips.

'The first time my father went to jail it was for dealing in contraband cigarettes. I was twelve. Since my mother wasn't able to put food on the table, I ended up in a boys' school run by nuns. Call them women if you want, but the prettiest one had a moustache worthy of a *carabiniere*. And they ate like pigs and then would make us do the washing up. Those brides of Jesus were all in love with Mussolini, every last one of them. Pray for the Duce, they would say . . . The Duce has saved Italy from the heathen communists and brought us peace. And they were obsessed with our willies. If you happened to touch your willy by accident – you know, say with your hand in your pocket – there was hell to pay. They'd drag you into a room, hold your wicked hand up in the air, and then lash it ten times with a little switch. You must never touch yourself down there, they would say, with their eyes big and round, if you touch yourself there you will go blind and be paralysed. And after the punishment they would bless you with a disgusted look on their faces. Then, one fine day, I went into the bathroom and found the Mother Superior . . . well, helping a friend of mine pee. I learned a lot during those years, a lot about the way the world works.'

They each lit another cigarette, and Bordelli tried to remember something from when he was twelve. Then a Sunday afternoon in the house on Viale Volta came back to him.

'All they were talking about on the radio was this blessed March on Rome, which had just happened the day before. Normally my father was a relaxed sort of chap, but that day it was as though he'd stuck two fingers into an electrical outlet. "Thank God for the Duce," he would say, taking a swig of grappa each time. My mother instead kept wandering about the house incessantly making the sign of the cross and muttering prayers. "What's got into you?" my father kept saying irritatedly. "I don't like him," she would whisper dramatically. "What don't you like?" my father roared. She would shrug and simply say, "I don't like him, I don't like him," and then resume her prayers. It took those prayers twenty years to reach God's ears,' Bordelli said by way of conclusion, smiling.

'Apparently Mussolini's curses were more persuasive,' Botta commented, emptying his glass in a single gulp. Then he stood up, put his hands on his hips, thrust out his lower lip and started springing up and down on his heels with eyes bulging.

'Fellow Italians! . . . Nincompoops on land, on the seas, and in the air! Blackshirts of idiocy and conformism! Men, women, children, grandparents, aunties, whores, dogs, cats, pimps, sheep and pigs of Italy, of the empire and the kingdom of Pinocchio! Lend me your ears! The hour of destiny chimes in the basements of our glorious Fatherland! The hour of *ir-re-vo-ca-ble* decisions!'

'You know, you really do look like the old fathead, come to think of it,' said Bordelli, amused. Botta carried on bouncing about, wild-eyed, fists pressed into his hips, talking in sharp cadences like the real Mussolini.

'There is only one watchword, imperative and binding for

all, flying overhead and already lighting up hearts from the Ponte di Mezzo to Coverciano: buy! And buy we will, to usher in at last a long period of debt for Italy, Europe, the world . . .!' And he imitated the roar of the crowd as it called out, '*Du-ce, Du-ce, Du-ce* . . .'

Then he dropped back down on the sofa and emptied the remains of the bottle into the two glasses.

'At last a sensible speech from the Duce,' Bordelli said, smiling.

Having polished off the wine, they moved on to the grappa, still travelling through time and coasting on memories. Ennio started telling the story of something that had happened to him one Sunday in August ten years ago, on the hill of Pian dei Giullari.

'It was hot as hell. Just blinking made you sweat. The Arno was so low it looked like a trickle of piss. Late one night I broke into a villa, certain that nobody was there. As I went down the corridor, I suddenly noticed light under a half-closed door. I turned off my torch and approached. Looking into the room, I saw a man sitting behind a large desk, staring into space. He was about fifty years old, had almost no hair, and was rather fat. He was sighing deeply and every so often ran a hand over his face. He looked desperate. I just stood there watching, wondering how a moneybags like him could be so unhappy. What, had he run out of champagne? Maybe the new Porsche hadn't arrived yet? Maybe the taxman had found out he was taking his money to Switzerland? I had no sympathy whatsoever for him. In fact, I laughed hard deep inside. Then the man suddenly looked down, opened a drawer, took out an enormous pistol and stuck the barrel in his mouth. It made my blood run cold. I waited to hear the blast and see his brain spattered on the wall . . . But then I pushed open the door and dashed into the room, screaming for him to stop. He spat out the gun and looked at me as if he'd seen a ghost. He stuttered and asked me who I was, then pointed the trembling pistol at me. I practically shat my pants for fear, but I remained calm.

I just sat down in front of the desk and crossed my legs. Tapping my fingers on the desk I said I was his guardian angel and asked him why he wanted to kill himself. He finally lowered the pistol and laid it down on the desk. My wife has another man, he whispered. Is that any reason to kill yourself? I asked, smiling. He smiled back, but it was frightening. She's doing it with a worker from my factory, he said. It was the fear of ridicule that tormented him. The humiliation of having his wife cheat on him with a man of lower rank. Don't you have anything strong to drink? I asked. He stood up, staggering, and went out of the room, and I took advantage of his absence to take the gun and put it in my pocket. He returned with a bottle and two glasses. He'd saved her from the gutter, he said, had made her a lady, covered her with jewels and furs, but she'd remained a scullery maid, always chasing after lower-class cocks, a communist . . . To make a long story short, we got drunk and carried on talking about his sweet wife all night. By the end we were laughing like two fools and calling each other by our first names. At daybreak I said I was going home to bed, but he begged me to stay and filled my glass again. He kept on talking about his wife, giggling in the naughtiest way. He said he'd never had so much fun in his life. I was so drunk that I fell asleep like a rock, right in the chair. When I woke up I had a headache and a terrible crick in my neck. The man was gone. I called his name, but he didn't answer. I patted my pocket, worried, but the gun was still there. So I started looking for him around the house, and finally I found him. He was sprawled on the floor of a luxurious bathroom in a pool of blood. He'd stabbed himself in the neck with a pair of scissors . . .'

Bordelli woke up in his bed, emerging slowly from a tiring, anguishing dream in which he'd done nothing but wander aimlessly through a vast, transparent palace full of people, going up and down stairs and corridors, through rooms large and small that were never the right room. His muscles ached. Without lifting his head from the pillow he saw the daylight filtering through the slats of the shutters. It was very cold. He glanced over at the alarm clock. Ten-twenty. He'd gone to bed past four o'clock, bringing the last inch of candle with him. He vaguely remembered accompanying Ennio to the so-called guest room, a square space crammed with depressing furniture he'd inherited from some old aunts.

He heard the sound of a powerful engine in the street and, defying his headache, summoned the strength to go and look out of the window. An amphibious army vehicle was passing at a walking pace, forcing its way through the wrecked cars and tree trunks, continually stopping to distribute emergency provisions. Other soldiers busied themselves removing animal carcasses, loading them on to a small truck. The street was already teeming with men and women hard at work removing debris from homes and shops and hoping to find things worth salvaging. About a foot and a half above their heads, the black band of heating oil was beginning to dry. Nauseating smells filled the air.

Bordelli dragged himself into the kitchen and made coffee with Botta's water. Just last Saturday he'd cursed the gas cylinder to the darkest circle of hell when it had run out. Now, of course, it was full, thanks to the gasman, who'd come by barely a week ago.

He turned on the transistor radio and heard the tail end of a news report. The Gavinana district was still flooded, and in the countryside around the city many people were still stranded on rooftops, awaiting rescue. President Saragat was supposed to visit Florence that morning to take stock of the situation in person.

There weren't any clean espresso cups so he drank his coffee from a glass, staring at the blue sky through the window. He went into the bathroom and, pouring a few drops of water at a time into the basin, tried to wash himself. He shaved, rinsed his face, washed his neck, chest, arms and feet as best he could. Then he put on a clean set of clothes, two pairs of socks, and pulled his rubber boots back on.

He heard snoring at the end of the hallway, and went and poked his head into the spare room. Ennio was sleeping with his mouth open and arms spread out like Christ on the cross. Bordelli gently closed the door again and went back to the kitchen. He wrote a note: *I've gone out and don't know when I'll be back. Make yourself at home. If you go out, please be sure to lock the door, as the world is full of thieves.*

It looked like one of those notes his mother used to tape on to the mirror in the entrance hall when she would slip out on tiptoe to go to mass on Sunday mornings. He placed the piece of paper well within view, next to the espresso pot. Then he put on his coat and went out. Splashing around in the oily muck, he headed for Piazza Tasso, passing silent people busy sorting out wreckage and rubbish. A boy holding a mattress over his head was trying to manoeuvre into a doorway and finally succeeded. The old lady with the grocery shop in Piazza Piattellina was whimpering like a wounded animal, emptying her shop of the last rotten remains.

The minute he got into the squad car he lit a cigarette. The Viali were just as clogged as the day before, if not more so. The only hope was to go through the centre of town. He flashed his badge to the soldiers on guard and they let him through. He'd never taken out his badge so many times as in the past few days.

He rolled along at a snail's pace, slipping and sliding through the slime. A number of streets were blocked by debris, but in the end he managed to cross the Arno by way of the Ponte Vespucci. On the streets in the centre of town, men in overalls were busy working on telephone exchanges and electrical transformers. Young people of both sexes were helping out with brooms and mops, emptying out houses and shops and piling rubbish on to the pavements. Students with rucksacks walked about in small groups, and there were many longhairs about.

Bordelli came to Piazza del Duomo, where a flood-damaged pharmacy had already miraculously reopened. He saw soldiers in front of the Baptistery door, protecting Ghiberti's panels, which had fallen off and were lying in the sludge. An elderly man was feeding pigeons on the steps in front of the church.

He turned down Via Martelli. When he was in front of the Prefecture, a young *carabiniere* turned and gestured for him to stop, then turned his back to him again. Bordelli was about to get out and ask him what was happening, but there was no need. Seconds later, a military jeep ridiculously crammed with people came out of the great door of Palazzo Medici-Ricciardi, followed by an RAI van full of television cameras. There must have been about fifteen people in the jeep, most of them standing, with the deputy mayor actually on the footboard, hanging on to the wing mirror with both hands. Bordelli realised the reason for all the hoopla when he recognised President Saragat and Mayor Bargellini next to the *carabiniere*, squeezed in by all the other people. Among the people standing he managed just in time to see the prefect, Commissioner Inzipone and a few other bigwigs whose names escaped him. He followed the grotesque caravan in his rear-view mirror as it headed towards Piazza del Duomo. Bargellini and the prefect would have sufficed to act as guides, but apparently nobody wanted to miss that Sunday-morning spin in the president's jeep.

He continued on down Via Cavour, and in Piazza San Marco he bought the day's edition of *La Nazione* from an old woman who'd set up a small wooden table in the mud.

A DISASTER WITHOUT PRECEDENT IN THE CITY'S HISTORY
FLORENCE DEVASTATED BY THE ARNO
CALM AMID THE TRAGEDY

He tossed the newspaper on to the passenger seat and drove off. A short while later he pulled up in the courtyard of police headquarters. There was less confusion than the day before. Mugnai told him the commissioner was looking for him, and Bordelli shrugged. He had no desire to see the man. He found Piras in the radio room, hollow-eyed and dishevelled.

'Did you get any sleep?' he asked him.

'I got enough, Inspector,' said Piras. 'On the night of the fourth I tried to phone you several times.'

'I wasn't feeling well and unplugged the telephone.'

'So much the better for you. It was a hellish night.'

'Your true love is lucky she lives in Via Trieste,' said Bordelli, referring to Piras's Sicilian girlfriend. He didn't stay long in the radio room. He wasn't cut out for sedentary lines of work. He would rather go to the worst-hit areas, scouting out potential emergencies.

He went out of the station again, got into the 1100 and headed for the centre of town, an unlit cigarette dangling from his lips. He parked in Via del Proconsolo and continued on foot, walking through crowds rummaging through smelly debris. People everywhere were muttering the same things. I have nothing left, I've lost everything, What will I do now? An elderly woman was whimpering that all she had remaining was her pension of fifteen thousand lire.

In Piazza San Firenze the muck was still deep, and the going was slow. A skinny little dog was hopping around in the mud, looking scared. The courthouse had been visited by the Arno, and the staircase in front was lined with young men and women passing large mud-covered folders to one another.

He turned on to Borgo dei Greci, leaning against the wall to keep from slipping. An old woman had lowered a basket on a rope from her window and a lad was filling it with bundles. A slender man with a pained expression was walking slowly with his head down and his trousers rolled up to his knees, splashing about in the mud.

'I lost my grandmother's ring . . . if anyone finds it, it's mine . . . it's got a diamond this big . . . it's a memento of my late grandmother,' he whined, as false as Judas. The people around him were giving him dirty looks and shaking their heads as they carried on with their labours.

Bordelli then went down Via dei Neri and saw Rosa from afar, made-up and well coiffed as always, sweeping away the mud together with the other flood victims.

'*Et tu, Rosa?*' he said, grabbing her arm.

'Argh! . . . Oh my God, you scared me!' said Rosa, a hand on her chest. Bordelli brought his mouth to her ear.

'You look fabulous even in the mud,' he whispered, ignoring the others' curious glances. Rosa blushed and giggled. At that moment a hunchback not more than four and a half feet tall walked by, and a big strapping lad leaned on his spade and turned to him.

'Hey, hunchback, is it true you've got a hump on your cock as well?' he called out, and everyone laughed. The hunchback turned round and looked at him.

'Damn, I told your mamma not to tell anyone!' he said, and everyone laughed even harder. The hulking youth merely glared at the hunchback as he hobbled away through the mud, and didn't have the courage to say anything else.

'Serves him right,' Rosa whispered with a titter.

Bordelli gave her a kiss on the cheek and continued his rounds. He was wandering randomly, without any precise destination. He wended his way through the wrecked cars in Via de' Benci and came out on the Lungarno. The river was calm and low, a pleasant little torrent flowing gracefully towards the Tyrrhenian Sea. It hardly seemed possible that just a few hours earlier . . .

He took a left turn in the direction of the Biblioteca

Nazionale. The parapet in Piazza dei Cavalleggeri had collapsed and the area had been cordoned off. He flashed his badge and was let through. Young volunteers had come in a flurry from all over Italy and the world and were still at work. There were even some children among them. They were passing to one another great tomes dripping with slime and then loading them on to army lorries. They were covered with mud from head to toe, and at times it was difficult to tell the men from the women.

He turned back, and after crossing the Ponte alle Grazie took a left. In Via dei Renai the mud was still nearly knee-high. Out of habit, he looked up to see the line left by the heating oil. The water had risen above the first floor. Together with Santa Croce, it was surely the lowest-lying part of Florence.

He turned the corner and come out in front of the church of San Niccolò. People from the neighbourhood were still emptying houses and shops of every manner of now-useless objects. Broken furniture, tables, chairs, bookcases, everything made of wood was being piled up outside Porta San Miniato. A man with big blue eyes ringed with fatigue and sparkling with irony was struggling to drag a pew out of the church with the help of a skinny lad staggering on his feet.

'Need a hand?' Bordelli asked, drawing near.

'A crane would be nice,' said the man.

The inspector helped them carry the pew up the incline. The blue-eyed man had a round white collar under his jacket, and Bordelli realised he was a priest. They laid the pew down beside the other wooden scraps.

'It's for making a fire at night. We're all sleeping outdoors,' said the priest. Then he introduced himself. He was called Don Baldesi, the local parish priest. Bordelli shook his hand.

'Pleased to meet you, I'm Inspector Bordelli, police. D'you have any urgent needs I could help you with?'

'We've already been to Campo di Marte several times, but it's never enough. Bread, water, blankets, medicine, we need it all.'

'I'll try to have a lorry come round as soon as I can.'

'I'll ask Saint Peter to shave off a few weeks in Purgatory for you.'

'You probably shouldn't bother, I may be going straight to hell,' Bordelli said with a smile. And he started walking towards the church with the priest beside him, already thinking he would continue on foot towards Campo di Marte . . .

At that moment the person he least expected to see came out of a building, and he felt his heart leap. Assisted by a tall young man with a handsome, shadowy face, the salesgirl from Via Pacinotti was carrying a mud-soaked mattress out into the street. She was wearing jeans, rubber boots and a heavy, over-sized jacket. He walked past her, but the girl remained unaware of the magnetic wave enveloping her and did not bother to look his way.

When he got to the church, the inspector felt weak at the knees, like a boy experiencing his first crush. He turned round to look at her again, but she was gone. He told Don Baldesi that he would go at once to Campo di Marte to look for food and medicine, then said goodbye and left without turning round. The minute he had turned the corner, he lit a cigarette. He was so excited that he no longer felt tired. Once again fate had pulled out another surprise for him. But he still didn't know whether it was a gift or a taunt. Who the hell was the shadowy young man? Her boyfriend? Better not think too much about it. At fifty-six years of age he could hardly compete with a handsome lad like that.

Along the Lungarno he took a right turn, walking towards Piazza Ferrucci and watching the students hard at work in front of the Biblioteca Nazionale. Lucky blighters, he thought. Young, beautiful, heroic. They had their whole lives before them, with all their hopes and dreams. Not like him, who felt like an old man no longer able to believe in illusions. All he had to look forward to was retirement, filling the long hours, dropping in at police headquarters to visit his busy colleagues. He'd better hurry up and decide to move to the country, so he could hoe the vegetable garden and raise chickens, and take long walks in the woods.

He crossed the San Niccolò bridge and continued down Viale Amendola, trying to keep his balance in the mud. It was as if he were walking through a car cemetery. He passed in front of the Cristallo, the ancient temple of the Rivista, the famous variety show, awakening prehistoric memories of his adolescence. Things were very different when he was young. Mussolini shouting from balconies, the Fascist Youth organisations, crystal radio sets, the empire, the African war, autarky, the songs about perfidious Albion . . .

After Piazza Beccaria he turned down Viale Mazzini, walking its entire length all the way to Via Mannelli. He clambered up the footbridge over the railway and then back down, and arrived at Campo di Marte out of breath. It was Sunday, but a number of grocery shops were open and people had formed long queues along the pavements. In the general chaos Bordelli presented himself to the camp commander and organised for a truckload of foodstuffs and medical supplies to be delivered to San Niccolò.

They unloaded the lorry in front of the Osteria Fuori Porta and, with the help of Don Baldesi and the students, distributed the contents down to the last bag of salt. The pretty salesgirl was nowhere to be seen, nor was the young man who'd been with her. Bordelli told the soldiers he wouldn't be returning to the stadium with them, then watched the lorry drive away up the hill. While helping the priest carry another few pews out of the church, he kept looking around in the hope of seeing the girl again. Don Baldesi was telling him naughty priest jokes in a low voice, his large, kind eyes sparkling with irony. After the fourth pew, he wiped the sweat from his forehead.

'I'm going to go and lie down for half an hour,' he said, exhausted. Since the night of the flood he'd slept barely two hours.

'I'll stay and lend a hand,' said Bordelli.

'Are you sure you're a police inspector?' the priest asked, two deep furrows in his brow.

'It's my only flaw.'

'I've got many – that's why I'm a priest,' said Don Baldesi with smiling eyes. He stood up unsteadily and disappeared into the shadows of a broad doorway.

Bordelli asked for a broom and started sweeping away the mud alongside the others. He was thinking of the salesgirl and felt like a fool, but he simply couldn't leave before he'd seen her again. He didn't have anything in particular in mind. He just wanted her to recognise him, look her in the eye, and see how she reacted.

After an hour of this, his back was a disaster and his hands were blistered, but he put his head down and carried on. There seemed to be no end to the slime. He helped a woman empty out her grocery shop. It was so sad to throw all that food out into the street, prosciutti, salami, cheese, pasta, crushed tins, boxes covered with oil . . .

Looking up from his labours for the hundredth time, he saw her at last. She was in front of the same doorway as before, sweeping the mud together with the shadowy youth, bantering with him and laughing. A beautiful couple, no doubt about it. One more beautiful than the other.

He was eyeing her surreptitiously, heart thumping in his ears. She looked beautiful even as she was, shabbily dressed, covered in mud, hair gathered behind her head. She had a light, graceful way of moving, natural and elegant . . . A pretty face alone didn't make a beautiful girl. Even a gorgeous body wasn't enough. You needed all the rest: the gaze, the voice, the smile, the bearing, the scent . . .

After a spell the lad went into the building, and she was left alone to sweep her broom across the cobblestones. Bordelli plucked up his courage and went over to her with a confident air. The girl was looking down and didn't see him approach. Noticing him suddenly in front of her, she frowned.

'Don't you recognise me?' Bordelli asked, feeling supremely embarrassed.

'Yes, but I can't quite remember . . .'

'I bought a blouse in your shop a few days ago.'

'Oh, right . . . though it's not my shop,' she said. She wasn't exactly aloof, but neither was she jumping for joy.

'I came to lend Don Baldesi a hand,' Bordelli lied.

'Don Baldesi has been wonderful,' the girl said.

'He's gone off to rest for a little while . . .'

'He's been working like a dog, poor thing.'

'Do you live here?'

'On the first floor. Luckily I managed to save a few things in time.'

'This mud is a nightmare.'

'We just have to be patient,' the girl said with a shrug.

The conversation was lagging, and Bordelli tried desperately to think of something intelligent to say, or something earth-shatteringly witty. He felt awkward and indiscreet and was waiting for her suddenly to say goodbye, fearing to see her eyes show the mild impatience of someone who is in a hurry or merely wants to be alone. *Come on, old fart, say something to make her laugh . . .* But what, indeed, was the use? In American movies there was always an old man who made the women laugh, though they certainly didn't fall in love with him for it. *It doesn't matter, take the plunge anyway. The worst that could happen is that you'll seem ridiculous.*

'Could I say something?' He faltered. What kind of way of talking was that? The girl gave him a perplexed look, waiting for his revelation.

'You're . . . such a nice girl . . .' he said, smiling stupidly.

'Thanks,' she whispered indifferently. And her eyes seemed to be saying: Is that all? God only knew how many other men had said the same thing to her, and more. Better to beat a hasty retreat, but with dignity.

'Well, I'm glad to have seen you again,' he said, giving a slight bow.

At that moment the shadowy beau appeared at the window. Seeing the stranger, he politely nodded in greeting.

'Chicca, I've dismantled it. Come and give me a hand,' he said.

'I'll be right there,' she replied, propping her broom against the wall. The lad disappeared inside. He didn't seem the least bit jealous. Indeed, how could he be, for Christ's sake?

'Your boyfriend seems nice,' said Bordelli, ready to leave. She started laughing, and her face seemed to light up.

'He's my brother,' she said, her small white teeth gleaming between her lips.

'You don't look very much alike,' Bordelli muttered, trying to mask his delight. But he realised at once that it wasn't any cause for rejoicing. Just because the lad was her brother, it didn't mean she didn't have a boyfriend.

'Some people say we're two peas in a pod,' she said.

'Chicca's just a nickname, I guess . . .'

'The family's always called me that. My real name is Eleonora.'

'And mine is Franco . . . If you like, I could give your brother a hand myself,' Bordelli suggested.

'Oh, thank you. There's a bed that has to be brought down and thrown away.'

'I'm happy to oblige.'

He went into the building and climbed two flights of stairs. After he had helped the brother bring down the dismantled bed, they went and put the parts on the pile of firewood. Eleonora asked them both whether they'd like a cup of coffee and then went upstairs to make it. They drank it quickly while standing on the pavement, then got back to work, speaking little and sweating a lot.

The Osteria Fuori Porta opened its doors at two o'clock. They bought some prosciutto and ate it with the bread from Campo di Marte. Before picking up their brooms again, they allowed themselves a glass of wine.

Don Baldesi returned with eyes puffy from sleep and resumed working alongside the others. Bordelli was always gravitating towards Eleonora, and every so often they would exchange a few words, without stopping their sweeping. Little by little they got to know each other, and before long Bordelli made an investigative comment.

'In that get-up your own boyfriend probably wouldn't even recognise you.'

'Why don't you speak more clearly?' she said, without looking at him.

'I don't understand . . .' he stammered hypocritically.

'Are you trying to find out if I have a boyfriend? Why don't you just ask me directly?'

'No, no . . . I . . . It was just to make conversation,' said Bordelli, blushing.

'Actually I have three boyfriends,' the girl said with a charming sort of sneer.

'Ah, well . . .'

'It's boring with just one,' she added.

The inspector took a few steps back, continuing to sweep the muck with an indifferent air. He even started whistling a song by Celentano, to show her that he wasn't the least bit troubled. A couple of minutes later the girl came up to him.

'It's not true, you know,' she said smiling.

'What's not true?'

'I don't have any boyfriends.'

'You don't?'

'I had one until a few days ago, but I dumped him.'

'At this point you also have to tell me why,' Bordelli said nonchalantly.

'I don't know . . . I got bored . . .'

'Had you been together for a long time?' Now he really did want to know.

'For ever . . . Almost a year,' she said in all seriousness. Bordelli forced a smile. For him a year was like the twinkling of an eye.

They worked until the last moment of daylight. When they couldn't see any longer, flood victims and students came together outside the San Niccolò gate, and Don Baldesi lit a big bonfire from the scraps of wood that had been piled up. They all sat down in a circle and began to eat, listening to the news reports over a transistor radio. There was yet another appeal concerning the inmates who had escaped from the Murate prison. More than fifty were still at large, and citizens were asked to report any suspicious individuals they might see.

The light of the fire cast a red glow on people's faces. It was bitterly cold, and many had wrapped themselves in blankets. The atmosphere was peaceful and almost light-hearted. The salesgirl had sat down between two young students who were talking to her non-stop, almost vying to see which one could make a bigger fool of himself. Bordelli had sat down on the opposite side of the human circle so that he could see her from the front, and every so often they would exchange a glance. When the cigarettes came out, he lit one too.

A while later a number of men went out on patrol, armed with large sticks, to discourage looters. A lad with long curly hair pulled out a guitar and started singing a very sad song in English.

'Why don't you sing us something by Gianni Morandi?' a woman asked. The long-haired lad ignored her and kept on singing his dirges. Don Baldesi was nodding off, chin on his chest, but every so often he would wake up and look around as though dazed. Bordelli stared at the flames, pretending to look thoughtful while secretly spying on the girl. He would have stuck his hand in the fire for a girl like her, like Gaius Mucius Scaevola.[42] When their eyes happened to meet, he would look down . . . But what if he stared straight at her instead? What would happen? He looked up again and waited for her to look at him in turn. He didn't have to wait long. They gazed into each other's eyes for a very long time, and he was the first to look away. Finally he couldn't stand sitting down any longer and stood up.

'I'm going to go and baste the lobster,' he said, and everyone laughed. He went up Via di Belvedere with his hands in his pockets. A moon shaped like a lemon wedge cast a placid pallor over the olive trees lined up along the wall.

His feet were cold and aching. The steep climb had him panting, but he didn't feel like slowing his pace. Calm down, old man. You're no longer a kid, you can't be wasting your time with this kind of crap . . . Stop fantasising and go home.

He made it up to the Forte Belvedere, legs buckling and out of breath. He stood there gazing at the dark silhouette of Costa San Giorgio, waiting for his heart to settle down. What the hell was happening? Nothing. Nothing was happening. He'd merely had the pleasure of talking to a beautiful girl . . . and would do best to get her immediately out of his head, or he was setting himself up for a fall. A good night's sleep was in order, and tomorrow would be another day.

Heaving a long, dramatic sigh, he headed back towards the bivouac of flood victims. He felt befuddled, but it wasn't only fatigue. He had to fight the absurd hopes that were insinuating themselves into his fantasies. Never had he felt so old as at that moment. Not to mention awkward, clumsy and even a little ridiculous. Like a bear chasing after a colourful little butterfly. The wisest thing was to say goodnight to the gang and go home to bed.

When he reached the bottom of the hill he saw the cause of his tribulations and bit his lip. The guitar was no longer playing. Some people had lain down to sleep, while others had formed little groups and were whispering in front of the smoking embers. Don Baldesi was snoring, wrapped in a blanket. Eleonora's hair was down. She was easily the most beautiful woman in the world. She was listening without much interest to the chatter of the two students, who were feasting their eyes on her. When she noticed Bordelli approaching, she looked at him with a hint of a smile on her lips.

'Did you find the big bad wolf?' she asked in a whisper.

'Just the blue fairy.'

'It might have been a witch.'

'I've always liked witches,' Bordelli said suggestively.

The two students seemed rather irked by the Methuselah's intrusion and were waiting impatiently for him to leave. The girl paid no attention to them and continued talking to Bordelli.

'Is it true you're a police inspector?'

'Who was the spy?'

'So it's true . . . I wouldn't have thought . . .' she said, looking him up and down. Her student friends didn't appreciate the news and looked quite put out. Bordelli stuck a cigarette between his lips.

'But they say you can spot a cop from a mile away.'

'I never can.'

'I have many other qualities,' said Bordelli, in a purposely paternal tone. He didn't want to seem like a hopeless suitor, like the two poor students.

'What's your area of expertise?' the girl asked.

'Murder.'

'Really? And when somebody is killed, you go and see the corpse?'

'I have to, I can't help it,' said Bordelli, shocked and pleased at all this interest on her part. The girl stood up and approached him, ignoring the murmur of disappointment from the lovesick youths.

'That's terrible,' she said.

'Somebody's got to do it, if the killer's ever going to get caught.'

They started walking downhill, side by side.

'Doesn't it ever upset you?' the girl asked, a furrow in her brow.

'The war was an excellent training course,' said Bordelli, playing the card of the man of experience. How could two little students ever compete with him, a sapper from the San Marco battalion?

'I was born during the war and don't remember anything,' said Eleonora.

'You're very lucky,' Bordelli whispered.

The girl stopped in front of the door to her building. In the wan moonlight her face seemed to emerge from the darkness.

'Are you married?' she asked, to his surprise.

'No.'

'Were you ever married?'

'No.'

'Then you must be a womaniser.'

'I wish I was, but I fall in love every time,' Bordelli had the courage to say, gazing straight into her eyes. They looked at each other in silence for an eternal second, and then the girl shrugged slightly.

'I suppose I'll go to bed.'

'In a flooded house?'

'I sleep on the third floor, with an elderly couple.'

'What about your brother?' He was trying to keep her for another second or two.

'Antonio's staying with my parents, but I'd rather stay here, alone . . . All right, I have to go. I'm exhausted.'

'Goodnight.'

'Will you come back and see us tomorrow?' she asked, again to his surprise.

'If I can get free . . .'

'G'night,' she said, then disappeared through the doorway, lighting her way with a pocket torch.

After a few minutes of bewilderment, Bordelli headed back towards the centre of town, sloshing through the mud, feeling light as a feather. He saw the men on patrol, moving through the narrow, dark streets with their heads down and clubs in their hands.

What was it Amelia had said? *You will meet a beautiful, dark young woman, but it won't last because something horrible will come between you . . .* Those were more or less her words. But there was a positive side to it. For something to come between them, they had to be together first. But was Eleonora really the *dark young woman* of the tarot?

Coming out on the Lungarno, he cast a glance at the young people still hard at work at the Biblioteca Nazionale under the glare of a powerful floodlight. He felt young and beautiful, just like them, a youth of fifty-six. He had to restrain himself from whistling a tune. He crossed the bridge in long strides, then continued down Via de' Benci, walking past the human shadows wandering silently between the heaps of debris. Farther ahead he saw a white light and heard a rumble of motors. In Santa Croce, too, they were working hard with the help of the army's floodlights.

The devastation around him was powerless to change his mood. He wended his way through the wrecked cars as if in a flowering meadow. As egotistical as anyone in love, he blessed the flood that had allowed him to meet Eleonora. The whole city had to be sacrificed so that they could find each other . . . Christ, what bollocks. He'd better curb his enthusiasm. It was possible the girl had chatted with an ageing police inspector merely out of boredom, at the end of a day spent sweeping mud. He decided to suspend judgement and sleep on it.

As soon as he got into the car he contacted police head-quarters, but there wasn't much news of importance. The requests for help kept coming in, especially from the country-side. There had been a few false alarms about the escaped convicts, and more than a few reports of looting.

He arrived home after a roundabout journey made necessary by all the flood-damaged cars and heaps of rubbish blocking the way. On the kitchen table he found some bundles of food, mineral water and a note from Botta:

I've found a bed at the house of a very kind lady. I couldn't refuse. If you need me, I'll be at home during the day, emptying out my private swimming pool, and if I'm not there, please leave word at the Bar del Chiodo. If it's urgent, you can call on me at the home of the kind lady . . .

An address followed.

In the bathroom there were three jerrycans full of water and a bottle of mineral water with another note under it: *Use this for brushing your teeth.* The toilet bowl was almost clean. Ennio must have poured a fair amount of water into it, and Bordelli sent him thanks in his mind. If only all ex-cons were like him . . .

He brushed his teeth and went straight to bed, pulling five blankets over him. He turned off the torch. He didn't even have the courage to read a page or two of Herodotus. In the total darkness he thought again of the girl and the words they had said to each other. He tried to interpret every phrase, to find hidden meanings in her tone of voice, or in a blinking eye

. . . And what about that long look she gave him? And when she curled her lip? However painful it was, he couldn't interrupt the game. Despite his fatigue, it took him a very long time to fall asleep.

At dawn he was already on his feet, ready to face a new day. He smelled like a beast; Rosa was right. He had to find a way to wash. He put two large pots of water on the stove to boil, then poured them into the bathtub and added some cold water. He tried his best to remove three days' worth of filth, without forgetting to lather up his head with shampoo. Then he shaved and slapped his cheeks with Aqua Velva. He felt reborn. Putting on what he considered his dressiest clothes, he returned to the mirror, boots on his feet. He wasn't exactly a raw youth any more, but he wasn't really so old, either. Nor was he a fashion plate. The only problem was that he could stand to lose a few pounds. He might not be as handsome as Mastroianni, but he had a certain charm . . .

All at once he felt like such a fool that he burst out laughing. A woman's smile was all it had taken to turn an ugly duckling into a preening swan.

Before going out he lifted the telephone receiver to see whether it was working, but it was still silent. He left and went to get the 1100. As soon as he set off, he contacted headquarters as usual, for the latest news. A few of the escaped convicts had been caught, others had turned themselves in at various different police and *carabinieri* stations, but more than forty were still at large. And during the night a number of looters had been arrested after being caught pillaging abandoned homes.

'Commissioner Inzipone's looking for you,' the dispatcher added.

'Don't tell him you heard from me. I'm going straight to Campo di Marte,' said Bordelli, hanging up.

He turned on the transistor radio and laid it down on the seat next to him, waiting for the news report. He recognised the voice of wild woman Rita Pavone, turned up the volume and sang along with her. Along the way he stopped to buy the newspaper and scanned it quickly while sitting in the car:

COUNTING THE DEAD – THE HUNGRY SEEK HELP
SARAGAT AMID THE RUINS OF FLORENCE
THE CITY CRIES FOR WATER AND BREAD

He plunged back into the traffic. As he waited in a jam on the Le Cure viaduct, the news report began. But the radio's batteries were losing power and he could no longer understand anything. He turned it off. At the end of Viale dei Mille he drove past Panerai's butcher shop, which was open and back in business. He caught a glimpse of the butcher inside, attending to customers, and it was like looking into a faraway world. Once the emergency was over, he would take the sordid affair in hand again, even though he was more and more convinced he would never get to the bottom of it.

When he got to the stadium, he put on army overalls and joined a rescue squad that was leaving for the Girone. He didn't want to rush immediately to San Niccolò. It was better to resist for a while. By the time they arrived in the flooded countryside, he was no longer thinking about the girl, and he rolled up his sleeves and got down to work.

They returned to Campo di Marte around two o'clock in the afternoon, all covered in mud. Bordelli took off his dirty overalls and had a bite to eat while sitting on a step alongside some exhausted soldiers. He'd succeeded in not thinking about her for the entire morning, but now he was dying to see her. He lit a cigarette and got into the car. There was the usual traffic on the Viali, but dozens of traffic police and soldiers were keeping a broad lane open in the middle for rescue vehicles and law enforcement to get through. The inspector put his badge on the dashboard and they let him through. In Piazza

Beccaria a number of breakdown lorries were hitching up the damaged cars, under the watchful eyes of the traffic police.

He crossed the Arno, turned on to Via dei Bastioni and then was in the San Niccolò quarter. He parked along the walls and continued on foot. Had he got too dressed up to be trudging about in the muck? Did he look ridiculous? Would Eleonora laugh at him? And what if she was cold and unfriendly instead? What if he didn't find her?

As he drew near he looked around at the groups of people to see whether he could spot her . . . At last he saw her. She was sweeping the street between two young men, but neither of the two was her brother. She was talking and laughing, and he felt a pang of jealousy. What was he imagining? That she would be religiously waiting for him to return? He went up to her with a relaxed demeanour, masking his agitation.

'Good afternoon . . .'

'Hello, Inspector.'

She didn't seem the least bit annoyed, but neither was she jumping for joy. The two lads eyed the intruder with suspicion. Bordelli nodded to them in greeting.

'Can I lend a hand?'

'You can even lend two,' she said, smiling and passing him her broom.

'I'm honoured . . .'

'Treat it well. I need it to fly over the rooftops.'

'Never fear, I have great respect for witches,' said Bordelli, amazed that he could speak with such nonchalance. The girl gave him a wry look.

'I'm going upstairs for a minute,' she said, and ran off.

The inspector was left alone with the two strapping young men. As he carried on sweeping, he moved a few steps away. He could hear them murmuring to each other and pricked up his ears. They were talking about the pretty girl and not refraining from making lewd comments. He pretended not to notice and moved even farther away. He waved at Don Baldesi in the distance. The priest was busy with two other men, emptying out a basement flat with buckets. On the wall of one building was a handwritten sign: *Rheumatism sufferers, try San Niccolò mud. Reasonable prices.*

Eleonora returned after five eternal minutes with another broom in hand. She dropped the two youths and started sweeping alongside Bordelli.

'Did she like the blouse?' she asked, without looking up.

'Very much, but unfortunately I got the size wrong.'

'Too big?'

'Too small.'

'You can exchange it when the shop reopens.'

'Thanks . . .'

'It's not easy to make women happy.'

'I learned how as a little boy, but every now and then I forget.'

'Is she your lover?'

'Just a friend.'

'A special friend?'

'Just a friend . . .'

They continued making small talk and joking around, working all the while. Bordelli was getting carried away making silly remarks that made the girl laugh, feeling more and more handsome. But he was also feeling the thrill of danger. Maybe he was only dreaming. Maybe she just felt like exchanging a few friendly words with someone.

They heard a person moaning and turned round to look. Two men were carrying an elderly woman, using a wardrobe door as a stretcher. The woman had a nasty wound on her shin, the blood dripping on to the mud. Some other people came and helped carry the improvised stretcher up the sloping street. Bordelli propped his broom against the wall and approached to have a look at the injured woman.

'Stop for a second,' he said, taking a clean handkerchief out of his pocket.

'Are you a doctor?' asked one of the stretcher-bearers.

'Police.'

Bordelli knotted the handkerchief about one palm's length above the wound and pulled it tight to block the flow of blood. Without letting the woman see him, he made a gesture to the others to indicate that the bone was broken.

'How did it happen?' he asked the woman.

'I slipped . . . against an iron spike . . .'

'You must take her to the hospital at once. With all this filth about she risks serious infection,' said Bordelli, searching for his car keys.

'Will I lose my leg?' the woman asked, frightened.

'Well, you've got two,' the inspector joked.

'Will they really cut it off?'

'Don't you worry, you'll be walking better than before,' the inspector reassured her with a persuasive tone. He told the men to wait for him in front of the *osteria*, cast a quick glance of goodbye at the salesgirl, then ran off to get the car. The sun was already setting. They laid the woman down on the back seat and put a blanket over her. As soon as Bordelli got into the car, the door on the passenger side opened and the girl got in.

'I'm coming too,' she said.

'As you wish,' said Bordelli, not showing how pleased he was.

They drove up the slope and then turned on to Via dei Bastioni. At each bump in the road, the woman groaned. The girl turned round and started chatting with her to distract her. She even managed to make her laugh.

They took the Viali all the way to the Fortezza da Basso and then went down Via dello Statuto. Bordelli turned to look at the extortionist's closed shop, remembering a proverb his mother used to quote: *He who wants too much gets nothing.* He, too, had to take care not to want too much.

'Thank you . . . thank you so much . . . you're angels, both of you . . .' the woman said between moans.

'Careful what you say, we might give you a knock on the head and steal your watch,' the girl said, laughing.

'I can tell from your eyes that you're a good person . . . like your father here . . .' the woman said, gasping in pain.

Bordelli saw the girl trying not to laugh, and gripped the steering wheel tightly.

'Actually, I'm not her—'

'Come on, Dad,' the girl interrupted.

'What?'

'Try to go a little faster, you always drive at a snail's pace,' she said, struggling to remain serious. Bordelli shook his head lightly and accelerated.

When they got to Careggi hospital, they were let through the blockade outside and parked near Casualty. In the area just outside the entrance, there was a crowd of people awaiting their turn. A few doctors were letting the most serious cases go first, then the elderly, the mothers with children, and pregnant women. Bordelli went to talk to one of the doctors, then walked him over to the car. Moments later two orderlies were carrying the old woman on a stretcher and took her inside.

'Well, that's done,' said Bordelli. ·

'We're a pair of angels, Dad,' the girl said, laughing. Bordelli took it in his stride. They got back into the car and, rolling slowly along, passed through the hospital's exit gate.

'Don't tell me you were offended by my little joke,' the girl said, after a long silence.

'No, no, not at all . . . I was just thinking . . .'

'What about?'

'I couldn't really say, to be honest . . .' Bordelli lied.

'I always know what I'm thinking about.'

'What are you thinking right now?'

'I can't tell you,' she said, staring at the road.

'You're more honest than I am,' Bordelli admitted.

They continued chatting and joking around, but neither suggested they use the informal address.

'Is this radio for talking with headquarters?' she asked.

'With the radio relay system I can talk to all of Italy,' Bordelli lied to impress her. Mostly he was avoiding asking the most important question of all, for fear of the reply. When they were at the tower in Piazza Piave, he summoned his courage.

'It's already dark outside, I guess we can't work any more without light,' he let drop, taking a roundabout approach.

'What we need is a floodlight like that one,' said the girl, gesturing at the beam of light shining down from Piazzale Michelangelo.

'Feel like eating something?' There, he'd managed to say it.

'I could eat a tyre,' she said.

'What do you say we go and get a bite?'

'Where?'

'I was thinking we could go to a restaurant.'

'Dressed like this?'

'What's wrong with that?'

'All right, then . . . Where shall we go?'

By eleven he was already in bed, head buried under the pillow. Herodotus could wait. Never had he felt like such a wreck, not even during the war. His bones were weary and his muscles ached. He felt as if he'd just sparred with Muhammad Ali. And as if that wasn't enough, he was agitated and even a bit frightened. He had a swarm of butterflies in his stomach and kept nervously shuffling his feet between the sheets. All because of the girl . . .

They'd gone to a little restaurant in the Arcetri district south of the city, surrounded by well-dressed people eyeing the two evacuees as if trying to figure out who they were. All the tables were reserved, and so he'd shown his badge to a waiter, asking politely that they not be sent away with empty stomachs. The waiter had almost sprung to attention, and then went and set up a small table in a corner. He even brought a candle, which made the girl laugh. The menu was limited to a few very simple dishes, and they hadn't taken more than a second to decide on their order. A nice plateful of pasta in tomato sauce, roast chicken, baked potatoes and red wine. After several glasses of wine, Bordelli had started talking about the war and, spurred on by the girl's curiosity, recounted some rather macabre stories . . . Like the time in the countryside of Le Marche when he and his men were de-mining a field to allow the armoured Allied troops to pass through, and a trip-wire connected to the ground had set off an anti-tank mine, sending Cavadossi flying through the air in pieces. Bordelli and the others had gone running to look for the human scraps and his identification tag. They'd managed to collect almost all of his remains, except a hand, and had put the pieces of Cavadossi in a sack and closed it with a rope. Only when they'd started heading back to camp had Bordelli found the hand. It was whole, intact, half open, cleanly severed as if by a hatchet. As the sack was already closed, Bordelli wrapped the hand in a handkerchief and put it in his rucksack.

'Good God, that's horrible . . .' she'd said.

They'd sat there for over two hours chatting, still using the polite form of address. Then the weariness of the day began to make itself felt, and after Eleonora's first yawn he asked for the bill. He drove her back to San Niccolò, and she asked him to stop the car at the corner of Via San Salvatore al Monte. He was hoping they might stay a little longer in the car, talking, but she opened the door at once and put one small foot on the ground.

'Leaving so soon?' he'd asked, blushing in the dark.

'I'm bone-tired. Thank you for a lovely evening,' she said, with a smile that looked a little ironic.

'It was a pleasure . . .' he muttered.

He got out to see her to her front door, but she said firmly that it wasn't necessary. She didn't want to be escorted home; there was no danger whatsoever. But the truth was perhaps that she didn't want to be seen with him by the people sleeping outside. What could it mean? Simply that she didn't want others to know her business? Or was she embarrassed of him because he was too old?

They stood face to face in the moonlit darkness, staring at each other in silence. Then she drew near, still smiling ironically . . . her lips parted . . . and at the last moment she took a step back.

'Goodnight,' she'd whispered, then turned and went down the sloping street. He watched her walk away, listening to her footsteps on the cobblestones . . . Was the beautiful Eleonora actually tempted for a moment to kiss him? Or was it only his imagination?

He'd got back in the car, puffed hard on a cigarette, and

gone home without knowing what he should be feeling. Maybe she was just amusing herself at his expense, taking him for a ride, trying to drive him mad, just for the hell of it, for fun, with the blitheness of youth, which often looks a lot like wickedness . . . But if, on the other hand . . . Come on, how could a beautiful girl of twenty-five . . . Although it was true that, sometimes . . . And why else would she have drawn near to him the way she did? In the end it was as if they really had kissed . . . They'd come close, very close . . . Or maybe she was just amusing herself at his expense, taking him for a ride, trying to drive him mad . . .

He was going round and round in circles. It would be better to sleep on the whole question. Thinking with a tired brain doesn't yield good fruit. He tried to occupy his mind by imagining Eleonora sweeping the mud on the street, counting the swipes of the broom . . . one . . . two . . . three . . . four . . . five . . .

He woke up with a start, realising that someone was knocking insistently at the door. It was still night outside. He turned on the torch and looked at the clock. Ten to one. Who the hell could it be? He heard the knocking again. He put both feet on the floor and ran his hands over his face. He felt as if he had spent the day shattering rocks in the hot sun. He went to open the door in his underpants and found a quite tall man standing before him.

'Hello, Inspector, I'm Bruno Arcieri.'

'Arcieri? Didn't we meet a few years ago?'

'In '57, when I came to ask you a favour. Could I come in?'

'Please do . . .'

He flung open the door to let him in and, running his fingers through his hair, gestured to him to follow. He went back to the bedroom and collapsed on the bed. Arcieri stopped at the foot of the bed, still standing and staring at Bordelli with a worried expression.

'Are you unwell?' he asked.

'Aren't they ever going to retire you, Colonel?'

'They're still keeping me on for a spell. I can't see you very well. Are you all right?'

'I'm just a little tired. I've been swimming in this shit for the past three days. Please sit down, Colonel.'

'No, I'd rather stand.'

'As you wish.'

'I have a favour to ask of you, Bordelli.'

'I scarcely imagined you came to chat about the flood . . .'

'It's a very delicate matter.'

'I'm all ears, but first I have to get a few hours' sleep or they'll soon be shipping me off to the madhouse at San Salvi,' said Bordelli, looking for his cigarettes. The colonel sighed.

'You're better at negotiating with Fascists than I am. I always get immediately enraged.'

'Are you kidding me, Colonel?' the inspector asked, smiling.

'Heaven forfend.'

'Still hunting down Fascists?' As Bordelli was lighting the cigarette, Arcieri dropped a small sheet of paper on to the bed.

'An old hand from the Salò days, who may have been chief of the secret service . . .'

'What do you mean, *may have been*?'

'There's no proof, unfortunately, so we can't touch him. But he probably knows some things that could be of use to me. I need to talk to him at once, but he has to be softened up first . . .'

'Why not send one of your own spies?'

'No. This is a personal investigation, Bordelli. Anyway, there's no time left. I can't have people coming up from Rome now. And more importantly, I don't trust anyone.'

'As usual. But what exactly am I supposed to do?'

'Just pay the gentleman a little visit. Find a plausible pretext for questioning him, something innocuous, an administrative check, whatever you can think of. But be sure you frighten him.'

'How much?' asked Bordelli. In the half-light he saw Arcieri smile.

'A lot, as much as possible. I'm sure you can think of something creative. But be quick about it, I have very little time left.'

'Is he one of the bad Fascists?'

'I didn't know there were any good Fascists in your book, Bordelli.'

'Some were just ignorant fools . . .'

He reached out and looked at the sheet that Arcieri had dropped: *Alfonso Gattacci, Via di San Domenico 71/A*. He knew this Fascist. Even personally. And he didn't like him one bit.

'I'll see what I can do,' he said, blowing smoke towards the ceiling.

Arcieri was fretting nervously.

'It's very urgent, Inspector.'

'I can imagine.'

'And I needn't mention how important it is that none of this matter—'

'Nobody will know anything,' the inspector cut him off, sitting up and arranging the pillow behind his head.

'I'm afraid I have to insist, Bordelli. I want you to go there . . . as soon as possible.'

'Of course. But now, if you don't mind, I'd like to get a little sleep.'

'I meant . . . right now, in fact. Every minute is precious,' Arcieri insisted, looking worried.

Bordelli knew the feeling well, having found himself a thousand times in the same situation. Even recently, in the case of the murdered boy. Perhaps it was best to make the anxious colonel happy, though he had no desire to do so. Heaving a sigh of resignation, he got out of bed, grumbling a half-curse. He started to get dressed, taking his clothes from the back of the chair.

'On second thoughts, I suddenly have a keen desire to have a little chat with a Fascist,' he muttered. Arcieri finally smiled. He was still standing at the foot of the bed, not moving, hands in his coat pockets.

'I'll wait for your call at the Prefecture, the number's on that piece of paper. I won't get a wink of sleep tonight. Goodbye, Bordelli.'

'You won't be the only one to go without sleep. There are still tons of mud to be shovelled, and who knows what we'll find beneath it?'

'Everything will go back to the way it was.'

'I wouldn't even bet a bowl of pasta on that,' said the inspector.

Lighting the way with his torch, he showed the colonel to the door. They shook hands, but had nothing more to say to each other. After a last nod Arcieri disappeared down the stairs. Bordelli closed the door and straggled into the kitchen to make coffee. A conversation with a Salò Fascist was the last thing he'd expected to be doing that night. But he'd decided to lend the unbending colonel a hand, and now he almost felt as if he himself couldn't do without it. He trusted Arcieri instinctively. The colonel seemed a survivor from another era, a man of another age. Perhaps he and Arcieri were more similar than at first appeared.

He knocked back his coffee and put on his coat. While descending the stairs he thought of Eleonora's mouth opening a couple of inches away from his own, and he bit the inside of his cheek. It was ridiculous for him to be so besotted at his age, but in a way he enjoyed feeling ridiculous.

The instant he stepped into the street he shuddered from the cold. Hidden behind clouds, the moon cast a spectral light over the building façades. He went and got the Fiat, lighting a cigarette as he drove off, holding the steering wheel with his knees. The unencumbered Viali were a pleasure. A rare car, a few tracked military vehicles, army lorries full of soldiers, and now and then a patrol car of the *carabinieri* or police, looking out for looters. Beyond the flood-damaged areas, the street lamps were on, and a few illuminated windows could be seen in some of the buildings.

He crossed the Cure viaduct and went down Viale Volta. As usual, he turned to look at the closed shutters of the house he'd grown up in, and felt a pang of nostalgia . . . As a child he'd never imagined that he would one day miss the years of runny noses and scraped knees.

At the end of the Viale he continued on towards San Domenico, thinking of that coxcomb Gattacci. In the days of the Duce he was a quite public personage, a puffed-up turkey who fancied himself a poet and boasted of being a friend of Pavolini. By no means a bore, he was actually quite cultured. His old haunt used to be the Giubbe Rosse, and he sat many a time at the tables of Vittorini, Landolfi, Montale, Gadda, Pratolini, Rosai . . . Once, in that same café, he'd dealt a back-handed slap to a young poet who had dared to speak facetiously about the glorious Ethiopian war and the necessity of empire. The blow had made the rounds of Florence, and Gattacci's fame increased. Somebody had introduced him to Bordelli in the late thirties, probably at a dinner party. He hadn't liked him, that much he remembered well. Some ten years later they'd crossed paths again, during an investigation into the murder of a woman, a very good friend of Gattacci and possibly his mistress. They'd recognised each other at once, and Bordelli had reacted coldly to the Fascist's friendly manner. And now he had to see him again. He hadn't even finished dealing with another fool pining for the old regime, and now this. It really seemed as if fate was having fun trying his patience.

He turned on to Via di San Domenico, reading the numbers of the buildings on the uneven side. He drove slowly past 71/A, a small villa with its front door directly on the street. Gattacci was still up, as a number of windows were illuminated. A great many cars were parked tightly along the pavement, bumper to bumper, most of them luxury models. He drove another hundred yards or so and turned left on Via Donati, a narrow little street which ran parallel to Via di San Domenico for a stretch. Stopping the car, he got out and heard some music coming from the ground floor of a large villa. It must have been a party, which would expain all those cars along the pavement. Bordelli approached a window and, peering through a shutter left ajar, he saw young people dancing amid clouds of smoke. Clean faces and pretentious looks. The girls were almost all wearing miniskirts and shaking their heads like she-devils . . . A cheerful little gathering of souls who didn't give a damn about the flood . . .

He shook his head, feeling as old as Methuselah, and headed off towards Gattacci's house with an unlit cigarette in his mouth. The dark sky was threatening rain, for a change. It was a pleasure to be able to breathe, far from the mud and heating-oil residues. As if by magic, he no longer felt tired. He was almost starting to enjoy his impromptu nocturnal outing. He was also pleased to be doing something concrete instead of losing himself in adolescent fantasies. What could be more concrete than having a chat with a Fascist at two o'clock in the morning? As soon as he stopped in front of Gattacci's house, he heard the sound of footsteps and two male voices behind the front door. He ran quickly away and hid between two parked cars, just barely in time to avoid being seen. Panting heavily, he remained crouched down and, watching the pavement, saw a man come out of Gattacci's front door. The man went off in the opposite direction, under the weak light of the street lamp. Bordelli noticed that he was limping slightly, and strangely, as if in fits and starts . . . Where had he seen somebody walk like that? He followed him with his eyes, trying to remember. A good cop was supposed to be able to recognise people, even at a distance of years. It might even be useful for Arcieri to know who the guy was, given that he was seen coming out of the Fascist's house . . . Suddenly he remembered . . . He was the client he'd seen at Panerai's butcher's shop, the first time he'd gone there. Bordelli no longer had any doubt. That was him, the polite gentleman who'd let the inspector go ahead of him.

The man continued down the pavement with his funny gait. Bordelli stood up and followed behind him, hands in his pockets, like someone out for a night-time walk. Running into the same person twice in a few days, in two such different places, was a very strange coincidence. Another odd detail was that the butcher and Gattacci were both Fascists. The simplest conclusion was the most banal: that the lame gentleman knew Gattacci and bought his meat from Panerai . . . So what? Nothing strange about that, really . . . and yet . . . A big fly was buzzing in the inspector's head . . . a detail which . . . What was it that was eluding his grasp? At last he got it. What he'd noticed that day, without grasping its meaning, was that the customer with the big nose had left the butcher's shop empty-handed . . . without buying anything . . . Nobody leaves a butcher's shop without buying anything. It wasn't like going into a shoe shop. Therefore the man had gone to Panerai's for another reason . . . Perhaps the two were friends, in which case the connecting thread might be merely a common nostalgia for the good old days. Fascists needing to come together to reminisce, to remember their beloved Duce while hoping for a brilliant, black-shirted future . . .

He was playing Sherlock Holmes and enjoying himself immensely. And to think that just an hour before, he had been sleeping like a log . . .

When the man reached the end of the long line of parked cars, he got into a large, bottle-green saloon which, at first glance, looked like a Jaguar. Bordelli picked up his pace. He got to the saloon just before it drove off and was able to read the number plate. It was a Jaguar, and a fine one at that. He waited for the car to get to the bottom of the hill, and after writing down the number on a box of matches, he headed back towards the Fascist's villa. Now came the fun part.

He walked slowly, trying to think of the best way to confront Gattacci. There was no name outside the house. He rang the doorbell and then stepped aside, leaning against the door, so he couldn't be seen through the spyhole. He heard some footsteps approaching cautiously. A moment later the spyhole opened slightly and a shaft of light cut through the darkness.

'Who is it?' a voice whispered.

Bordelli stood there in silence, blowing his smoke into the ray of light. The spyhole opened all the way, but Gattacci still couldn't see anybody.

'Eh, is that you?' he asked, alarmed. Bordelli then stepped in front of the spyhole and Gattacci leapt backwards.

'Long time no see,' said the inspector, blowing a mouthful of smoke into the house. Gattacci looked pale.

'Who are you?'

'Don't you recognise me, Gattacci?' said Bordelli, taking a couple of steps back to allow him a better look. Two wrinkles appeared on Gattacci's forehead.

'Inspector . . . Bordelli . . .'

'In all my glory.'

'What do you want?' asked Gattacci, at once reassured and alarmed.

'I'd like to have a little chat with you.'

'At this hour?'

'Dirty business is best taken care of at night, don't you think?'

'What the hell are you talking about?'

'It's not polite to keep your friends waiting on the doorstep, Gattacci,' the inspector said, in a vaguely menacing tone.

'And what if I decided not to let you in?' asked the Fascist, trying to recover some dignity.

'I'll pretend I didn't hear that question,' Bordelli whispered icily. Gattacci sighed and decided to open the door. He was wearing a Bordeaux-red dressing gown and his face glistened with sweat. The inspector entered the house without taking his hands out of his pockets, a wicked smile playing on his lips.

'I'm sure you've got something special in your closet,' he said, looking the Fascist straight in the eyes. Gattacci led him into an elegant, dusty little sitting room furnished in the thirties style. Despite his age he moved with unusual agility, though nervously. They both remained standing, staring at each other.

'I'm listening, Inspector,' Gattacci blurted out, tying to hide his agitation.

'Aren't you going to offer me something to drink?' Bordelli asked, looking around for an ashtray. Gattacci was tense and didn't understand.

'Just put your ash in that little dish,' he muttered.

Then he went to the drinks trolley and grabbed a single snifter and a bottle of French cognac, and set them down on the coffee table. Bordelli served himself and then leaned back in a big armchair, noticing the same odour of the past that he used to smell in the home of his father's old aunts. Taking a sip, he raised his eyebrows slightly.

'This is magnificent . . .' he whispered, rolling the cognac around in the glass.

'What do you have to tell me?' Gattacci asked impatiently.

'It's not good news, I'm afraid.'

'Why? What happened?'

'You're in big trouble, Gattacci.'

'I've got nothing to do with it,' the Fascist said, terrified, then bit his lip.

'Who knows if we're even talking about the same thing?'

'Well, whatever it is, I've got nothing to do with it.'

'Did you have a nice time in Predappio, on the twenty-eighth?' Bordelli tossed out, bluffing. Gattacci stiffened.

'What? Are you spying on me?'

'It's just a show of affection.'

'Just leave me alone . . . I haven't bothered anyone for twenty years.'

'You can't erase the past, Gattacci. Not even with Togliatti's sponge.'[43]

'I've never done anything to be ashamed of.'

'Oh, it does you honour, I'm sure,' said the inspector, crushing his cigarette butt in the little plate and smiling compassionately.

'No one will ever write on my tombstone that I was a turncoat . . . like that renegade Malaparte.'

'If you carry on that way I'm going to start crying.'

'You know as well as I do how many so-called anti-Fascists used to grovel at the Duce's feet.'

He was excited, his round eyes darting nervously.

'Poor dear Gattacci . . .' Bordelli said softly.

'You haven't yet told me what you want from me, Inspector.'

'Not everyone has lost his memory, Gattacci. Violence leaves deep wounds.'

'Get to the point, Inspector. I would like to go to bed,' said the Fascist, summoning all his courage. Bordelli downed his glass and crossed his legs, sighing as though bored. He calmly lit another cigarette and blew the smoke towards the ceiling.

'I can already see the front page of *La Nazione*: BODY OF ANOTHER FLOOD VICTIM FOUND . . .'

'What on earth are you talking about?'

'The case will be shelved as an *Accidental death caused by the Arno's fury* – a little folder that'll quickly start gathering dust . . . How terribly sad.'

'What is the meaning of this? I've done nothing . . . nobody can possibly have anything against me . . . I've done nothing . . .' Gattacci protested in a falsetto voice, a bead of sweat dangling from his chin.

'You have no idea how stubborn some people can be . . . and now you haven't got Mamma Pavolini's skirts to hide behind any more,' said Bordelli, standing up.

'But who is it? Who are you talking about?'

'Watch your step very carefully, Gattacci, if you don't want to end up with four candles around you,' said Bordelli, pouring himself more cognac.

'Is that a threat?'

'On the contrary, I'm trying to save your skin. But if the big bad wolf suddenly shows up, don't come running to me, because I won't be able to do anything.'

'Why won't you speak clearly?' Gattacci asked, clenching his fists.

'Speaking any more clearly . . . might be fatal,' Bordelli whispered, smiling like a real bastard. Who knew what Eleonora would make of it, if she could see him in this guise? He downed his cognac in a single gulp and headed for the door. Gattacci followed behind him, panting as if he had just run up many flights of stairs. Bordelli opened the door and went out without turning round.

'Sweet dreams,' he said, a moment before the door closed behind him. As he walked away he heard the sound of locks and bolts turning, and he broke out laughing. Now he had only to ring Colonel Arcieri.

He got into the car, and as soon as he drove off he contacted police headquarters via radio. There wasn't much news. No more prison escapees had been found, but to make up for it, a number of other looters had been arrested. The telephone lines had been back in working order since the afternoon, the electricity for a couple of hours.

'Is Piras there?' Bordelli asked.

'Yes, Inspector.'

'Tell him to wait for me, I'll be right there. Over and out.'

He stepped on the accelerator, having fun making the Fiat's tyres screech. It was ten minutes to three and there was nobody about. He was still thinking of the man he'd seen leave Gattacci's villa, feeling more and more curious to find out who he was. Maybe he was nobody and Bordelli was thinking too much like a cop, but he couldn't help it. Actually it wasn't the only fixation gnawing at his brain . . . Had Eleonora really been about to kiss him?

Minutes later he pulled into the station, greeted Mugnai with a nod, and went upstairs to his office. It smelled stuffy, and so he opened the window. It had been scarcely four days since he'd sat at his desk, but it felt like a century. Everything from before the flood seemed irretrievably remote in time. He picked up the phone and called Colonel Arcieri. He told him in a few words about his pleasant nocturnal meeting and mentioned the limping man who'd come out of Gattacci's house.

'I'll know his name very soon, if you're interested,' said Bordelli.

'If Gattacci tells me what I want to know, I won't need it, but if I do I'll be back to bother you. Thank you so very much, Inspector.'

'Not at all, it was a pleasure. Good luck.'

'Thanks,' said Arcieri, who then said a hasty goodbye and hung up.

Gattacci's nocturnal surprises weren't over yet, Bordelli thought with a smile. He called the radio room and told Piras to come to his office straight away. While waiting he extracted from his pocket the matchbox with the Jaguar's licence plate number: FI 176090. Who knew how much a car like that cost? He lit a cigarette and went to the window to smoke it, so as not to offend Piras's nose. A dense flock of clouds was passing slowly through the night sky, faintly illuminated by the moon. He imagined Eleonora sleeping under many blankets, curled up against the cold, oblivious to what she had unleashed inside a police inspector close to retirement . . .

Piras knocked and opened the door without waiting.

'Hello, Piras, I'll get straight to the point. I want to know the name of this gentleman, what he does, where he lives, and if he has anything on his record,' said Bordelli, passing him the matchbox with the Jaguar's number on it.

'When do you need it by?'

'Tomorrow morning would be fine.'

'No problem.'

'I'm going to dash home now. I need to lie down for a few hours.'

THE FIRST PROVISIONS BEGIN TO ARRIVE FOR FLOOD VICTIMS STRANDED ON ROOFTOPS

Bordelli tossed *La Nazione* on to his desk, leaned back in his chair, yawning, and read Piras's report, which was typewritten and perfectly error-free:

```
Moreno Beccaroni, born in Florence on 9
July 1922. Registered with the Bar
Association since 1952. Home: Via di Santa
Maria a Marignolle 96B. Office: Via dei
Servi 50. Married in 1947 to Maria
Migliorini. One daughter, born in 1949,
called Claretta. Separated from wife in
'53. Charged in '53 with sexual molestation
of a minor (a certain Gualtiero Cioni,
born 1939) and acquitted at the inquest
when the charges were dropped. That's all
I can find for now. Piras.
```

'Well, well, well . . .' he mumbled to himself, staring at the sheet of paper. This little detail about sexual molestation certainly gave one pause. The lawyer was probably a friend of Panerai's, who'd lost his telephone bill in the same wood where the boy's body was found. The connection was as flimsy as a hair, but Bordelli wasn't about to ignore it. Without it he had nothing. He lit a cigarette and started thinking. Beccaroni knew both Gattacci and Panerai, both Fascist reactionaries, and he too probably felt nostalgic for the bygone days, given his daughter's name.[44] In short, the link between the three men had a clear explanation, nothing strange about that . . . But sexual molestation was another matter. Acquitted or not, the shadow of the original charge remained. There was always something odd about cases where the charges were dropped . . . it usually hid the fact that a large sum of money was exchanged.

He had to try to find out whether the three comrades had any common interests of another nature . . . of *that* nature, that is. He had to give it a go, even if it was like playing roulette. There were no precedents of the sort in Panerai's past, but what about Gattacci? The inspector knew nothing about his private life. Given his past Fascist escapades, he'd certainly left some deep tracks in the state archives and those of the Secret Service. All Bordelli had to do was ask another favour of his friend in the SID, Pietro Agostinelli, nicknamed Carnera for his size.[45] They hadn't seen each other for years, but every so often they would talk over the phone just to stay in touch or for some work-related matter. It was past 8.30. The inspector looked up his number and called Rome. A very polite secretary answered, as warm as a slab of marble.

'I'm sorry, the admiral is in a meeting.'

'Will he be long?'

'I have no way of knowing . . . If you like, I can have him call you back as soon as he's free.'

'All right, thank you. Please tell him it's extremely urgent.'

'And could you please repeat your name for me?'

'Inspector Bordelli.'

'And your telephone number?'

'Pietro knows it.'

'I'll pass this on to the admiral. Goodbye, Inspector.'

'Goodbye.'

He hung up, sighing impatiently. Waiting, always waiting. He started pacing back and forth, daydreaming about the possible meaning of the coincidence. From the very start of this nasty affair, chance had been amusing herself by casting her ambiguous bait here and there, and he had bitten each time.

Smoking avidly, he tried to piece together the few elements he had available, launching into hasty hypotheses that lasted as long as a match flame. It was like seeing a faint light at the end of a dark, endless tunnel.

The ring of the telephone startled him, and he ran to pick up.

'Yes?'

'Is that you, Franco?'

'Hello, Carnera.'

'Hello, old boy, how are you?' Agostinelli asked cheerfully.

'Not too bad, and you? Still playing spy?'

'It's a thrilling job, you really ought to try it.'

'Just the thought of it makes me shudder,' Bordelli said, smiling.

'I really mean it. Why don't you quit the police force and come and work for us?'

'I'd rather wait for my pension and retire to the countryside.'

'Well, think about it anyway.'

'I'm not made for sitting cooped up in an office all day, Pietro.'

'How are things in Florence? I saw Burton's appeal on the telly last night . . . A fine mess . . .'

'Saragat came to have a look for himself, but we're still waiting for Rome's timely help.'

'The hallways in Rome are long and tortuous, and people sometimes get lost in them,' Agostinelli said sarcastically.

'Never mind . . . Guess who just paid me a visit.'

'Brigitte Bardot?'

'One of yours: Colonel Arcieri,' said Bordelli.

'An excellent fellow, one of those who never breaks and doesn't even bend,' said the admiral.

'He was pretty upset.'

'I know, I know . . . We're working on a sensitive case.'

'I don't want to know about it . . .'

'I couldn't tell you even if you did.'

'So much the better . . . Listen, as to the matter at hand . . . I wanted to ask a favour.'

'Tell me.'

'I would like to know everything you know about three people, even though I doubt you've got much on two of them . . .' And he gave him their names – Livio Panerai, Moreno Beccaroni and Alfonso Gattacci – as well as the public information he had on them. As for Gattacci, he mentioned only that he was about seventy years old.

'All right, I'll have someone search the archives and let you know.'

'Thank you so much.'

'I'll call you back shortly,' said the admiral, hanging up.

Bordelli seized the moment to go and have a coffee at the bar in Via di San Gallo, then paid in advance for one for Mugnai. Back in the office, he resumed pacing back and forth in front of the window, thinking about the girl. Maybe it was better to stay away, so she could see how much she missed the old Methuselah . . . But what if one of those students then . . . No, she wasn't the type to waste time with snotty-nosed little boys . . . Which didn't mean of course that she was the type who liked old police detectives, either . . . And yet, last night after dinner, in front of the car . . . Was she just having fun at his expense? But what if instead . . .

The ring of the telephone pulled him out of the swamp into which he was sinking. As he'd hoped, it was Agostinelli.

'On Livio Panerai there's hardly anything.'

'As I expected.'

'All we've got is that he's a butcher by trade, a member of the MSI,[46] a staunch Fascist and makes frequent visits to Predappio.'

'More or less what I already knew.'

'On to Moreno Beccaroni. Not much on him, either. Son

of the barrister Romano Beccaroni. Fascist Youth, Avanguardia, and all the rest. Basically like everyone else who grew up under the regime. Carducci middle school, the Liceo Dante Alighieri after that, followed by law school. Temporarily interrupted his studies in 1940. Didn't serve in the war because of an older brother who died in the Greek campaign. An adherent of the Republic of Salò, without any special posts. No documented atrocities . . . No Black Brigades, just to be clear. He's suspected of having taken direct part in the confiscation of the possessions of a number of Jewish families in the Veneto in '44, keeping some of it for himself, but there's no proof of this. After the war he resumed his studies and graduated in '49. Passed the bar in '52. In '55 he was charged with sexual molestation of a minor, the son of peasants—'

'Gualtiero Cioni?'

'That's right.'

'Our research shows that it never went to trial because the charges were dropped . . .'

'That's what we've found, too, but, given the situation, I'm taking the liberty of assuming that the family was paid off handsomely.'

'I thought the same thing.'

'And that's all for Beccaroni.'

'All right.'

'As for Alfonso Gattacci, we've even got a rather detailed dossier from the OVRA.'[47]

'I'm all ears.'

'He was an active participant in the Fascist project from the very start. The paramilitary *Fasci di combattimento*, the March on Rome, and so on . . . he didn't miss a thing. University degree in literature and philosophy. A man of culture, not a thug à la Dumini. In '32 he founded a publishing house which went bankrupt after one year and folded. A failed poet who used to rub elbows with important writers and painters, including Marinetti and Boccioni. He was a minion of Pavolini, who protected him during some unpleasant moments. Under the Salò regime he was one of the founders of the PDM, a clandestine organisation of the Salò gang which we know little about. And during the pathetic days of the Valtellina Redoubt,[48] he escaped to Switzerland . . .'

'Is there anything more personal on him?'

'Let's see . . .' said Agostinelli, leafing through the pages of the file.

'There ought to be . . . The OVRA used to know how many times a person pissed a day.'

'Here we are. And I quote: "A pervert. Prefers very young males. Spends a great deal on his sexual pleasures . . ."'

'That's exactly what I was looking for,' Bordelli interrupted him, fumbling for his packet of cigarettes.

'So now you know everything,' Bordelli said, after telling Piras of his latest discoveries. For the whole time, the Sardinian had been squeezing his lower lip between two fingers.

'Very interesting,' he said under his breath.

'We have to keep an eye on all three; it's the only thing we can do.'

'Right . . .'

'Let's get started straight away – I'll leave it to you to organise the shifts. If anything happens, contact me immediately, even via radio. I've been using a squad car, the grey 1100.'

'All right, Inspector.'

'And you know what? We never did start looking for the owner of the flat in Via Luna . . .'

'Would that help?'

'You never know. But I imagine the Land Registry office was flooded.'

'It was, and so was the records office. Destroyed,' said Piras, who was always very well informed.

'And there's no point looking at the Conservatory. Without a name, it would be like looking for a needle in a haystack.'

'We could try asking the neighbours, if you like.'

'All right. But use the utmost discretion.'

'We could ask Canu to do it. He's very good at that sort of thing.'

'Yes, send him. And fill me in as soon as you can,' Bordelli said, standing up.

They went down the stairs together, and he was pleased to note that Piras was limping less and less. He nodded goodbye and drove away in the 1100. The flow of traffic on the Viali was decidedly better. He glanced at his watch. He'd resisted the call of the wild until almost noon, but now he had to see her again. When she was beside him he forgot about old age and death . . . Well, not really, perhaps, but at least they seemed far away, unreal, not to be taken seriously. Every woman he'd ever taken a fancy to had had the same effect on him, but this one even more, much more. Amelia's prediction came back to him again, in full this time, and he suddenly felt overwhelmed by sadness. The fortune-teller had said that the *dark young woman* was not the woman of his life, and that it wouldn't last . . . What a bloody fool . . . Nothing had even happened yet and here he was getting lost in the hocus-pocus predictions of a card-reader.

When he got to San Niccolò he looked around through the crowd. She wasn't there. The windows of her flat were wide open, like so many others, to air out the rooms. He felt a tap on the shoulder and turned round. It was Don Baldesi, and his eyes looked even more ironic than usual.

'Hello, Inspector.'

'Hello . . .'

'Chicca's gone to her parents' place for a bath and a bite to eat.'

'What's that?'

'She should be back soon.'

'Oh, right . . . Such a nice girl,' Bordelli muttered.

'Don't tell me that's the only thing you noticed.'

'No, of course not . . . She's also very intelligent.'

'Let me treat you to a glass of wine, I need to warm up,' said Don Baldesi, smiling. They went uphill to the Osteria Fuori Porta, ordered two glasses of red, and sat down at a table.

'The Church and the state, drinking together . . .' said Don Baldesi, raising his glass.

'It's sure to be in all the papers,' Bordelli said, smiling.

'Have you heard the one about the pope who went to see the Pyramids?'

'No . . .' said Bordelli, still smiling and ready to listen. At that moment Eleonora walked in and approached their table. Her hair was clean and she smelled of soap.

'Mind if I sit down with you two?'

'I don't know . . . What do you think, Inspector?'

'Just this once . . .' Bordelli said, hiding his embarrassment.

'Oh, I'm so honoured,' the girl said. She settled into her chair and asked the waiter for a glass of red.

'How's your flat coming along?' Don Baldesi asked her.

'Everything's drying out, but it still stinks of heating oil. I'll have to scrape down all the plaster,' she said, shrugging in resignation.

'It would have been worse if you lived on the ground floor.'

'Who ever expected twenty feet of water?' said Eleonora, making a gesture of thanks to the tavern owner, who'd just brought her wine. People were starting to pour in for refreshment after the morning's work, muddying the *osteria*'s floor. Every now and then Bordelli felt the girl's knee lightly touch his. He couldn't tell whether she was doing it on purpose or not, and remained stock still. He was also trying not to look at her too much, for fear of being unmasked. Don Baldesi finally told his pope joke, at high volume, and everyone laughed. He put two hundred lire on the table for the wine, emptied his glass, and stood up.

'I'm going to get the remaining furniture from the sacristy,' he said, caressing Eleonora's face in a fatherly way.

'He's a very special priest,' she said after he was gone.

'I've noticed.'

'Do you believe in God?'

'I've never really been sure . . . Do you?'

'Sometimes yes, sometimes no, it depends on the day,' the girl said with a hint of a smile.

'That's the first time I've ever heard anyone say that,' Bordelli admitted, and again he felt her knee touch his. The girl stared into space.

'It's sort of the same with love. One day I think I've found the man for me, then the next morning I don't care for him any more.'

'*La donna è mobile*,' said the inspector, feeling a twist in his stomach.

'Men have always slandered women, because they're afraid of them.'

'Quite true,' Bordelli acknowledged. He found every tiniest detail about her fascinating, even the way she moved her lips when speaking.

'I slept really badly last night,' the girl said.

'I'm sorry to hear that.' Good God, was he profound. He had to try to be a little more original if he wanted at least to arouse her curiosity.

'I had a terrible nightmare . . .'

'No man was wooing you any more?'

'Oh, that would be a relief.'

'For a week, perhaps, but then you would start crying, I'm sure.'

'What rubbish . . .'

'What did you dream?' Bordelli asked, curious.

'You were in the nightmare, too.'

'Me?'

'I was surprised too, since I barely know you.'

'Was I a monster chasing after you?'

'It was much worse than that, but I couldn't possibly tell you,' said Eleonora, staring into his eyes. Bordelli grabbed his glass and downed the last sip. The girl sighed.

'I guess I'll have to start emptying out the cellar today.'

'I don't envy you.'

'Would you lend me a hand?' she asked, standing up.

'If you like . . .'

He followed behind her like a little dog. They went down the street together to San Niccolò, amid the usual chaotic hustle and bustle. And straight away they got to work, which consisted of repeatedly going down to the cellar with two buckets, filling them up, and then pouring them out in the street. Ever so slowly the level of the smelly muck began to descend.

'What we really need is one of those motorised contraptions that suck the water out,' said Eleonora.

'Maybe they'll arrive by Christmas.'

It was a thankless, laborious task, but Bordelli rolled his sleeves up and tackled it. He was ready to do whatever it took to be by her side. He wondered whether he was in love with the girl or with the fact that she could fall in love with him. Deep down, however, there wasn't much difference between the two. He simply felt besotted and that was enough for him.

Every so often the long-haired little students came over and tried to buttonhole Eleonora, but when they saw that she wasn't giving in an inch, they would leave, to the great joy of the old inspector.

They spent the afternoon getting all muddy and checking the results of their efforts. When night at last began to fall, they had managed to free up the third step of the staircase. Leaving their buckets in the building's entranceway, they picked their bones up off the ground. They felt like wrecks.

'I would love to have another dinner like last night,' she said, wincing in pain.

'Will you allow me to take you out again?'

'Are you sure you don't have any other engagements?'

'Not that I know of . . .'

'But first I'd like to run over to my parents' house . . . I'd like to change clothes.'

'I'll follow your example.'

'Eight-thirty in front of the church of San Miniato?'

'Perfect . . .' Why couldn't he just have said *all right*?

As he was driving to the station he contacted the radio room. The surveillance operation was already under way. He asked to be connected with the cars out on duty, but they had nothing important to relay. Gattacci's house was in darkness, without even a light over the front door.

At headquarters he went up to his office. Deciding to contact Colonel Arcieri, he dialled the same number as the night before, to find out how his visit with the Fascist had gone. A nasal voice told him that the colonel was not in and that nobody knew where to find him.

Bordelli imagined that Gattacci had fled very far away, and he couldn't really blame him. Perhaps it was pointless to keep a watch on his house, but in that kind of situation he couldn't afford to let the tiniest thing escape him. He tried ringing Rosa, but the phone lines around Santa Croce were still down. He would pay her a visit as soon as he could, to see whether she needed anything.

The commissioner rang, asking him where the hell he'd been hiding. Bordelli dispensed with him in a few seconds, saying a new lead had developed in the Pellissari case and he didn't have time to stay on the phone. He hung up before Inzipone could reply.

As he was looking for the number of the restaurant near Arcetri in the telephone book, there was a knock at the door. It was none other than Canu, a tall, blond Sardinian with green eyes.

'I did what you asked round Via Luna, sir.'

'Come in . . .' said Bordelli. Canu entered the room and plonked himself down in front of the desk.

'A neighbour told me the owner of the flat is a certain Cesira Baiocchi who lives in Via del Gelsomino, but she didn't know the number. She also didn't know whether the place was rented out or not. So I went to Via del Gelsomino and started knocking on all the doors. I found a lady who used to know her. She said Signora Baiocchi died two years ago. She didn't have any children but had a niece who lives in France. The lady'd never seen this niece and didn't know her name. She didn't know about any other relatives, either. That was all I could gather.'

'Well done, Canu.'

'Need anything else, sir?'

'No, that'll be all for now, you can go.'

'At your service, sir,' said the Sardinian, dashing off.

Bordelli leaned back in his chair. He'd requested that little investigation so as to leave no stone unturned, but he'd expected all along that it would come to nothing. It was better to concentrate on the three Fascists.

He remembered the restaurant. Looking the number up in the phone book, he reserved a table for nine o'clock, then jotted the number down so he could leave it with the lads in the radio room.

'If there's any news, I'll be at this place having a bite between nine and eleven.'

'A lovely flood victim?' asked Inspector Bonciani, winking.

'A boring work dinner.'

'If you like, I could go in your stead.'

'I'm happy to make the sacrifice myself.'

'So she must be very pretty . . .'

'After eleven you should try the car radio or come straight to my place, since I don't think the phones are working in San Frediano,' said Bordelli, who then left without saying goodbye. He never could stand male camaraderie on the subject of women.

He raced home. In order to wash he had to heat up another big pot of water on the stove. He selected a nice suit, put his best shoes in a bag and went out wearing boots. He trudged through the mud to get to the car, then took off the boots and put on his shoes. He drove up Viale Machiavelli at thirty kilometres an hour, ignoring the horns and the flashing high beams of the nervous drivers behind him. He was in front of the iron gate of the church of San Miniato at twelve minutes past eight, but he didn't stop the car. To kill a little time he went down to Piazza Ferrucci and turned round. Eight-twenty-four. He parked and started pacing back and forth, smoking a cigarette. A great many cars drove by on Viale Galileo. He turned round to look at the church of San Miniato, which stood out against the dark sky. Its magnificent medieval façade soared white in the night, with its geometric patterns and the eagle of the Wool Guild on top, in the place of the cross. The most beautiful basilica in Florence, if not the world . . . but at that moment he was in no condition to appreciate it.

He tossed aside his cigarette butt, but she still hadn't arrived. What if she didn't come? What if she'd changed her mind? Worse yet, maybe she was hiding behind a bush with her friends and laughing at the old fart who'd deluded himself into thinking he could sink his teeth into some young flesh . . . But enough of this defeatism. It was perfectly normal for a woman to be late. And anyway, it was only 8.31. He needed to calm down. He continued walking around, hands in his pockets, trying to think of other things. The three Fascists were under close surveillance, and maybe something interesting would come of it . . .

At 8.40 he leaned his elbows on the marble parapet and looked out over the valley. What was keeping Eleonora from running into his arms? He decided he would wait until 8.50 . . . or nine at the latest . . . If, by a quarter past nine, she still hadn't arrived, he would go down to San Niccolò and look for her. He lit another cigarette, found it disgusting, but kept on smoking it.

He heard a car coming up the Via delle Porte Sante and turned round. He saw some headlights approaching, and then a white Fiat 500 parked behind his squad car. The engine went off at the same time as the lights, the door opened, and out stepped Eleonora's slender, sinuous figure.

'Hello,' she said, coming slowly towards him. No mention of her tardiness. Bordelli went up to her.

'Hello.'

'I'm famished . . .'

'Then let's not waste any time.'

They got into his car and drove off. She was wearing very close-fitting black trousers and a short coat gathered at the waist, but would have been beautiful even in a hauberk.

'Have you arrested any murderers in the meantime?'

'We're working on it . . .'

'Are you serious?'

'Absolutely.'

'Who are you looking for?'

'If you've read the papers you should know.'

'The boy they found in the woods.'

'That's right.'

'What a horrible story . . . And you're about to catch the killer?'

'I hope so,' said Bordelli, without revealing that there were at least three killers.

'Would you believe it if I told you I really am a sort of witch?'

'In what sense?'

'You'll find the killer, I'm sure of it.'

'Thanks for the encouragement.'

'It's not just encouragement. It's what I feel.'

'Then I hope you really are a witch.'

'You mean you still have doubts?'

'No, on the contrary . . .'

'I'm also a vampire, when I need to be,' said the girl in a more or less serious tone.

They arrived at the restaurant and Bordelli led the way inside. He helped her with her coat, and they sat down at the table. They ordered more or less the same things as the night before. There wasn't much else available.

All they did was talk during the meal. Family anecdotes, not very serious discussions about politics and Florence, films, books, painters, a passing mention of the war, the youth of today, long hair, modern music, the flood . . .

When they got up from the table it was past eleven, and they'd drunk almost two bottles of wine and several small glasses of *vin santo*. Bordelli felt as light as a feather. As they were walking out of the restaurant, the girl look his arm, laughing.

'Oh my God, my head is spinning a little.'

'It must be the salad . . .' he said, overcome by a wave of heat from the unexpected physical contact.

'Shall we go for a walk?'

'I'd love to.'

And they headed down the narrow, dimly lit road under a dark sky.

'Do you like to walk?' she asked.

'I often go for long walks in the woods,' Bordelli boasted.

'It must be so quiet . . .'

'Every now and then I need that.'

'I'd already realised you have a bit of the bear in you,' said Eleonora.

Seconds later she let go of his arm, leaving him alone in the cold. They walked on for a bit, passing between high stone walls and large, silent villas. A little farther ahead there was a small, low wall outside an olive grove, and they stopped. She turned round to look at him, but said nothing. In the darkness Bordelli saw two tiny diamonds glitter in her jet-black eyes. He had to find the courage to kiss her. He had to take the plunge. What was happening to him? Had he forgotten he was a man? What was he waiting for to take her in his arms? If he didn't kiss her in two seconds . . . But she took care of it herself in the end, as if it was the most natural thing in the world. She drew near and parted her lips. It was a delicate kiss, at first, but little by little it went deeper and deeper . . .

He heard her breathing in the dark. She'd fallen asleep a short while before, her warm feet intertwined with his. The room was cold, but it felt good under the covers. It was no longer a fantasy. Eleonora was there beside him. He could smell her scent. They'd made love sweetly, violently, continuing to address each other in the polite form just for fun. After blowing out the candles, they'd amused themselves revealing what had been going through their heads at certain moments. Know what I thought the first time I saw you? And when I touched your knee under the table at the *osteria*? Is it true you were about to kiss me that time?

'Today's girls certainly move fast,' he'd said. Barely half an hour had passed between the first kiss and the bed, the time it took to get to San Frediano and climb the stairs to his flat.

'The world is changing. Haven't you noticed?'

'I have, but I can't always keep up with it.'

'Try to stay on top of it instead of following behind,' she said in a sing-song voice, pulling the hair on his belly.

'Who knows what your mother would say if she saw you now?'

'She'd say I sleep with old men.'

'How very kind . . .'

'You're the one who asked.'

'It was a rhetorical question.'

'Did you know that my mother is younger than you?' she said.

'Do you do it often?'

'Do what?'

269

'Sleep with older men.'

'Oh, no, are you now going to ask how many men I've been with and what I did with them?'

'It's the farthest thing from my mind.'

'And what do you think? That I'm a tart?'

'Of course.'

'Oh, thanks . . .'

'You're the one who asked.'

'It was a rhetorical question,' she'd said, laughing, and they'd started making love again in the dark . . .

He got out of bed, moving slowly so as not to wake her. He groped around for his clothes on the floor and managed to take a blanket from the wardrobe, shivering with cold all the while. Grabbing the torch, he didn't turn it on until he was out of the room. He went into the dining room and got dressed in a hurry, teeth chattering. He had to remember to buy a small gas heater. He lit two candles and sat down on the sofa to smoke a cigarette, wrapped in his blanket. Slowly he began to warm up. He felt good, perhaps too good, but he was also worried. At his age he would rather avoid particularly stinging defeats. He hoped he would know soon whether she was serious about him or only playing around. He didn't want to be left high and dry. An old man's concerns, these. He was well aware of that. She seemed not to worry herself too much about things. She probably didn't need to. He had to be careful not to spoil everything with his apprehensions. He was probably better off not clinging too much or chasing wild illusions . . . What was he hoping for, anyway? For her to move in with him? Perhaps in an old country house with mice running about in the kitchen?

He'd been away from her for just a few minutes, and already he felt like going back. He stubbed out the half-smoked cigarette and blew out the candles. He returned to the bedroom, hand shading the light of the torch, then turned it off and slipped under the covers with his clothes still on. Slowly he took his trousers off and let them slide down from the bed. Eleonora moved, making a slight moaning sound, and cuddled next to him without waking up. She was warm and smelled of youth.

He lay awake, staring into the darkness, gently stroking her back. He didn't feel like asking himself any more pointless questions. It made no sense. He should let whatever happened, happen. Actually he was quite curious to know how old Inspector Bordelli was going to deal with this one. He would force himself to live one day at a time, without tormenting himself. However it turned out, nothing would ever erase this night from his memory.

Eleonora moved again and slowly turned away. He got closer to her and delicately pressed his chest against her back. The moment he closed his eyes he started thinking of the murdered boy, the killers, his new hope for the case. He could imagine what fun the men in the surveillance cars were having. Now patience alone would yield fruit, if there was any to be had. At moments he thought he was on the right track; he had a sort of feeling about it . . . Yes, they were the killers: Panerai, Beccaroni and Gattacci . . . Gattacci too? Really? At his age? But what could an elderly, cultured Fascist have in common with a butcher, assuming they knew each other? And a lawyer with an office in the centre of Florence, what kind of relationship did he have with Gattacci and Panerai? Were they really a clique? And, if so, was their common bond merely a devotion to the Duce? Or also a passion for young boys?

He woke up gently and reached out for her. The bed was empty. For a moment he thought he'd dreamt the whole thing. He opened his eyes. It was day. Eleonora's clothes were gone. The door was open, and he heard noises in the kitchen. He got up and put on his trousers. He tried hastily to arrange his hair and ran a hand over his unshaven face, then tiptoed towards the bathroom.

'Ciao!' she yelled from the kitchen.

'You been up for long?' he asked loudly.

'Just a few minutes. I'm making coffee.'

'I'll be right there.'

He rinsed his face in a hurry, brushed his teeth with mineral water, and combed his hair. Then he came out of the bathroom to meet his destiny. The pleasant aroma of coffee filled the kitchen. Eleonora was already dressed and had even put on her coat. Obviously she was as beautiful as the sun.

'Did you sleep well, signorina?'

'Not really, it felt like there was an ogre in the bed,' she said, smiling. Bordelli came towards her with his hands in his pockets, repressing the desire to kiss her. He looked her in the eye.

'Were you cold?'

'The ogre made sure I was warm.'

'Not all ogres are out to cause harm,' said Bordelli.

She smiled and went to shut off the burner under the boiling espresso pot.

'What are you doing today?' she asked, pouring the coffee into the cups.

'Well, I'll be going to the station now, but after that I don't know.'

'Will I see you again tonight?'

'If you insist . . .' he said. Eleonora took a step forward and kissed him.

'You wouldn't want to leave me alone with all those young students and soldiers . . .'

'Never. I'd rather die.'

'What time will you come by?'

'Excuse me for just a second,' said Bordelli.

He went into the entrance hall and got an extra set of house keys from a drawer in the small table there. Returning to the kitchen, he handed them to her. They were merely little pieces of metal with teeth, but at that moment they were charged with meaning. Eleonora was surprised. After a moment of hesitation, she took the keys and put them in her pocket without saying anything.

They drank their coffee and went out. In the streets the people had already been at work for a while. The piles of debris hauled out of the buildings were getting taller and taller, and nobody was coming to take them away.

Bordelli drove Eleonora to San Miniato to get her car and didn't smoke along the way. Before saying goodbye they exchanged a long kiss. He watched her little Fiat drive away, and the moment it vanished round the corner his mood darkened. He felt alone again. Up until a second ago he would have sworn that she, too, was in love, but now he already no longer believed it. He got in his car and drove off, trying to think of other things.

There were soldiers in the centre of town, lending people a hand, but there were still far too few of them. More importantly, they lacked the machines that the mayor had so loudly called for.

At the station he went upstairs to his office with the day's edition of *La Nazione* under his arm. On his desk he found the night's reports on the three Fascists. Nothing of note. One had to be patient, though this was no guarantee of results. But for the moment, at least, the commissioner wouldn't be on his back, busy as he was with the flood disaster.

Bordelli lit a cigarette and went out again. He needed to throw himself back into the fray, if only so he wouldn't have the time to torment himself with his usual doubts. After arriving at the stadium he left with a military convoy headed for the countryside around Lastra a Signa, where there was still a great deal to be done. He spent the whole day handing out provisions and never once felt tired.

As they were headed back he suddenly buckled under the fatigue and leaned back against the side of the lorry. Eight-fifteen. He wouldn't race straight to San Niccolò. It was better to leave the girl in peace a little . . . Or maybe he just wanted her to miss him.

At the stadium he climbed out of the lorry, said goodbye to the soldiers and drove off in the 1100. He radioed headquarters: nothing new, as usual. He told them he would call again later and signed off. He hoped Cesare's trattoria would be open, since the flood waters hadn't reached it. Turning on to Viale Lavagnini, he felt relieved to see its window lit up. He really felt like chatting a little with Totò.

Almost all the tables were taken, and a dense hum of voices filled the room. He exhanged a few words with Cesare, the usual stuff about mud and slime.

'I'm going to see Totò.'

'There isn't much choice tonight.'

'I'm fine with anything.'

He waved goodbye to Cesare and slipped into the kitchen. Totò gave him an enthusiastic welcome, as if he hadn't seen him for a year. He told him the flood waters had risen to six inches away from his flat, and he'd been stranded inside for an entire day.

'And what about your Nina?'

'Safe and sound. She's at Serpiolle.'

'So when are you getting married?'

'You'll have to be patient. It's been barely a year . . . How hungry are you, Inspector?'

'All I've had to eat all day was a panino.'

'How does *ribollita* and *osso buco* sound?'

'Sounds great . . .'

'Just as well, since that's all there is.'

'I would've gobbled up even an onion.'

A minute later he found a big pot of steaming *ribollita* in front of him, and as Totò spoke and he listened, he ate it all, with the help of several glasses of wine. He then set to work on the *osso buco* with its side dish of beans, feeling even hungrier than before. He had all the bread he could eat. The cook's stream of words was flooding the kitchen. Bordelli limited himself to grunting, his desire to see Eleonora again growing all the while. When the cream pie arrived, he had trouble swallowing it, unlike the *vin santo*, which flowed nicely. As usual, he had eaten and drunk too much, and he swore that the next time . . . At ten o'clock he turned down a glass of grappa and stood up.

'Just one little glass, Inspector.'

'You're trying to kill a dead man, Totò,' said Bordelli, and he patted him on the shoulder by way of goodbye.

He got into the 1100 and raced to San Niccolò. From a distance he scanned the group of flood victims talking and laughing round the fire, but she wasn't there. Maybe she'd already gone to sleep with the elderly couple on the third floor, or to her parents' house. Or maybe . . . He swept away the other hypotheses, pulling hard on his cigarette. What was this stupid mania for theorising, anyway? Did he always have to play police detective and look behind appearances? He was a fool not to have come earlier, nothing more.

He felt restless and had no desire to go home. He thought he would take a hike up to Diotivede's house and hoped he would be at home. Stopping in front of the doctor's gate, he looked at the house, which stood about ten yards back from the street. There was light in the windows, and the pathologist's black Fiat 1100 was parked in the garden. He rang the bell. After a good wait, the door opened, and the silhouette of a woman appeared against the light in the entrance hall. Tall, broad hips, long hair.

'Who's there?' a beautiful voice called out.

'Good evening, forgive me for coming so late. I was looking for Peppino, but it's not important . . . I'll come back another time.'

'Who shall I say called?'

'Franco.'

'Wait just a minute.'

The woman closed the door gently, and her shadow passed behind the curtains at the window. A good two minutes later, the door opened again, and the unmistakable form of Dr Diotivede appeared.

'I hope you haven't brought me a dead body,' he said, seriously concerned.

'I dropped by to have a little chat over a glass of wine, but I see you have company and I don't want to—'

'I've never denied a glass of wine to anyone,' said the doctor, pressing the button to release the lock on the gate.

'Your lady friend won't mind the intrusion?' Bordelli asked, remaining outside the gate.

'I'm sure you're just dying to meet her.'

'I'm mostly curious to see what you're like when you're in love.'

'As silly as everyone else, but not in front of witnesses.'

'Such tenderness . . .' said Bordelli, going into the garden.

'I can only give you half an hour. I spent the whole day at the lab, and I have to be back there tomorrow at dawn.'

'Are you working on the dead or the living?'

'Still the dead, God willing,' said the doctor, and he stood aside to let Bordelli in before closing the door.

Bordelli had always felt comfortable in Diotivede's house. It was sober, clean, and simply and tastefully furnished. A few antiques, a few beautiful paintings, valuable carpets, and here and there a Chinese vase or a bronze statuette. But the real masterpiece was the lighting, which was never harsh and yet able to make every nook, even the most neglected, seem welcoming.

'I only ask that you don't smoke,' said Diotivede, heading down the hallway.

'I wouldn't dare.'

Bordelli looked around in wonder. This was the sort of atmosphere he would like to create in the country house he dreamed of buying. He followed the doctor into the sitting room, and the girlfriend stood up from the sofa and smiled. Diotivede was right. She was beautiful. Refined, chestnut hair, dark eyes, the oval face of an actress and a lovely Junoesque body.

'Pleased to meet you, I'm Marianna.'

'Franco . . .' He shook her hand.

'I've heard a great deal about you.'

'I can only imagine the nasty things Peppino says about me.'

'On the contrary . . .'

'Wine or grappa?' Diotivede asked, approaching the drinks trolley.

'Wine for me,' said Marianna.

'For me too,' said Bordelli.

They all sat down and got comfortable, sipping their red wine. Bordelli in an armchair and the two lovebirds on the sofa, thigh against thigh. They talked about how they had made it through the flood, what they'd seen and what they'd heard. Bordelli glanced over at Marianna often. The woman was a gift from heaven, especially for a man over seventy like Diotivede. She wasn't just beautiful, but likeable and intelligent. She was wearing a skirt with a slit up the side, and when she crossed her legs, Bordelli had to make an effort not to look . . .

He left the car in Viale Petrarca and continued on foot. It still wasn't possible to park near home, as the wrecked cars and mountains of rubbish were still there.

He'd stayed at Diotivede's house until after midnight, drinking wine and chatting, above all trying not to look at Marianna's legs.

He reached his front door, lighting the way with his torch. As he climbed the stairs he imagined he would find Eleonora waiting for him in bed. She had the keys and could let herself in whenever she liked.

He opened the door ever so slowly, peered through the crack, and saw only darkness. He headed down the corridor, holding his breath, and looked into the bedroom, lighting up the bed with the torch . . . It was empty. He'd been seriously hopeful, and now felt terribly let down, like when a promise is not kept.

He was knackered. It had been a long, hard day. He brushed his teeth as best he could with half a glass of mineral water. Lighting a couple of candles on the bedside table, he got undressed and slipped under the covers, consoling himself with Herodotus. That was what he'd forgotten: to buy a little gas heater. With all the cold and damp he'd absorbed, it was a miracle he hadn't got sick again. Perhaps the fever of a few days earlier had made him more resistant. Not against women, though . . .

He woke up very early, and his first thought was of Eleonora. It was still dark outside. He dragged himself into the kitchen, legs aching. He made coffee by the light of the torch, as he used to do during the war . . . and in the penumbra he saw file past all his comrades who'd been blown up by mines, killed in battle, or torn to shreds by mortar shells. Who'd died to offset Mussolini's infantile dreams of glory, of an Italy that would never come to be . . .

Weighed down by melancholy, he drank his coffee and went back to the bedroom to get dressed. He opened the wardrobe. There wasn't much choice. Another week of this and he wouldn't have anything clean left to wear.

Day was beginning to break as he went out, and the street was already peopled with shadows. The cold seat of the Fiat 1100 made him miss his bed. The Viali were almost deserted. There was one kiosk already open, and he bought the day's edition of *La Nazione*.

'OPTIMISM IS MEANINGLESS'
SAYS DEPUTY MAYOR LAGORIO
FLORENCE FIGHTING A DESPERATE BATTLE AGAINST HALF A MILLION TONS OF MUD

While driving, he contacted headquarters via radio, to see whether the surveillance cars had any news. Still dead calm. Waiting . . . waiting . . . always waiting . . .

Though it was still very early, he dashed over to San Niccolò to look for Eleonora. Many people were already hard at work, but there was no sign of her. She was probably still sleeping. He waved hello to Don Baldesi from afar and then quickly drove off, feeling embarrassed. Crossing the Arno again, he went to Campo di Marte. As usual there was a great commotion. A helicopter was landing on the football pitch, making an infernal racket, while people were already queuing up at the provisions stands. A great quantity of K Rations had arrived from the United States, miraculous tins that each contained a whole day's nourishment. The most unusual thing was the arrival of a lorry during the night. After hearing about the flood, an Italian who had opened a pizzeria in Finland had bought a truckload of rubber boots and driven all the way to Florence to deliver them in person.

The Red Cross nurses were looking for volunteers to take medical supplies to different quarters of town, and so Bordelli loaded up the Fiat with small bags and boxes. They gave him a list of names and addresses, and he headed downtown, where he met with a surprise: bulldozers and road scrapers had arrived from Rome, and there were now hundreds of soldiers and firemen working alongside the Florentines and students. Bargellini's pleas had finally been heard.

He dropped by Via dei Neri to say hello to Rosa, but she was neither at home nor in the street. He left a note on her door: *If you need anything, find a working phone, call the station, have them send for me. My best to Gideon and the one-eyed kitten.*

He continued his rounds, and by late morning was back in San Niccolò. Still no sign of her. He went to check the basement of her building and found it still full of mud.

He ordered a panino at the Osteria Fuori Porta and ate it standing in front of the window, keeping a close eye on the street. Nothing. She was nowhere to be found. Vanished.

He got back in the car with his tail between his legs. He could hardly spend all evening waiting for her, not even knowing whether she would appear or not. It was better to come back tomorrow.

To avoid thinking about her, he went and ate in Totò's kitchen, determined to stuff himself to bursting. The cook was in excellent form, dancing amid clouds of steam and having no trouble talking. Bordelli just nodded and chewed. *Spaghetti alla carbonara*, grilled sausages, red wine. This time he didn't refuse the grappa. Not the first glass, nor the second, nor the third . . .

He left the trattoria at half past ten, with two tree trunks in place of his legs. It was starting to rain. He got in the car, lit a cigarette, and sat there watching the street. The night spent with Eleonora seemed a distant memory. Maybe it hadn't even happened. He rolled down the window to let out the smoke.

To escape his torment he turned on the radio and contacted headquarters.

'I've been looking for you, Inspector. Piras called a short while ago and wants to talk to you,' said the officer on duty.

'Get him for me now, would you?'

'Straight away, sir.'

He heard some crackling and, a few seconds later, the Sardinian's voice.

'Can you hear me, Inspector? This is Piras.'

'I hear you loud and clear.'

'Beccaroni went out around half nine in his Jaguar. He drove straight to the Parco delle Cascine and picked up a youth who popped out from behind the trees. We followed them as far as Via Bolognese, where the Jaguar disappeared behind a gate that immediately closed again. The villa is set back from the road, you can barely see it through the trees . . .'

'Is that all?'

'No, now comes the good part . . . You know what car went through the same gate shortly afterwards?'

'I don't feel like playing guessing games, Piras.'

'Panerai's Lancia.'

'Where on Via Bolognese?' Bordelli asked, starting up the car. Piras gave him the number, and they signed off. It was raining harder and harder, but compared to the night of the flood it was just a little sprinkle. Turning uphill on to Via Bolognese, he chewed his lips. He felt like a wolf that had scented its prey. If Colonel Arcieri hadn't asked that favour of him . . . Here at last was some interesting news: the butcher and the lawyer were meeting at a villa along Via Bolognese, bringing along a boy picked up at the Cascine. With the owner of the villa, that made three, the same number as Giacomo's rapists . . . But he was getting ahead of himself. They might just be a group of perverts who liked to hold orgies.

He spotted the first surveillance car parked at the side of the road about thirty yards from the villa's entrance gate. Rolling on a little farther, he saw the Fiat Multipla with Piras and Tapinassi in it. After making a U-turn, he pulled up behind them, made a dash through the rain to avoid getting wet, and got in the back of the Multipla. The two policemen turned round and sketched a military salute.

'Did you read the name on the doorbell?' Bordelli asked.

'It says *Signorini*,' said Tapinassi.

'You've already reported this to headquarters?'

'Yes, sir. They should be calling back soon.'

'Who knows what time their little banquet will end,' Bordelli mumbled, stifling a sausage-flavoured burp.

'We're going to have to be very patient.'

'May I smoke?' Bordelli asked, a cigarette already between his lips.

'I'd rather you didn't,' said Piras, polite but blunt.

'Shit, Piras. Let's open the windows, but you can't ask me not to smoke . . . Not tonight, anyway,' said Bordelli, rolling down his window.

'Yes, sir,' said Piras, and he rolled down his window as well. Beside him Tapinassi was chuckling. It was freezing cold with the two windows open, and Bordelli tossed out his cigarette.

'You're a menace, Piras.'

'If you ask me, smoking is a senseless vice,' said the Sardinian, without taking his eyes off the villa's gate. Every so often he turned on the windscreen wipers to clear his view.

'All this fuss over a cigarette . . .' Bordelli said.

'You're the one who makes such a big deal of it.'

'No, I just like it, that's all.'

'It's an addiction.'

'Oh, come on, an addiction! I can quit whenever I want.'

'You'll have to forgive me, sir, but I don't believe it.'

'All right, then, from this moment on, I won't smoke. Here, take the cigarettes,' said Bordelli, dropping the packet on to Piras's lap. Without a word the Sardinian shut it inside the glove compartment. The rain drummed monotonously on the roof, as the headlights of the rare passing car shone brightly on the wet asphalt.

After a few very long minutes of silence, Bordelli held out his hand.

'Okay, you win, Piras. Give me back the cigarettes. I'll go and smoke out in the rain,' he said dramatically.

'It's not raining that hard,' said Piras, passing him the packet. At that moment there was a call from headquarters with the information on the villa's owner: *Italo Signorini, born 10th November 1939, son of Beatrice Ciacci and the textile manufacturer Emanuele Signorini, both deceased. No record.*

'Today's his birthday,' Bordelli observed.

'Twenty-seven years old,' said Piras. 'He's a lot younger than the other two.'

'Bloody rain,' the inspector grumbled, a cigarette between his lips. He really wanted to smoke, but not to get wet.

At about one o'clock it finally stopped raining. Bordelli had barely managed to smoke half a cigarette outside the Multipla before the butcher's Flavia came out of the gate, followed closely by two other cars, the lawyer's Jaguar and a white saloon. All three descended down Via Bolognese, towards Florence.

'I'll follow the sedan,' said Bordelli, and he ran towards his car and drove off, cigarette between his teeth. When he drove past the gate, it was already closed. The three cars proceeded slowly as far as the Ponte Rosso, followed at a distance by the police cars. The lawyer's Jaguar stopped at the corner of Viale Milton. The passenger's side door opened, and a slender figure slid out of the car and set off along the banks of the Mugnone, swaying like a ballerina. The Jaguar continued on towards Piazza della Libertà.

'Piras, can you hear me?'

'Loud and clear, Inspector.'

'Is that the kid from the Cascine?'

'I'm pretty sure it is.'

'Stay on his tail and find some excuse to pick him up. Take him to the station and have him waiting in my office.'

'All right, Inspector.'

'I'm going to see where the white saloon goes, then I'll return to headquarters. Over and out.'

The Jaguar turned on to Viale Lavagnini, the butcher's Lancia headed towards Le Cure, while the white saloon took Viale Matteotti. The coming and going of cars and military vehicles actually made it easier to tail them. Bordelli accelerated and drew closer to the saloon. It was a Peugeot 404. Just to be sure, he read the numberplate: FI 451025. He couldn't find a pen so tried to memorise it: 45, the end of the war; 10, the year of his birth; 25, the day in July when Mussolini was arrested . . . End of the war, year of birth, Mussolini's arrest . . . End of the war, year of birth, Mussolini's arrest . . .

The Peugeot came to the end of the Viali, crossed the Ponte San Niccolò, and turned on to Viale Michelangelo. After the intersection with Via dei Bastioni, it indicated right, braked and slipped in between two plane trees, pulling up with the nose of the car in front of the entrance gate to an immense villa shrouded in darkness. Bordelli slowed down and turned to look at the guy who had just got out of the car. He caught a glimpse of a tall, well-dressed man sticking a key in the lock of the gate. Prompted by the horn blasts behind him, he drove on, continuously turning round to look, but by now a hedgerow blocked his view. He stopped his car at the start of Via Tacca and went back on foot, along the pavement on the other side of the street. By the time he was opposite the villa, the gate was already closed. A moment later, two windows lit up on the first floor.

He crossed the Viale to see if he could read the name on the gate. On a brass plaque was just the surname *Sercambi*. He returned to the car, repeating the formula . . . End of the war, year of birth, Mussolini's arrest . . . End of the war, year of birth, Mussolini's arrest . . .

The moment he arrived at the station he found Tapinassi waiting for him in the courtyard. They'd picked up the youth who had got out of the Jaguar.

'Where is he now?'

'In your office with Piras, sir.'

They both headed up the stairs.

'What's he like?'

'He's a hysterical little fairy who wears sunglasses even at night. You oughta smell the perfume the guy's got on,' Tapinassi said, chuckling.

'Has he made a fuss?'

'Not really, but he's not exactly thrilled.'

They were just outside the office door and could hear talking inside.

'Write down this registration number and find out who owns the car: FI . . . 45 . . . 10 . . . 25 . . .' said the inspector, helping himself with his mnemonics. Tapinassi didn't have a pen, and he walked away muttering the number. Bordelli heaved a big sigh and went into his office, interrupting the lad's litany of complaints. The whole room smelled of perfume. Piras, who was standing leaning back against the wall, pulled himself up and gave a military salute.

The youth was sitting in front of the desk, back straight, and turned round to see who had come in. Behind his dark glasses he had a nervous little head and feminine features. He looked barely seventeen.

'Maybe now you'll tell me what horrible crime I've committed?' he said, in a high-pitched little-girl's voice and a heavy Milanese accent, writhing in his chair. He was wearing a pastel-green velvet jacket and a purple silk scarf pulled too tightly around his neck.

'Please take off your glasses,' said Bordelli, sitting down.

'Yes, sir!' said the boy, tearing off his glasses with rage and sticking them in his pocket. He had two big, round dark eyes full of resentment. An angry child blinking as if he had a bright light shining in his face.

'Name?' Bordelli asked. He had nothing against the boy, but he was ready to do anything to find out what had happened in the villa on Via Bolognese.

'Mind telling me what I've done wrong?'

'This is just a routine check.'

'Are we not allowed to walk on the street any more?'

'Calm down and answer my questions. Name?'

'Nando Rovario,' the boy said in a defiant tone.

'How old are you?'

'Twelve . . . I ran away from home.'

'I'm warning you, Rovario, I'm not a patient man.'

'What do you want to do? Beat me up? Okay, go right ahead,' said the boy, offering himself like a martyr. Piras observed the scene in silence.

'Don't be silly. Have you got your papers on you?' Bordelli asked.

The boy pulled out an ID card and threw it on to the desk. Bordelli picked it up with a sigh of forbearance and read: *Ferdinando Rovario, born 17 August 1945 at Binasco (MI), height 5 feet 5 inches, brown eyes, dark brown hair, distinguishing features* . . . this part was scratched out.

'Became a legal adult only a few months ago,' he said, glancing at Piras.

'Exactly. I can do whatever I please,' the boy mewled.

'Do you live in Florence?'

'I come and go.'

'Do your parents know what kind of life you lead?'

'They can die for all I care . . .' said Rovario, snapping his head back.

Bordelli had noticed that the boy kept rubbing his fingers nervously under his nose. He leaned forward to look at his pupils. They were almost as wide as the irises.

'Did you finish the cocaine?' he asked, smiling.

'What are you talking about?'

'Empty your pockets on to the desk.'

'Why?'

'Don't make me repeat myself.'

'I want a lawyer,' the boy said, stubbornly. Bordelli sighed in annoyance. Lighting a cigarette, he stood up calmly and came towards the youth with his hands in his pockets.

'Piras, leave us alone for a minute, would you?' he said, without taking his eyes off the boy. Piras went out, and Bordelli sat down on the edge of the desk.

'I can have you searched, and if I find any cocaine on you, you could be in a lot of trouble. But I can also let it slide, if you tell me what I want to know.'

'What do you want to know?' the boy asked, alarmed.

'Tell me how you spent the evening.'

'That's none of your business.'

'I'll help you, then. Around ten o'clock, a Jaguar came to the Cascine to pick you up—'

'You were following me?' said Rovario, round eyed.

'Calm down. The two of you then went to a villa along the Via Bolognese—'

'What do you want from me? You seem to know everything already.'

'Aside from you, there were four men there, am I right?'

'So what if you are?'

'Did you have fun?'

'I certainly hope that's not against the law.'

'Having fun, no, but cocaine, yes,' said the inspector, expelling smoke through his nose. The boy bit his lip.

'You're a monster . . .' he whispered. Bordelli calmly stubbed out his cigarette in the ashtray, staring at the boy all the while.

'Listen to me, Rovario. I have nothing against you, and I don't give a shit how you live and what you do with your backside. I just need some information and I haven't got time to waste fucking around with you. If you're a good boy I'll let you go. Otherwise I'll have you searched, and if I don't find anything on you I'll have you take a nice urine analysis and then lock you up for using narcotics. Is that clear?'

'Yes . . .' said the youth, intimidated by Bordelli's calm, decisive tone. It was clear he couldn't wait to get out of the room.

'All right. Now that we're friends, will you answer my questions?'

'Yes.'

'At the first whiff of bullshit from you, I'll call my colleagues and have them turn you inside out like a sock, and I assure you it won't be pleasant.'

'Ask me whatever you want,' said the boy, giving up the fight.

'Let's start again. At ten o'clock you got into the Jaguar and went to Via Bolognese . . .'

'I don't know whether it was Via Bolognese or the moon we went to . . .'

'Are you trying to pull my leg?'

'The moment I got in the car, the guy had me put on a blindfold.'

'Really . . .'

'For me it was sort of fun.'

'Do you know the names of these gentlemen?'

'No, they use nicknames.'

'What kind of nicknames?'

'Piglet, Sheepie, Giraffe . . . obscene stuff like that. I never even saw their faces, they were wearing carnival masks.'

'What about the man in the Jaguar? Didn't you see him when you got into the car?'

'He was wearing dark glasses with a scarf pulled up to his eyes and his collar turned up.'

'Why did they disguise themselves?'

'That happens to me a lot, when I go with rich men. Many of them are married with children, maybe they're important people . . . At any rate, they're keen not to be recognised.'

'Had you ever been to that villa before?'

'Yes, once.'

'When?'

'Last spring, I think.'

'So you were still a minor . . .'

'I've been making my own decisions for a while now,' the boy said with a hint of mischievousness.

'To continue. Were the same people present at the spring party? I advise you not to lie, since, as you've seen, I already know a lot.'

'I've got no reason to lie, because I've done nothing wrong.'

'Just answer my question, please.'

'There were the same four as tonight and a few others.'

'Was there a sprightly old man of about seventy with a crew cut?'

'Yes.'

'Describe the other four for me.'

'One is fat and hairy, a brute who loses his head when he gets aroused. The guy who picked me up is about the same size as you and has a slight limp. Then there's a tall bloke, very smart, with an icy voice, a real sadist. Then there's the young guy, who's very attractive, thin as a rail, and always seems sad. He lives all by himself in that big villa . . . Brrr, I wouldn't live there even after I died . . .'

'Why not?'

'It's like a museum. I'd rather live in a cemetery.'

'Did they pay you well for the evening?'

'I've got no complaints.'

'Did you have . . . group sex?' asked Bordelli, mildly embarrassed.

'Do I really have to give you the details?' the youth asked, half smiling.

'Just give me a rough description of the troop formations,' Bordelli said metaphorically.

'Well . . . me and the cute guy play the girls, if that's what you're asking.'

'Tell me a little more.'

'So you're a voyeur . . .' the boy said with a mischievous glint in his eye.

'Just go on, please.'

'Me and the cute guy dress up as little children, in shorts and knee-high socks . . .'

'And then what?' the inspector insisted, a shiver running up his spine.

The youth, for his part, appeared calmer than ever. He was finally convinced that nobody had anything against him, and now he seemed almost to be enjoying recounting his exploits. He moved in his chair like a snake, accompanying his words with sinuous gestures.

'We could hide anywhere in the villa we wanted. There are dozens of rooms, not counting the attic and cellars. A little while later the others came looking for us, growling like the giants in fairy tales, going *Ugh ugh* and stuff like that. And then when they found us . . . well, they got all excited and started yelling *Viva il Duce!*' Rosario concluded with a complacent smile, looking at Bordelli with a docile expression.

'Is that how it went at the party in the spring, too?'

'No, we played a different game that time.'

'What was it?'

'Me and the cute guy were little children who needed to be punished, but the ending was the same.'

'Did the old guy get in on it too?'

'Yes, he took part in his own way . . . he stood aside, watching, and did it alone . . . if you know what I mean.'

'Nice little party,' the inspector blurted out in disgust.

'What harm is there in it? To each his own.'

'That's for sure.'

'If you haven't experienced something directly you can't know if you like it or not,' said the boy.

'You're right . . . Maybe you should try living a less depressing life, you might like it.'

'My life isn't the least bit depressing.'

'Are you so sure?'

'What about you? How can you stay cooped up in this squalid, dusty office? I'd kill myself.'

'To each his own,' said Bordelli. The lad shrugged and leaned his head to one side.

'Can I go now?'

'One more thing. Did you hear any of those nice gentlemen make any mention of children?'

'In what sense?'

'Did any of them boast about *having fun* with a little boy?'

'After the riding party the fat one said they used to fuck little Negroes in Eritrea, and then he kissed his fingers in delight.'

'The true soul of Fascism . . .' Bordelli whispered.

'I don't give a damn about those things.'

'And what about the cocaine, who obtains it?'

'The sad young man, I think.'

'Very well. That's all I have to ask you. I'll have someone take you wherever you wish to go,' said Bordelli, standing up. The boy also rose to his feet, and arranged his scarf.

'Inspector . . .'

'Yes, what is it?'

Deep down he rather liked the poor kid.

'I wanted . . . yes, it's true . . . I think you're a good person.'

'I wouldn't be so sure.'

'You pretend to be mean, but under your shell . . .'

'Never mind, Rovario.'

'I mean it.'

'I'll have someone take you home.'

'You're too kind,' said the boy.

Bordelli circled round behind the desk and put a call through the internal line.

'Find Piras for me and send him up to my office,' he said, then hung up.

'I like that Piras, a lot . . .'

'Stay away from that villa, Rovario. I'm telling you as a friend.'

'You don't have to tell me.'

'I'm going to keep an eye on you, and if I see you talking to those people you're going to be in big trouble.'

'I swear to God that if the Jaguar comes back I won't even let them see me,' said the boy, crossing his fingers over his mouth and kissing them.

At last Piras arrived.

'Have someone take him wherever he wants to go and then come back here,' Bordelli said to him, pulling out another cigarette.

'Yes, sir.'

'Goodbye, Rovario, I wish you my very best.'

Bordelli held out his hand, and the youth shook it ever so lightly.

'Bye bye, Inspector,' he said, giving a little bow and then going out with Piras. Bordelli lit the cigarette and dropped into his chair. It was almost three . . .

If Rosario was telling the truth, he couldn't identify the villa on Via Bolognese even if he wanted to. As long as they didn't come back for him at the Cascine, there was no way for him to alert the four friends. But what if he was lying and knew how to get in touch with them? What if he filled them in on the situation? There was no choice, Bordelli had to take that chance. He couldn't very well throw the kid in jail and leave him there. Deep down, though, he wasn't worried. Something told him that Rovario was telling the truth. The monsters would never find out . . .

But he was reasoning as if he now knew for certain that they were the killers . . . He had to go about this much more slowly and take care not to let himself fall prey to suggestion . . . But it was hopeless. He was unable to rid himself of the terrible sensation that he had the maniacs who had raped and killed Giacomo Pellissari in the palm of his hand. He blew the smoke up to the ceiling, trying to put his thoughts in order and work out what his next move should be.

Piras came back a few minutes later with a typewritten page that he laid down on the desk. It was the information gathered from the number plate of the Peugeot. The car was registered in the name of Gualtiero Sercambi, born in Parma, 16 February 1922, residing at 12 bis Viale Michelangelo since '49. No record.

'Does that name mean anything to you?' Bordelli asked.

'No . . .'

'Let's drop Gattacci's house from our surveillance. He hasn't reappeared, at any rate . . . and let's keep an eye on this Sercambi.'

'What'd the kid tell you?' asked Piras, squinting with disgust at the smoke floating in the air.

'I'll sum it up briefly . . .'

And he quickly recounted the things he'd learned from

Rovario, admitting at the end that he felt he was on the right track.

'But even if they are the killers, how are we going to prove it?' asked Piras, uncharacteristically pessimistic. Bordelli remained thoughtfully silent for a moment, then stood up with bones cracking.

'We'll have to sleep on it, Piras. We'll talk again in the morning.'

Driving home, he kept on thinking about the little party in Via Bolognese. Were they really the killers? Were they the gang of monsters who'd killed the boy? Had the phone bill he'd found actually worked a miracle? Had that silly piece of paper actually turned out to be Ariadne's thread that led out of the labyrinth? What the hell should he do now? Even if they really were the monsters, years of surveillance might not yield a thing. And they could keep on picking up boys at the Cascine and playing hide-and-seek . . . So what? They could do whatever they liked in their own homes. Maybe Giacomo Pellissari had only been an accidental victim, and with a murder on their hands the fun-loving friends would be very careful not to take any more risks. Surveillance wasn't very useful, unless they happened to kidnap another little boy.

In spite of everything, Eleonora continued to hover above his thoughts. Who knew where she was at that moment? He had to find the time to go and look for her tomorrow. All of a sudden, he slapped his forehead . . . the gas heater, dammit! He'd forgotten about it again.

Crossing the Ponte alla Vittoria, he saw a few human shadows looking out over the parapets at the river. A couple of drops of rain had sufficed to reawaken fear, even though the Arno was so low you could barely see it. When he reached Viale Petrarca he parked the Fiat along the walls, as usual. He proceeded through the darkness, lighting his way with the torch, when to his great relief he saw that the scrapers had also passed through San Frediano. A few wrecked cars and several mountains of debris had been carried away.

He went through the front door and started up the stairs.

Three-twenty. He was exhausted and desperately needed to rest his weary bones. He reached the third floor panting heavily. Entering the flat, he went straight to the bedroom and his heart skipped a beat. In his bed lay Eleonora, sleeping, her hair spread out over the pillow and her lips slightly parted. He felt so emotional he had to flee to the kitchen. He started smoking a cigarette, trying to calm down. He would never have had the courage to surprise her like that, for fear of appearing over-eager. Whereas she hadn't given it a second thought, had come into the flat and got into bed. That was what modern girls were like.

Suddenly, what he hadn't even dared to hope just a short while ago now seemed perfectly normal. She was sleeping in his bed as if it were the most obvious thing in the world. He crushed his cigarette in a small dish and went back to the bedroom. He set the torch down on the floor, so as not to make too much light. He undressed, turned off the torch, and in total darkness gently slipped under the covers, trying very hard not to brush against her. He didn't want to wake her up. Suddenly she moved, faintly moaning, then stopped. She must have woken up. He thought he could feel her smiling, and a small hand reached out in the darkness and touched his stubbly face. He took her hand and kissed it.

'What time did you get here?'

'Shhh . . .' she said, and pressed her body against his. They exchanged a long kiss, caressing each other all the while. Eleonora then jumped on top of him and they made love in an entirely different way from the first time. Afterwards they fell immediately asleep.

When Bordelli opened his eyes, the room was bright with daylight. He found Eleonora's face half an inch away from his, more beautiful than ever. She was already awake and looking at him without saying anything. He opened his mouth to speak, but she put a hand over his lips.

'Shhh . . .' She pulled him on top of her and forced him to resume the discussion interrupted by sleep. For the whole time Bordelli managed not to think of the monsters of Via Bolognese, but the moment he collapsed on to the bed, there they were again in his mind. She turned her back to him and pressed up against him, hot and wet with sweat. A well-deserved rest after the battle. They were both a bit out of breath. Bordelli would have liked to speak, perhaps to tell her what he'd done the night before, but he didn't dare breathe a word. They lay there in silence, pressed together like two spoons in a cutlery box. From the street came the sound of an approaching bulldozer, then some voices, but all the bustle outside only made the bed seem more intimate and secret. The bulldozer drove past, then another followed, stopping almost directly under the window, and began shovelling debris.

Eleonora bent her head back to graze his cheek with her lips, then got out of bed. It was the first time Bordelli had seen her standing completely naked, and he found her much more beautiful than he had imagined. Perhaps the right word was 'gorgeous'.

The girl got dressed in a hurry, because of the cold, amusing herself by imitating a stripper's movements. Bordelli cursed himself for not having bought a heater.

'You are so beaut—'

'Shhh,' she said, finger over her lips. She left the room and went into the kitchen to get the coffee pot going.

Bordelli couldn't help but think about the day ahead. He had an idea what he needed to do to find out whether *they* were really the killers. He had to find the weak link in the chain and try to make it break – that is, make him confess. The butcher seemed like a tough customer, someone who couldn't be shaken so easily. The lawyer was no doubt accustomed to lying and dissimulating, and must certainly know a thousand ways to defend himself from baseless accusations. Gattacci had fled who knew where, and despite appearances, he wasn't without resources. Which left the others: the distinguished man with the Peugeot and the youngster who lived in the villa. Which was the weaker of the two?

Hearing Eleonora lock herself in the bathroom, he got out of bed and dressed in a hurry. He would have paid pure gold to take a hot shower with her. He ran to the kitchen to take the coffee pot off the burner and then rinsed two little cups as best he could with a little mineral water.

Eleonora came into the kitchen and signalled to him not to talk. They drank their coffee in silence, looking into each other's eyes. She then set her cup down on the table, drew near to give him a light little peck on the lips, and left. Bordelli sat there for a few seconds, stunned, staring at the empty hallway. Then he roused himself and looked at his watch. Ten past eight. He went into the bathroom to try to wash. As there wasn't much water left in the drum, he decided not to shave.

He went out and passed by a bulldozer at work as he headed for Piazza Tasso. He felt like a lion. As if he were twenty years old. Turning round to cast a glance towards Via del Campuccio, he saw Ennio in the distance, emptying a bucket of mud into the street. He didn't have time to shout a greeting before Ennio disappeared back into the building. A patient man, poor Ennio.

He got into the Fiat 1100, then contacted headquarters as he was turning on to the Viali. The morning surveillance shift had just begun: Piras was in Viale Michelangelo at Sercambi's villa, and the car that had been watching Gattacci's house had moved to Via Bolognese.

He stopped in Piazza della Libertà to buy *La Nazione*.

A GLIMMER OF HOPE
IN THE CITY'S GREAT BATTLE
MACHINES BEGIN TO ARRIVE
TO FREE FLORENCE OF DEBRIS

At headquarters he shut himself in his office. Grabbing a clean sheet of paper from a drawer, he lit a cigarette and wrote down the five names that were now lodged in his brain: *Livio Panerai, Moreno Beccaroni, Alfonso Gattacci, Gualtiero Sercambi, Italo Signorini*. He sketched a sort of caricature of each, even the young owner of the villa, whom he'd never seen. Were they really the monsters? He rolled the paper up into a ball and tossed it into the rubbish bin. He had to learn more about Sercambi and Signorini, find out what kind of people they were. By now he was ready to try anything to get to the bottom of this. He could always bluff if need be. He just had to find the right target.

There was a knock at the door. An officer delivered a message from Piras and quickly left. The inspector read the handwritten note:

The Peugeot 404 came out of the gate in Viale Michelangelo just before nine, with two people inside: one in the driver's seat, the other seated in the back. It went as far as Piazza del Duomo and stopped outside the front door of the Episcopal Curia. ('Holy sh—' Bordelli muttered, goosebumps on his arms.) *The passenger got out. Under his coat he was wearing a cassock. He opened the main door with a key and disappeared inside. The Peugeot drove away, and we followed it to the San Lorenzo market. The driver calmly did some shopping and then returned to Viale Michelangelo.*

'Bloody hell . . .' Bordelli raced out of his office to the radio room, where the men on duty were still coordinating rescue efforts for victims in the surrounding countryside. He called

Piras and asked him to describe the driver in his report, and the man who'd gone into the Curia building.

'I only saw them from far away,' said the Sardinian.

'Tell me anyway.'

'The driver looks about forty, and he's short, sort of fat, chestnut hair. The prelate is tall, slender, upper-class and doesn't have a hair on his head. That's about all I can tell you.'

'It's good enough for now,' said Bordelli.

'Any orders, sir?'

'Never mind about the driver, but keep tailing the prelate. Over and out.'

He went back upstairs to his office and stood in front of the window, looking at the sky. Who was Gualtiero Sercambi? A villa in the hills of Florence, a personal chauffeur, a priest's cassock . . . It all pointed to his being a high-ranking prelate in the Curia, but Bordelli needed to know more. Given his haste, he had no choice but to ask Batini, an old journalist who knew every corner of Florence as well as he did the insides of his pockets. He called the brand-new offices of *La Nazione*, flooded barely a month after their inauguration, and asked to speak to him.

'Yes?'

'Hello Federico . . . It's Bordelli . . .'

'Oh, hello, copper. How are you?'

'Not too bad. How are things going at the paper?'

'We're printing in Bologna, but everything else is fine. Tell me everything.'

'I need to ask you a favour.'

'If I can be of help . . .'

'Who is Gualtiero Sercambi?'

'You mean Monsignor Sercambi?'

'That's the one.'

'What would you like to know?'

'Everything there is.'

'Well . . . For the past few years he's been a kind of personal assistant of the archbishop's, a sort of grey eminence, not much in view but very powerful. To give you an idea, he has a direct line to the pope, the president, and all his ministers.'

'What kind of person is he?'

'Cold as ice. He speaks very little and weighs every word before he utters it. I'm almost certain he's a Freemason, but I have no proof of it, I'm just going by smell. In Florence, above a certain level of power or wealth, they're all Freemasons.'

'Thanks . . . I'll let you get back to work.'

They said goodbye, and Bordelli laid siege to a cigarette. Well, the weak link in the chain certainly wasn't Monsignor Sercambi. That left only the youth, the owner of the villa where they played hide-and-seek. He called the radio room and asked who was on duty in Via Bolognese.

'Tapinassi and Biagi, sir. Car thirty-five.'

Bordelli reached up and took a set of naval binoculars from a shelf. They had nine magnification settings. He'd brought them home with him from the war together with a San Marco regiment dagger and a couple of pistols. He went down to the courtyard and got in the 1100. The moment he was out in the street he called Tapinassi on the radio.

'Any news?'

'Nobody's come out of the villa. At half-eight a fat lady opened the little gate with a set of keys and went in. From the look of her and the way she's dressed she must be the cleaner. She hasn't come back out yet. At half-nine the dustbin lorry passed. In the last half-hour two errand boys came with groceries, one after the other . . . And that's all, Inspector.'

'I'm on my way to see you now. Over and out.'

Driving up the Via Bolognese, he thought of the night he'd spent with the beautiful Eleonora, wondering when he would see her again. They hadn't said a single word to each other, and had made no arrangement to meet again. It was she who'd wanted the silence, and he'd played along. It wasn't easy for people of his generation to live suspended in mid-air, but he had to admit that it was thrilling. Every moment held the possibility of surprise, though it did make one suffer . . .

He drove past Villa Triste,[49] with its big empty squares of cement looming over the road, where the Nazis and their Fascist collaborators had tortured resistance fighters during the occupation, and his love pangs seemed more ridiculous than ever. He remembered something his father had told him right after the war. As Mario Carità was torturing partisan fighters in the building's cellars, a Benedictine friar banged out Neapolitan songs on a piano to cover the screams. He was known as Father Ildefonso, but his real name was Alfredo Epaminonda Troia. It was impossible to forget a name like that.

He sat alone in the 1100. That way he could smoke freely without disturbing anyone. He'd parked far from the gate, at the top of the hill. The other car was some fifty yards farther down.

At noon the cleaning lady came out on to the pavement and headed down the hill. Ten minutes later a sporty, fire-red Alfa Romeo emerged from the property and stopped on the pavement, engine running. Bordelli already had the binoculars in hand. He saw a young man of about thirty get out, rather good-looking, medium height, slender build, gloomy expression, regular features, straight black hair that half covered his ears . . . He fitted the description Rovario had given. The man closed the gate and got back into the two-seater convertible. He drove off, tyres screeching, towards Florence. Bordelli followed behind him and called Tapinassi on the radio.

'I'll follow him myself.'

'Very well, sir.'

'You stay here at the villa. Over and out.'

There was traffic, and the Alfa tried to overtake the other cars without success. When it reached Piazza della Libertà, it took a right turn on to Viale Lavagnini, grinding the gears. Bordelli could count on the 1100's souped-up engine and had no trouble keeping up with the other car. At a red light he read the number plate and wrote it down on his matchbox. The Alfa went the entire circuit of the Viali up to the Arno and then took the Lungarno Vespucci at a crawl, stuck behind an army lorry. It crossed the bridge and turned right on to the Lungarno on the opposite bank, following the flow of the traffic. It passed under the arch of Santa Rosa, and two hundred yards farther on it pulled up on the right, under some trees. Bordelli slowed down, and when he realised the young man wanted to cross the street he stopped to let him by, ignoring the furious blasts of horns behind him. As he started up again he watched the man in his rear-view mirror and saw him disappear into the blind alley of Via della Fonderia. He parked the car a hundred yards up the boulevard, hiding it behind another vehicle. Contacting headquarters, he gave them the number plate of the Alfa Romeo, just to be on the safe side. In order to get a better view of the entrance to the alley, he moved across and sat sideways in the passenger seat. He kept the windows open and blew the smoke outside. He had no idea how long he would have to wait there, and the seconds passed exasperatingly slowly. He was sick of waiting, always waiting . . .

Signorini reappeared just a few minutes later, got back in his car and drove off, spinning the wheels on the muddy asphalt. Cocaine, thought the inspector. He lay down on the seat to avoid being noticed by Signorini, then waited for him to pass before hopping back over to the driver's side to follow him. It wasn't hard to spot the bright red Alfa amid the rest of the dull-coloured traffic, and he was able to follow it from a distance of about thirty yards. The Alfa crossed the Ponte alla Vittoria, continued up the Viali, then at Piazza della Libertà turned towards Via Bolognese. Bordelli stopped along the kerb and called Tapinassi.

'Signorini's heading home . . . Any news at your end?'

'Nothing, sir.'

'I'm going to go and have a bite to eat.'

'Lucky you, sir,' said Tapinassi.

The inspector headed straight for Totò's kitchen. He managed not to eat too much, and half an hour later he was already back at the office with a cigarette between his lips. On his desk he found the information on the owner of the Alfa Romeo, which was the same as that on the owner of the villa in Via Bolognese.

He rang the radio room and gave the order for all the surveillance vehicles to come back to headquarters, except for the one tailing Signorini. For the moment the policemen could turn their attention back to the rescue efforts.

So there was his target: the sad-faced young man. Bordelli knew he might have to use some rather unorthodox methods, but he had no alternative. He had to proceed very carefully. He couldn't afford to make even one wrong move. He was also hoping for a little luck.

First of all he had to verify whether Signorini was indeed buying drugs in Via della Fonderia, so he could gain the upper hand. There was only one person who could help him: Botta, as usual.

He went at once to look for him in Via del Campuccio and found him with a bucket in hand and covered with mud from head to toe.

'I need you for something, Ennio,' said an anxious Bordelli, getting right to the point.

'Another lock?' asked Botta, wiping his hands with a rag.

'We're changing category this time . . . Can you pinch a wallet without getting caught?'

'Are you trying to offend me, Inspector?'

'You're not that kind of thief?'

'Are you kidding? I could do it by the time I was ten! In all modesty, I've even given lessons.'

'Are you serious?'

'Do I ever lie, Inspector? I can lift a wallet and put it back any time and any way I want.'

'Do you do it often?'

'I'm *no longer* that kind of thief,' said Botta, laughing.

'Are you sure you haven't lost your touch?' the inspector asked with concern. Ennio made a gesture of irritation, lost his balance, and grabbed hold of Bordelli.

'I'm sorry, Inspector . . . this damned mud . . .'

'I was already imagining you on the ground.'

'I've dirtied your coat,' said Botta. He pulled a handkerchief out of his pocket and tried to repair the damage.

'Never mind . . .'

'You're better waiting for the mud to dry, it comes off easier then.'

'So will you help me out, Ennio?'

'First open your wallet and give me back the rolled-up thousand-lira note I just put in it,' Botta said, smiling.

'You're joking, of course . . .' Bordelli took out his wallet, opened it, and found a one-thousand-lira note rolled up inside it. His jaw dropped.

'Now do you believe me?'

'I believed you before,' said Bordelli, giving him back the thousand lire.

'You seemed a little sceptical.'

'Force of habit,' Bordelli explained.

'Who's the sucker?'

'A rich, melancholy young man.'

'I've heard the sulphur mines are a good cure for melancholy . . .'

'I'm almost certain the guy goes and buys cocaine in the blind alley of Via della Fonderia. Are you aware of any dealers on that street?'

'I've nothing whatsoever to do with that stuff, but if you want I can ask a friend.'

'When?'

'Give me just one minute.'

Botta walked away, towards Via Romana, an area the flood waters hadn't reached. A hundred yards or so farther up, he disappeared into a doorway. Moments later he reappeared and returned to the inspector, whistling. He spoke in a very low voice, without moving his lips.

'A bloke from Genoa, thirty-five years old. He's a bartender at a nightspot and does a little business on the side as a top-up . . .'

'Cocaine?'

'A bit of everything, but he's small potatoes. Not even worth the cost of a day at Murate.'

'I couldn't care less about a dope-dealing bartender, I'm looking for something else.'

'Tell me what you want me to do.'

'The next time the guy goes to Via della Fonderia, I want you to grab his wallet before he gets back in the car. And let's hope we find some cocaine in it.'

'How will I know when he goes there?'

'Tomorrow morning I'll send an unmarked car to keep you company, and when the time is right, I'll call you on the radio.'

'Having policemen around isn't exactly my idea of fun, but if it can't be avoided . . .'

'It'll only be during the day. At night I'll leave you in peace.'

'Thanks for being so sensitive, Inspector.'

He didn't leave the station until after midnight, feeling dead tired and wondering whether he would come home to the same surprise as the night before. The same stale smell of heating oil and sewage hung in the air, but the situation in the streets was much improved. In the glow of the street lamps one could still see the thick black line running across the fronts of the buildings, getting higher and higher the closer one came to the Arno.

When he got to San Frediano, the neighbourhood was still in darkness, but he was finally able to park the 1100 just outside his door. Only two or three other cars were parked along the street. It felt like the late forties again.

He'd finally remembered to buy a little gas heater, along with a small gas canister that was as heavy as a boulder. He reached the third floor out of breath and was greeted only by darkness when he opened the door. He went to look in the bedroom, convinced he would find her in his bed. He was wrong. On the pillow lay a note: *Shhh*. Well, it was better than nothing. He sniffed the piece of paper and thought perhaps he could smell her scent. He was dying to hold her in his arms but didn't feel like going to look for her. He would play along and patiently wait for her to decide.

He lit the heater to warm the room up a little, then went into the dining room and sat down to smoke his last cigarette. What time had Eleonora come by? Why hadn't she stayed? Had she got tired of waiting and left? Or had she already known she wouldn't stay?

He returned to the bedroom, determined not to tax his brain

307

with pointless questions. The air was barely less cold than before, but to make up for it, it now stank of hot metal. He didn't have the strength to read even one page of Herodotus. He closed the gas bottle, turned off the torch and got into bed. How long would it take for him to fall asleep? In the silence, every so often he thought he heard a key turning in the lock, but it was only his imagination.

MASSIVE CLEARANCE OPERATION
BUT SITUATION REMAINS CRITICAL
HOPE RETURNS TO THE STREETS OF FLORENCE
INCIDENTS AT SENATE AS MORO SPEAKS

He left the house very early the next morning and went to watch the gate in Via Bolognese in person with Piras. He felt the need to follow developments from up close, to keep from thinking about Eleonora. An unmarked car with Tapinassi and Rinaldi in it was still shadowing Ennio, with the radio on.

The cleaning lady, the dustbin lorry, the delivery boys, the same things as the previous morning. A lethal bore. In order to smoke in peace, Bordelli got out of the 1100 and went for a little walk. The cleaning lady came out at twelve on the dot and headed down the pavement towards town.

Waiting, waiting . . .

The red Alfa popped out on the street at 3.25. As usual, Signorini got out to close the gate, then drove off with a roar. He always opened and closed the gate himself, therefore had no one to perform this service for him. Piras called Tapinassi's car to tell them to get ready. Across from the Trattoria da Cesare, the Alfa turned on to Via Nazionale. It then parked in Piazza Indipendenza, and the driver got out and continued on foot towards the centre of town.

'Call Tapinassi again and tell him it was a false alarm,' said Bordelli, and he got out to tail Signorini on foot. He watched him walk with a hesitant step, bent slightly forward.

The young man went on a long hike through the flood-stricken areas, a bit like a tourist visiting the ruins of an ancient city. He was smartly dressed and rather conspicuous amid the filth. As he walked by, the people toiling in the mud watched and whispered comments to each other. When the daylight began to fade, Signorini went back to his Alfa and drove home.

Bordelli decided to call off the night-time surveillance. He wasn't interested in where Signorini went at night. He had another purpose: to scare the kid, threaten him, force him to talk. It was his last hope for keeping the case from being shelved. He had to give it a try, even though he had no evidence to hand, no real clue at all . . . Was his intuition corrrect? Had he really cornered Giacomo's killers? He was ready to do anything to find out. It was do or die.

When he went home that evening, he noticed with relief that electrical power had returned to the neighbourhood. It seemed like the end of a nightmare. In some ruined shops there were still a few insomniacs keeping busy, while above he saw a number of heads hanging motionless over the windowsills. He looked up at his bedroom window . . . it was illuminated. He raced up the stairs and opened the door with his heart in his mouth. Lights were on in the hallway and kitchen as well.

'Is that you?' he called out, going into the bedroom with a half-smile on his lips. The bed was exactly as he had left it, and there wasn't even a note on the pillow. What a nincompoop . . . The light switches had been on since the day of the flood. He should have remembered.

Maybe he wasn't cut out for this game of expectations and surprises, he thought to himself, putting the very last cigarette of the day between his lips.

He made his way around the flat, seeing by the light of the lamps the state it had been reduced to. Muddied floors, kitchen sink overflowing with plates and cups, dirty clothes on the backs of chairs. The bathroom smelled like a sewer. He tried turning on the tap in the bathroom basin, and after some gurgling, a stream of dark water started to come out. He really hadn't expected it, and couldn't help but smile. He let the water run for a while. He pulled the chain to flush the toilet, and the familiar sound was a joy to hear. The tap water was becoming gradually clearer, though there wasn't much pressure. As he always left the water heater on, he turned off the basin tap and opened the one on the bath. Waiting for it to fill up, he went and grabbed the gas heater and lit it.

Easing himself into the hot water, he moaned with pleasure. He lay back, eyes closed, enjoying this unexpected well-being. Realising he was in danger of falling asleep, he pulled himself up. He grabbed the soap and scrubbed himself long and hard, scraping his skin.

When he got out of the tub, the water was black with all the filth he had been carrying around for the past few days. He felt five pounds lighter.

The air in the room was stifling, and he turned off the little heater. Then he shaved, standing naked in front of the mirror. He felt like a different man. Wrapping himself in a bathrobe, he raced to the bedroom. He quickly changed the sheets, put the blankets on top, and slipped into bed. He managed to read only a few pages of Herodotus, before turning out the light. After all those days in the dark, the glow of the street lamps through the slats of the shutters gave him a warm feeling. The only thing missing was her . . .

BARGELLINI TAKES STOCK OF THE DISASTER
MANY PARTS OF TUSCANY STILL ISOLATED

At 7 a.m. that morning the unmarked cars took up their positions. Same formation as before. Piras and Bordelli in Via Bolognese, Rinaldi and Tapinassi in San Frediano outside Botta's place.

It was a Sunday. The cleaning lady didn't show up; no dustbin lorries, no delivery boys. The waiting was more boring than ever. Bordelli had great difficulty restraining himself from lighting one cigarette after another, as when he had been on the cruiser *San Giorgio* staring at the empty horizon . . .

Finally, at 11.25, Signorini's Alfa two-seater came out of the gate and headed towards town. The sports car went to the gardens of the Fortezza, hugged the wall, went through the railway underpass and then turned on to Via Belfiore. Piras exchanged a glance with the inspector and called Tapinassi on the radio.

'I think this is it . . . Get yourselves to the Lungarno Santa Rosa.'

'Roger.'

Signorini crossed the Arno and parked in the same spot as before, across from the blind alley of Via della Fonderia. The traffic on the street was continuous. Bordelli had already pulled over to the pavement, eyes following the young man as he hastily crossed the street and went down the alley. There was no sign of Botta, and the inspector grabbed the radio microphone and called Tapinassi.

'Where are you? I don't see Ennio . . .'

'We just dropped him off on the Lungarno. We're sitting tight at Porta San Frediano.'

'All right, then, over and out . . . He must be hiding,' Bordelli said to Piras. Despite his great faith in Botta's abilities he felt rather nervous and stuck a cigarette in his mouth. Feeling Piras's eyes boring a hole through him, he sighed and put it back in the packet.

'There's another solution to this problem, Piras.'

'What problem?'

'Smoking.'

'And what would the solution be?'

'If you started smoking yourself. That way it wouldn't bother you any more.'

'Go ahead and light your firecracker, Inspector. As long as the window's open . . .'

'The Lord will reward you in heaven,' said Bordelli, rolling down the window and lighting up.

A few minutes later Signorini came back out of the alley. As he was trying to make his way across the busy street between cars and motorcycles, a bearded tramp with matted hair appeared on the other side. He looked filthy and staggered as though drunk. But it wasn't a tramp . . .

'Here we go,' Bordelli whispered. Ennio was standing right in front of the Alfa Romeo's door. Signorini finally managed to get across, looking all the while at the tramp with an expression of disgust. When he reached the car, Botta took a step forward and pretended to fall to the ground, grabbing Signorini's coat. The young man pushed him away, ignoring his drunken apologies, then got into the car and drove off, spraying mud with the tyres.

'I have a hard time believing he actually did it,' said Bordelli, starting up the car. He waited until the Alfa was out of sight, put the car in gear and drove up to Botta with the window down.

'Did you manage it, Ennio?'

'Don't ask me pointless questions, Inspector,' said Botta, dropping Signorini's wallet between Bordelli's legs.

'You're a genius . . . Come on, get in, I still need you for something.'

As Botta was getting in the car, the inspector opened the wallet and rifled quickly through it.

'Bingo,' he said, showing the others a bulging piece of folded-up tinfoil. He handed it to Piras and drove off, hoping to catch up with Signorini's Alfa. He honked the horn to get the other cars out of his way, swearing between clenched teeth. Ennio was combing his hair in the back seat, looking in the rear-view mirror. Piras opened the foil packet carefully, then brought it to his nose to smell the white powder.

'It's not cocaine, sir.'

'It's not?'

'Morphine.'

'Bloody hell . . .' Bordelli muttered, thinking of the traces of morphine found in the little boy's blood.

'And rather high quality, I'd say.'

'How many grams?'

'About five, more or less,' said Piras, folding the foil back up.

'Fifty thousand lire?' Bordelli asked. Ennio leaned forward to give his own opinion.

'If it's good stuff, even a hundred.'

'Didn't you tell me you steered clear of the nasty stuff?'

'It's true, but I still know the going rates.'

'You know you really looked like a proper tramp, Ennio?'

'I was an actor in my youth, Inspector.'

'Sooner or later I'll find out you sang with Celentano,' said Bordelli, giving a smile. Piras kept rifling through the wallet but found nothing else of interest. He put the morphine back inside it and then laid it in the glove compartment.

They spotted the red Alfa on Viale Strozzi and followed behind it, hidden by the traffic. Signorini then went up Via Bolognese and stopped in front of his gate. He got out to open it and, after driving the car through, got out again to close it.

Bordelli turned round in a space at the side of the road and went back towards the villa, parking the car some distance away from the gate.

'Let's see how long it takes him to discover the trick,' said Bordelli, glancing at his watch. Twelve minutes past twelve.

'I'll give him five minutes,' said Botta, leaning forward for a better look.

The Alfa came back out of the gate at sixteen minutes past the hour. Signorini hurriedly reclosed the gate, then got back in the car and blasted off.

'You follow him, Piras. I'm sure he's going back to his dealer . . . Ennio, you come with me,' said Bordelli, putting Signorini's wallet in his pocket. He got out of the 1100 with Botta. Piras got behind the wheel and was off like a rocket.

'This time I have a feeling there's a nice big lock to contend with,' said Ennio.

'You're wrong. There're two.'

'I can handle as many as you like, Inspector. The more the merrier.'

They descended the incline of Via Bolognese and stopped to chat right in front of Signorini's gate like two friends discussing football. Botta studied the lock and smiled. Bordelli squeezed his arm.

'Need much time to open it?' he asked in a whisper.

'As much as if I had the key,' Ennio blustered. Bordelli took a last look at the road to make sure nobody was watching.

'Let's go . . .'

They approached the gate. Botta quickly pulled from his pocket his passepartout, a piece of thick iron wire tapered at the point. He stuck it into the lock, which clicked almost at once. They hurried through, closing the gate behind them. A small pebbled driveway climbed up towards an immense eighteenth-century, three-storey villa surrounded by centuries-old trees.

'If this was my place I don't think I'd be so melancholy,' said Ennio.

They looked around to check whether anybody could see

them, but the closest homes were hidden behind trees and high garden walls. They could move about freely. They headed for the villa, walking between two rows of plants in large terracotta pots. It felt like a world apart, far from the noise and smell of common mortals. The only incongruous element was a beaten-up Fiat 600 parked under a huge oak. They climbed the stone staircase and arrived outside the great door. Botta bent down to look at the lock.

'Shit, this one's *trouble*,' he said, in the tone of a connoisseur.

'How long will it take to open it?'

'That's not easy to say.'

Grabbing his passepartout, he got down to work. Bordelli looked at his watch impatiently.

'If you haven't managed in ten minutes . . .'

'I need silence, Inspector. This is a delicate procedure.'

'Sorry.'

The minutes went by, with Botta more and more absorbed in his task. His thick fingers moved quite delicately, as if he were applying plaster with a lizard's foot. Finally they heard a metallic click, and the door opened.

'There we are. How long did it take me?'

'Six minutes.'

'Could have been worse.'

'Thanks, Ennio, I don't know what I'd do without you.'

'Piece o' cake,' said Botta.

'I'm going inside to wait for Signorini. Sorry to send you away on foot, but at the moment I have no choice.'

'No problem, a brisk walk never harmed anybody.'

'Ciao, Ennio.'

'Good luck, Inspector.'

Bordelli went inside and turned the doorknob to make the lock catch. The daylight streamed in through the slats in the closed shutters, and visibility was pretty good. The entrance hall alone was four times as big as his flat. Patterned floors, dark furniture, antique paintings, fancy ceramics . . .

Every detail oozed wealth. A monumental staircase led to the upper floors. Reaching the top of the first flight, he went down a broad corridor with a number of doors. He started wandering about the rooms. He'd never been inside a house like this before. Vast salons, silk Persian rugs, Renaissance suits of armour, statues, tiger and lion skins with embalmed heads and glass eyes, modern television sets and lamps, glass-fronted cabinets with lead-lined panes, paintings ancient and modern, elegant little sitting rooms with sofas and low tables, a music room with a grand piano, other doors and other rooms connecting with one another in an unending labyrinth . . . A perfect setting for playing hide-and-seek.

He stopped in a study lined with dark-wood bookcases soaring up to the ceiling and crammed with books. It looked like one of the more frequently used rooms. Two large modern armchairs, a low, small crystal table covered with books and bottles, an antique grandfather clock almost six and a half feet tall. Between the two windows, somewhat aslant, a magnificent desk with a typewriter on it. There was a sheet of paper in it, and he bent down to read the only written line: *At that moment Ruggero understood what had actually happened and felt a* . . . Beside the typewriter were more pages, face down. He picked them up, and on the first page saw: Italo Signorini / *He Who Does Not Die Repeats Himself.* Odd title. It must be a novel. He read the opening lines:

Ruggero was not made to be in the company of others. In fact he hated people. Hated them because he was afraid of them. As a child he was so shy that if anyone ever spoke to him he would turn bright red. He sought solitude, darkness, silence. He'd never known his mother, who died when he was only a few months old. His father was an imposing, wealthy man who never laughed. They lived in a large, dark villa surrounded by a park . . .

The outpourings of a spoiled child, he thought, putting the pages back. In a drawer he found a few new syringes and a large wad of cotton. Towards the back of the drawer and partly hidden was a nine-calibre Beretta wrapped in a piece of deerskin and loaded with a full magazine. An illegal weapon. He put it in his pocket and continued his visit.

On the second floor were more sitting rooms and countless bedrooms that smelled rather musty. Four-poster beds, tapestries, wardrobes with time-blackened mirrors. The only lived-in room was the one in which Signorini surely slept. Shoes on the floor, clothes strewn everywhere, books, bottles, glasses . . .

Almost twenty minutes had gone by. Bordelli went calmly down to the first floor and back to the study. He collapsed into an armchair and lit a cigarette. All he could do was wait, but the wait was completely different this time.

Finishing the cigarette, he lit another. In the silence he could hear the slow ticking of the grandfather clock. Extracting the tinfoil with the morphine from Signorini's wallet, he set it down on the arm of the chair. Leaning his head back, he started staring at the crystal chandelier hanging from the ceiling in the middle of the room. He was about to play his last card, and if he lost he would have to give up. He'd proceeded blindly, coincidence by coincidence. Starting with a phone bill, he had ended up at a villa in Via Bolognese, but he still didn't have a speck of proof, only hunches and feelings . . .

At last he heard a car engine approaching. A braking on the pebbles, the car door slamming, the front door opening, hurried steps up the stairs and down the corridor . . . Signorini entered the study, turned on the light and froze in disbelief. Before he was able to say anything, Bordelli held up the foil with the morphine.

'I believe this is yours,' he said with a cold smile, remaining comfortably seated.

'Who are you?'

'There was no need to go back to your Genoese friend in Via della Fonderia.'

'How did you get inside?' Signorini stammered, turning pale.

'Your door doesn't close properly.'

'Who are you?'

'It depends. I could be a good friend, or I could be your downfall,' said Bordelli, fiddling with the tinfoil.

'That stuff's not mine.'

'But it was right here in your wallet,' he said, taking the wallet out of his pocket and tossing it on to the little table.

'You must leave at once, or I shall call the police,' the young man threatened, terrified.

'Go right ahead. But with the drugs you've got here, I'd think twice if I were you,' Bordelli insinuated, tossing the foil next to the wallet.

'What do you want?' Signorini asked brusquely. He had gentle features, a weak chin and a dissolute gaze. Clearly he'd never worked a day in his life.

'Please sit down and let's talk.'

'I have no time to waste with you,' said Signorini, and he ran over to the desk, opened the drawer and searched around inside for something he couldn't find.

'Are you looking for this?' Bordelli asked, pointing the Beretta at him.

'What are you doing? Are you mad?'

'That's enough fooling around, now sit down,' the inspector ordered him, gesturing with the barrel of the pistol at the free armchair. After a few seconds of indecision, the youth sat down in the chair, his legs shaking.

'What do you want from me?'

'You know what they do to young guys like you at the Murate?'

'Are you trying to blackmail me?'

'Sort of,' said Bordelli, laying the Beretta on his thigh while still squeezing the butt.

'How much do you want?'

'Normally you ask prostitutes—'

'How much money do you want?' the young man repeated.

'You want to know how much my silence is worth?'

'Silence about what?'

'Giacomo Pellissari,' said the inspector, looking him hard in the eye. Signorini shuddered and for a few seconds seemed out of breath. He tried to remedy the situation with a horrific smile.

'I don't understand . . .' he mumbled, despair in his eyes. He looked as if he felt cold, and his nose was running.

'Who strangled Giacomo Pellissari?' Bordelli asked, more and more convinced he was on the right track.

'What? I don't know any Giacomo by that name.'

'Was it Panerai? Or Beccaroni?'

'What are you talking about?'

'Or maybe it was that old Fascist Gattacci? Or Monsignor Sercambi?'

'I have no idea what you're talking about . . .' said Signorini, pale as a ghost.

'Well, whoever killed him, you're all guilty.'

'You're insane. I don't—'

'All right, then, I'll have you arrested for drugs trafficking,' Bordelli interrupted him, flashing his badge. The young man's eyes widened.

'What trafficking? I just buy some every now and then for myself.'

'And for your orgy mates.'

'Orgy?'

'Never mind, you'll have all the time in the world to explain these things to the judge. And while you're waiting you can rest on a nice little bunk in Murate prison.'

'I haven't done anything,' Signorini whispered, white as a corpse. The inspector smiled.

'Unfortunately the Italian justice system is as slow as treacle. It's not uncommon for some unlucky wretches to be forgotten for a long time in prison.'

'I haven't done anything . . .'

'You'll see what a wonderful experience it is. There are some lifers who haven't seen a woman for twenty years, but they don't have any problems with the other sex . . . Especially with a pretty boy like you.'

'Why are you telling me this?'

'You'll get used to it soon enough, if that's any consolation.'

'I don't want to go to jail . . .' Signorini muttered, standing up robotically.

'Who killed the little boy?' Bordelli insisted. It was the first time he had said that the victim was a young boy, but Signorini showed no surprise. Therefore he knew perfectly well. They *were* the monsters, Bordelli was sure of it now.

'I don't know anything . . .' Signorini babbled, dropping back into the chair.

'I'm afraid you won't be playing hide-and-seek with your friends for quite a long time,' Bordelli said stingingly.

'But who . . .'

'Don't be so surprised, Signorini. I know everything. I'm still missing a few details, but I know exactly what happened,' he bluffed. He'd seized his prey by the throat and was waiting only for him to succumb.

'I . . . don't . . .'

'You kidnapped the boy, took him to the flat in Via Luna and—'

'No!' Signorini was terrified.

'You all had your fun raping him for three or four days—'

'That's not true!'

'Then you got bored with it and so you killed him and buried him in the hills of Cintoia . . . Have I left anything out?'

'No, no, that's not right!'

'It's not? Did you rape him and kill him in this beautiful villa?'

'No, no, no, no . . .' the young man groaned, his voice cracking.

'What were you thinking when the little boy screamed and cried, Signorini? That he was having as much fun as the rest of you? That they were moans of pleasure?' the inspector asked in a terrifying voice. The young man merely looked around with his mouth open, bewildered.

'You tortured a thirteen-year-old boy to satisfy your cocks, you showed him what hell was like, and then you swept him out of the world like a pile of dog shit . . . If it was up to me, I would kill you all one by one,' Bordelli concluded, squeezing the butt of the pistol.

Signorini sat there in a daze for a few seconds, then buried his face in his hands and burst out crying, howling like a beaten dog. He slid out of the armchair and ended up face down on the Persian rug, sobbing more and more violently. It seemed he would never stop.

Bordelli observed the spectacle in disgust, thinking that Signorini's tears pretty much sealed the fate of the band of monsters. Slowly he began to feel an inrush of immense pity for this spoiled young man swimming in wealth, but it seemed to him an unhealthy emotion, to be driven back into the shadows.

He patiently waited for Signorini to stop whimpering. When the sobbing was beginning to wind down, he stood up and put the Beretta in his pocket. Pulling Signorini up by one arm, he sat him back down in the armchair.

'Who killed the boy?' he asked again, forcing himself to assume a fatherly tone. The young man was trembling, and his eyes were red and swollen, his cheeks wet. He kept his eyes lowered and every so often his chest heaved.

'Livio . . .' he muttered.

'Ah, our friendly butcher,' Bordelli said with a shudder, having trouble believing he'd got to the bottom of the whole dirty business.

'It was . . . an accident . . .'

'Oh, of course it was. You really only wanted to have an evening of light-hearted entertainment.'

'It's true . . . it was an accident,' Signorini whined.

The inspector started pacing back and forth on the Persian

rug, hands in his pockets, never once turning his back to Signorini.

'You'd better tell me the whole story from the beginning.'

'I need a little morphine,' the young man whispered, jaw trembling.

'If you tell me everything, I'll let you shoot up all the morphine you want afterwards.'

'Do you promise?'

'I promise.'

'All right . . . I'll tell you everything . . . I'll tell you everything . . .'

'I'm listening,' the inspector said softly, showing patience. He calmly lit a cigarette, eyes following a smoke ring as it floated slowly up to the ceiling. Signorini was panting, trying to summon the courage to begin. He kept running his hands over his eyes, his forehead, his hair. At last he made up his mind to talk, and he started with the very distant past . . . It was a confession, but it closely resembled a personal unburdening that had been a long time coming . . .

Italo Signorini's mother died when he was only a few months old, like the protagonist of the novel he was writing. His father had several mistresses but never remarried. Italo met Panerai, Beccaroni and Sercambi at Forte dei Marmi in the summer of '53, when he was just under fourteen years old. He had recently discovered the guilty pleasures of masturbation, and during those moments his fantasies were peopled only by men. Young girls meant nothing to him.

He used to spend holidays with his father at the Villa Roma Imperiale, which belonged to his paternal grandparents, who in summertime used to go away on long journeys. That summer, at the start of the holidays, he and his father met the three men, friends since early adolescence, on the beach. A butcher, a lawyer and a secondary-school Italian teacher. At the time Panerai, Beccaroni and Sercambi were just over thirty, while Italo's father was a few years older.

The three friends were often invited over to the villa. They would have elaborate dinners, play billiards, poker and tennis on the private court. With the addition of his father, they became a rather harmonious foursome. Young Italo was always hanging around with them, enjoying the company of these men who had the power to lighten the moods of his normally gloomy, severe father. The three new friends often used to joke around with the boy, patting him on the head and slapping him on the back.

The carefree days went by, each one better than the last.

One evening Italo's father told him that the following morning he had to leave to settle an annoying row that had erupted in one of his textile factories, and he had asked his friends to keep his son company while he was away. He drove off, leaving Italo on the beach with the three friends. They had lunch at the villa then all went into the billiards room, where Panerai offered to teach the boy how to play the 'stick-and-balls' game. He leaned over him from behind to show him how it was done, whispering his instructions directly into his ear, and running his hands over the boy's naked arms to direct the shot. The other two were playing at another table, watching the scene and smiling. Italo realised that he didn't mind the contact at all, and that actually he felt a strange void in his stomach, as he used to feel when on a swing as a little boy. Panerai was laughing and every so often inserting his hand into the boy's bathing suit and tickling him. Italo wasn't very good at billiards, and after a while Panerai suggested they play another game that was a lot more fun. They had to take all their clothes off, and then one of them had to put on a blindfold and try to identify the others by touching their bodies. They all agreed to play, Italo included, who felt excited and proud to be allowed to play a grown-up game. Before they started, Panerai told the boy that never in a million years should he tell his father about the game they were about to play, or they wouldn't be his friends any longer. Italo swore on his own head that his father would never find out. He knew how to keep a secret; he was hardly a little boy any more. All right then, said Panerai, that's very, very good, I like a boy like you. You're a very good boy, and worthy of our friendship.

They stripped down naked, drew lots, and the one whose turn came first was none other than him, young Italo. They blindfolded him, and each came forward, one at a time, to be touched. Breathing heavily, they would guide his hands between their legs, where Italo always found a surprise. He sensed that he was doing something forbidden, and this fact excited him and made him laugh. Then Beccaroni said they could play another game that was even more fun. He knelt in front of the boy and started licking him, as the others egged him on with obscene little comments. Italo felt himself sinking into an unknown world where pleasure and fear disturbingly merged. Soon the game took strange new turns, and he found himself bent over the edge of the billiards table. You're a big boy now, they said, you're ready to learn some new things.

Italo tried feebly to resist, vaguely frightened by the transformation of the three men, who had abandoned their usual politeness for a much ruder manner . . . But the desire to discover what there was beyond caresses held him prisoner. The moment he felt himself being penetrated by Sercambi, great pain became suffused with unimaginable pleasure. It wasn't just a physical thing, but rather as if he had at last found his place in the world. Yes, that was it . . . He liked feeling submissive, dominated. Sercambi whispered into his ear to rebel, to try to break free, that would make the game more fun. So to please him Italo squirmed and struggled, pretending he was being raped, and his own pleasure increased. Sercambi let out a stifled groan and collapsed on top of him. Beccaroni was very fast, and then it was Panerai's turn. He'd saved himself for last, he said, smiling, because his thingy was huge and he wanted the road cleared before him. He proved to be the most violent of them all, and he took for ever. Italo started to feel tremendous pain, tried to rebel in earnest, crying and kicking. But Panerai wouldn't hear of it and kept murmuring sweet and lewd things, crushing the boy's head against the billiards table and hitting him hard. As he was reaching orgasm he squeezed Italo's neck almost to the point of strangling him, then detached himself with a wheeze and slapped his bottom, whispering that he was truly a beautiful boy. You hurt me, Italo said to him, and he started to put his clothes back on with a crushing sense of guilt. I guess I was maybe a little naughty there, said Panerai, caressing the boy's cheek with a sweaty hand. Friends again? Now we'll all go to Viareggio for some good ice cream. But first we must sign a pact in blood among men, he added, and we must take our secret to the grave with us. And they turned off the lights, to make the whole thing seem more solemn. Panerai heated the tip of a penknife over a candle flame and they each held out a finger to be pricked. They mingled their blood, and Sercambi proposed sealing the oath with a sign of the cross.

Italo kept his word and said nothing to his father. A strange feeling of frenzy had remained inside him. His father, however, didn't absent himself again for the rest of the summer, and there were only rare occasions for brief little games, though these were *equally thrilling. They took place out at sea, in beach huts, and in the dark corridors of the villa.*

The three friends returned to Florence in early September, promising to stay in touch, and Italo was left alone with his secret. He knew with absolute certainty that he would never say a word about it to his father. It was a matter that concerned him and him alone.

Despite their promises, he didn't see the men again for several years, not even during the summer holidays. Little by little, the memory of that afternoon began to fade and nearly vanished under the weight of other experiences.

A few years later his father suddenly died, making Italo the heir to a vast fortune. He was rich, and free, at long last.

One spring morning when he was twenty-two, he ran into Beccaroni by chance on a street in the centre of town. They greeted each other with a touch of embarrassment, sizing each other up, but it took only a few moments for the old familiarity to return. You certainly have grown, said Beccaroni; you've really become a good-looking lad. Ah, so your father died? I'm so sorry. Listen, what do you say we get together with our other friends? Even tonight, if you like. They exchanged telephone numbers, knowing full well why they were doing so, and that same evening they met up again. The merry brigade from Forte dei Marmi was reunited, and the amusements began almost at once. Italo discovered to his surprise that Sercambi was not a professor of Italian but a monsignor of the Episcopal Curia. He would never have imagined it from the way he remembered the man playing poker and billiards. But deep down he found it amusing.

One evening they introduced him to Gattacci, who shared with the three friends a nostalgia for the good old days. Italo wasn't the least bit interested in politics but was seeking only familial warmth and sexual amusement. Aside from certain choreographical variations, the essence of their games remained the same as the very first time. He was on the bottom, and they were on top, in every sense. Submission was the very greatest pleasure for him. The others, too, liked him best this way. Gattacci only rarely took part in their *soirées,* and on those occasions he never joined the fray. He preferred to stand apart, watching and masturbating.

Panerai's and Beccaroni's families were of course unaware of anything and simply thought they were out playing poker with friends. Sercambi had no wife to answer to, being a priest, and Gattacci had never married. In short, it was smooth sailing for their little banquets of sex, champagne and a smorgasbord of drugs.

After a couple of years of this, the three friends began to grow bored with the usual arrangements, and more and more mention was made of the need to find a new 'female'. Italo was terrified of being left alone and abandoned, and to keep the little group from disbanding he offered to try to procure new young flesh, boys who hustled for a living and even kids who only occasionally sold themselves just to raise money for their next meal. The others greeted this proposal with enthusiasm, but Beccaroni wanted to establish a few safety rules to protect this secret part of their lives. He liked to make a show of his professional skills and started to dictate rules. No one must ever know their true identities. A scandal could sweep them away for ever, especially Monsignor Sercambi, who had made morality his personal banner. Therefore anyone recruited for their 'games' had to be blindfolded before being escorted into and out of the villa. Italo then had to get his hands on a very commonplace model of car, a Fiat 500 or 600, with which to pick up boys off the street. And, most importantly, during the fun and games they had to use nicknames and wear carnival masks. Beccaroni's suggestions were unanimously approved, and the new pact of secrecy further consolidated their group.

Italo bought a second-hand white Fiat 600 and got down to work at once. A man of independent means, he could spend all the time he wanted on these matters. To make his search more interesting, he would sometimes imagine he was living an adventure. At times he was a secret agent looking for boys to recruit as spies to send on dangerous missions. At other times he was a film director looking for actors. But what he liked best was to view the whole thing as a mission to save their group and therefore himself. He couldn't stand the idea of ever being separated from the others. The bonds *between them must remain unbreakable, eternal. The four men were his family, the only one he'd ever had.*

He would go out looking for boys on the street, abandoned waifs willing to sell their bodies in full for a few thousand lire. Such quarry was rare, unfortunately. While waiting for a stroke of luck they made do with a low-class young hustler they'd snagged in the Parco delle Cascine. The job of picking him up would sometimes fall to Beccaroni or Panerai as well, but Italo's role never varied. He on the bottom, the others on top.

One time he managed to bring home a gypsy boy of sixteen, as beautiful as the moon. Things didn't quite work out, and they had to take him by force. After the performance the young gypsy made a terrible scene, threatening to kill them with his knife and screaming that he would call the carabinieri. To calm him down, they had to stuff him with money. They'd dodged a bullet, but the whole experience had become a sort of obsession for them, an ideal to aim for. Violence was the most exciting thing of all.

Italo had been more frightened than the others by the gypsy boy's threats. He suggested they move their parties to another house, fearing that, despite their precautions, one of the boys might be able to identify his villa. Until they found a new venue, they should suspend their search.

It was Panerai who resolved the problem, renting for little expense an apartment in Via Luna quite appropriate for their purposes. It had the only door giving on to a small, hidden piazza, and there was a canopy roof covering the doorway that prevented anyone from the surrounding buildings from seeing who went in and out. There was even a cellar, with a door at the top of the stairs and another at the back. It was in that basement room that they outfitted their torture chamber: a bed, a rug, a few pieces of antique furniture, and a big bronze bust of Mussolini. No sound made in there could be heard outside. They'd even conducted a test: two of them locked themselves up in the cellar and started screaming at the top of their lungs. Nothing was audible outside, not even if one pressed one's ear to the door giving on to the street. They all shared the rental expenses and each had a set of keys.

By this time there were no more obstacles, and Italo resumed wandering about the city in search of meat for the butcher's block. He tried hard to look for younger and younger boys, knowing that this would please the others. He found an orphan who'd run away from an orphanage, a nasty little urchin just released from juvenile prison, a poor abandoned boy who lived in the cellar of a building on the edge of town, and even a mentally disabled lad. He would take them to Via Luna like so many pounds of beef and feed them to the lions. It didn't happen too often, two or three times a year at the most. The rest of the time they made do with the usual boys picked up at the Cascine.

Then came that accursed day in October. It was raining buckets. Italo had gone to Fiesole, invited to supper by the adminstrator of his estate, an old Jew who'd been a friend of his father's and had miraculously escaped deportation. But he'd got the day wrong, and the trustee's wife told him that her husband was in Rome. Italo apologised for the oversight and left. On his way home he happened to go down Viale Volta. In that downpour there were hardly any other cars on the street. At one point he noticed a boy drenched to the bone and running along the pavement, his coat pulled up over his head and a satchel slung behind his back. He instinctively slowed down, saw the child turn on to an uphill street, and followed behind him from a distance. Every so often the boy would stop running to catch his breath, then start up again. He crossed a deserted little square and ducked down a narrow alley between the very high wall of the Parco del Ventaglio and the façade of a large building with iron bars over the windows. At a certain point the boy slipped on the wet asphalt and fell flat on his face. When Italo pulled over to help him, he was crying like a baby. He tried to comfort him and managed to persuade him to get in the car. They were both dripping wet.

Italo didn't know yet that he would take him to Via Luna, couldn't even imagine it. He wasn't looking at one of their usual little wretches; this was a rich boy, clearly. Then he suddenly thought with a shudder: nobody saw me. He imagined his friends' delight at the sight of such a catch, and that was enough to make up his unhappy mind. He stood there motionless in the downpour . . .

I'll take you straight home, he said, but first you must stop crying. You certainly wouldn't want your parents to see you in such a state, would you? You're a proper little man by now, no? What's your name? Giacomo? What a nice name. Who's your father? Really? You're the son of Pellissari the barrister? I know your father, I know him quite well. Where do you live? Oh, of course I know where Via Barbacane is, my old girlfriend lives there. A blonde girl, with green eyes. Her name is Sara, do you know her? No? Well, isn't that strange. And you, do you have a girlfriend? Of course you do. How could you not? You certainly needn't feel embarrassed to say so. Are you cold? Soaked to the bone as you are, you'd better be careful or you'll get a sore throat. Ah, but I've got some powder for sore throats. It's a little bitter, but you'll feel better at once. It's a medicine made by monks, who know about these things. You know what? I'm going to give you some, as a present. It's really expensive, you know. But I'm happy to give you some. Here, just do as I do. Lick your finger, swirl it around in the magic powder, then suck it like a sweet . . . Like this, see? Come on, now it's your turn. Yes, just like that. There's a good boy. Now suck. What did I tell you? It's pretty bitter, but good medicine is always bitter . . .

Sigorini stopped talking and buried his face in his hands. The chime of the clock startled him, but he did not remove his hands from his face. Bordelli had listened to his tale without breathing, feeling sick to his stomach. Poor Giacomo. Fate had played all her cards in delivering the boy into the arms of death . . . If it hadn't been raining so hard, if his mother's car hadn't broken down, if his father hadn't got stuck on the Viali because of an accident, if a perverse, drug-addicted young man hadn't gone to lunch on the wrong day . . .

Signorini dropped his hands to his knees and, taking a deep breath, resumed speaking in a feeble voice.

The morphine took effect in less than a minute. The child couldn't keep his eyes open and was drooling from the corner of his mouth. Italo sped to Via Luna, entered the flat and carried the child down to the cellar. Laying him on the bed, he gave him a shot of morphine and locked him inside. He would sleep for several hours, but even if he woke up, it wasn't a problem. He could scream all he liked and nobody would hear him.

He phoned the others to tell them he'd found a tasty little titbit, and they arranged to meet there that evening, just after supper. Italo went much earlier and injected more morphine into the still-drowsy boy, taking care not to administer too much, for fear of killing him.

The first to arrive was Beccaroni. Peering in through the basement door, he realised that this time Italo had gone too far. This was a textbook kidnapping, for Christ's sake, it could land them in jail for thirty years. They locked the door and went back upstairs to wait for the others. Panerai arrived shortly afterwards with Monsignor Sercambi. They were told the situation, and all were in agreement that it was madness, but no one was able to make a decision. Then Gattacci also arrived, and as soon as he knew the situation, he left in terror.

The atmosphere was charged with electricity, and every so often one of them started laughing hysterically. They snorted a bit of coke mixed with morphine, and a short while later Panerai came out with his idea . . . By now the damage was already done . . . they should think about it . . . an opportunity like this happens only once in a lifetime . . . they would be very gentle . . . only once . . . slow and soft . . . with masks on, as always . . . The only person whose face he's seen is Italo, but it's unlikely he could ever recognise him . . . we'll just have a little fun, what could ever come of it? Then we'll put him into a deep sleep with the morphine and drop him off somewhere . . . Maybe we'll open up some car at random and put him inside . . . I know how to break into a car, that's not a problem . . . Tomorrow morning our little boy will be back in his mother's arms, and in a few days he'll forget about the whole thing and go back to playing with toy soldiers . . . What do you say?

It was so silent they could hear their hearts beating. They sighed, they shook their heads, they bit their lips. When Monsignor Sercambi made the sign of the cross, they lost their heads. After a quick *exchange of glances they put on their carnival masks and went down to the cellar. The boy was still groggy but by now he understood, and there was terror in his eyes.*

Come on now, don't be afraid ... We don't want to hurt you ... not in the least ... Now now, hold still ... Don't scream, you little brat ... Come on, you know you like it ... Good ... Ah, fuck! ... the little pup bites ... Hold him still for me ... Look at that beautiful little bottom ...

The boy was dragged to the ground and stripped. He kept kicking and trying to elude their grasp, grabbing on to the carpet and scratching the wall as if he wanted to dig a hole in it, trying to bite the hand pressed over his mouth ... but it was all useless, and Sercambi was the first to penetrate him.

Italo stood to the side and watched the bullfight, his heart racing. He was hoping to catch a gleam of pleasure in the boy's eyes, the same as he'd felt that summer afternoon at Forte dei Marmi ...

All at once the boy stopped struggling, exhausted. A grimace of pain and fear remained on his face, but his fingers moved very slowly, almost imperceptibly, like a crab's legs in the sun.

After a long moan, Monsignor Sercambi collapsed on to the boy, huffing like a locomotive. Then it was Beccaroni's turn, and as usual he was done in a hurry. When Panerai's turn came, Italo left the room and went upstairs to give himself a shot of morphine. He couldn't wait for it all to be over, and he felt remorse for having made it happen. From now on only quiet affairs, he thought, floating in his morphine paradise.

Suddenly he heard Beccaroni coming up the stairs in a hurry, muttering something. The lawyer charged into the room in vest and trousers and, trembling in fear, said that Panerai had killed the boy. He didn't mean to, bloody hell, he really didn't. Italo felt a river of anguish course through his veins and dashed downstairs. Panerai and Monsignor Sercambi were putting their clothes back on. The butcher was pale and kept shooting glances of what looked like anger at the boy's lifeless body. The prelate's eyes burned with bitterness over this disastrous inconvenience.

Italo laid the boy down on the bed, closed his eyes, and covered him with the sheet. Then he went back upstairs with the other two. There they were again, standing before one another, exchanging anxious glances, as they had a little while ago . . . before the murder.

Now what? There was no turning back. All they could do was find a solution. There was a strange sense of calm in the room, but you could almost hear the sound of their brains whirring.

Panerai was biting his lips and pacing back and forth, opening and closing his hands. It was he who'd killed the boy, of course . . . but they were all implicated, that should be clear to all. An unfortunate accident. He'd just wanted to squeeze the boy's neck a little, as he always did when he came . . . Damn it all . . .

Once again, it was he who took the initiative. He already had a plan for getting rid of the body. Listen closely . . . The first thing we do is put him in the refrigerator, so we're not forced to rush things, and at the right moment we'll go and bury him in the hills of Cintoia. I know those woods like the back of my hand, I've been going hunting there for years. If we do things right, they'll never catch us . . .

They were all in agreement. They didn't have any choice. And so they took everything out of the refrigerator, including the shelves, then turned the thermostat down as far as it would go and put the body inside. All that was left to do was to find the right moment for burying it, and in the meantime they should each continue to live their normal lives. Beccaroni said that Alberto Sordi would be appearing on Studio Uno *on Saturday night; he'd read the announcement in the newspaper. Everyone would be glued to their television sets, and if it kept raining as the reports said it would, the circumstances would be perfect.*

Saturday came and it was raining hard, just as they had hoped. At nine o'clock Panerai and Italo left Via Luna with the corpse in the boot of the butcher's Fiat 850, wrapped in a sheet. They had worked everything out, down to the last detail. All they needed now was a little luck and they would be home free. They had two spades, a pickaxe, a torch, and some rags and wire to wrap round their boots so that they wouldn't leave tracks. Taking the boy's stiff body out of the fridge was horrible. His skin had taken on a grey cast, but luckily he didn't smell too bad.

They left the city and reached Upper Cintoia without any trouble. They took the dirt road that led to Monte Scalari, and after about a mile and a half, they stopped the car. Wrapping their boots with the rags and iron wire, they went out and very silently climbed a small hill, lighting their way with the torch. They found an appropriate spot and hastily dug a quite shallow grave, impatient as they were to leave. They buried the child and went back to the city.

To be safe, the following day they cleaned all the mud off the car, tools and boots. Once their clothes had been through the washing machine, the operation was definitively over. No one could ever trace the killing back to them. All they could do was wait for the body to be discovered, though it was possible it might never be found . . . The woods are full of boar, thought Panerai . . .

'There, now you know everything . . . Now you must keep your promise,' Signorini said in a soft voice, exhausted.

'What are your nicknames?' Bordelli asked.

'I'm called Sheepie, though I won't tell you why. Gualtiero is Giraffe, because he's so tall. Livio is called Piglet, and Moreno is the Penguin because of the way he walks . . .'

'What about Gattacci?'

'He's Benito.'

'Such imagination . . .'

'Can I, now?' the young man asked anxiously.

'Go ahead,' said the inspector. There was no harm in letting him have his last dose of morphine. If anything it would make him more docile. Signorini stood up with effort, dragged his feet as far as the desk and collapsed into the chair. Taking a spoon out of the pen-case, he started preparing the morphine with trembling hands.

Bordelli attacked another Nazionale cigarette. He'd been chain-smoking all the while, and the room smelled like a snooker hall. One reassuring thing had emerged from Signorini's confession: Giacomo died on the night of the kidnapping, not after three days of sexual abuse, as he had imagined. The inspector inhaled the smoke angrily. He still had the images evoked by Signorini in his head and couldn't wait to arrest the three comrades. Who knew how long they would survive in jail? Even the most hardened criminals were disgusted by those who preyed on children, and in prison their disgust turned magically into the most atrocious sort of violence. But he certainly wouldn't shed any tears over them . . .

Once again he was getting ahead of himself. He was already imagining the monsters being sodomised with the handle of a spade, castrated with a flick knife, and torn to shreds in their jail cells with the approval of the prison guards. But he hadn't even arrested them yet. In order to do this he needed Signorini's signature on the transcript of an official interrogation with a lawyer present. Until that moment, no word of any of this must get out. In that sense the flood was a big help; the news reporters had other things to think about.

Signorini rolled up a sleeve and tied a haemostatic tube around his arm, enlarging the vein. He inserted the needle with a sure hand and pressed the plunger. One second later his face turned into a mask of bliss. Rolling his sleeve back down, he turned towards Bordelli.

'How did you find us?' he asked in a whisper.

'By chance.'

'The death of that boy . . . weighs on my mind like a boulder . . .'

'Well, you've got Mamma Morphine to coddle you.'

'It's as if I killed him with my own two hands,' the young man continued, ignoring the provocation.

'That's only just occurred to you?' said Bordelli.

'You can believe what you like, but I was about to turn myself in many times.'

'Why didn't you?'

'Prison frightens me . . . And whatever the case . . . no justice can raise the dead.'

'Pretty good excuse,' said the inspector, wishing he could slap him.

'What's done is done . . .' Signorini whispered, staring into space through heavy eyelids. The inspector stood up and went over to the desk.

'At police headquarters you're going to have to repeat everything before a witness and a lawyer. Naturally, someone other than your friend Beccaroni.'

'I'll do everything you ask,' the young man muttered, rubbing his nose slowly with his fingers.

Bordelli picked up the telephone and calmly dialled the number for headquarters. He had them ring Piras and then asked him where he was.

'In Via Bolognese, Inspector.'

'Wait for me outside the gate in the car.'

'All right, sir.'

'See you in a few minutes.'

He hung up. Justice had prevailed, but the satisfaction of having found Giacomo's killers did nothing to cancel out his bitterness and disgust. He gestured to Signorini to let him know that it was time to go. Signorini stood up, leaning with his hands on the desk.

'First I'd like to show you something.'

'What?'

'It'll only take a minute,' the young man mumbled, staggering towards the door.

Curious to know what it was, Bordelli followed him. They went down the hall to the landing without saying a word, then went up to the second floor and into Signorini's bedroom. The inspector remained in the doorway, awaiting the revelation. The young man went and opened the window, threw open the shutters and, with a surprising leap, threw himself out without a cry. Before he could make a move, Bordelli heard the dull thud of the body striking the stone pavement below. He dashed to the window and looked down. The ground around Sigorini's head began to stain red. The inspector clenched his fists and raced down the stairs, swearing. He'd let himself be walked over like a rookie. Bloody hell. If Signorini died, goodbye confession . . .

He went out of the front door and ran behind the villa. Signorini lay motionless, in an unseemly and almost light-hearted pose. His eyes were open and he had a beatific expression on his face. Bordelli put two fingers on his jugular and felt no pulse. He sat down on the edge of a large flowerpot and lit a cigarette. It had all gone to the dogs. No transcript, no charge, no proof. He was back to square one, the only difference being that now he knew for certain who the killers were. He'd never found himself trapped inside such a paradox before. He could, of course, repeat Signorini's confession under oath, but what would be the use? Without any evidence, even a court-appointed lawyer would send him home with his tail between his legs. And a good lawyer would make him look like a pathological liar . . .

What should he do? Become a vigilante and personally kill Panerai, Beccaroni and Monsignor Sercambi? He would have been delighted to do so, but that wasn't why he'd joined the police force. In spite of everything, he believed in the state and couldn't take justice into his own hands. Giacomo Pellissari deserved a proper public trial; he deserved to have the names of his tormentors plastered over all the newpapers; he deserved justice . . . not three anonymous gunshots.

It occurred to him that Piras must be already outside the gate. He cast a final glance at Signorini and went back into the villa. Climbing the stairs to the study, he removed his cigarette butts from the ashtray and with a handkerchief wiped down everything he'd touched. He put the Beretta back in its place and threw open the window to let the smoke out. He went to the second floor as well, to wipe away any trace of his having been there. Then he left, closing the front door behind him. He walked calmly down the pebbled driveway, in no hurry. By now he'd made up his mind. Except for Piras, no one would know that Signorini had killed himself before his very eyes.

He would let someone else find the corpse. It seemed the only real solution, if he was to avoid creating a firestorm of controversy. The other members of the clique would think their little friend had taken his life out of remorse, but they wouldn't be alarmed. They had no way of knowing that a pig-headed cop had unmasked them.

He went out on to the pavement and found Piras there

waiting for him in the 1100. There wasn't a soul about. He opened the door and stuck his head inside.

'I don't need a lift any more, Piras. I'll walk back.'

'All the way to Via Zara?' the Sardinian asked in surprise.

'I need to think.'

'Did you talk to Signorini?'

'I'll tell you later, Piras. Just wait for me at the station, please.'

'All right, sir,' said Piras, setting aside his curiosity for the moment. There was no point in insisting when the inspector had that look on his face. He started up the car and drove off.

Bordelli headed down the street, his thousandth cigarette of the day in his mouth. Just a few hours ago he had been in bed with Eleonora, and now it felt as if he hadn't seen her for a century . . .

He passed by Villa Triste again, thinking that the flat in Via Luna was also a Villa Triste. Who knew how many other Ville Tristi there were in the world? Buildings that looked normal from the outside, but inside which . . .

Not far from there, in Via Trieste, lived the beautiful Sonia Zarcone, Piras's girlfriend. Certainly the nights the Sardinian spent there were anything but sad.

Almost without realising, he found himself in Piazza della Libertà, but instead of crossing it and going to the station, he headed up the pavement on Viale Lavagnini. He suddenly felt an urgent need to eat something and drink a glass of wine. It was late, but maybe Totò had some leftovers.

The moment he returned to the station he shut himself up in his office with Piras to tell him about Signorini's confession and suicide. The Sardinian listened in silence without batting an eyelid, his face as stony as a nuragh.[50] Bordelli lit a cigarette and blew the smoke upwards.

'Nobody must know. I mean it.'

'Sardinians don't talk, Inspector.'

'Tomorrow morning the cleaning lady's going to come and discover the body.'

'At least we know who the killers are now.'

'That's not much help, if we can't find any proof. Our only hope was the flat in Via Luna, but the river took care of that by washing all the evidence away.'

'What are you going to do?'

'I don't know yet.'

'They can't get away with this.'

'They won't get away with this, Piras. I just need some time to think,' said Bordelli. The Sardinian realised the inspector wanted to be alone, and so he left without another word.

Bordelli began pacing back and forth in front of the window, hands in his pockets. Smoking cigarette after cigarette, he evaluated the situation from every angle. What did he have in hand? A bill from the telephone company, a male prostitute's story about the parties at the villa in Via Bolognese, and a dead man's confession. A handful of flies would probably have been more useful in a courtroom. His word against that of a high-ranking prelate of the Curia, an influential lawyer, and

340

an honest citizen who sold meat. He would never overcome such odds. Now it really made no more sense to tail the other three, waiting for them to commit more crimes. The little boy's death had been a 'damned accident', and they would never put themselves in the same situation again. It had always been Signorini, moreover, who took care of finding unusual young boys, and now he was no longer around. And so? What could the right move possibly be? To set a trap for them. How? Those sorts of things were long and complicated, and often didn't work.

In the end he realised there was only one thing he could do. To hound those three sons of bitches until they gave themselves up, even if it meant spending the rest of his life doing so. They mustn't have a minute of peace. He couldn't see any other solution. And he might as well start right away. He looked at his watch: ten to seven. He drove off in the 1100 and took Via Cavour to the centre of town. A long queue had formed in front of the pharmacy. The city looked as if it had just emerged from the war. In Piazza del Duomo there was a great coming and going of people and military vehicles. Two tankers, surrounded by crowds, were distributing water.

He passed behind the baptistry and parked just outside the front door of the Episcopal Curia. He rang the bell. A couple of minutes later a spyhole opened.

'What can I do for you?' asked the eye in the hole.

'I would like to speak to Monsignor Sercambi.'

'Your name?'

'Inspector Bordelli, police.'

'Do you have an appointment?'

'It's about a rather urgent and delicate matter.'

'I'm sorry, but I doubt the monsignor can see you.'

'Tell the monsignor I'm a dear friend of Piglet's.'

'I beg your pardon?' The eye scowled.

'Tell him exactly that: a friend of Piglet's.'

'Please wait.'

The spyhole closed abruptly. A good five minutes went by before the door opened.

'Come,' said the man. He was short with rather dramatic eyes and a soft step, even though he walked a bit askew. They went up a stone staircase and then down a long, silent corridor with a coffered ceiling until they came to a large inlaid door which the little man opened with a solemn motion.

'You can wait here. Monsignor will see you as soon as he can.'

'Thank you,' said the inspector.

He went into the room and the door closed delicately behind him. It was a luxurious little waiting room, with a wooden Madonna in a niche and a large crucifix hanging on the wall. Poor Jesus, he thought. Too often men have used him as a sword, a purifying fire, a hammer for nailing coffins. Now he was even being waved about to gain votes for a political party. If he ever came back to earth to speak his mind, they would lock him in a loony bin. Poor Jesus.

He sat down in one of the small armchairs, waiting patiently for the monsignor to deign to receive him. Meanwhile he thought of Eleonora . . . when would he see her again? He needed her kisses, he needed to fall asleep in her warm embrace. Sooner or later he had to pluck up the courage to ask her to come and live with him, perhaps in an old country house. But he had to find the right moment . . .

The door opened and the same little man as before appeared. He invited Bordelli to follow him and took him to the floor above. He knocked on a dark door and then opened it to let the inspector in. Bordelli entered and found himself in a large room with just a few pieces of antique furniture that made the space at once sumptuous and sober. A scent of incense and dead flowers floated in the air. Monsignor Sercambi was seated behind an antique desk and did not move. His long neck rose up from the collar of an impeccably tailored cassock, and on his straight, slender nose rested a pair of round spectacles in a very fine gold frame. His utterly bald head sparkled as if it had been polished with floor wax.

The inspector approached with his hands thrust deep in his pockets and remained standing in a wilfully boorish pose. The prelate eyed the stranger in silence, his gaze as cold as steel. On the wall behind him hung another poor Christ on the cross, looming over his head like a dagger. Bordelli decided to let the monsignor have the first word and returned his stare. They kept glaring at each other for a very long time, without either of them showing any sign of embarrassment whatsoever. In the end it was the prelate who broke the ice.

'With whom do I have the honour of speaking?' he asked, in a deep, steady voice.

Bordelli put a cigarette in his mouth and lit it, blowing the smoke through his nostrils.

'Chief Inspector Bordelli, murder squad.'

'What can I do for you? I haven't got much time.'

'Mind if I smoke?' Bordelli asked, trying to be as unpleasant as possible. Sercambi didn't answer, limiting himself to a slight, haughty movement of the eyebrows. The inspector smiled.

'Actually, we both deal in death, don't we? Though for different ends, I'll admit . . .'

'I beg your pardon?'

'I look for killers to lock them up in jail, and you absolve them in the name of the Father, the Son and so on . . .' said Bordelli, miming a sign of the cross in the air.

'Please get to the point.'

'Tell me, Monsignor . . . Can someone who rapes and kills a little boy actually go to heaven?'

'God's mercy is infinite, if the sinner is moved by genuine repentance,' Sercambi said icily.

'That's fantastic news. I can't wait to tell Sheepie, Piglet and the Penguin . . .'

'I'm afraid I don't understand,' said Sercambi, unruffled.

'Oh, I'm sorry, I forgot Giraffe . . .'

'I don't follow, Inspector.'

'The masked parties, the drugs, the unpleasant incident in Via Luna . . . Now do you follow?'

'Even less than before, I must say.' He was harder than stone.

'In fact, I've come to give you a chance to confess. For a man of the cloth it must be a good healthy habit.'

'Please stop making insinuations and speak clearly,' said the monsignor, but in his eyes one could read the question: *who is the traitor?*

'Kidnapping, rape, murder, concealment of a corpse, drug abuse . . . I think that's everything.'

'And so?'

'On the night of the twelfth of October, you and your playmates raped and killed thirteen-year-old Giacomo Pellissari in a cellar in Via Luna . . . Is that a little clearer?'

'You don't know what you're talking about.'

'It happens to me sometimes . . .'

'This has nothing to do with me.'

'I'm going to prove it and drag the lot of you into court.'

'I advise you to get your facts straight,' said the prelate with the vaguest hint of a smile.

'And I advise *you* to have a little chat with that poor Christ hanging over your head. He might have some very important advice for you.'

'I'm afraid I have to end our discussion now,' said Sercambi, pressing a button screwed to the edge of his desk.

'Deep down I understand you. It must be very exciting to rape a little boy while he's screaming for help.'

'I have nothing more to say to you.'

The door opened and the little lame man reappeared.

'Please show the gentleman out, Vito,' said Sercambi, showing no sign of agitation. The inspector smiled, even though he really didn't want to, then he leaned forward and lowered his voice so that only the prelate would hear him.

'Remember me in your prayers, Monsignor. I am God's instrument for saving your corrupt soul.'

'Goodbye, Inspector,' said the prelate.

Bordelli tapped his ash on to the magnificent desk and left the room. The little man led him down the same corridors and stairs as before, not saying a word. He had the sort of frowning and vaguely arrogant demeanour that the servants of the powerful often have. He showed him to the exit and, after a vague gesture of goodbye, locked the door behind him. Amen.

It was nine o'clock when he turned on the telly.

As soon as he'd got home he'd lit the gas heater in the bedroom, to warm the air for sleeping. He took off his shoes and collapsed on the sofa with a reheated dish of lasagna that Totò had given him. He didn't feel like seeing anyone except her. He was hoping to wash away the disgust of his day, but it wouldn't be easy. He couldn't stop thinking about Signorini's confession, his suicide, the lifeless body with its head cracked open still lying on the pavement outside the villa, the repulsive conversation with Sercambi and everything else . . .

He ate the lasagna while watching the evening news on Channel 2. They said things were getting back to normal in Florence. The Florentines, however, knew that this was a lie. There were still tons of mud and debris in the streets and thousands of wrecked cars to be removed. Some areas still had no electricity, telephone, gas or even water. Many shopkeepers and craftsmen had lost everything, with no hope of going back to work. Hundreds of families still couldn't get back into their homes and were being put up in hotels at public expense. Fire engines were working day and night, pumping the mud out of the basements of public buildings, and thousands of men, women, soldiers and students were still splashing about in the stuff. There were queues for food at the stadium, queues outside the few open shops and stores, queues around the tankers. Careggi hospital was bursting at the seams. Not to mention the works of art and thousands of ancient books covered in mud and heating oil. And in the provinces things were even worse . . . Back to normal, indeed.

He flipped through the newspaper to see what was on the television, and stood up to switch to the National channel. He started watching the second instalment of *The Count of MonteCristo*, accompanying it with a glass of wine and a cigarette. He missed Eleonora, her smile, her scent . . . and everything else. It was better not to think about her. One needed patience with today's girls.

When the episode ended, it was followed by a variety show featuring Orietta Berti. By the second song he had fallen asleep sitting up on the sofa and begun to snore, chin resting on his chest. He missed the goals in *This Sunday in Sports*, did not watch the late edition of the news, and did not hear the key turn in the front door. He didn't even hear Eleonora approach and turn off the television. He didn't know she was looking at him and could never have imagined what was going through the mind of the beautiful girl he had lost his head over. Had he known, he would have woken up and asked her to come and live with him.

Eleonora watched him with tenderness, thinking that the grumpy inspector was a wonderful man. She had to accept it: she was wild about him. But she didn't want him to find out too soon, for fear of frightening him. At his age it was anybody's guess how many women he'd been with, and he certainly wouldn't want a clingy young girl beside him all the time. The evenings she hadn't spent with him had cost her a great deal of effort. But she wanted to show him she was a mature woman, not an insecure teenager in need of constant reassurance. If their relationship continued, maybe they could try living together . . . Why not? It would be the first time for her, and the very idea gave her butterflies in her stomach. She sat down beside her man and caressed his brow. Bordelli woke up, but it took him a few seconds to realise he wasn't dreaming.

'I must've fallen asleep,' he mumbled.

'You mean you weren't contemplating the universe?' she said, laughing.

After a long kiss, Bordelli lay down and rested his head on her thighs.

'I had a terrible day,' he let slip.

'Tell me . . .' she said, stroking his cheek.

'No, I beg you. I'm trying not to think about it.'

'Was it really that bad?' Eleonora insisted.

'A lot worse than you can imagine. Let's talk about something else . . . How's your cellar coming along?'

'I've almost finished. A handful of good-looking boys gave me a hand.'

'Out of sheer altruism, I expect.'

'You're the only one who sees me as irresistible . . .'

'Liar. Every man in the world fancies you and you know it.'

'If that were true I wouldn't be here with an ageing, melancholy cop.'

'I'm not at all melancholy,' Bordelli protested.

'Then I stand corrected: an ageing cop.'

'Thanks, that makes me feel a lot better.'

'I bet you've been with hundreds of women and probably can't even remember all their names.'

'That's why I set up an archive.'

'Really?'

'Unfortunately it was destroyed by the flood. I kept it at the Biblioteca Nazionale. There were too many volumes for me to keep it at home.'

'Come on, tell me the truth . . . How many women have you been with?'

'Please don't make me count them.'

'Are there really so many?' she asked, worked up.

'One really has to be careful with you women. You're all in love with Don Juan and Casanova, and at first you're thrilled that your man is a skirt-chaser. Then as time goes by you're liable to get jealous of a chicken . . . I mean the kind that cluck.'

'I'm not jealous at all,' said Eleonora, shrugging.

'I wish you were, at least a little.'

'Sorry to disappoint you . . .'

'You mean I can sleep with all the women I want?'

'Of course, but if you do I'll chop off your head.'

'That's what I call consistency,' said Bordelli. He was finally starting to relax.

'Have you ever lived with a woman?' she asked.

'I've come close, but it's never happened.'

'Are you usually the one to cut and run, or is it the women who leave?'

'It's always the women who leave.'

'Well, that's something to think about.'

'Ah, you mean women can think?'

'Silly . . .' said Eleonora, rubbing his face with her hand. He stuck his hand under her jersey to tickle her, and between the yelps and laughter the skirmish continued in bed. The air in the bedroom was hot and dry from the gas heater, but they didn't even notice. In the half-light they indulged in a thousand different games, whispering sweet nothings and obscenities to each other. They felt free, they could do whatever they liked . . .

When Bordelli got to the office, Signorini's cleaning lady had phoned just a few minutes before. Tapinassi and Rinaldi had gone to the villa, and Diotivede had already been alerted. The inspector got back into the 1100 together with Piras and calmly drove off. He didn't tell his young assistant about his pleasant visit to Monsignor Sercambi or his intention to pay a call on the other two as well. For the moment he preferred to set out alone on this desperate and perhaps pointless adventure.

When they arrived at Via Bolognese, the gate was open wide. They pulled up in front of the entrance staircase, alongside the run-down Fiat 600. As soon as they got out of the car, Tapinassi popped out from behind a corner of the villa.

'It's the guy we were tailing, sir,' he said. Piras and Bordelli exchanged a fleeting glance of understanding.

'Have you already searched the house?' Bordelli asked.

'Yes, sir. The cleaning lady let us in. And in the victim's study we found a nine-calibre Beretta, a syringe and a few grams of morphine,' said Tapinassi, leading them to the corpse.

'Any signs of a break-in?'

'No, sir.'

'Can you tell what window he threw himself out of?'

'From his bedroom, Inspector.'

'Any signs of a struggle?' Bordelli asked, pretending to assess the possibility of murder.

'At a glance, I'd say no, Inspector.'

They went round to the back of the villa and stopped near the body. Signorini was in the same position in which Bordelli had left him, looking as if he were executing a dance step. The puddle of blood had dried, the facial colour was tending towards grey, and the blackened tip of the tongue was sticking slightly out of the half-open mouth. Bordelli looked up at the fatal window, feigning thoughtfulness.

'Where's the cleaning lady?'

'Inside with Rinaldi.'

'I'm going to go and talk to her.'

He went into the house with Piras at his side. They found the woman in the study, talking to Rinaldi. She was frightened and sorrowful over the young man's death, and had clearly been crying. Bordelli asked her a few questions. Using round-about turns of phrase and vague hints, he tried to find out whether the woman knew about Signorini's drug abuse and sexual habits, but she genuinely seemed to know nothing.

'He was always so sad . . . It was almost to be expected . . . Poor boy . . .'

'For the moment I have nothing more to ask you, signora.'

Bordelli told Rinaldi to accompany the lady to headquarters for her witness statement, then went up to the second floor with Piras. Now they were alone.

'I've got half a mind to fabricate evidence to implicate his friends in throwing him out of the window,' Bordelli whispered.

'I'm with you,' said Piras.

'It's not so easy, unfortunately. Just write a report declaring it a suicide and let's close the book.'

'Yes, sir.'

As they were going out of the house they saw Diotivede's 1100 coming down the driveway towards them. The doctor parked alongside the department's 1100 and got out with his inevitable black leather bag.

'Don't tell me you've got a new car,' he said.

'The farthest thing from my mind. That's a squad car. It's only useful 'cause it's got a radio.'

'You could have a radio installed in the Volkswagen.'

'Sooner or later I will.'

'Where's my client?'

'Behind the villa. No need to waste much time on the post-mortem. It's a suicide.'

'How can you be so sure?'

'I'll tell you another time. I have to go now. Give my regards to your girlfriend.'

'Did you know that Marianna said you were handsome?' said the doctor, perplexed.

'I guess she knows men.'

'I was thinking she should probably see a psychiatrist.'

'Your sensitivity is touching.'

'Oh, sorry . . . Maybe she only needs a pair of glasses,' said Diotivede with a sly smile, before walking away whistling.

'He's not being mean. That's just the way he is,' Bordelli said to Piras as they were getting in the car. They didn't say a word the whole way back to the station.

The inspector went up to his office and opened the Pellissari file. On a sheet of paper he wrote down Beccaroni's two addresses, the lawyer's office and home. He picked out a few photos of Giacomo Pellissari's dead body, put them in his coat pocket, and drove off again. The moment had come to pay a little visit to the other two. Surely the monsignor had already alerted them, and surely they must be alarmed.

Reaching the end of Viale dei Mille, he parked in front of the butcher's shop and noticed a few customers queuing up. Around the stadium there was the usual bustle of people and army vehicles, but at that moment his thoughts were elsewhere. He went into the shop and greeted Panerai with a friendly smile. The butcher returned the smile, but it was clear he was anything but cheerful. While serving the customers he eyed Bordelli suspiciously. He was almost certainly asking himself: *Is he the police inspector who paid a visit to the Giraffe? This likeable gentleman who is loyal to the Duce and likes his steaks four fingers thick? Is it possible? And yet he fits Gualtiero's description . . .*

Bordelli strolled about the shop while awaiting his turn, humming a tune. He noticed a small frame hanging in a corner. Printed on tricolour paper were three lines of verse that aped a tercet of the *Inferno*:

> *By the true light do we still abide,*
> *the same that shone across our land:*
> *so bright still shines our supreme Guide.*[51]

It must have been a nice little souvenir of Predappio, like the bust of Mussolini in the cellar on Via Luna. He waited patiently for the last customer to leave, then approached the counter with a jovial air.

'Now, to us . . .'

'What can I get for you?' Panerai asked guardedly, knife in hand.

'I'd like a nice leg of little boy,' Bordelli said, as if it was the most natural thing in the world.

'Whaa . . .?' said the butcher, open-mouthed, a thick furrow across his brow. It was finally clear to him that the ball-busting police inspector was indeed the steak man, and he realised he'd been under surveillance for quite some time. Bordelli pulled out one of the photos of Giacomo's dead body and thrust it under his nose.

'Young meat is always more tender, wouldn't you say?'

'What the hell is this?' Panerai muttered, turning pale. Bordelli put the photograph back in his pocket.

'Who knows what your beloved Fathead would think of you and your friends? At least he bragged about fucking women, not little children.'

'Who are you, anyway? What the hell do you want from me?' the butcher spat out, terrified.

'Come on, Piglet, you don't expect me to believe that the monsignor didn't forewarn you, do you?'

'You're mad.'

'I may well be, but soon I'll have proof that you raped and killed that boy,' Bordelli lied, knowing the butcher wouldn't believe him. But that sort of statement always had an effect.

'I don't know what you're talking about,' said Panerai, squeezing the handle of the knife.

'You'll find out soon enough. Tell Penguin the lawyer that I'm on my way to see him, maybe he'll get in some pastries.'

He walked away whistling, and when he got back in the car he shot a glance at the butcher's counter. Panerai was gone, probably already phoning Beccaroni.

He drove back downtown to continue his work. The three friends must certainly have gone looking for Signorini, and when they couldn't find him they'd grown suspicious. They were probably wondering whether it wasn't indeed the rich young fool who'd snitched on them. Before long, however, they would hear the news of his suicide on the radio or television, and they would breathe a sigh of relief. So the question on Bordelli's mind was now: with Signorini dead, which of the three left was the weakest link? Certainly not the prelate. Perhaps it was Panerai, with his tough-guy façade . . .

He felt as if he had set out on a path of no return, as in certain wartime operations. He had no hope of gaining anything, other than the fact that the three killers now knew that he knew. A miserable consolation. But what else could he do? Take revenge? He imagined himself lurking in the bushes in front of Monsignor Sercambi's villa, with a precision rifle with a silencer on it. Head in the cross-hairs . . . Zap! . . . Meet your maker, Monsignor. The lawyer he would wake up in the middle of the night, make him get down on all fours, and then slit his throat. For the butcher, special treatment: a big stick up the arse and wire round the neck. Amen.

He stopped the car in Piazza Santissima Annunziata in front of Palazzo Budini Gattai and continued on foot. A breakdown lorry was removing the last wrecked cars from the square, and here and there could be seen the usual little mounds of debris gathered together by the bulldozers. Turning the corner of Via dei Servi, he stopped in front of number 50. He rang the buzzer for the Beccaroni law offices, but nobody replied. He tried again twice, then went back to the car.

He took the Viali to the end, then crossed the Arno and went as far as Porta Romana. Turning up Via Ugo Foscolo, he continued on to Via di Marignolle . . . 4 . . . 18 . . . 36 . . . 62 . . . 80 . . . 92 . . . 94 . . . 96 . . . 96A . . . He pulled up in front of 96B and got out. A high stone wall, a closed gate, a villa immersed in greenery. He stuck his head through the bars to have a look at the garden. Two large dobermans trotted over and, growling softly, they sat down one beside the other a few yards from the gate. He heard some cautious steps in the gravel and Beccaroni appeared, in gardener's overalls and holding shears. He stopped at a distance from the gate. He was frightened, but forced himself to appear composed.

'If you're looking for the barrister, he's gone on holiday,' he said with a vague hint of menace.

'When he gets back, tell him his gardener likes to amuse himself by raping children.'

'I'll tell him,' said Beccaroni, trying to imitate the Giraffe's cold aplomb.

They stared at each other long and hard, with no need for any more words. Bordelli stepped away from the gate and got back in his car.

While descending the Via Foscolo, he felt like a pathetic fool. What did he hope to gain from this farce? The three killers were well aware there was no proof. The only hope was that one of them would lose his head and trip up somehow . . . but it was like waiting for apples to grow on a cypress. Gattacci knew everything, even though he hadn't taken part in their happy little banquet. He wouldn't talk, either, assuming it was even possible to track him down . . . Perhaps he was already in Brazil . . .

So what the hell was he looking for, then? A way to vent his personal feelings? To pretend he was avoiding defeat? A servant of the law couldn't afford to fall into such traps. His job was to find evidence, not to play chess with killers. Maybe he'd gone down the wrong track. Maybe he should rather have been patient and spun a web for them. But now it was too late, and it made little sense to torment himself with doubt. He had let things get away from him and now he had to follow them through to the end. He would prod the three comrades every so often, if only so that they wouldn't sleep well at night . . . And what if one day he actually managed to bag them? One thing was certain. He didn't intend to tell Giacomo's parents anything, to avoid making them suffer needlessly and consequently risk turning them into avengers.

When he got to Porta Romana, he took Viale Petrarca. As

he was approaching Piazza Tasso, he thought of Botta. After a morning like this, he needed to talk calmly with a friend. He took a right turn down Via del Campuccio. Ennio was still emptying out his lair, one bucketful at a time.

'Inspector, what's wrong? You should see your face . . .'

'I'm trying to digest an elephant turd, Ennio. I assure you, it's not easy.'

'I try every day, and I'm starting to get used to it.'

'I wanted to thank you for your help,' said Bordelli, to change the subject.

'Was it useful to you?'

'You can't imagine how much . . .'

'Meaning?' Botta asked, curious.

'I'll tell you the next time we get drunk together.'

'As soon as I've got my flat back in order I'll come calling on you with such a grappa you have no idea—'

'I can't wait, Ennio. And maybe before Christmas we'll arrange a dinner at my house.'

'Whenever you like, Inspector. I could cook Lebanese.'

'You can cook whatever you like, I trust you.'

'I learned when I was on holiday in Marseille with two really nice guys from Beirut.'

'Were they on holiday for drugs or armed robbery?'

'Murder, actually, but they could cook like gods,' said Botta, kissing his fingertips.

'Are you asleep?' Rosa asked in a whisper, still massaging his neck.

'I wish,' Bordelli groaned. He was lying belly-down on the sofa with his shoes off. That morning the electricity had finally returned to Santa Croce as well, but Rosa still amused herself by using candles, and the room was full of quivering shadows. The cats were chasing each other around the flat as usual, slipping on the floors like in the cartoons. Briciola had gained weight and looked like a little ball.

'You seem strange . . .' said Rosa.

'Why?'

'You've been frowning all evening.'

'I'm just a little tired.'

'I know you too well, monkey. You're hiding something from me.'

'All right, I'll tell you. But you have to believe me.'

'Why, what's happened?' said Rosa, dying of curisoity.

'I've fallen in love . . .'

'Oh my God, is it possible? It's never happened to you before,' said Rosa, breaking into a hysterical laugh.

'What can I do if that's how it always ends up?'

'He who always falls in love never falls in love . . .'

'Let me have a little hope, Rosa.'

'Hope is the virtue of the dead.'

'Are you going to spend the evening stabbing me with a knife?'

'And who's the unlucky girl this time? Is she pretty?'

'Gorgeous.'

'So she's obviously young.'

'Thirty-five,' Bordelli lied, adding a good ten years.

'Come on, you could be her father.'

'Age doesn't matter,' Bordelli said in self-defence, thinking he could actually be her grandfather.

'Is she tall?'

'No, not really, but she has something about her . . . how shall I put it? . . . like a Greek statue.'

'Dark or fair?'

'Raven-haired.'

'You see? Amelia was right!' Rosa said, as if she'd just won a battle.

'Pure coincidence.'

'I hope so, for your sake.'

'Why do you say that?'

'Because she said it wouldn't last.'

'Thanks for reminding me . . .'

'What do you care, if you don't believe in the stuff?' she said, messing up his hair.

The massage, unfortunately, was over. Bordelli pulled himself up to a sitting position. He felt as if he'd been used as a bell clapper. He glanced at his watch. Almost eleven. Maybe Eleonora was waiting for him at home . . .

'I'm going home to bed, Rosa.'

'Come on, one last little cognac . . .'

'Just a finger.'

'Good God, are you ageing badly . . .' said Rosa, filling two little glasses to the brim.

'I'll be going now . . .'

'What's the big hurry . . .?'

'I'm a wreck, Rosa,' said Bordelli, putting his shoes back on. Rosa grabbed the kitten and accompanied him to the door.

'Say bye-bye to the inspector, Briciola. He's the man who saved you.'

'Bye, one-eye,' said Bordelli, stroking her head with a finger. He kissed Rosa on the cheeks and started down the stairs.

'Give your sweetheart my best,' she said coquettishly, and after blowing a burst of kisses she closed the door.

Bordelli bit his lip, hoping Eleonora really was waiting for him at home. He needed her now as never before. But he didn't want to make it too much of a habit, and so he prepared himself for a solitary night.

While driving towards San Frediano he started contemplating Botta's Lebanese dinner, just to keep all his other thoughts at bay. Next Sunday, perhaps? Or was Saturday better? He would invite Dante, Piras and Dr Fabiani, as on all the other occasions. And maybe after dinner he would tell the happy tale of the butcher and his friends, glass in hand . . .

He glanced often in the rear-view mirror, under the impression a dark car had been following him for too long. He was thinking like a cop again, but perhaps it was better to make sure. He pulled over abruptly to let the car pass, then turned to see who was inside. Nothing alarming. A Lancia Appia with a sixtyish-looking couple inside. He calmly drove off again. Where was he? Ah, yes, the Lebanese dinner and the uplifting story of the butcher and his friends . . . Why not? Spreading the rumour might actually be a good way to torment them. The word would spread from mouth to mouth across the city, slowly creating a clearing around the three blackshirts. It didn't compare to the satisfaction of throwing them in jail, but at least they wouldn't be able to live in peace.

He parked just outside his front door, determined to leave these thoughts in the car. He climbed the stairs, praying to heaven that she would be there. He reached the third floor out of breath and noticed that the door to his flat was ajar. Careless girl, he thought with a smile. Once inside he noticed that the light was on in the bedroom but he couldn't hear a fly breathing. He headed down the corridor . . .

'Here comes the big bad wolf,' he said in a monster's voice, stepping into the doorway . . . and his playful mood was swept away in an instant. Eleonora was curled up under the covers with a pillow over her head, trembling lightly. Her clothes were scattered about the room in tatters.

'What the hell's happened?' Bordelli gasped, slowly raising the pillow. There was no need for her to answer. It was enough to see her empty gaze, the bruises on her face, her shrivelled lips.

He felt an animal rage take hold of him and dig deep down into his viscera . . . like during the war, when he would follow the trail of horrors the Nazis left behind on their northward retreat. A ferocious desire to kill, to slaughter, rose up inside him, in his very blood . . . but for now it was Eleonora who must command his attention. He clenched his teeth, knowing it was not the right time for questions. He took off his coat and dropped it on to a chair, then lay down beside her and embraced her with all the tenderness he could muster in a sea of hatred. Eleonora pressed up against him, shivering. She seemed like a small animal on the verge of death. He stroked her hair, trying to be gentle. His fingers ran over a large lump, and she flinched with a moan.

'I'm sorry . . .' he whispered, lightly brushing her cheek. He bit his lip until it bled. So they wanted to play rough, did they? Very well. He would launch a war without quarter, even if it meant getting himself killed . . . Calm now, he had to remain calm. Losing his head was pointless.

It didn't take much to figure out who had done it. In his show of bravado he'd stepped on some very important toes without giving much thought to the consequences. Why didn't that son of a bitch of a priest take it out on him directly? Batini had told him. Monsignor Sercambi was very powerful and almost certainly a Freemason. Perhaps all it had taken was one phone call to take care of the troublesome nuisance. Easier than pulling out a nose hair. *Hello, old boy. I have a little problem on my hands . . .* A few people had briefly conferred as to the best way to satisfy the monsignor, and in the end they'd decided to send someone to beat up and rape a girl who had nothing to do with anything, just to send the ball-busting inspector a message. It wasn't just to intimidate, this contemptuous show of force from people who knew they were untouchable. The powerful don't like long, boring discussions; they prefer swift violence and blood . . .

He could tell that Eleonora wanted to free herself from his embrace, and so he let go. She barely moved away at all, just far enough to look him in the eye. In her gaze he read disgust, anger, humiliation, and above all, fear. She almost seemed a different person. Bordelli said nothing. At that moment any word at all would have seemed to him useless or stupid. Eleonora got out of bed, wrapping herself in a blanket, and left the room in hurried little steps. Bordelli heard the bathroom door close, and immediately the hiss of the shower. He couldn't help but feel guilty. He sat up and lit a cigarette. While Eleonora was being raped, he was lying on Rosa's sofa getting his neck massaged. It was a strange feeling for him, guilt. He was always getting into things he ought not to, and when he rightly should have been present he wasn't. Only rarely did he act with any consistency, as he had done with Signorini.

He got up to look for an ashtray, and his gaze fell on the bed. In a shudder of horror he tore off the the bloodied, sperm-stained sheets, gathered up Eleonora's tattered clothes, went into the kitchen and thrust it all in two plastic bags. Then he returned to the bedroom and started pacing back and forth, clenching his fists.

The noise of the shower suddenly ceased, and a tomblike silence ensued. A good five minutes went by before Eleonora emerged from the bathroom. She was wrapped in the same blanket, and had the same look in her eyes as before. She walked past him, avoiding his gaze, and went to open the wardrobe. She took out a white shirt, a pair of dark trousers and a belt, then got dressed without removing the blanket from her shoulders. She rolled up the trousers and shirtsleeves, then put on her boots. Even dressed like Stenterello[52] and with bruises all over her face, she was still beautiful. But it wasn't the right time to say so.

'Do you feel up to talking?' Bordelli asked, trying to get her to look at him. She sat down on the edge of a chair and wrapped her arms round her knees. At last their eyes met.

'What's the use?' she said, barely shrugging a shoulder.

'They won't get away with this.'

'It's you they were pissed off at.'

'I know . . .'

'They told me to tell you to stop sticking your nose in matters that don't concern you.' She spoke in a calm, detached voice.

'How many were there?'

'Two.'

'And they both . . .?'

'Yes, both.'

'How did they get inside?'

'I don't know, they were already here.'

'What time did you come in?'

'Ten-thirty.'

'Would you be able to identify them?'

'They were hooded.'

'Florentines?'

'Yes,' she said, shrugging, with a shudder.

'It's all my fault.'

'Don't ask me anything else,' Eleonora whispered.

'You'll have to report this . . .'

'No . . . leave me alone . . . I just want to forget . . .'

'Maybe in a little while . . .'

'Take me home . . . to my parents . . .'

'Please, I beg you, don't leave.'

He hadn't wanted to say it, but it had slipped out. She put on her jacket as if she hadn't heard, then left the room without turning round. Bordelli grabbed his coat and went after her. They descended the stairs in silence, without touching. They got into the car.

'Via d'Annunzio . . .' she whispered, as if speaking to a taxi driver. When the 1100 started moving, she pulled up her feet and wrapped her arms round her legs. For Bordelli began the shortest and longest drive of his life. The silence weighed terribly on him, but he couldn't find anything meaningful to say. After asking his inspectorly questions, his tongue had gone dry. Eleonora stared at the road indifferently, every so often resting her chin on her knees.

They drove across Florence, passing by a few cars and the usual military vehicles, then turned on to Via d'Annunzio, and about half a mile later, Eleonora pointed to a small, three-storey building. Bordelli pulled up alongside the pavement and turned off the engine. He summoned the courage to take her hand.

'You want to get out right away?'

'I'd rather . . .'

'If you need me you only have to—'

'Don't worry about it,' she cut him off.

'But you'll at least let me know you're all right?'

'I'm going,' she muttered, grabbing the door handle.

'I know it's not the right moment, but . . . Will I see you again?'

'Don't ask me anything,' she said. And all of a sudden she burst into tears. Her throat filled with all the sobs she'd been holding back, and she started whimpering like a dog. Not knowing what to do, Bordelli squeezed her hand. He always felt lost in the presence of a weeping woman.

After a few minutes of this, she finally calmed down. She wiped her eyes and heaved a big sigh, staring at the road. Bordelli squeezed her hand more tightly.

'Eleonora . . .'

'Leave me alone . . . I'm fine . . .'

And she withdrew her hand, got out of the car, and gently closed the door behind her. She unlocked the door of her building, slipped inside, and a second later it was as if she had never existed.

Bordelli lit a cigarette, took a deep drag and headed home. Monsignor Sercambi had succeeded in destroying the most beautiful thing in his life. He could always kill the priest, but it wouldn't make any difference.

He drove back across the city, crushed by anguish. The mud and desolation he saw around him seemed an emanation of his soul. Would Eleonora ever recover? Would she remain the free-spirited girl full of life he had known? Would she continue to make love joyfully?

When he closed the door of his home behind him, he felt as if he had entered a prison. He looked into the bedroom. That was where it had all started, where it had all ended. He didn't dare hope she would return, and even if she did, it would never be the way it was before. All he wanted was for her to be safe and to start to forget. That was enough.

He remade the bed with clean sheets and put the blankets back on. He took off his shoes and lay down still dressed, leaving the light on. Now he wanted more than ever to leave this flat. He felt annihilated. Even the idea of revenge gave him no satisfaction . . .

He suddenly realised that there was a sheet of paper taped to the windowpane with something written on it. He didn't remember noticing it before he went out. He got up to see what it was, and he felt his heart sink. It was a typewritten list of names. At the top was *Eleonora B.*, which had been struck out with a pen, and this was followed by *Rosa Stracuzzi, Ennio Bottarini, Dante Pedretti, Elvira Bandini, Pietrino Piras* . . . He realised that the war was over before it had even begun. And he had lost. He crumpled up the sheet of paper and dropped it on the floor.

He lay back down in bed and turned off the light. He had failed. He had to accept it. He couldn't forgive himself for the fact that Eleonora had got dragged into it. The idea that other people might pay for his mistakes prevented him from carrying on the fight. The long arm of Freemasonry could strike again, possibly even killing innocents. The case was closed. All that remained was to bury it and give it a tombstone . . .

A thought slowly worked its way into his head and stayed with him until he was lucky enough to fall asleep.

He woke up very early and washed the dirty dishes, humming popular tunes. But his mood was darker than the bottom of a well. After drinking an entire pot of coffee, he went out in the car for a long drive through the hills, ending up at La Panca. He needed a little time alone to reflect. He left the 1100 by the side of the road and walked up the slope. The sky had a sort of greenish glow that was anything but cheerful, and a cold breeze was blowing. When he reached the top of the ridge, he was out of breath and drenched in sweat. Seeing these woods again was like going back in time, to when he still had hopes of winning.

He continued to follow the path, and when passing along the plateau where he'd found the kitten, he peeked behind the brambles. The carcasses of the other kittens were gone; some animal must have eaten them.

He walked under the boughs of the great oak and reached Monte Scalari. Looking at the ancient abbey, he decided once and for all that he would sell the flat in San Frediano. Immediately. As soon as possible. He would go and live in the country, spending his time reading and gardening, far away from everybody.

He pushed on a bit farther, then stopped at the fork for Pian d'Albero. He stood there for a few minutes, looking at the trees, the rocks, the thorny shrubs scattered across the carpet of dead leaves. He'd grown very fond of the peace and quiet of these hills, and thought once again that he wanted very much to explore them in every detail.

He calmly began to make his way back down. By now he'd

made his decision and would never turn back. Returning to La Panca, he got into the car and drove off along the dirt road with a disgusting cigarette in his mouth. It wasn't quite ten o'clock.

When he got to the station he felt devastated but calm. He went into his office and, without sitting down, took his regulation pistol out of a drawer. He'd never used it, and often left it at work. Grabbing an old bag, he started putting his personal effects in it, trying not to forget anything. He left the bag on his chair and went out. On his way up to the second floor he ran into a colleague and asked him whether Commissioner Inzipone was in his office.

'He should be, I saw him just a few minutes ago.'

'Thanks.'

He arrived outside the commissioner's door, knocked softly, and let himself in without waiting for a reply. Before Inzipone could open his mouth, he dropped his pistol and badge on to the desk. The commissioner looked at him as if he was mad.

'What is the meaning of this, Bordelli?'

'I'm going to start raising chickens.'

'What the devil is wrong with you?'

'The police force is no longer for me.'

'You can't just quit like this, Bordelli.'

'Goodbye, Mr Commissioner,' said the inspector, heading for the door.

'You've an ongoing investigation, dammit!' Inzipone shouted. Bordelli stopped on the threshold and turned round.

'You can shelve it,' he said, and he walked away, ignoring the commissioner's protests.

He passed by his office to get the bag and then went down to the courtyard. He looked over at the 1100, thanking it for its company. Leaving the station on foot, he waved goodbye to Mugnai, as usual. Who knew whether he would ever see him again. Perhaps by chance, going into a cinema or at a pizzeria. He almost felt as if he were running away, but he had no desire to go and say goodbye to all his colleagues. They would ask too many questions he wouldn't want to answer. He would tell only Diotivede and Piras how things actually stood, and certainly wouldn't lose touch with them.

He started walking towards the centre of town, in no hurry. Twenty years on the force were all contained in that bag. Now he had all the time in the world to finish Herodotus's *Histories* and read all the other books he'd never read.

Passing by the baptistry he glanced up at the windows of the Episcopal Curia, imagining Monsignor Sercambi behind the curtains, looking down at him and gloating. He felt a wave of heat envelop his chest, followed at once by a sharp chill. Would he ever manage to swallow this ignoble abuse of power? Would he ever be able to forget? At the moment he didn't want to think about it.

He pushed on towards the Arno, distractedly watching the busy military vehicles and lorries with wrecked cars in tow. He didn't want to think of the murdered boy or Eleonora, but it wasn't easy.

Without realising it, he was back in San Frediano, like a horse returning to its stable. Passing under his own windows, he crossed Piazza Tasso and went to Via Villari, where he'd abandoned the Beetle. He hadn't driven it since the day after the flood, but it started up on the first try. He turned on to the Viale, with the familiar, reassuring sound of the Volkswagen buzzing in his ears.

He arrived in Santa Croce and parked right outside Rosa's building. There was still a viscous patina of slime on the street and pavements.

He went up to the first floor and knocked at the door. There was music inside, but nobody came to the door. He knocked harder; at last he heard the sound of high heels approaching. Rosa opened the door and let out a cry.

'I don't believe it – I was thinking about you just one minute ago,' she said, giving him a smacking kiss on the lips.

'Feel like going out, Rosa?'

'If you ask me with a face like that, the answer is no,' she said, pulling him inside.

'I'm sorry, I'm in a bad mood.'

'Because of your sweetheart?'

'Rosa, let's make a deal. No questions today.'

'Well, aren't you a barrel of laughs . . .'

'I'll get over it soon enough. Come on, let's go.'

'Give me a minute,' said Rosa, then dashed off like an actress to her dressing room.

Bordelli went and sat on the sofa, resigned to a long wait. He felt strange without the badge in his pocket. He felt naked, but also lighter. Getting out was the only right thing to do. Like the forty-year-old boxer who loses the title to a youngster. It was the first time in his life that he'd lost a battle in such a definitive way. The most humiliating part of it was knowing who the killers were and not being able to . . . But enough. He had to stop thinking about it. He was no longer a chief inspector of police, but a common citizen like everyone else.

The one-eyed kitten drew near on the sly and, leaping through the air, attacked his shoelaces, chewing them as if they were the bars of a prison. The little ball of fur felt like a tiger. Bordelli grabbed her and lifted her high in the air. He let her flail about for a second or two, then set her down, and she shot off like a rocket.

'Rosa, you ready yet?'

'I'll be right out . . .' she said from the bathroom.

She came out some forty minutes later, completely made up and as fragrant as a prostitute, then disappeared again into the bedroom for another half-hour. When she reappeared she was as beautiful as the sun, as striking and luminous as ever. She went into the kitchen to fill the cats' bowls and returned to the sitting room.

'Shall we go?' she said impatiently, like someone who'd been waiting for hours for her escort. They descended the stairs arm in arm, like husband and wife, then got in the Beetle and drove off.

'Where are you taking me?' Rosa asked, feeling content.

'No questions,' said Bordelli. He turned on to the Viali and went as far as Novoli. When he picked up the Firenze–Mare motorway, Rosa went back on the attack.

'Are we going far?'

'No questions, Rosa.'

'Bah!'

'Sing me a song,' said Bordelli, stepping on the accelerator. Rosa didn't have to be asked twice. She cleared her throat and started singing.

'*Con ventiquattromila baci-i-i . . . Oggi saprei perché l'amore-e-e . . . Vuole ogni tanto mille ba-a-ci . . . Mille carezze all'ora all'o-o-raaaa. . . . Con ventiquattromila baci-i-i . . . Felici corrono le ore-e-e . . . Un giorno splendido perché-è-é . . . Ogni secondo bacio te-e-eee . . . Niente bugie meravigliose, Bu-bum-bu-bum . . . frasi d'amore appassionate, Bu-bum-bu-bum . . . Ma solo baci chiedo a teeeee-eeeee . . . ie. . . . ie. . . . ie . . . ie . . . ie . . . ie . . . ie! Con ventiquattromila baci-i-i . . . Così frenetico è l'amore-e-e . . .*'[53]

She knew the whole thing. Too bad she was tone-deaf.

With one song after another, they arrived at last in Migliarino. Bordelli turned on to the *lungomare*, the seafront road, and half an hour later they were at Marina di Massa, the small seaside town where as a child Bordelli used to spend his summer holidays with his parents. It was like a second home for him, as he'd spent at least four months a year there for many years. He'd gone back a few times as an adult to look up old friends, and once he'd even gone there for an investigation. Casting a quick glance at Piazza Betti, he continued down the *lungomare*, until the asphalt ended. On the right was a restaurant with big picture windows and a green sign: Da Riccà. He turned into the car park lot and found a space among the other cars.

'Are you hungry?'

'As a wolf,' said Rosa.

'Do you like fish?'

'I love it . . .'

They got out of the car, and Bordelli led the way into the restaurant. A large dining room, with crabs and conches hanging in the corners over large sections of fishing nets. Almost all the tables were taken. Bordelli stuck his head into the kitchen, and was greeted with such enthusiasm that it was audible outside. A blue-eyed Hercules came towards him and embraced him with his greasy hands.

'Ciao, Nobody,' said Bordelli, using Riccà's partisan *nom de guerre*.

'Hey, old copper, nice to remember your friends now and then.'

'From now on I promise I'll come more often.'

'Nice little paunch you've put on there, old man,' said Riccà, slapping Bordelli's gut with the back of his hand. Then he looked at the beautiful blonde next to his friend.

'This is Rosa,' Bordelli hastened to say. Riccà gave her a firm handshake and didn't let go.

'I'd be careful with this one if I were you. He's actually a stubborn mule who needs a few kicks up the arse now and then.'

'What?' said Rosa.

'He's no good . . . A bandit . . .'

'Oh, I'm well aware of that,' she said, chuckling.

'A good-looking lady like you deserves better.'

'Don't worry, he's not my man . . . Far from it,' Rosa said with a sneer.

'How are things down in Florence?' asked Riccà, accompanying them to a table.

'I'd rather not think about it today.'

'Then we won't mention it any more. What would you two like to eat?'

'You decide, we trust you.'

'And I'll take good care of you . . . I have to return to the kitchen, but later we'll drink a glass of some good white wine of mine,' said Riccà. He gave Bordelli a pat on the back and then left.

'Nice guy,' Rosa whispered.

'I've known him since we were little kids.'

'You should learn from him . . . He's not a sourpuss like you.'

'Everyone's different, Rosa,' said Bordelli.

He looked up through the window and was spellbound by the white peaks of the Apuan Alps standing out against the sky . . . How was Eleonora doing? Would he ever see her again? He'd rather not think about it; he didn't want to be poisoned with bitterness. It wasn't Monsignor Sercambi's fault that she was gone. He preferred to think it was fate, as the fortune-teller had said. If that hadn't been the reason, there would have been another. The tarot never lied.

He kept his eyes fixed on the distant mountains, lost in other thoughts. Giacomo Pellissari . . . Piglet the butcher . . . Rich-boy Signorini . . . the telephone bill in the woods . . .

'What are you thinking about?' Rosa asked, squeezing his wrist.

'About Briciola . . .'

If not for the kitten, he would never have discovered anything.

La Nazione, Monday, 20 February 1967
Page three

HILLS OF HORROR
SUICIDE IN THE WOODS
FLORENTINE BUTCHER, 44 YEARS OLD
SHOOTS HIMSELF IN MOUTH AT CINTOIA ALTA
MOTHER AND DAUGHTER GRIEF-STRICKEN

Yesterday morning Livio Panerai, a butcher of 44, killed
himself by firing a shotgun into his mouth near the abbey
of Monte Scalari. Shortly before 7 a.m., a hunter found
the butcher's lifeless body in the woods, still holding the
double-barrelled shotgun. Signora Cesira Batacchi
Panerai, the victim's wife of nineteen years, had no
explanation for her husband's extreme act. He had left
before dawn that morning to go hunting in the hills of
Cintoia, as had long been his custom on Sundays.
Livio Panerai had no apparent causes for distress in his
day-to-day life. A hard worker, always cheerful and
beloved of his customers, he led a transparent existence.
The inhabitants of La Panca, the site of the tragedy, now
speak of 'hills of horror'. Not only was the area the scene
of atrocious massacres by the Nazis at Pian d'Albero
and other locations nearby, but the horror hasn't let up
since. The suicide victim was found not far from the
spot where the lifeless body of Giacomo Pellissari,

the young kidnap victim who had been raped and murdered, was discovered a few months earlier. Pellissari's killer has never been apprehended.

The mortal remains of Livio Panerai have been transferred to the chapel of the hospital of . . .

Acknowledgements

Leonardo Gori: without the material on the flood that he was kind enough to let me borrow, and without his generous and decisive help on a few crucial points in the plot, this novel would have had more than a little trouble emerging from its cocoon, and might never have been written. I even used the encounter between Arcieri and Bordelli from his novel *L'angelo del fango* (Rizzoli, 2005), in a sort of reverse-angle shot that respected the dialogue without changing so much as a comma.

Enneli Haukilahti: by now she has become one of my most precious consultants.

Laura Bosio: a highly gifted line editor at Guanda publishers, possessed of infinite patience.

Adolfo Mattirolo: a comrade of my father's in the San Marco batallion, he has told me many stories about the war.

Alessandro Coppola: a police officer in the DIA (Direzione Investigativa Antimafia), his technical observations on the police procedures of the 1960s have been invaluable to me.

Alberto Severi: for having put me in touch with Angela Motta.

Angela Motta: the kind director of the Teche Rai of Florence, she provided me with material on the flood surpassing all expectations.

Bruno Casini: for his critical reading.

Carlo Zucconi: for having directed me to useful witnesses to the events of Cintoia and for his critical reading.

Curzio Malaparte: for *Mamma marcia* (Vallecchi, 1959).

Daniele Cambiaso: for his historical review and other useful pointers.

Dante Falleri: for the story of Giuggiolo, heart-rending and true.

Divier Nelli: for his reading and observations.

Domenico Antonioli: for translating into Massese dialect the dialogues between Bordelli and the former partisan fighter Nobody – that is, Riccà, who was his father.

Don Gamucci: for accounts of the flood.

Emiliano Gucci: for his uncompromising critical reading.

Enzo Fileno Carabba: for his help on mushrooms.

Francesco Leonardi: a Florentine policeman in service in 1966, he told me many stories about the flood.

Grazia Collini: for putting me in touch with Alessandro and Raffaele Coppola.

Laura del Lama: for her critical reading.

Luca Scarlini: for information and a variety of pointers.

Mariangela Zucconi: for her critical reading.

Max Aub: for the story of the mouse (in his version it was a crow).

Paolo Ciampi: for the extremely useful book he got for me.

Piernicola Silvis: for putting me in touch with Dante Falleri.

Raffaele Coppola: for his stories about the flood.

Stefano Miniati: for his critical reading and more.

Valerio Valoriani: for his critical reading.

Principal Sources:

La Nazione – Various editions from November 1966.

Teche Rai – Television and radio documentation.

DOC, the review – Year 5, number 20 (Arno '66 – *Fango e ideali*).

L'alluvione di Piero Bargellini, Bernardina Bargellini Nardi, Polistampa (2006).

L'inondazione di Firenze del 4 novembre 1966, Ilario Principe – Paolo Sica, Istituto Geografico Militare, Florence (1967).

NOTES

by Stephen Sartarelli

1. – *Ça va sans dire*: It goes without saying.
2. – Calimero is a cartoon character created by Italian television advertisers, a little black chick who first appeared during the nightly *Carosello* adverts programme. Once a normal chick, he falls into a mud puddle and turns black, after which his mother no longer recognises him. His black colour leads him into a number of misadventures before he is washed in the detergent Ava, the sponsor of the spot, which turns him white again and puts an end to his troubles.
3. – The road linking Florence and Siena and passing through the Chianti wine region.
4. – Potente was the *nom de guerre* of Aligi Barducci (1913–1944) a Florentine who joined the partisan resistance after the Armistice of 8 September 1943 and became a leader and hero of the struggle against the Nazi occupation around Florence and in Tuscany generally. He was killed by an enemy grenade just as the Germans were being routed from the city.
5. – *Se vai a funghi, a parlar non ti dilunghi* (Tuscan saying).
6. – A cartoon kitten. *Briciola* means 'crumb'.
7. – A famously sonorous line, redolent of troubadour verse, from the famous Paolo and Francesca episode of the *Inferno* (Dante, *Inf.*, Canto V, l. 103). Tantalisingly ambiguous in meaning, it is usually rendered in English, in accordance with the traditional Italian interpretation, as roughly 'Love, which absolves no beloved from loving'.
8. – An Italian breed of cattle.

9. – That is, a supporter or functionary of the Republic of Salò, the puppet government set up by the occupying Nazis in 1943 with the recently deposed Mussolini as a figurehead, after the Germans sprang the disgraced dictator from an Italian prison in a spectacular raid. The government had its seat in the town of Salò in the Alpine lakes region of northern Italy.

10. – Piazza Venezia is the square in Rome in which Mussolini used to address crowds from his famous balcony on the façade of Palazzo Venezia. Piazzale Loreto is the square in Milan in which the body of Mussolini and his mistress Clara Petacci were hung on public display on 29 April 1945, after they'd been captured and shot by partisans in the country-side near Lake Como. Their corpses were put on public view in the same place where, one year before, Fascists had displayed the bodies of fifteen Milanese partisans whom they had executed for participating in the resistance.

11. – September 8 1943 was the date of the official announce-ment of the so-called armistice – in actuality an uncondi-tional surrender – whereby the nation of Italy would cease all hostilities against Allied forces. The Germans, however, already controlled the northern half of the peninsula and sprang Mussolini, who had been deposed and arrested some six weeks before, from his mountain prison just four days later, on 12 September, guaranteeing more than another year of Fascism and bloodshed for Italy.

12. – See note, no. 4

13. – The famous Fascist 'battle cry', invented during the First World War by the poet Gabriele d'Annunzio, who claimed it was once the battle cry of the ancient Greeks. The latter part of the cry, *alalà*, derived from the Greek verb ἀλαλάζω (*alalázo*), is found in Pindar and Euripides and appears in the work of nineteenth-century Italian poets Giovanni Pascoli and Giosuè Carducci as well. Mussolini later adopted the *eja eja alalà!* as the vocal equivalent of the Fascist salute, itself derived from the Roman era.

14. – 'Bighead' (It. '*il Testone*') was one of the nicknames by which Italians referred (at first affectionately, then disdainfully) to Benito Mussolini, who appeared to have an oversized head on his rather diminutive though stocky frame.

15. – The 10th Assault Vehicle Flotilla (known in Italian as *La Decima Flottiglia MAS*, for *Mezzi d''Assalto*, or simply as *La Decima* or X^a *MAS*) was an Italian commando frogman unit of the Italian Navy created during the Fascist regime, one of whose symbols was a death's head with a rose between its teeth.

16. – Literally, 'I don't give a damn.' Another 'rallying cry' first used by d'Annunzio (see note, no. 13) in the First World War in one of the many pamphlets he wrote for aerial distribution, by Italian airborne squadrons, over certain cities under Austrian rule, usually those with a majority Italian-speaking population. It became a common slogan of Fascist Party stalwarts. The intended meaning, in a wartime setting, of this otherwise common expression is revealed in the poet's account of how it first occurred to him. As the story goes, during a discussion between a certain Captain Zaninelli and a certain Major Freguglia on 15th June 1918, at Giavera del Montello, Freguglio ordered his subordinate to take his company and attack an Austrian stronghold at Casa Bianca, adding that it was a suicide mission, but that it had to be undertaken no matter the cost. The captain supposedly looked at the major and replied, '*Signor comandante, io me ne frego, si fa ciò che si ha da fare per il rè e per la patria*' ('Commander, sir, I don't give a damn, we do what we must for the king and the nation'). And he dressed in his finest parade uniform and went to his death.

17. – Another Fascist motto, which means 'Quitters are murderers!', it was, paradoxically, first coined by Eleonora Pimentel Fonseca during the Neapolitan revolutionary uprising of 1799 known as the Parthenopean Republic and later revived by Milanese revolutionaries during the

1848 riots that echoed many of the other uprisings occurring across Europe that year.

18. – Some of the lyrics to the famous song 'Mamma', originally written in 1940 by Bixio Cherubini (1899–1987), though popularised in the US by Connie Francis and later covered by such famous tenors as Luciano Pavarotti and Andrea Bocelli. The lyrics here quoted translate as: '. . . Mamma I'm so happy / because I'm coming home to you . . . My song tells you it's my greatest dream . . . Mamma I'm so happy, why live far away?'

19. – Orgosolo is in Sardinia, and Mesina is Graziano Mesina (born 1942), a former Sardinian bandit and proponent of Sardinian independence famous, among other things, for his many prison escapes.

20. – 'Beautiful Sicilian' in Sicilian dialect.

21. – A Fascist song that imagines, in Marinettian-Futurist fashion, modern warfare as music. Translation: '. . . and the part of the violins / [will be played by] magnetic mines and submarines, / and instead of horns, / bombs, bombs, bombs, bombs . . . / The tenor sax / will be the cruiser, / and instead of drums [we'll have] / missiles, missiles, missiles galore . . . / missiles, missiles, missiles galore! / A great serenade, a great serenade / for perfidious Albion!'

22. – Dante, *Inf.*, Canto V, 121–3 ('*Nessun maggior dolore, / che ricordarsi del tempo felice, / ne la miseria . . . / e ciò sa'l tuo dottore*'). The words of Francesca da Rimini to Dante during the Paolo and Francesca episode of the *Inferno*. The 'teacher' (*dottore*) here mentioned is Virgil, Dante's guide.

23. – That is, the infamous March on Rome on 8 October 1922, when about thirty thousand Fascist militants marched on the capital city, demanding that their party be handed the reins of power if the country wished to avoid a violent coup. While a rather messy, inglorious affair amid the rain and mud, the march succeeded, and power was handed over to Mussolini.

24. – The term *trinariciuto* ('three-nostrilled') was coined by ultra-conservative author and satirist Giovannino Guareschi (1908–1969) to characterise the militants of the Italian Communist Party. (The third nostril served two functions: to drain brain matter, and to allow the party's directives direct entry to the brain.) The application of the adjective to Jews here is not Guareschi's, but Panerai's. Though solidly reactionary, Guareschi, best known for creating the character of Don Camillo, was not a Fascist or an anti-Semite. Indeed, the fictional Don Camillo, based in part on a real priest, was a partisan in the Second World War and interned at Dachau and Mauthausen.

25. – Totò has the same name (a diminutive of the names Salvatore and Antonio) as the much-loved Totò (born Antonio de Curtis, 1898–1967), perhaps the greatest Italian comic actor of the twentieth century.

26. – A television variety show broadcast from 1961 to 1966 on the national television station of the RAI (Radiotelevisione Italiana). The popular singer Mina was the show's mistress of ceremonies in 1965/66.

27. – Cigarettes are controlled by a state monopoly in Italy, giving rise to a thriving black market of smuggled and even counterfeit brand-name cigarettes. Neapolitan-made fake Marlboros, for example, were long legendary for their seeming authenticity, being nearly impossible to distinguish from real American Marlboros smuggled in, as both lacked the *monital* stamp found on all state-issued cigarettes.

28. – Amedeo Nazzari (1907–1979) was an Italian actor of the screen and the stage, one of whose most famous roles was in *La cena delle beffe* (1941, directed by Alessandro Blasetti), a Renaissance-era costume drama derived from the stage play of the same name by Sem Benelli, in which Nazzari's character's famous line 'Whoever won't drink with me, a plague on him!' (*'Chi non beve con me, peste lo colga!'*) became a popular saying. Under the title

of *The Jests*, Benelli's play was a big success in New York in 1919, featuring Lionel and John Barrymore in the lead roles.

29. – A Sicilian greeting of respect, meaning literally 'I kiss your hands'.

30. – All Souls' Day in Italy is called *Il giorno dei morti*, the Day of the Dead.

31. – As Italian morale sank during the First World War, the high command instituted a policy of literal decimation – that is, every tenth man of a recalcitrant unit was shot for refusing to jump out of the trenches to a certain death. See Mark Thompson, *The White War: Life and Death on the Italian Front, 1915–1919*, Faber & Faber, 2009.

32. – *Bordello, casino* and *postribolo* all mean 'brothel'.

33. – Man is the maker of his own luck.

34. – Nationalist poet Gabriele d'Annunzio famously planned and participated in a daring flight over Vienna on 9 August 1918, to distribute flyers featuring a text written by the poet himself, in effect to taunt the Austrian enemy by showing that the Italian air force could fly unimpeded over their capital city. Some fifty thousand of these flyers were released into the air. What is less well known is that d'Annunzio's text had been judged ineffective and untranslatable into German, and 350,000 copies of a second flyer with a less provocative and more conciliatory message, written by Ugo Ojetti, were also released on the same mission.

35. – The Balilla was a parascholastic and paramilitary Fascist Youth organisation founded by the party in 1926.

36. – The Alto Adige is the Italian name for the South Tyrol, a majority German-speaking area north of the province of Trent. At various times since its annexation by Italy in 1919, there have been radical Tyrolean militants willing to use force to achieve independence from Italy. Tempers have cooled in more recent times, since the region has gained considerable autonomy from Italy.

37. – Ciacco is a mythic character who appears in Dante's

Inferno (VI, 52–4) and Boccaccio's *Decameron* (Novel VIII, Ninth Day) as a personification of gluttony.

38. – Mattonella was a famous pastry chef from the town of Prato near Florence, noted among other things for his *biscottini*. These are what are now called *biscottini di Prato*, but originally they were called, as Rosa calls them, *biscottini del Mattonella*. *Brutti ma boni* (literally, 'ugly but tasty') is the name of a traditional Italian biscuit.

39. – Dante, *Inf.*, Canto XIV, 116. '*Lor corso in questa valle si diroccia, fanno Acheronte, Stige e Flegetonta.*'

40. – The Porcellino ('little pig') is a bronze fountain statue of a boar in the Mercato Nuovo in Florence, whose snout one is supposed to rub for good luck. The current statue in the Mercato is actually a copy of the Baroque original by Pietro Tacca (1577–1640), itself a copy of an Italian marble copy of a Hellenistic marble original. Tacca's original is now in the Museo Bardini.

41. – Dante, *Inf.*, Canto III, 109, '*Caron dimonio, con occhi di bragia . . .*'

42. – A semi-legendary Roman youth of the sixth century BC who is said to have thrust his hand into a fire to prove his valour and bravery and willingness to die in battle.

43. – A reference to to the famous 'amnesty' granted in June 1946 by popular communist leader and anti-Fascist Palmiro Togliatti (1893–1964) to those guilty of political and common crimes, including conspiracy to commit murder. Togliatti was Minister of 'Grazia e Giustizia' ('Pardons and Justice') in the post-war government.

44. – Claretta was the name of Mussolini's mistress, Claretta Petacci.

45. – The SID (Servizio Informazioni Difesa) is a division of the military intelligence apparatus in Italy. Primo Carnera (1906–1967) was a famous Italian boxer who was world heavyweight champion in 1933/34 and known for his tremendous size.

46. – The MSI is the Movimento Sociale Italiano, the

neo-Fascist party founded in 1946 by diehard survivors of the puppet Republic of Salò regime and the original Fascist party itself.

47. – The OVRA were the secret police apparatus of the Fascist regime from 1930 to 1943 and of the quisling Salò government from 1943 to 1945.

48. – Also known as the Republican Alpine Redoubt (*Ridotto alpino repubblicano*), this was a fortified stronghold where the remaining Fascist diehards planned to stage their final defence of the Republic of Salò as the end drew near. A few thousand loyalist soldiers actually did begin to gather there in the winter and spring of 1945, but the whole plan came to naught after Mussolini was captured by partisans on 25 April 1945.

49. – From September 1943 to August 1944, the Villa Triste ('House of Sadness') at 67 Via Bolognese in Florence lodged a unit of the German 'political police', the SD (*Sicherheitsdienst*), and a section of the Milizia Volontaria per la Sicurezza Nazionale (the Voluntary Militia for National Security) of the Salò government. This ruthless Italian militia was commonly known as the Carità Gang, after its leader, Mario Carità. The Germans let the Italians use the lower floors of the building, where Carità created his 'Special Services Unit', made up in large part of criminals seeking amnesty for their crimes by serving the Nazi occupation government, and other mentally unbalanced individuals. The Villa Triste of Florence was one of several buildings so called in the Italy of the occupation, the others being in Rome, Milan, Trieste, Genoa and elsewhere.

50. – The nuraghi are the archaic conical megaliths of central Sardinia.

51. – Dante, *Inf.*, Canto X, 102. Dante's original says, 'We see, like those who have imperfect sight, / the things,' he said, 'that distant are from us; / so bright still shines our Supreme Guide.' In Dante, the word I have translated

as 'Guide' (intended as God) is *duce*, thus allowing the exploitation and adaptation of the passage here to Fascist purposes. Indeed, the last line in the original tercet reads: '*cotanto ancor ne splende il sommo duce*'.

52. – Stenterello is a traditional character of the Florentine carnival, clownish and often dressed in unmatching clothes.

53. – The song 'Ventiquattromila baci' ('Twenty-four thousand kisses') was written by Pietro Vivarelli and Lucio Fulci to music by Andrian Celentano, and was sung first by Celentano, then by various other Italian entertainers. The lyrics translate as follows: 'With twenty-four thousand kisses / I should know today why love / Now and then wants a thousand kisses / a thousand caresses per hour, per hour / With twenty-four thousand kisses / the hours pass happily / It's a splendid day because / Every second I'm kissing you. / No wonderful lies ... / [sound effects] / passionate words of love / [sound effects] / Only kisses I ask of youuuuuuuuu / you ... ou ... ou ... ou ... ou ... ou ... ou! / With twenty-four thousand kisses / Love is so frenetic.'

Shortlisted for the Crime Writers' Association
International Dagger 2013

Death in Sardinia

Marco Vichi

Florence, 1965. A man is found murdered, a pair of scissors
stuck through his throat. Only one thing is known about him –
he was a loan shark, who ruined and blackmailed the vulnerable
men and women who would come to him for help.

Inspector Bordelli prepares to launch a murder investigation. But
the case will be a tough one for him, arousing mixed emotions:
the desire for justice conflicting with a deep hostility for the
victim. And he is missing his young police sidekick, Piras, who is
convalescing at his parents' home in Sardinia.

But Piras hasn't been recuperating for long before he too has a
mysterious death to deal with . . .

Out now in paperback and ebook

Death and the Olive Grove

Marco Vichi

April 1964, but spring hasn't quite sprung. The bad weather seems suited to nothing but bad news. And bad news is coming to the police station.

First, Bordelli's friend Casimiro, who insists he's discovered the body of a man in a field above Fiesole. Bordelli races to the scene, but doesn't find any sign of a corpse.

Only a couple of days later, a little girl is found at Villa Ventaglio. She has been strangled, and there is a horrible bite mark on her belly. Then another little girl is found murdered, with the same macabre signature.

And meanwhile Casimiro has disappeared without a trace.

The investigation marks the start of one of the darkest periods of Bordelli's life: a nightmare without end, as black as the sky above Florence.

Out now in paperback and ebook

HODDER

Death in August

Marco Vichi

Florence, summer 1963. Inspector Bordelli is one of the few policemen left in the deserted city. He spends his days on routine work, and his nights tormented by the heat and mosquitoes.

Suddenly one night, a telephone call gives him a new sense of purpose: the suspected death of a wealthy Signora. Bordelli rushes to her hilltop villa, and picks the locks. The old woman is lying on her bed - apparently killed by an asthma attack, though her medicine has been left untouched.

With the help of his young protégé, the victim's eccentric brother, and a semi-retired petty thief, the inspector begins a murder investigation. Each suspect has a solid alibi, but there is something that doesn't quite add up . . .

Out now in paperback and ebook

HODDER

The best books live on in your head long after they are finished. As you read, you are turning the pages faster and faster to find out what happens next, only to feel bereft when you reach the end.

If that is how you feel now, you might like to join us at www.hodder.co.uk, or follow us on Twitter @hodderbooks, and be part of our community of people who love the very best of books and reading.

Whether you want to find out more about this book, or a particular author, watch trailers and interviews, have the chance to win early limited editions, or simply browse our expert readers' selection of the very best books, we think you'll find what you're looking for.

And if you don't, that's the place to tell us what's missing.

We love what we do, and we'd love you to be part of it.

www.hodder.co.uk

@hodderbooks

HodderBooks

HodderBooks